THE FIRST DAY OF HER SECOND CHANCE

"Sign here, Kyla," the man says, and points to a blank line at the end of a long document, *Kyla Davis* is typed underneath.

"What is it?" I ask, the words out before I can *think before you speak* like Dr. Lysander is always telling me.

"The man at the desk raises his eyebrows, as surprise then irritation crossed his face. "Standard release from mandated treatment to external sentencing. Sign."

"Can I read it first?" I say, some stubborn streak making me go on even as another part whispers *bad idea*.

His eyes narrow, and he sighs. "Yes. You can. Everyone, prepare to wait while Miss Davis exercises her legal rights."

Dad puts a hand on my shoulder, and I turn. "It's all right, Kyla. Go on," he says, his face calm, reassuring; his words and Mum's the ones I must listen to from now on. And I begin to remember a nurse patiently explaining this all to me last week: that listening to them is part of what is in this contract.

I flush, and sign: *Kyla Davis*. Not just Kyla, anymore: the name picked by an administrator when I first opened my eyes in this place nine months ago, after her aunt who she said had green eyes like mine.

"Let me carry that," Dad says, and takes my bag. Amy links her arm in mine again, and we go through one last door.

Just like that, we leave behind everything I have ever known.

OTHER BOOKS YOU MAY ENJOY

S L A T E D

TERI TERRY

speak

An Imprint of Penguin Group (USA) Inc.

SPEAK
Published by the Penguin Group
Penguin Group (USA) Inc.
375 Hudson Street
New York, New York 10014, U.S.A.

USA / Canada / UK / Ireland / Australia / New Zealand / India / South Africa / China
Penguin Books Ltd, Registered Offices: 80 Strand, London WC2R 0RL, England

For more information about the Penguin Group visit www.penguin.com

Published in Great Britain by Orchard Books, 2012
First published in the United States of America by Nancy Paulsen Books,
a division of Penguin Young Readers Group, 2013
Published by Speak, an imprint of Penguin Group (USA) Inc., 2013

THE LIBRARY OF CONGRESS HAS CATALOGED THE NANCY PAULSEN BOOKS EDITION AS FOLLOWS:
Terry, Teri. Slated / Teri Terry. p. cm.
Summary: In a future England, sixteen-year-old Kyla is one of the "Slated," those whose
memories have been erased usually because they have committed serious crimes, but as she
observes more and more strange events, she also gains more memories, which put her and her
boyfriend, Ben, in danger.
ISBN 978-0-399-16172-8
[1. Memory—Fiction. 2. Identity—Fiction. 3. Family life—England—Fiction. 4. High schools—
Fiction. 5. Schools—Fiction. 6. Science fiction.] I. Title.
PZ7.T2815Sl 2013 [Fic]—dc23 2012020873

Speak ISBN 978-0-14-242503-9

Printed in the United States of America

5 7 9 10 8 6

The publisher does not have any control over and does not assume
any responsibility for author or third-party websites or their content.

For Graham

PROLOGUE

I RUN.

Fists of waves claw the sand as I force one foot to pound after the other. Scramble up, slip down, repeat. Faster. Eyes fixed on dunes ahead. Don't look back. Mustn't look. Ragged breath; in, out; in, out. Still I run.

Just when lungs might burst and heart explode, a crimson star on the sand, I stumble.

A man turns back. He pulls me to my feet and urges me on.

It's getting closer.

I cannot stand, and fall again. I can run no more.

He kneels to hold me, and looks in my eyes. "It's time. Quick, now! Put up the wall."

Closer.

So I build it, brick by brick. Row by row. A high tower, like Rapunzel's, but this has no window, nowhere to lower my hair.

No chance of rescue.

"Never forget who you are!" he shouts, grips my shoulders, and shakes me, hard.

A blanket of terror obliterates the sea. The sand. His words, the bruises on my arms and pain in my chest and legs.

It's here.

WEIRD.

All right, I haven't got much experience on which to base this judgment. I may be sixteen and I'm not slow or backward and haven't been locked in a closet since birth—as far as I know—but Slating does that to you. Makes you lacking in experience.

It takes a while for everything to stop being firsts. First words, first steps, first spider on the wall, first stubbed toe. You get the idea: first *everything*.

So today feeling weird and unknown could just be that.

But I am biting my nails and sitting here waiting for Mum, Dad, and Amy to pick me up at the hospital and take me home, and I don't know who they are. I don't know where "home" is. I don't know *nothing*. How can that not be . . . weird?

Bzzzz: a gentle warning vibration from the Levo at my wrist. I look down: I've dropped to 4.4, the wrong side of happy. So I have a square of chocolate, and it starts a slow climb up as I savor the taste and watch.

"Much more of your nerves, and you're going to get fat."

I jump.

Dr. Lysander is framed in the door. Tall, thin, and white-coated. Dark hair pulled straight back. Thick glasses. She glides, silent as a ghost the whispers say, always seems to know *before* it happens when someone's about to fall into red. But she's not like some of the nurses, who can bring you back with a hug. She isn't exactly what you would call *nice*.

"It's time, Kyla. Come."

"Do I have to? Can't I stay here?"

She shakes her head. An impatient flick of her eyes says *I've heard this a million times before.* Or, at least, 19,417 times before, as 19,418 is the number on my Levo.

"No. You know that isn't possible. We need the room. Come."

She turns, walks out the door. I pick up my bag to follow. It is everything I have but it's not heavy.

Before I shut the door, I see: my four walls. Two pillows, one blanket. One wardrobe. The sink with a chip on the right side the only thing to mark my room as any different from the endless row of boxy rooms on this floor and others. The first things I *remember*.

For nine months, the boundaries of my universe. This and Dr. Lysander's office and the gym and school one floor down with others like me.

Bzzzz. More insistent now, it vibrates up my arm, demanding attention. Levo's dropped to 4.1.

Too low.

Dr. Lysander turns, clucks under her breath. She bends down so we are eye to eye, and touches a hand to my cheek. Another first.

"Truly, you will be fine. And I'll see you twice a month to start with."

She smiles. A rare stretching of lips across teeth that looks uncomfortable on her face, as if unsure how it got there or what to do once it did. I am so surprised, I forget my fear and start to climb away from red.

She nods, straightens, and walks down the hall to the elevator.

We go silent down ten floors to Ground, then down a short hall to another door. One I haven't been through before for obvious reasons. Over the top it says P&R: Processing and Release.

"Go on," she says.

I hesitate, then push the door part open. I turn to say good-bye, or please don't leave me, or both, but she is already disappearing into the elevator with a swish of white coat and dark hair.

My heart is thumping too fast. I breathe in and out, and count each time to ten until it begins to slow, like they taught us; then square my shoulders and push the door open wider. Over the threshold is a long room with a door at the far end, plastic chairs along one wall, two other Slateds sitting with regulation bags like mine on the floor in front of them. I recognize both of them from lessons, though I've been here much longer. Like me, they are out of the pale blue cotton overalls we always wear and into actual jeans. Just another uniform, then? They are smiling, thrilled to be leaving the hospital at last with their families.

Never mind that they've never met them before.

A nurse at a desk on the other wall looks up. I stand in the doorway, reluctant to let it shut behind me. She frowns slightly, and flicks her hand to beckon me in.

"Come. Are you Kyla? You must check in with me before you can check out," she says, and smiles widely.

I force my feet forward to her desk; my Levo vibrates as the door shuts with a *swoosh* behind me. The nurse grabs my hand and scans my Levo just as it vibrates harder: 3.9. She shakes her head and holds my arm tight with one hand, and jabs a syringe into my shoulder with the other.

"What is that?" I ask, pulling away and rubbing my arm, though I am pretty sure I know.

"Just something to keep you level until you are somebody else's problem. Sit down until your name is called."

My stomach is churning. I sit. The other two look at me with wide eyes. I can feel the Happy Juice begin to ease through my veins, taking the edge off, but it doesn't stop my thoughts even as my Levo slowly rises to 5.

What if my parents don't like me? Even when I really try—which, to be fair, isn't all the time—people don't seem to warm to me. They get annoyed like Dr. Lysander when I don't do or say what they expect.

What if I don't like them? All I know are their names. All I have is one photograph, framed and hung on my hospital room wall, and now tucked in my bag. David, Sandra, and Amy Davis: dad, mum, and older sister. They smile at the camera and look pleasant enough, but who knows what they are really like?

But at the end of it all, none of this matters, because no matter who they are, I have to make them like me.

Failure is not an option.

2

"PROCESSING" DOESN'T INVOLVE MUCH. I AM SCANNED, photographed, fingerprinted, and weighed.

It turns out "Release" is the tricky bit. The nurse explains on the way that I need to say hello to my mum and dad, that they and I will sign some papers to say we are all now one big happy family, and then we will leave together to live happily ever after. Of course I spot the problem, straightaway: What if they take one look at me and refuse to sign? What then?

"Stand up straight! And *smile*," she hisses, then pushes me through a door.

I paste a wide smile on my face, convinced it won't transform me from scared and miserable to angelic and happy; more like, demented.

I stand in the doorway, and there they are: I almost expect to see them posed like they are in the photograph, like dolls. But each of them is in different clothes, different positions, and the details fight for notice: too much at once, all threatening to overwhelm and send me into the red, even with the Happy Juice still lingering in my veins. I hear the teacher's bored voice, over and over again with the same words, as if she were standing there next to me: *One thing at a time, Kyla.*

I focus on their eyes and leave the rest for later. Dad's are gray, unreadable, contained; Mum's soft, flecked light brown, impatient eyes that remind me of Dr. Lysander, like they miss nothing. And my sister is there, too: wide, dark, almost black eyes stare curiously back at mine, set in glowing skin like chocolate velvet. When the photo was sent weeks ago, I'd asked why Amy was so different from my parents and me, and was told sharply that race is irrelevant and not worthy of notice or comment under the glorious Central Coalition. But how can you not see?

The three of them sit in chairs at a desk, opposite another man. All eyes are on me but no one says anything. My smile feels more and more like an unnatural thing, like an animal that died and is now stuck on my face in a death grimace.

Then Dad jumps out of his chair. "Kyla, we're so pleased to welcome you to our family." And he smiles and takes my hand, kisses my cheek, his own rough with whiskers. His smile is warm, and real.

Then Mum and Amy are there, too, all three of them towering inches taller than my five foot nothing. Amy slips an arm through mine and strokes my hair. "Such a beautiful color, like corn silk. So soft!"

And Mum smiles then too, but her smile is more like mine.

The man at the desk clears his throat and shuffles some papers. "Signatures, please?"

Mum and Dad sign where he points, then Dad gives me the pen.

"Sign here, Kyla," the man says, and points to a blank line at the end of a long document, *Kyla Davis* typed underneath.

"What is it?" I ask, the words out before I can *think before you speak* like Dr. Lysander is always telling me.

The man at the desk raises his eyebrows, as surprise then irritation crosses his face. "Standard release from mandated treatment to external sentencing. Sign."

"Can I read it first?" I say, some stubborn streak making me go on even as another part whispers *bad idea*.

His eyes narrow, and he sighs. "Yes. You can. Everyone, prepare to wait while Miss Davis exercises her legal rights."

I flick through but it is a dozen pages of long, close-typed print that swims before my eyes, and my heart starts thumping too fast again.

Dad puts a hand on my shoulder, and I turn. "It's all right, Kyla. Go on," he says, his face calm, reassuring; his words and Mum's the ones I must listen to from now on. And I begin to remember a nurse patiently explaining this all to me last week: that listening to them is part of what is in this contract.

I flush, and sign: *Kyla Davis*. Not just Kyla, anymore: the name picked by an administrator when I first opened my eyes in this place nine months ago, after her aunt who she said had green eyes like mine. An actual second name that belongs to me, as part of this family. That is in this contract someplace, too.

"Let me carry that," Dad says, and takes my bag. Amy links her arm in mine again, and we go through one last door.

Just like that, we leave behind everything I have ever known.

Mum and Dad study me in the car mirror as we spiral up out of the parking lot under the hospital toward the exit. Fair enough, as I study them back.

They are probably wondering how they got two such mismatched daughters, and nothing to do with the skin color I'm not supposed to notice.

Amy sits next to me in the backseat: tall and busty and three years older at nineteen. I am small and slight with wispy blond hair; hers is dark and thick and heavy. She is *va-va-voom*, like one of the male nurses says about another nurse he fancies. And I am . . .

My brain searches for a word the opposite of Amy and comes up empty. Maybe that, in itself, is the answer. I am a blank page. An uninteresting one at that.

Amy is wearing a flowing red patterned dress with long sleeves, but she pulls one up now so I can see the Levo on her wrist. My eyes widen in surprise: So she was Slated, too. Her Levo is an older model, chunky and thick where mine is a thin gold chain with a small dial, meant to look like a watch or bracelet but fooling nobody.

"I'm so happy you are my sister," she says, and she must mean it as it says 6.3 in big digital numbers.

We get to the gate; there are guards. One comes up to the car and others watch behind glass.

Mum, Dad, and Amy pull up their sleeves and hold their hands out the windows, so I do the same. The guard looks at Mum's and Dad's empty wrists and nods, then he goes to Amy and holds a thing over her Levo, and it beeps. Then he does the same thing to mine, and it beeps, too. He looks in the trunk and slams it shut.

A barrier in front of the car rises, and we go through.

"Kyla, what would you like to do today?" Mum asks.

Mum is round and pointy, and no that isn't ridiculous. Her shape is round and soft, but her eyes and words are sharp.

The car pulls onto the road, and I look back. The hospital complex I know, but only from the inside. It stretches side to side and up and up. Endless rows of little barred windows. High fences and towers with guards at regular intervals. And . . .

"Kyla, I asked you a question!"

I jump.

"I don't know," I say.

And Dad laughs.

"Of course not, Kyla; don't worry. Kyla doesn't know what she wants to do; she doesn't know what there is *to do*."

"Now, Mum, you know," Amy says, and shakes her head. "Let's go straight home. Let her get used to things for a bit, like the doctor said."

"Yes, because doctors know *everything*." Mum sighs, and I get the sense of a long-standing argument.

Dad looks in the mirror. "Kyla, did you know that fifty percent of doctors finished in the bottom of their class?"

Amy laughs.

"Honestly, David," Mum says, but she is smiling also.

"Have you heard the one about the doctor who couldn't tell his left from his right?" Dad says, and launches into a long story of surgical errors that I hope never happened in my hospital.

But soon I forget all they are doing and saying, and stare out the window.

London.

A new picture begins to form in my mind. New London Hospital is losing its central place, shrinking in the sea of what surrounds it. Roads that go on and on, cars, buildings. Some near the hospital are blackened and boarded; more are full of life. Washing on balconies, plants, curtains billowing out windows. And everywhere: people. In cars, walking along the street. Crowds of people and shops and offices and still more crowds of people, rushing in all directions, ignoring the guards at the corners who get fewer the farther away we are from the hospital.

Dr. Lysander has asked me many times: Why do I have a compulsion to observe and know *everything,* memorize and map every relationship and position?

I don't know. Maybe because I don't like feeling blank. There are so many details missing that need to be set right.

Within days of remembering how to put one foot in front of the other and not fall over, I'd walked and counted and mapped with pictures in my mind every floor of the hospital that was access allowed. I could have found each nurses' station, lab and room by number blindfolded; I could close my eyes now and see it all before me.

But London is a different matter. A whole city. I'd have to go up and down every street to complete the map, and we seem to be on a direct trip to "home," a village an hour west of London.

I'd seen maps and pictures, of course, at the hospital school. Hours every day they'd spoon-feed us as much general knowledge as our blank brains could soak up to prepare us for release. I eagerly gripped each fact, drawing and writing things over and over again in a notebook so I couldn't forget. Most of the others were less receptive. Too busy smiling great dopey grins at everything and everybody. When we were Slated, they upped the happy in our psychic profiles.

If they upped the smiles in mine, they must have been nonexistent to start with.

3

DAD PULLS MY BAG OUT OF THE TRUNK AND WALKS TOWARD the house, whistling, keys in hand. Mum and Amy get out of the car, then turn back when I don't follow.

"Come along, Kyla." Mum's voice is impatient.

I push at the door, hard and then harder, but nothing happens. I look up at Mum, my stomach beginning to twist, as the look on her face matches her tone.

Then Amy opens the door from the outside. "You pull this handle down, on the inside of the door, and then push it open. All right?"

She shuts the door again, and I grasp the handle and do as she says. The door swings open and I step out, glad to straighten my legs and stretch after so long in the car. The one-hour trip had turned to three due to traffic delays and diversions, and had Mum getting more annoyed as each one passed.

Mum grabs my wrist. "Look. 4.4 just because she can't work out a door. God, this is going to be hard work."

And I want to object, to say that is unfair and it isn't just the door but how you are being about it. But I don't know what I should or shouldn't say. Instead I say nothing and bite the inside of my cheek, hard.

Amy slips an arm across my shoulders as Mum follows Dad inside. "She doesn't mean it; she's just cranky that your first dinner is going to be late. Anyhow, you haven't been in a car before, have you? How should you know?"

She pauses and I don't know what to say, again, but this time it is because she is being nice. So I try a smile, a small one, but it is for real this time.

Amy smiles back, and hers is wider. "Have a look around before we go in?" she says.

The car is parked along the side of the house on a driveway made up of small stones that crunch and move underfoot as we walk. A square of green grass covers the front yard, a massive tree—oak?—to the left. Its leaves are a mix of yellow, orange, and red, some spilling messily underneath. *Leaves fall in autumn,* I remind myself, and what is it now? The thirteenth of September. There are still a few red and pink straggly flowers on either side of the front door, petals dropping on the ground. And, all around me, so much space. So quiet after the hospital, and London. I stand on the grass and breathe the cool air in deep. It tastes damp and full of life and the ending of life, like those fallen leaves.

"Come in?" Amy says, and I follow her through the front door into the hall. Leading off it is a room with sofas and lamps, tables. A huge flat black screen dominates one wall. A TV? It is much bigger than the one they had in recreation at the hospital, not that they let me near it after the first time. Watching made my nightmares worse.

This room leads to another: There are long counters, with cupboards above and below. And a massive oven that Mum is bending over just now, putting a pan inside.

"Go to your room and unpack before dinner, Kyla," Mum says, and I jump.

Amy takes my hand. "This way," she says, and pulls me back to the hall. I follow her up the stairs, to another hall with three doors and more stairs going up.

"We're on this floor; Mum and Dad are upstairs. See, this is my door." She points at the one to the right. "That on the end is the bathroom, we'll share. They have their own upstairs. And this is your room." She points left.

I look at Amy.

"Go on."

The door is part open; I push it and go in.

Much bigger than my hospital room. My bag is already on the floor where Dad must have put it. There is a dressing table with drawers and a mirror above it, a wardrobe next. No sink. A big wide window that looks out over the front yard.

Twin beds.

Amy comes in and sits on one of them. "We thought we'd put two in here to start with; I can stay with you at night if you want me to. The nurse said it might be a good idea, until you get settled."

She doesn't say the rest but I can tell. They must have told them. *In case I have nightmares.* I often do and if no one is there fast enough when I wake, I drop too low and my Levo knocks me out.

I sit on the other bed. There is something round, black, and furry on it; I reach out a hand, then stop.

"Go on. That's Sebastian, our cat. He is very friendly."

I touch his fur lightly with a fingertip. Warm, and soft.

He stirs, and the ball unwinds as he stretches out his paws, puts his head back and yawns.

I have seen pictures of cats before, of course. But this is different.

He is so much more than a flat image: living and breathing fishy breath, silky fur rippling as he stretches, big yellow-green eyes staring back into mine.

"Meow," he says, and I jump.

Amy gets up, leans across.

"Stroke him, like this," she says, and runs a hand along his fur from his head down to his tail. I copy her, and he makes a sound, a deep rumbling that vibrates from his throat through his body.

"What is that?"

Amy smiles.

"He's purring. It means he likes you."

Later it is dark out the window, and Amy is asleep across the room. Sebastian still purrs faintly beside me when I stroke him. The door is part open for the cat, and sounds drift up the stairs. Clattering kitchen noises. Voices.

"She's a quiet little thing, isn't she." Dad.

"You can say that again. Nothing like Amy was: She wouldn't stop giggling and talking from the first day she came through the door, would she?"

"Still won't," he says, and laughs.

"She is a different girl, all right. A bit odd if you ask me; those great green eyes just stare and stare."

"Oh, she is quite sweet. Give her a chance to get settled."

"It is her last chance, isn't it."

"Hush."

A door shuts downstairs, and I hear no more. Just a faint murmur.

I hadn't wanted to leave the hospital. Not that I wanted to stay there forever, but within those walls, I knew where I was. How I fit, what was expected.

Here, all is unknown.

But it isn't as scary as I thought. Already I can see Amy is lovely. Dad seems all right. I'm guessing Sebastian will be better than chocolate to pull me back from the edge if I get low. And the food is much better. My first Sunday roast dinner. We do this every week, Amy said.

Dinner and not a shower, but a bath—a whole hot tub to soak in—had me at nearly 7 by bedtime.

Mum thinks I am odd. I must remember not to stare at her so much.

Sleep settles around me, and her words drift through my brain.

Last chance . . .

Have I had other chances?

Last chance . . .

I run.

Waves claw at the sand under my feet as I force one foot to pound after the other, again and again. Ragged breath sucked in and out until my lungs might burst, and still I run. Golden sand gives way under my feet and stretches on and on as far as my eyes can see, and still I scrabble up and slip down and run.

Terror snaps at my heels.

It's getting closer.

I could turn and face it, see what it is.

I run.

$\bullet$ $\bullet$ $\bullet$

"Shhh, I've got you."

I struggle, then realize it is Amy whose arms are around me.

The door opens and light streams in from the hall.

"What is going on?" Mum says.

Amy answers. "Just a bad dream, but you're all right, now. Aren't you, Kyla?"

My heart rate is slowing; vision, clearing. I push her away.

"Yes. I'm fine."

I say the words, but part of me is still running.

4

I DRIFT THROUGH TREES, SPIN AND SPRAWL DOWN ON GRASS
and daisies on the ground, alone. I stare at clouds drifting across the
sky, making half-known shapes and faces. Names slip away if I grasp
at them, so I let them wash past: just lie still and be *me*.

It is time. Like mist I bleed away until I am gone. Trees and sky are
replaced by the darkness of closed eyelids, tickling grass by solid bed.

Quiet. Why is it so quiet? My body knows it is later than five A.M.
but no buzzer has sounded, no breakfast trolleys clang up and down
the hall.

I lie very still, hold my breath, and listen.

Gentle, even breathing. Close by. Did I black out last night, is there
a Watcher in my room? If so, it sounds like they sleep rather than
watch.

There are faint cheerful sounds in the other direction, a distant
rise and fall, like music. Birds?

Something warm by my feet.

I'm not in my room at the hospital. My eyes snap open as I
remember.

Not a Watcher at all across the room: Amy, sound asleep and
breathing deeply, like Sebastian at my feet. She is a new sort of the
same thing, maybe.

I slip quiet to the window, pull the curtain.

Dawn.

Red streaks cross the sky, pockets of pink in wisps of cloud, like corrugated twists of metal, light shining through on grass and wet leaves, a riot of color. Orange, gold, red, and all in between.

Beautiful.

My hospital window faced west. Sunsets I've seen—mostly blocked by buildings, true—but never a sunrise.

And the birds! They have friends, and the faint song from earlier becomes more as they join in. I push the window open wide, lean out and *breathe*. The air is fresh, no metallic or disinfectant smells. Damp greenness, of garden below and fields beyond that shimmer in the early light.

And somehow, I know. The city was never mine. I was—am—a country girl. Sure of it like breathing, certain this is a place that is more like home to me.

Not *like* home, it *is* home: Yesterday, today, how many more future days I do not know.

But before I became who I am now, too. Dr. Lysander says I fancy things in my subconscious, that there is no way to know if they are true or not. Applying sense to the unknown to order it, just the way I draw diagrams, maps. Faces.

Below, the glistening grass, fallen leaves in swirling patterns of rich colors, and most especially the fading flowers along the house, all beckon. All yearn to be captured, ordered, to become lines on paper. I slip across the room. Amy lies silent and still, chest movements slight and even.

Two green eyes watch me from the end of my bed. "Meow!"

"Shhh. Don't wake Amy," I whisper, and run a hand across Sebastian's fur. He stretches and yawns.

Where are my sketching things? Amy unpacked my bag yesterday afternoon. I was too fuzzy-headed to get involved, all the new things and people taking too much attention.

I open one drawer, then another; carefully and quietly, until I find them: my folder of drawings, paper and pencils.

I lift them out and underneath spy chocolates. Given to me as a parting gift by the tenth-floor nurses that last morning. Just yesterday, I realize, surprised. It seems longer ago than that; already part of my past.

My levels are 6.1. Not low at all. I don't *need* a chocolate. But who needs an excuse? I open the lid.

"Interesting choice for breakfast," Amy says, then sits up and yawns. "Are you an early bird?"

I look at her blankly.

"Do you always wake up early?"

I consider. "I think so," I say, finally. "Though that could be because at the hospital you have no choice."

"Oh, I remember that. Horrible morning buzzer. Breakfast by six." She shudders.

"Want one?" I hold out the box.

"Oooh, tempting. Maybe later, when I'm more awake. What is that?" She points at the folder in my other hand.

"My drawings."

"Can I see?"

I hesitate. I rarely show them to anyone, though Dr. Lysander insisted on checking through them now and then.

"You don't have to show me if you don't want to."

I sit next to her and open the folder, pull out the sheets of paper.

Amy exclaims at the one on top. A self-portrait. Me, but different: half as I am in the mirror, the other half with skin missing, eyeball hanging from an empty socket.

"May I?" She holds out a hand, and I pass the drawing to her.

But that wasn't on top before. I start flipping through the sheets.

"You're so good; this is amazing."

Not enough of them, not as thick a sheaf as it should be. Where are they?

"What's wrong?"

"Some of my drawings are missing."

"Are you sure?"

I nod. And look through them more slowly.

Those of me, my room, imagined people and places, are present and accounted for. Many others are not.

"I'm sure. Almost half of them are gone."

"What were they of?"

"All sorts of things. Nurses. My floor of the hospital, maps of different areas, rooms. Dr. Lysander. And—"

"Did you say, Dr. Lysander?" Amy's eyes open wide.

I nod, still looking through the sheets, convinced if I look hard enough, they will all be there.

"*The* Dr. Lysander? Do you actually know her?"

I stop looking. They're not here. Gone.

Bzzzz. A warning from my wrist: 4.3 and falling.

Amy slips an arm across my shoulders. I'm shaking, but not from cold. Who would do this? Take the only things I have that are *mine*.

"You can make more drawings. Can't you?"

3.9 and falling.

"Kyla! Look at me." Amy gives me a shake. "Look," she repeats.

I tear my eyes from my self-portrait, from the dead eye in the socket. To Amy. Worry and fear for me in her eyes, whoever I am.

3.4 . . .

"Kyla, you can draw me. Do it, now."

She pulls the blank sheets from the back, puts a pencil in my hand.

I draw.

5

"Can I see?" Amy asks. She cranes her head forward, but I angle the sketch away.

"Not yet. Hold still, or I won't be able to finish it."

"Bossy thing." She laughs.

"It won't be long now," I say, glancing back at Amy, then down to my drawing for a few final strokes of my pencil.

Amy smiles. "Are you level?"

I turn my wrist to check. "Yes. 5.2 and steady."

The door opens but I don't look up.

"Are you girls ready for breakfast?" Mum says.

"Nearly," I say, looking at Amy one more time, then at the sketch in my hands. A final stroke, *there*. "Done," I say, and put the pencil down.

"Let me see!" Amy springs up, and Mum walks over.

"Oh. That is so good," Amy says.

Mum's mouth is in a round O of surprise. "That is Amy; you've captured her, just so. I want to frame this and hang it on the wall. May I?"

I smile. "Yes."

Breakfast is pancakes. Eaten with butter melting in streaks, and syrup or strawberry jam. I try both, together: *very* nice.

"Don't think you'll be eating like this every day," Mum says. My sketch of Amy is on the fridge with a magnet instead of a frame on the wall, and Mum has reverted to her pointy self.

"Amy, you've got twenty minutes before the bus and you don't look even a bit ready to me."

"Can't I stay home with Kyla today?"

"No."

"Where's Dad?" I ask.

"Work, of course. Where I should be, but had to take time off to mind you."

I do the math. Amy is going to school, Dad's at work; that leaves Mum and me for the whole day.

"When can I start school? Can I go today?"

"No."

Amy explains. "You've got to be assessed by the area nurse first; she has to think you are ready. Then the school tests you to work out where to put you, what year. Though they've sent some books for you to read."

"Oh."

"The nurse is dropping in this afternoon to meet you," Mum says.

I vow to act as well-adjusted as possible.

Amy dashes upstairs in a flurry of finding schoolbooks, uniform. She is in her last year of high school. At nineteen she should be done already, at the University, studying nursing like she wants to. But she needed an extra year to catch up. And she was fourteen when she was Slated. I'm sixteen now. How many extra years of school will I have?

"You can wash up," Mum says.

"Wash what?"

She rolls her eyes.

"The dishes."

I stand and look at them on the table.

She sighs. "Pick up the dirty dishes from the table and put them there." She points at the counter next to the sink.

I carry one plate across and go back for another.

"No! That will take forever. Stack them up. Like this."

She stacks plates, pulling out knives and forks and clattering them on the top of the pile, then brings it all to the counter.

"Fill the sink. Add soap, just a little." She squeezes a bottle into the sink.

Bubbles!

"Wash them with this brush." She scrubs a brush across the plate. "Rinse it under the tap, put it in the rack, like so. Repeat. Got it?"

"I think so."

I plunge my hands in the hot water.

So this is washing up.

I carefully clean a plate of the sticky remains of pancakes and syrup, rinse it and put it in the rack.

"Pick up the pace or you'll be there all day."

I stop, and look around.

"Pick up what?"

"The pace. It means *go faster.*"

Plates, then cups. This isn't so bad. I speed up, and Mum starts wiping them with a towel. Amy clatters down the stairs as I start on the cutlery.

I gasp, and look down: A thin line of red drips down from a knife clasped in my right hand.

Amy bounds in. "Oh no! Kyla."

Mum turns and clucks under her breath. She grabs a sheet of paper towel.

"Press it against the cut, don't bleed everywhere."

I do as she says, and Amy rubs my shoulder and looks at my Levo: 5.1.

"Doesn't it hurt?" Amy asks.

I shrug. "A little," I say, and it does, but I ignore the jagged heat that throbs through my hand, and stare, fascinated. Bright red soaks into the paper towel, slows, then stops.

"Just a nick," Mum says, peeling it back to look. "The nurse can check it later. She's all right, Amy. Run or you'll miss the bus."

Mum wraps a bandage around my hand as Amy bounces out the door.

Mum smiles.

"I forgot to mention, Kyla. Knives are sharp. Don't hold them by the pointy end."

So many things to remember.

Nurse Penny unwraps my hand later for a look.

"It should be all right without stitches," she says. "I'll just put some antiseptic on it. Sorry, it might sting a bit." She splashes some yellow stuff on my hand that smarts and makes my eyes water, then wraps it up again.

"It was weird," Mum says, "when she cut it. She just stood there looking at the blood running down her hand. No tears, no reaction."

"Well, she's probably never cut herself before. Never seen blood like that."

Huh. I just love it when people talk about me as if I'm not even there.

"It didn't send her low or anything. And—"

"Excuse me." I smile my best well-adjusted smile. They both

jump as if I am a ghost that materialized before them the moment I spoke. "When can I go to school?"

"Don't worry about that yet, dear," Penny says. "Have a look through the books they sent." And she turns back to Mum. "You have to try to remember to point out hazards, like knives. She may not look it, but in some ways she is really like a small child, and—"

"Excuse me." I smile again.

Penny turns.

"Yes, dear?"

"Those books the school sent. I looked through them this morning. They're too easy, all stuff I already know from the hospital school."

"A genius then, are you?" Mum says, with a look on her face that says I'm quite the opposite.

Penny pulls a netbook out of her bag. Frowns and taps the screen on the side, then runs her finger across the screen, searching files.

"Well actually, she isn't far off. Tested age-appropriate before she left the hospital. That is most unusual; most of them are years behind. I'll get the school to send some more stuff. Or Amy might have old schoolbooks around? We need to work out what subjects you should take."

She shuts her netbook and turns back to Mum.

"Where was I? Oh yes. There are no sharp corners, no hazards at the hospital. So everything dangerous needs to be pointed out. Like crossing the road, and—"

"Excuse me." Even to me my smile is starting to feel stretched. Dislocated.

"What is it this time?" Mum says.

"I already know what subject I want to take."

Penny raises an eyebrow. "Oh, you do, do you? What, then?"

"Art."

She smiles. "Well, you may need a few more practical subjects. And they'd have to assess you to take you in art."

Mum points at the fridge. "She drew that, this morning. Of Amy."

Penny gets up to look; her eyes widen. "Well. I should think they'll let you, dear."

She turns back to Mum.

"You did such an amazing job with Amy; she is a delight. I'm sure, with time, Kyla will adjust to your family."

I cross my arms. Kyla will adjust; what about everyone else?

"She had a nightmare last night," Mum says. "Screamed the house down."

Penny opens her netbook again. Asking *me* might be an idea; I am the one who knows all about it.

"There is a history of that, I'm afraid. No doubt why they kept her so long at the hospital. Nine months instead of the usual six. We'll look at some ways of controlling that in Group. They tried all the usual meds at the hospital, but those made it worse if anything. And—"

"Excuse me. Could you talk to me, instead of about me?"

The smile slips from Penny's face.

"You see what I'm up against," Mum says, and sighs.

"Part small child, part moody teenager," Penny says. "Now, Kyla, dear; let me chat to your mum. Why don't you run along upstairs?"

I shut the door, hard, and plonk myself down on the bed. No sign of Sebastian, and it is hours before Amy gets home.

My folder of drawings sits on the dressing table. I pick up a sketch pad.

Now that the shock is over, it is no matter about the ones that went missing. If I close my eyes, they are all in my mind. Every detail. I will draw them again.

I grasp a pencil, but it is no good: It rests between my thumb and index finger, just where I cut my hand, the hand I draw and write with. Time for an experiment: pencil in the left hand. It feels awkward at first, wrong. I do a few quick sketches and it starts to loosen up, but I can't shake the feeling of *wrongness,* an edge of fear almost, that something will happen if I continue.

But I can't stop.

A fresh page: who first?

Dr. Lysander. Getting her right is all about the eyes. Tricky eyes, she has; mostly shielded and cold, but she peeks out now and then. When she does she seems more startled about it than I do.

I begin, hesitant at first with an unfamiliar hand. Line, shading, all. Faster and surer as confidence increases. Dr. Lysander begins to look back at me from under my pencil. Goose bumps rise along my arms, my neck.

Strange.

I draw much better with my left hand.

6

VOICES DRIFT INTO MY MIND. OUT FRONT?

I put down my pencil, and go to the window. A boy and two girls stand in the yard below, wearing school uniforms like Amy's: maroon jackets and black pants. I hide my drawing under others in a drawer, and head for the stairs. Amy and Mum stand in the hall below.

"We're just going for a walk. Why ever not?" Amy.

"I don't think it's a good idea; she hasn't been out of the house yet. What about traffic?" Mum.

Talking about me, again.

"I do actually know not to jump out in front of cars," I say when I reach the bottom step.

"Oh bother, take her then! Just watch her very carefully."

"I know, Mum," Amy says. After Mum leaves the hall Amy adds, in a low voice, "I know better than you."

She turns to me. "Kyla, come meet my friends."

I start for the door.

"Put some shoes on, first."

Oh. All right. Amy finds me the sneakers I wore from the hospital yesterday, and waits while I struggle with the laces. We head outside.

"This is Jazz," she says, and points at the boy. "And Chloe and Debs. Everyone, meet Kyla."

"Oh, she's cute. I wish I could trade my sister in," Chloe says. "How old is she?"

"Talk *to her* if you want to know something," Amy says.

"I'm sixteen," I say.

"Sweet sixteen and never been kissed," Jazz starts singing as we walk up the road, and my cheeks burn.

Amy slugs him in the arm. "Shut up, you numbskull, she's off-limits to you."

Jazz grabs her hand. "Sorry, I was joshing. Forgive me?"

"I suppose," she says, and he slips an arm around her waist. Amy is tall but Jazz is taller; broad-shouldered with an easy way of walking. Now that I'm closer, I'm guessing he is not so much a boy, more like eighteen, so years older than any I met in the hospital. And he is different not just because of that: His smile has an edge of mischief that I've never seen on Slated boys. He's cute.

We walk through the village, back the way we came in the car yesterday. Past freestanding houses like ours, then rows of terraced cottages, a pub with White Lion on a painted sign. Until we get to a sign that points out a green way, marked footpath.

"Fancy a walk?" Jazz says.

Chloe and Debs evidently do not, as they say good-bye.

Amy links one arm with mine and the other with Jazz. "Come on," she says.

The ground is soon uneven and rough, and I have to concentrate on placing my feet. There is a tall hedge on one side, sloping fields covered in dead stubble of whatever was growing there on the other. The path narrows, and Amy lets go of Jazz and hangs on to my hand.

He protests.

"Shut it, numbskull," she says, and he leads the way.

We climb up, higher and higher; I breathe harder. The hedge and fields give way to trees, and I drink in the riot of orange and red leaves, brown and gray trunks, some with red berries and spiky leaves that prick if you touch them. Holly?

"The view is this way, ladies," Jazz says.

We round a bend and look across woods and fields, down over distant tiled roofs, gardens, roads.

"Look, Kyla," Amy says. "You can see the whole village from here. That is our place. See? Second from the left." She points, and I see the tiled roof and brick walls of our house.

There is a log and we sit on it. Jazz wraps his arms around Amy from behind, with a resigned look on his face. I get the feeling they usually come here alone.

She prods him in the ribs with her elbow.

"So, Kyla. How are you getting along with the Dragon?" he says.

"The Dragon?"

"He means Mum," Amy says.

"Uh . . ."

"Say no more! I understand *Uh*. It means you have noticed that she is not a sainted mother figure as advertised, but actually a fire-breathing mythical green beast."

I giggle.

"That's not fair," Amy says. "Mum's not that bad; you have to get to know her. I used to be scared of her, and then all at once, she was all right."

"You know, the weird thing to me is how you both straightaway call her *Mum*," Jazz says.

"Why is that weird?" I ask.

"Well, you just met her, didn't you?"

Amy shakes her head. "That doesn't matter. It is what you are told at the hospital, right from the beginning. That your mum and dad are coming to take you home."

"A prefab kid," Jazz says, then ducks when Amy twists to smack him.

"So we're different from everybody else," I say.

"Unique," Amy says.

"My special girl," Jazz says, and kisses her cheek.

"There are just two of us in this village," Amy says. "That is why I'm so happy you came. I'm not the only one anymore. Though there are a dozen or so of us at our school, from all over the place."

Soon with a look at his watch and a curse, Jazz disappears at speed down the path the way we came.

"His parents have a farm; some days he has to help after school. We'll walk back the long way," Amy says, and we set off in the other direction. "Seriously: How did you get along with Mum today?"

I shrug. "I don't think she even likes me. Why take me if she doesn't want me?"

"Oh, but she does want you. She just doesn't show it very well. It's complicated."

"Simple is hard enough. Who needs complicated?"

"Don't worry about it now. One thing, though: Mum doesn't always hear things, unless you say them. Don't be afraid to tell her what you are thinking. It's easier that way."

The path steepens and Amy slips in front; I have to concentrate on my feet again as we descend. I think about what she said about Mum: the Dragon, Jazz called her.

"Is Jazz your boyfriend?"

"Yes. Don't tell Mum. She doesn't like him."

Jazz: He sang to me. *Sweet sixteen and never been kissed.* Or have I? If I can't remember, does it count?

"I was told very sternly at the hospital to avoid boys at all costs. Mess up your levels."

"Oh, they do that!" Amy laughs. "Probably best to leave them alone for a while. The secret, though, is to start with one you're not that bothered about."

What is the point in that?

"Where've you been?" Mum is waiting in the door, arms crossed.

"Told you: We went for a walk," Amy answers as we walk in and take off our shoes.

"Those shoes are muddy. You didn't go up the footpath on your own, did you? I've told you it's not safe."

"No, of course not; we weren't alone," Amy says, and with her back to Mum rolls her eyes.

"Kyla? Is that true?" Mum turns to me with a full dragon glare.

"Yes," I say. And it is true: Jazz went with us. He didn't come back with us, but that isn't what she asked.

"Listen to me, both of you. You know it isn't safe for you on your own. You can't protect yourselves."

Amy nods, and I remember lessons on *personal safety* at the hospital. It is part of being Slated. You can't defend yourself any more than you can attack someone, so you have to be extra careful.

But what is up the footpath, but trees and more trees?

"You've been ages. I was worried. And you've almost missed Dad," Mum says, and I notice she is standing next to a suitcase in the hall.

Her arms are still crossed and her skin has a strange tinge: slightly dragon-green. I can imagine scales in the light crisscross of lines about her forehead, by her eyes. Is there a bit of smoke coming from her nostrils?

"What is so funny, miss?" she says to me.

I wipe the smile off my face. "Nothing. Sorry."

"Leave the poor girl alone," a voice says from the living room: Dad.

Amy crosses the room and kisses him on the cheek. I stand uncertain in the doorway.

"Come in, Kyla. Have a seat. Tell me about your day, and I'll tell you about mine."

So we swap stories. And he seems as interested in me cutting my hand, Nurse Penny's visit and going for a walk, as I am in his.

Dad works with computers. He travels a lot, installing and testing new systems, and is about to leave and won't be back until Saturday. Five whole days from now. And then he tells me about family stuff. That he has two sisters, one visiting with her son on Saturday so I can meet them. The other lives far away in Scotland and we might visit her next summer. And Mum is an only child; her parents died many years ago in a car accident. She was just fifteen.

Later that night when Amy and I go up to sleep, I fish out today's drawing from where I hid it under the others.

"Amy, this"—I hold up my afternoon's work—"is Dr. Lysander. Why were you surprised I know her?"

Amy takes the sheet from my hand.

"She looks scary!"

I shrug. "She can be. But sometimes she's all right."

"I'd love to work with her when I'm a nurse; she's amazing."

"Why?"

"Don't you know? She started it all: Slating. She invented it. We learned about it in science at school."

I look back at the picture in my hands, at her hooded eyes that stare back at mine. I didn't know that. Or did I? Everyone always deferred to Dr. Lysander; got out of her way in a hurry. All Slateds have a main doctor assigned to them at the hospital, and she was mine. But now that I think about it, there was never anyone besides me in her waiting room. No one else I knew saw her. If she is so important, why would she bother with me?

They taught us the basics about Slating in the hospital school. We were all criminals, sentenced to Slating—wiping our memories and personalities—so we could start over again. With the Levo in place to make sure it all worked, until it is removed the year we turn twenty-one on the anniversary of our Slating. So Slating is a second chance, for which we should be grateful: It kept us out of jail, or off the chair.

But at least if you were in jail, you'd know who you are. Not for long on the chair, though, if you'd done something bad enough to warrant that.

I bite my lip. "Don't you ever want to know?"

"What?"

"Why you were Slated."

"No. If the past is unbearable, why choose to bear it?"

I shrug. *Because it is mine.*

"Anyhow, that solves the mystery of what happened to your drawings."

"It does?"

"Security must have taken them before you left the hospital. They wouldn't want anyone to know what Dr. Lysander or anyone else who works there looks like, or where things are in the hospital. It's too dangerous."

Whispers overheard mix together in my mind; snippets, rumors, and distant loud noises at night. Guards and towers. Burned-out buildings.

"Terrorists?"

"Exactly."

Amy switches out the light. Soon her even breathing says she sleeps. Sebastian curls along my side.

So. Dr. Lysander is important, and they stole my drawings to keep her face hidden from the world. And now, I've drawn her again. Maybe I should hide it? This likeness of her is the best I've ever done.

Even though I used the wrong hand.

I am in a small space, alone. Wood surrounds me. It is dark, but I hold a flashlight in my right hand.

Cross-legged on the floor, I'm hungry and it is cold and damp. My legs are stiff and there is no room to stretch out, but I don't care. The pages lie across my knees, kept flat by a piece of wood underneath. The pencil flies across the paper, a dance of magic that is mine alone. Creating an imaginary place so far from this one, in distance and in time: a place I long to be.

So absorbed, that at first, I don't hear the footsteps coming down the stairs over my head. I turn off the flashlight and hold my breath.

They stop at the bottom; pause. Then they start again, coming closer and closer to my secret place. I should do something, hide my drawings, anything, but I am fixed like stone.

A light switches on in my face. Blinding me.

"There you are."

I say nothing. He can see it all: the drawings, the pencil. The hand that holds it.

"Get up!" he snaps.

I scramble out, the light still dazzling my eyes.

"You know the reasons; you know how important this is. Yet still you disobey."

"I'm sorry. I won't do it again, I won't. I promise!"

"Enough of your promises. You can't be trusted."

His voice is full of regret; sadness, even.

"Give me your left hand," he says, and when I don't, he grabs it.

"You have to learn. I'm sorry."

And I almost believe he means it, as he smashes my fingers, one by one, with a brick.

8

AGONY STABS MY EYES, TWISTING LIKE THE BLADE OF A KNIFE.

There is a metallic, bitter taste under my tongue. I cough.

"She's coming around." A male voice. Who?

I try to open my eyes, but they burn as if the sun has fallen from the sky. I groan.

"Kyla?" A hand touches mine. Amy.

"Turn out the lights," she says. The light dims, and I squint between my lids.

"There you are," she says, and smiles.

I'm on the floor. I try to sit up.

"Don't move yet," the male voice says again, and I turn my eyes to the source. A paramedic? And another. Mum, white-faced, stands in the doorway.

They lift me back into bed while Amy holds up an IV bag. One of them fixes it up, the other injects something into it, and warmth slides into my veins, starts to take the pain away. My eyes close.

Voices mix and fade.

A nightmare did *that*? Disbelief.

She could have died . . .

Keep in bed for a day or two . . .

Pain management . . .

If Amy hadn't woken when she hit the floor, she would have died . . .

Last Chance.

9

"CAN I AT LEAST HAVE A BOOK?"

"No. You're supposed to be resting," Mum says, and crosses her arms.

"I can rest, and read."

"No."

"They would let me in the hospital," I lie.

"You're not in the hospital, you're on my watch, and you are resting. Go to sleep," she says, and leaves again, shooing Sebastian out and shutting the door.

I can convince myself she means well. But it is hard to rest with someone sneaking up on you every two minutes to make sure you are resting.

I close my eyes. My head still feels like it is being crushed in a vise, though it is better than this morning, when even the sound of Sebastian purring vibrated through my skull like drums, and I'd asked for him to be kept out. But I'm afraid to sleep. Afraid that dream will find me again. Now that the injection has worn off, *anything* could happen.

My nightmares in the hospital were terrifying, but vague. Most of the time I couldn't remember much of what happened; I just woke up screaming. Often running from something, without knowing what it was.

But this one was different. I remember it as vividly in my mind as if it is happening on replay before my eyes, right now, over and over again. I can feel the pain, see my broken, bloody fingers. It is so real.

Real like a memory etched within, stark and clear; the kind so horrible you can never forget, no matter how hard you try. But memories are one thing I am not supposed to have. Nothing from before being Slated. It is almost like drawing with my left hand yesterday brought it back, from some hidden place, up to the surface.

Who is he? Is he real, or just some nightmare creature that inhabits my mind? In the dream I never see his face. First the light dazzles my eyes, then I can't see through the pain and tears. But my dream self knew him, even recognized his footsteps.

One thing is certain and sure: If he is real, I don't want to know.

"Hmmmm?"

"Sorry. Did I wake you?" Amy.

I was actually asleep; in a black and silent place, dreamless and still. Maybe the drugs haven't worn off.

"It's okay. I'm sick of being in bed. Can I get up?"

Amy shakes her head. "She'll never let you. They said you were to stay in bed for a few days. Mum always follows to the letter, whether she believes it, or not."

"I'm so bored."

"Poor you. How is your head?"

"Not great."

"Can I get you anything? Are you hungry yet?"

"No."

Amy turns to go.

"Wait. There is one thing you could do for me."

"Yes?"

"My sketch pad. She took it away so I can't draw."

She hesitates. Goes into her room and comes back. "Is this any good?" She holds out a small blank notebook and pencil.

"Perfect. Thanks."

"Keep it hidden." She winks.

I prop myself upright on pillows, and turn away from the door so my body shields the notebook. Listening carefully for any little creak that might be Mum sneaking up the stairs.

But with the comforting scratch of pencil on paper, I get more and more absorbed. Escaping from myself, the dream; everything.

I am somebody else.

"Lucky that was me."

I jump.

Amy shuts the door and puts a tray with soup on the table next to me.

"What are you drawing?"

I show her. Half Mum, half dragon. In a variety of poses. Breathing fire; flying over the house.

She laughs. "Oh, God. Don't let her see those. We'll have to hide this away, and—"

She stops and frowns, looking at my hand. My left hand, holding the pencil. Dread trickles into my stomach.

"I thought you were right-handed. When you drew me, you used your right hand."

"I am! I was drawing with my right hand. I just shifted it across to pass you the notebook."

"Oh. Sorry; of course," she says, and smiles again.

My Levo vibrates; 4.6.

"Chocolate?" she asks.

I shake my head. "Can you bring me Sebastian?"

She opens the door and moments later returns carrying Sebastian, and dumps him on my lap. He meows, indignant at being kept out all day. I pet him and he flops down on my lap, purring. His paws knead against my side through the quilt, claws in and out.

"Will you eat a little?" Amy says.

"In a while."

Once my levels get back to 5 she leaves to watch TV downstairs. I wrap myself so tight around Sebastian that he squirms and protests until I loosen my arms.

Without even thinking about it, I was drawing with my left hand. Why did I lie?

In that moment, I was afraid. Of Amy? This is insane. But the fear was there, it was real. As if Amy could be another one wielding a brick.

I hold up my left hand. Turn it side to side. The fingers are whole and perfect; there are no scars. I can almost convince myself it never happened, that my subconscious mind made it all up. That realizing I could draw better with my left hand somehow triggered the dream. It can't be a memory. I'm Slated; I don't have memories.

But somehow a sick certainty sits like a crushing weight on my chest, making it hard to breathe. Every instinct of self-preservation screams inside and won't be ignored.

No one must know.

10

"**Everyone, we've got somebody new today!**" Nurse Penny says, her voice almost bright enough to match the yellow cardigan she wears.

"Everyone" is a dozen or so Slateds like me, gathered from surrounding villages near and far, sitting in a loose circle in a drafty, high-ceilinged hall.

Nurse Penny gives me a push. "Go on. Introduce yourself, and grab a chair."

"Hi. I'm Kyla," I say, and find a chair in a corner, pull it into the circle.

The others smile at me and one another; most are years younger. Except one girl, about my age, sitting with her arms crossed and looking out the window into the darkness.

Oh, joy. First day at Group. Just what I need with this blackout headache still heavy behind my eyes. They usually take a few days to go away. Mum had said maybe I could leave this until next week, but then I decided I felt well enough to come tonight. At least this way I finally get out of the house. Besides, there is no point putting it off; it will be every Thursday at seven until further notice. Amy doesn't have to go anymore, so I'm assuming "further notice" is until they are convinced you don't need constant monitoring.

We had Group at the hospital, also, so I know the story. We're supposed to talk about our feelings in a "supportive, nonjudgmental atmosphere," but it usually seems to me that they tell us what we are supposed to be feeling.

Penny crosses her arms. "Does anyone remember what you need to do now?"

They look at one another.

This is painful.

Until finally the older girl turns away from the window, and rolls her eyes. "You all are as exciting as watching paint dry. Introduce yourselves before we all die of old age."

I feel my eyes widen along with everyone else's in the circle. She was saying, out loud, the kind of stuff I say in my head. How did she dare?

Penny frowns. "Thank you for setting us straight. Perhaps you'd care to begin?"

"Sure. Greetings, dear Kyla; I am Tori. Welcome to our happy group."

The others begin to chime in with their names, one after another. Smiling. Unaware that Tori's voice was dripping with sarcasm. All, that is, except for Penny, who still frowns at Tori.

Once the introductions are over, Penny glances at the clock: ten past seven. "Well, I suppose we had better—"

But then the door flies open at the back.

"Sorry I'm late," a voice says. Male. I turn just as a chair is dragged across the floor; Tori pushes hers to one side to make room, and he sits next to her.

Penny pretends to look stern. "You must learn to be punctual, Ben. How's the training going?"

"Good, thanks." He smiles, and as Penny smiles back, I see it in her eyes: nurse's pet. He's not the least bit worried that he is late, and neither is she. He is the favored one.

Not surprising. He's obviously been Slated longer than everyone here, except perhaps Tori. His smile is real rather than dazed, the sort of smile that makes you want to give one back. Training, Penny said: He is wearing shorts although it is a cool night; his legs are well muscled; a long-sleeved T-shirt clings to his back and shoulders. His skin is a light bronze that says he is outside more than in. And Tori is smiling her first real smile of the night at Ben. It transforms her face: She is stunning.

"Hello, are you the new girl? I'm Ben," he says, and I realize I've been staring. Color climbs up my cheeks.

"Kyla?" Penny prompts, and I jump.

Tori rolls her eyes. "Yes, Ben, you've missed the introductions. Ben, this is Kyla; Kyla, this is Ben."

"Welcome," he says, and smiles right into my eyes.

"Thanks," I say, and look at my feet.

"Shall we get started, then?" Penny says. She looks around the circle at every face, then stops on mine. "Kyla, why are you here? Why are we all here?"

I stare at her blankly.

The answer in my mind—*because we have to be*—may be factual, but isn't the right answer. I'd figured out at the hospital Group that although it is meant to be a safe place where you can say anything, it is best not to be too honest. Too much honesty landed me several times in with Dr. Lysander for a tinker in my brain that left me exhausted and fuzzy for days.

I smile widely and don't answer. Nurses usually fall for that if they don't know me too well.

"Kyla, we are here to support one another in our transition from the hospital to our families and society," she says, answering her own question. "Now, why were you in the hospital?" She smiles brightly.

This is more interesting. I mean, I know what they did to me, in general terms. They wiped the synapses and linkages in my brain that added up to *me*: my personality, my memories. And I know the usual reasons Slating is done, danger to society being the most common. But I don't know why they did it in my particular case. Is this in Nurse Penny's files someplace?

"Well, Kyla?" she says.

"You tell me."

Tori looks up, meets my eyes. Interest and amusement dance in hers.

Penny frowns. I've been to enough of these things to know no real answers will be forthcoming. Before she can react, I am saved by Ben putting up his hand.

"We were given a new beginning," he says. As he smiles at me again, I feel a shock, a recognition: liquid brown eyes, dark hair pulled back that curls just past his ears, all somehow familiar. As if I already know him. I shake myself internally, force my eyes away.

"Exactly," Penny says. "Now today, everyone, we are going to pick up where we left off last week. Does anyone remember what we were talking about to tell Kyla?"

She looks around, but nobody volunteers.

"We were talking about maintaining our levels. What is everyone right now?"

We dutifully check and call out. I am lowest at 4.8.

Penny looks concerned. "What are your strategies?"

"What do you mean?"

"If your levels are dropping. What do you do to bring them up again?"

"Eat some chocolate. Hugs from people. Or, lately, stroke the cat."

"These are all external things to make you feel better. What about things inside yourself?"

Well, maybe we are actually going to learn something useful.

"What level are we aiming for?" She addresses the group. Discussion follows, and I tune out. I've heard it before, many times.

Level means between 5 and 6. 10 is complete joy; 1 is anger that could kill or misery so black you can't move. If you go below 3 you are heading for la-la land: The Levo zaps the chip they put in your brain when you are Slated, and you black out like I did the other night. Just in case there are any violent impulses lurking within that Slating somehow missed, if you somehow drop below 2 without blacking out, it gives more than a zap. More like a barbecue. Seizures follow, and if you come around at all, you'll be a drooling idiot.

Penny scans through files on her netbook, *tsk-tsk*ing. "I see you have quite a history, of nightmares and blackouts. Let's see if we can help Kyla with strategies. Everyone?"

She doesn't seem to know anyone's actual name. Doesn't she know even Slateds don't answer to "everyone"?

She points at one after another for an answer, and I listen, interested despite myself.

A range of suggestions follow; some I already use.

Distraction: Focus on something else. Repeating times tables, counting tiles on the floor. Ben runs: I know that one. I used to spend hours on the treadmill at the hospital gym, until feelings faded away and all that existed was the *thump-thump* of feet. Or my other version: organizing the unknown into faces made up of lines and shade, drawing maps of corridors and doors and everything between to create boundaries. Is that why I do it?

Visualization: Go some other place in your mind. A Happy Place, in nurse-speak.

Transference: Put your feelings on someone else.

Dissociation: Become somebody else, leave your feelings behind.

I'm becoming an expert at that one.

Aren't we all?

Later Penny tells us to split into small groups, to practice conversation. Today's assigned topic: to talk about our families.

And everyone begins to move their chairs around into twos and threes, without discussion: They all know where they belong. I hesitate, unsure what to do, then jump as a warm hand rests on my shoulder: Ben. He leans over.

"Join us?" he says, smiles, and I find myself staring up into his eyes. Close up there are warm gold flecks mixed in with the brown; they'd be a challenge to paint, to get the colors mixed right, and—

Amusement crosses his face. "Well?"

"All right," I say, and stand. His hand drops from my shoulder, and he lifts my chair and puts it next to Tori, then pulls his to sit opposite us both.

Tori's eyes narrow. She starts to say something, but stops as Penny comes over to join us.

Soon I learn that Ben's dad is a teacher, his mum is an artist and works in the workshop at a dairy; Tori's dad is a government councilor in London, and she stays with her mum in the country. He's just home some weekends and the way she says it, sounds like she thinks it is a good thing. At seventeen they are both a year older than me, and know Amy from school. The same school I'll be going to as soon as they let me.

"Where'd you really come from, then?" Tori demands as soon as Penny moves out of earshot to see how the next group is getting along.

"What do you mean?"

"Where were you, before here."

"At the hospital. I just got out last Sunday."

"I don't believe you."

"Tori," Ben interrupts. "Play nice."

She smirks at him. "There is no way she was just released, the way she talks. You know it as well as I do. We've both been out for years; you know how the new ones are."

"I was in the hospital longer than most," I say. "Because of nightmares."

"How long?"

"Nine months, or so they tell me."

"Even so. You're different."

And I want to protest, argue. My mouth half opens, but then shuts again. There is the proof. Most new Slateds would just smile and agree with anything you said to them. What is the point in denying what is so obviously true?

I shrug. "So what if I am?"

"Aha!" Tori says.

Ben leans forward, searches my eyes with interest. "What is wrong with being different?"

Tori scowls, then Ben gives her a hug and the scowl goes.

"Want to meet up with us on Sunday?" Ben looks at me, his arm still across Tori's shoulders. "We're going to the Thame Show."

Tori looks both surprised and annoyed.

"I don't know. I'll have to check if I'm allowed."

She rolls her eyes. "Sure. Whatever."

And I get the distinct impression that if I want to get along with Tori, I'll need to keep well clear of Ben. And somehow, I don't think that's what I want to do.

Penny corners me as everyone is leaving.

"Kyla, stay. I want to talk to you alone."

She waits until the last one goes, then sits next to me.

"I heard about your blackout a few nights ago. I need to check your Levo."

She pulls out a handheld scanner, like the ones in the hospital but smaller, and plugs it into her netbook. She holds it over my Levo and graphs flash across the netbook screen.

"Oh my God."

"What?"

"Look, Kyla. See for yourself." She touches the screen, selects a graph marked *09/15*. A whole section of it, in the early hours of Tuesday morning, is in the red. She touches the points and numbers appear on the screen.

"Kyla, you were 2.3. That is too close. What happened?"

I stare back at her. Just 0.3 away from not waking up *at all.* My stomach twists.

"Well?"

"I don't know. I had a nightmare, that's all. I didn't wake up. Next thing I knew the paramedics were there, injecting me with Happy Juice. I still have the headache to prove it."

"Your Levo isn't affected by dreams, you know that. It is when you wake up afterward."

I shrug. "I don't remember waking."

"What was the dream?"

"I don't remember," I lie.

She sighs. "I just want to help you, Kyla. You're not due for your first hospital check until the weekend after next, but maybe we should move it up to this one."

"No! I just need . . ." How do I put this in nurse-friendly words? "I need *distraction*, to fill my time and my mind. Can I start going to school? Please."

She leans back, and looks in my eyes as if searching for something.

"It's too soon. You need to get used to things at home, first. And—"

"Please." I don't say what I am thinking, that it is being home all day alone with Mum—*the Dragon*—that worries me. These last days in bed with her and Sebastian my only company made even my nightmares seem good.

"Distraction is all well and good, but you need redirection as well. I'll give you some exercises to do, all right? If you'll do them—really do them, and try hard—then we'll get you in school next week. Deal?" She holds out her hand.

I stare back at her. It is Thursday today; Monday is only four days away.

"All right. Deal," I say, and grasp hers.

Amy peeks in at the back of the hall, probably sent to find out why I haven't come out yet.

Penny spots her. "Amy? Come in. You can help."

Soon they have me visualizing a Happy Place. I choose my dreaming green place of trees and flowers, lying back and looking up at clouds in the sky. Whenever I am upset or scared, I am to go there in my mind. Until it becomes automatic.

Easy, right?

11

"**Are you sure you're all right watching both of** them?" Mum says, turning at the door.

"Yes, I told you," Amy says. "Go on."

Me, I'm not convinced about this. The noise is getting into my head. How can someone so small make so much noise? Screaming *Mummy* over and over.

The door shuts, and out the window I see Mum and Dad walking off down the road to the pub, with Dad's younger sister, our aunt Stacey, who seems immune to the wailing of her small son.

He draws in a shuddering breath to fill his lungs for another onslaught.

Amy bends down. "Robert, want a cookie?"

His mouth wobbles. She holds out her hands and he looks up at her, indecision playing across his tear-stained face. She scoops him up and into the kitchen. In seconds he is giggling and chomping on cookies on the floor.

"How does he go from screaming to laughing in a minute?"

"He's just a baby; easy to distract."

Sebastian wanders in, takes one look at Robert, and jumps out of reach up on the counter.

"Kitty?" Robert points. "Kitty!"

He drops his cookie and pulls himself up holding the legs of a chair, pointing at Sebastian. He takes a few steps, then falls on his backside, looking startled. His face screws up.

"You're okay, Robert!" Amy scoops him up and holds him so he can reach one hand to Sebastian, who looks resigned.

"Pet kitty nicely, like this," she says. And shows him much like she did with me on my first day.

But he doesn't get it, more thumps him than strokes, then runs his hand the wrong way so his fur stands up. Sebastian jumps down and disappears out the cat flap.

Amy sits with Robert on her knee and starts tickling him before he can get upset. He giggles.

An hour or so of playing with cupboard doors and banging pots with wooden spoons follows. Robert starts rubbing his eyes, and falls asleep in Amy's arms.

"Tea?" she says, and I get up to fill the kettle, put it on the stove.

Amy turns in her seat, and I see her watching. Like Mum said. She is watching *both of us*. Like I might burn my hand on the stove, or wobble and fall over on my backside like Robert.

Nurse Penny said to Mum I am like a small child. But look at him: He can't learn things as fast as I can. He couldn't even pet the cat right. Amy says he's been taking his first steps for weeks, yet he still falls over; he is a year old, but can barely talk.

When I was Slated, I could walk in weeks, no wobbles. Talking in complete sentences days after my first words. I was faster than many, true, but even the slowest ones can hold basic conversation in a month or two.

My memories are gone, but parts of me remember. My body, my muscles. Like my left hand with a pencil. It knew what to do with it once I put it there. So it isn't the same thing as starting over, at all. It is more that given the right trigger, you can do things you forgot. Who knows what else I am capable of?

I put cups of tea on the table, and sit down.

"Ow, my arm is falling asleep. Can you just hold his head?" Amy motions and I slip my hands under Robert while she shifts in her seat. He doesn't wake.

"Thanks. Isn't he adorable?" she says.

I shrug, unconvinced. "Too noisy, when he's awake. I like him better this way."

"True. How he howled for his mother."

"She didn't seem bothered to leave him; she and Mum practically flew out of here."

"Yeah. Mum finds him hard to be around."

I'd noticed this, too, and somehow it wasn't just the obvious things, like the fact that the baby screamed and needed a clean diaper before they left. Mum seemed to want to have space between them as fast as possible; she was the one who suggested they go off to the pub, leaving us three behind.

"Why?"

"I'm not sure I should say."

"What? Tell me."

Amy stares back, eventually nods. "Okay, but this is a family secret. You can't tell anyone you know."

I nod. "All right."

"Aunt Stacey told me last spring when I was babysitting; Mum doesn't know I know everything. But before Mum and Dad got together, Mum was with somebody else, and they had a child named

Robert. They split up when he was little. Stacey was friends with Mum back then; that is how she met Dad. After they got married, Robert died. And Stacey named her baby Robert after him. She meant well, but I think whenever Mum sees him, she thinks about her son that died."

"How awful!" My throat constricts. First her parents when she was fifteen; then, years later, her son died, too. No wonder she is such a dragon.

"I know Mum can be difficult, but there are reasons," Amy says.

"She never talks about her Robert?"

"Never. Not to me, anyhow."

I stare back at Amy, confused. Mum is a contradiction. Everything about her is on the surface, yet she hides all this inside.

"I don't understand her," I say, finally.

"Look at it this way: You'll get along with her better if you don't act so scared around her. Speak your mind like she does. It is how she gets by."

Soon we hear voices and footsteps out front.

Amy holds a finger to her lips, and I nod.

The front door opens, and moments later Mum and Aunt Stacey walk into the kitchen.

"There's my boy," Aunt Stacey says, and she does look like she missed him. She eases him out of Amy's arms and soon says her good-byes.

"Where's Dad?" Amy asks.

Mum rolls her eyes. "He got a call; some emergency at work. He took off halfway through lunch."

Mum starts sweeping Robert's cookie crumbs off the floor;

Sebastian reappears through the cat flap and rubs around her ankles. "Dinnertime for Sebastian?" she says, and reaches for a tin in the cupboard. That is when she focuses on the remains of our lunch and tea things on the counter.

"Really. It wouldn't have killed you to wash up, would it?" Mum snaps.

I flinch and just stop myself from jumping up, starting them right away. She'll stand and watch and tell me what I'm doing wrong. But then some voice inside me says *just tell her what you think*.

"We've been too busy looking after Robert to do the dishes," I say.

Mum turns to me, eyes surprised. Then nods.

"Fair enough; what a handful. Glad *you* didn't come in diapers," she says, and laughs. And I laugh with her. Amy winks her approval when Mum isn't looking. We all make dinner, together, and for the first time I almost feel relaxed in her presence.

Later Amy and I have said good night and are heading for the stairs, when Amy turns back.

"I almost forgot to ask. Mum, can we go to the Thame Show tomorrow?"

The show: Isn't that what Ben suggested? That I go too, with him and Tori. I spin around.

Mum puts down her book. "Who with?"

"Everyone is going, Mum. You know: Debs, Chloe, Jazz; everyone."

Her eyes narrow. "Well, so long as it is *everyone*, I can't see why not. But I'll take you."

"Thanks," Amy says, but her face says something else.

She shuts the door when we get upstairs. Rolls her eyes. "I can't believe she still insists on *taking* us. Like we're *twelve*."

"She looked suspicious."

"What of?" Amy says, and laughs. "If you mean me and Jazz, that is only half of it."

"What do you mean?"

She throws a pillow at my head. "Why *Ben,* of course."

"What?"

"He asked me in school yesterday. If you could get out tomorrow, to go to the show. I think you've made an impression there."

"Oh."

"Just *oh*? He is rather cute, isn't he?"

"I guess." And of course he is; beyond merely cute, to some other category. And there is something else about him, some feeling I can't put my finger on, that I want to know more about. But there is no point kidding myself with Tori in the picture.

"Even some of the girls in my year chase him. Not that I've noticed anyone catching him."

I shrug. "I think he is busy with Tori."

"I doubt it. She's not his type."

"Why not? She's gorgeous." And she was, especially when she smiled. She had that perfect bone structure and proportions, and long flowing dark hair. She could be a model, if that weren't one of the things you aren't allowed to do when you are Slated.

"I just know. She's bitter and twisted; he's nice. It is obvious."

"Well, if that is so, she doesn't know it."

Amy laughs. "Then she's an idiot. But even she will work it out eventually."

Amy switches off the light and is soon asleep. Later I hear scratching at the door, and open it: Sebastian meows and jumps on my bed. Apart from him, the house is dark and silent.

Sleep is keeping away. There are too many things to process. Everything is so complicated; nothing is what it appears on the surface. Amy seems to understand Mum in ways I do not, yet I am sure she is wrong about Ben and Tori. As much as I might wish her right.

12

IT TURNS OUT THE THAME SHOW IS A VERY BIG DEAL.

When Mum, Amy, and I finally get there after inching along in traffic on rambling country lanes through fields and farm buildings, there is a long line of people waiting to go in. Everyone is in high spirits, chatting and jostling as they move slowly closer to the front. When we pass into the tent that covers the entrance, though, all fall silent.

There is a security gate that must be passed. Mum seems surprised. "They've upped this since last year," she says in a low voice.

But it doesn't seem to be this that has silenced the crowd. Overseeing it all are several men in gray suits, standing behind the security grill, unsmiling. Scanning the crowd. No one meets their eyes or looks at them directly, yet when everyone carefully looks everywhere but one place, it becomes obvious that is the place to watch.

Mum had explained on the way that the Thame Show began centuries ago, but had started to die down with the decline of the farming industry early in the twenty-first century, until it stopped altogether. With the big agricultural push for self-sufficiency by the Central Coalition decades later, it and other country shows were reinstated, and this is now one of the biggest. Bigger than it ever was.

When we get to the front we have to walk one at a time through the gate. Amy and I both set it off, of course, with our Levos. We are taken to one side, closer to the gray-suited men, and scanned head to toe.

With no reason for fear that I can identify, my hands start to shake. When they are done and wave us in, Amy takes mine in hers and almost has to drag me on wobbly legs toward Mum, who waits.

"What's with you?" Amy says. "You've gone all white."

I shrug, and look down at my Levo: a little low at 4.6, but holding steady, now that I've remembered to start visualizing *green trees blue sky white clouds, green trees blue sky white clouds* . . .

Mum squints at me as we walk into the show. "Are the crowds too much for you, Kyla?" she asks, and slips her arm across my shoulders.

"I'm fine," I say, and with Amy on one side and Mum on the other, soon I am. And I'm not sure what even bothered me in the first place.

The show is all noise, with people and animals everywhere. Rich country smells fill the air. I find I am quite content to stick close to Mum, even when Amy disappears with her friends.

There are endless displays and competitions of fruit and vegetables and baked goods; crafts and wood carving; livestock of all sorts in pens and in rings. Mum seems to know almost everyone, and says a few words now and then as we go along.

"Kyla! You made it," a voice calls from behind.

We turn, and there is Ben, and Tori. His smile is warm, but her hand is curled around his arm. *This is mine,* she is saying, and he is allowing it to be there.

Mum smiles. "Is that Ben? I haven't seen you since Amy stopped going to Group. You've gotten taller."

"Yes, Mrs. Davis."

"Good timing," Mum says, waving at someone. "Can you keep an eye on Kyla? I'm going to have a drink with a friend."

I flush in embarrassment. Someone else asked to babysit.

"Of course," Ben says. "We were just thinking of going to the Sheep Show, if you'd like to come?"

Tori rolls her eyes. "Oh, joy. It is billed as the Miss World of sheep. I can hardly wait."

Mum raises an eyebrow. "You'd do well to take care with your words here today, young lady," she says, her own words now so quiet it is hard to hear them over all the voices and noise surrounding us. Then she disappears with her friend.

Tori's mouth drops open. "Who does she think she is?" she says, loud and bristly, ignoring Ben's *shhh.*

"If you don't know, little girl, then I'll tell you," says a man standing behind us, who must have heard every word. "*That* is Sandra Armstrong-Davis."

"So?" Tori says, a hand on each hip.

"The daughter of William Adam M. Armstrong."

Understanding starts to cross Tori's face, but I am none the wiser.

"What does he mean?" I say, as we walk away.

"Don't you even know who your own mother is?" Tori says.

I look up at Ben, confused.

"She is the daughter of Wam the Man, who showed no mercy and crushed the gangs way back in the 2020s," he says. "He was the Lorder prime minister, before the terrorists blew him up."

"But they told me her parents died in a car accident," I say.

Tori laughs. "They did, if you call blowing up the highway an accident."

"Are you all right?" Ben asks, and links his other arm with mine. "This is all stuff that happened a long, long time ago. I figured you'd know all about it."

"I'm fine," I lie.

We go to the Sheep Show. There are a variety of attractive sheep—if you're into that sort of thing—with interesting names, like Lady Gaga and Marilyn Monroe, all paraded about while their virtues are extolled, and then a prize ceremony. It seems so silly, that soon all of us—even Tori—are laughing and cheering along with the crowd. Marilyn wins.

Next is a sheep-shearing demonstration. The ewe struggles at first. Then there is realization in her eyes: This man pinning her down is too strong. She can do nothing but lie limply while sharp blades so close to her skin relieve her of her wool; nothing to keep her warm through the winter. Maybe that doesn't matter as she is nearing the end of the line.

Wonder if she is visualizing her Happy Place to get through it?

Mum and Amy find me there. "Ready to go?" Mum asks, and I nod.

Leaving is easier than arriving; there are no security checks, and we just spill out a gate. But off to one side are a few men in gray suits, watching the exit. Checking faces, one by one, as everyone leaves. And as if they are standing in a collective blind spot, the crowd pretends they don't exist.

Late that night I stare at the ceiling. Amy confirmed Mum's family history. Why hadn't anyone told me?

Maybe it is because they knew I'd connect the dots in a way Amy would not. Mum's parents were killed by terrorists; her dad's life work was routing out and annihilating the gangs that almost destroyed this country, long before Slating was a treatment option. Back then they were all put to death.

Yet now she is fostering two Slateds. Two new daughters that were criminals, no matter what they remember now. Who could very well have been gang members, terrorists, or even both.

And just when I am starting to feel like maybe, at least some of the time, I understand her and what she is about, now this. I find I don't get her, at all.

The other thing keeping me awake is those men in gray suits that everyone ignored. Somehow I couldn't quite bring myself to ask who they were, but for some reason, their mere presence filled me with cold dread and fear. So much so it was hard to even move. But some small kernel of self-preservation inside made me go on, to avoid attention, screaming *don't make them notice you.* Did I succeed? Amy had to help me walk when we arrived.

There is a slight sound, downstairs: Sebastian? He is not curled along my feet as usual; maybe he can help me sleep. I slip out of bed and down the steps.

"Sebastian?" I call softly, and walk into the dark kitchen, the floor cold under my bare feet. Goose bumps walk along my arms and up my spine.

I turn toward a movement, not so much a sound as a disturbance of air that is the wrong size and shape for a cat.

Light floods my eyes.

I open my mouth to scream.

13

"**Are you sure you don't want some tea?**" Dad asks.

"I'm fine, really," I say, and back toward the door.

"I didn't mean to frighten you." He smiles, but it doesn't quite reach his eyes. He looks very tired, like he hasn't slept since he left yesterday. Rumpled like he hasn't changed, either, but the black pants and pullover he wears are not what he had on when he left for the pub.

For one so tired, he moved very fast across the room. His hand had clamped swiftly over my mouth, stopping the scream that was working its way up my throat, so all that came out was a small strangled whimper.

He released me as soon as I stopped struggling. Once the dazzle left my eyes enough to see that it was him.

Now he seems to be thinking something over, then nods to himself.

"Sit," he says, and puts two cups next to the kettle.

I sit.

He makes tea, unhurried. Glances at me now and then. He's normally so talkative, but the silence stretches around us.

"I am curious about a few things," he finally says.

"Like what?"

"First of all, why were you up?"

I shrug. "I couldn't sleep."

He stirs his tea, seems about to ask something else, then shakes his head slightly.

"I see. Second question: Why did you come downstairs?"

"I was looking for Sebastian."

He seems to consider this answer, then nods.

"Third: Why were you so scared when I turned on the light." He says it like a statement, not a question; one that he is trying to figure out.

"I don't know. You startled me," I answer, truthfully. Though maybe it had something to do with my dream, when I'm dazzled by the light, and can't see who it is, and—

"Speak what you just thought," he says, and I jump.

"In my nightmare last week, a light shines in my eyes and I can't see, and I'm really scared. I think that might be why," I say, all in a rush. Surprised to hear my voice answering the question, about the dream I'd told everyone else I couldn't remember.

"You blacked out then, didn't you."

I nod.

"Yet, despite a fright just now, however silly, you're not even low."

"No."

My Levo is a quite contented 5.1.

"Interesting," he says. Pauses, then smiles his usual happy smile. "Go to bed, Kyla. Aren't you starting school tomorrow? You must get some rest."

I dash upstairs, both relieved and confused, tea left untouched. What was that about? I'd almost felt like I was being interrogated. And I answered his questions more than I would have thought possible; almost felt *compelled* to do so. Nearly even told him about having my fingers smashed in my nightmare.

But for some reason I held that back. And I got the distinctly unpleasant feeling, that somehow, he knew I didn't tell him everything. And despite his smile, he wasn't happy about it.

14

MONDAY MORNING AT LAST.

"I can't imagine why you are so keen to go to school," Amy says. "It's not that great."

I pull on my uniform: white shirt, black pants, and maroon jacket. Bought new on Friday when it became apparent that even Amy's old ones were far too big for five-foot-nothing me.

"I like learning things," I say, brushing my hair. Which is true, though not the whole answer. I want—no, need—to know *everything*. Every fact and detail I can find out and categorize, draw and file away, is one more step.

"Well, that's good, I guess. But it's all the rest of it."

"What do you mean?"

Amy sighs. "It's not like the hospital school. Not everyone will be *nice*."

Mum is fussing about in the kitchen when we go down for breakfast. I look about, suddenly nervous that Dad will be here, or won't be here, and what that might mean, either way. Did I dream the whole thing?

"Keep it down," she says. "Dad got in late last night; he's asleep." Not a dream.

Amy and I have cereal; finally Mum comes to sit with us.

"Kyla, listen. Are you sure you want to go today? You don't have to yet, you know."

I look at her in surprise. She'd been happy to hear I was to start school, *get out of her hair,* she'd said, so she could get back to work herself.

"Yes, I'm sure," I say.

"Yesterday at the show, you seemed nervous about all the crowds of people. Lord Bill's is a big school: there are over a thousand students. Are you sure you are up for this?"

"Please let me go," I say, suddenly worried she won't, and I'll be home for days, that days will stretch into weeks. A long march of monotony to winter with no one to talk to and nothing to do.

She stares back, then shrugs. "All right. If you are sure this is what you want. Do you want me to drive you instead of getting the bus?"

"No. I'll be fine with Amy."

I get up and start stacking the bowls.

"Leave them. I'll do it."

Well.

I look at Amy. She smiles as Mum carries the dishes into the kitchen. "See, I told you she isn't that bad," she whispers.

I get on the school bus, Amy behind; it's nearly full.

Heads turn; ripples of low voices follow as we walk down the aisle. I feel eyes like footprints walking up my spine. There are two empty seats opposite each other. I move toward one of them, and the girl by the window narrows her eyes. She puts her bag across the empty seat.

Amy crosses her arms. The bus lurches as it pulls away from the curb, starts up the road, and I grab the back of the seat to stop myself from falling over.

"You know, I think that was a bit rude," Amy says.

The girl stares back at Amy and swings her feet up across the seat. Voices hush; eyes swivel and stare.

A hand waves at the back of the bus. "Kyla? There's room here."

I look across heads: It is Ben. Relief fills me, to see a face I know. A safe place.

Amy still stares at the girl.

"It's all right," I say to Amy, and move back. Thinking *green trees blue sky white clouds green trees blue sky white clouds* . . .

"Hi," I say to Ben, and sit down next to him. There are a few others from Group also, all sitting in a smiling tight cluster together at the back of the bus. All in the same maroon and black uniform as everyone else, though somehow on Ben it is different. Everything looks better on Ben. But no Tori?

He leans down, close to my ear. "Best to keep away from that girl," he says in a low voice.

"Why?" Apart from the obvious.

"She's a Slater Hater."

"Oh."

Green trees blue sky white clouds green trees blue sky white clouds . . .

"I'm sorry about that," Amy says when we get off the bus.

"It's not your fault."

"Well, I should have warned you. I—"

"You've been warning me of things all weekend."

"Most of the time we'll get a lift with Jazz, anyhow. He's at the dentist this morning."

Relief unknots my stomach.

Amy and Ben show me to the door of the Unit, then go off to classes.

"Don't look so worried; you'll be fine," Ben says. Waves as he goes.

The SEN Unit: for students with special educational needs. Apparently that is me, until proven otherwise.

Inside there is a woman sitting at a desk, tapping at a screen.

"Uh, hello," I say.

She looks up, doesn't smile. "Yes? What do you want?"

"I'm a new student."

"Another one? Name."

I stare back at her. Name . . . what?

She focuses on my Levo, and sighs. "Your *name*?" she says, slower and louder.

"I'm Kyla. Kyla Davis." The new second name, same as Mum, Dad, and Amy, still feels odd, like it doesn't go with *Kyla*. But who knows what either of my names were before. Did they go together better?

She shuffles some papers in a box and pulls out a file.

"Oh, yes. Brought forward a few weeks, weren't you? I have just been trying to schedule you in with a whole day's notice." She sighs. "Have a seat." She points at a chair, gets up, and disappears through another door with the file in her hand.

I sit.

And so goes most of the day. I don't get out of the Unit. I sit in chairs. People come and say hello occasionally; one tells me I'll get a tour of the school tomorrow and do some tests, and where the bathroom is. I get pointed toward a room at lunchtime and eat the sandwiches Mum gave me that morning with a bunch of other Slateds, all younger than me; there is no sign of Amy, or Ben. Everyone smiles and chews, like a bunch of placid cows we drove past in a field this morning. Not much conversation with unnamed teaching assistants—TAs—posted at both ends of the table. Watching and listening.

In the afternoon I get handed a *History of Lord Williams's School* to read through. Mum had called it Lord Bill's. It is old, really old; founded in 1559, so it will soon be five hundred. A boys' school, then coed. It used to have an autism unit: Is that where I am now? Before autism was eliminated. The school was shut for five years or so after the county riots; it was reopened by the Central Coalition with much fuss and ceremony twenty years ago, with new fields and a running track in annexed land. Now it is a specialist agricultural college, like most secondary schools.

Amy and Jazz come for me at the end of the afternoon. I smile relief at Jazz, back from the dentist: no bus.

"Well? How'd it go?" Amy says.

I shrug. "It was boring. I just sat around all day, waiting for something to happen."

"Welcome to school," Jazz says, and laughs.

We walk down a footpath between brick buildings to a parking area, and along to a dented two-door car. It is mostly red, but with bits patchworked here and there in other colors.

"Ladies, your chariot," Jazz says, and bows.

I grab the door handle, and then think I've got it wrong.

"Allow me; there is a bit of a knack," Jazz says. He pulls the handle, puts one foot up on the side of the car for leverage, and yanks hard.

Amy holds the front seat while I climb into the back, wondering if this is a good idea.

"Where's the seat belt?"

"There isn't one; it broke. Just hold on tight," he says.

Good advice, as Jazz screeches off up the road, then brakes hard at a corner. I lurch forward and grab at Amy's seat in front. Gears crunch, and we jerk along. I haven't been in many cars, so maybe this isn't fair. But Slater Haters aside, I think I'd rather take the bus.

Jazz turns off the road and goes down a winding back lane, then pulls in front of a lone house down a long drive.

"We've got to get Kyla home soon," Amy says. "Mum isn't back at work until tomorrow."

"Just a quick one, then," he says. "We'll beat the bus."

Jazz yanks the car door open again; Amy and I climb out.

"We're just visiting my cuz," he says to me.

"Cousin," Amy translates.

He knocks once and opens the door.

"Mac, you home?" he yells, walks through, and leads us to the back door.

"Yeah. Grab yourselves a drink and come out," a voice answers.

Jazz turns back, opens a cupboard and takes out brown bottles. "Come on," he says.

I follow them into the backyard. There are cars and parts of cars everywhere. Mac pulls himself out from underneath one, and Jazz introduces us.

"Mac built my car from bits of other cars," Jazz says. "Drink?" He holds a bottle toward me. No label.

"Have you ever had beer?" Amy says, and I notice she isn't having one.

"No."

"Want to try it?" Jazz says. "Mac makes the stuff; it's brilliant."

I look at Amy and she shrugs, pulls a face that suggests it is not so brilliant.

"All right," I say, and he takes the top off. I tip the bottle back like Jazz did with his, and it hits the back of my throat in a rush. I cough.

"Well, what do you think?" Jazz says.

Coughing still against the bitter taste, I shake my head and hand back the bottle.

Mac laughs. "Not for little girls, this stuff; it is seriously strong."

Despite what he said, it is hard not to like Mac. His grin is contagious and a bit mad, though he looks a lot like one of his cars: made up from salvaged parts that don't match. His arms and legs seem longer than they should be; his brown hair a tangled uneven mess, as if he cuts it himself and isn't worried if it is straight, only that it is out of his eyes.

"We really can't stay," Amy says, looking at her watch. "The bus will be nearly there."

"Oh yes, the Dragon!" Jazz downs his drink, then mine, and jumps up. We head back through the house.

"Should you be driving?" Amy says.

"I'm fine."

"You shouldn't have had two."

"Well, I couldn't let it go to waste, could I?"

"Let me drive," I say.

They both laugh.

"Did you get your license at the hospital, then?" Amy asks, smiling.

"No. But can I?"

"Why not let her try?" Jazz says. "Just on this back lane."

Amy rolls her eyes. "You're both bonkers. But it's your car."

Jazz yanks the door open.

"Get in the back," he says to Amy, and she climbs into the backseat.

I slip into the driver's seat, Jazz next to me in the front. He starts a long explanation. Gears, clutch, brake . . .

I turn the key in the ignition. I don't really understand what he is saying, but my hands and feet know what to do. Clutch, gear: reverse into the lane.

"A natural, she's a natural," Jazz says, stunned as I ignore Amy's protests and neatly continue on to the main road.

"Must be my excellent teaching," Jazz says.

No. I *remember*. So long as I don't think about it too much, my hands and feet take over; some memory locked into muscle that my brain has nothing to do with.

I know how to drive. And I'm better at it than he is.

15

"Hi, Kyla? I'm Mrs. Ali. I'm the teaching assistant who will be helping you get settled over the next few weeks, starting with a tour." She smiles and actually looks into my eyes with her dark ones, holds out her hand. I shake it.

School might be more interesting today.

I follow her out the door and around the school grounds.

She chatters and points out buildings: English block, library, agricultural center. Math, fields for sports and agricultural projects—growing new crop strains in the spring. The school's ancient brick buildings mixed with newer additions are scattered about the large site, with grass and a maze of crisscrossing paths between.

"Don't worry if you get lost to start with; everyone does. I'll be shadowing you for a few weeks, and can show you around."

No. I won't get lost. The map is firmly in my mind, laid out in a grid of paths and buildings. But I just smile.

She takes me to the administration building from the far side of the school grounds, through other buildings and past class after class of students, to the main office. There is a jumble of desks and cabinets, computers; ringing telephones; half a dozen harried workers.

"This is Kyla Davis, here for processing," Mrs. Ali announces to the room. Moments later a tall, unsmiling man with thick glasses appears from behind a row of filing cabinets.

"Come this way," he says, and we follow him through another door.

Processing? I look at Mrs. Ali.

"Just getting your school ID sorted," she says.

But it is more involved than that. First my fingers are pressed one by one on a small screen for digital fingerprint storage. Then my head is held firm and I am ordered not to blink; a bright light shines endlessly in my right eye for a retinal scan. My eyes tear and vision blurs when it is over. A ghostly afterimage like the branches of a tree lingers, black on the white wall, white on the dark floor, then gradually fades. Finally a normal photograph is taken. Then he fusses with a computer for a moment, and a plastic card spits out the other end.

"You must wear this at all times," he says, and slips it into a holder and puts it around my neck.

I hold it up, and there I am: Kyla Davis, it proclaims under the photo, and there is a red *S* after my name. An uncertain smile on my lips that Mrs. Ali managed to elicit just before the flash.

"There. You are officially a student of Lord Williams's now," she says, like it is an accomplishment, or a choice. "Now we must go back to the Unit."

We go out the front door this time. Nestled alongside the building is a large stone monument, rosebushes around, with 2048 carved on top: six years ago.

"What is that?" I say.

"It's a memorial. To some students who died."

I walk closer, somehow drawn to see, and Mrs. Ali follows.

There is a list of names carved into the stone, with ages after. So many, from Robert Armstrong, 15, to Elaine Weisner, 16, and thirty or so names between. All my age or near enough. Stopped, still, silent forever.

"What happened to them?"

"They were on a class trip to the British Museum in London, and there was an AGT attack. Nothing to do with them; there were traffic diversions that put them in the wrong place, and the bus got hit. Not many survived."

I stare back at her, unable to take it in.

"AGT?"

"Antigovernment Terrorists: Fodders." Her lip curls when she says the words, as if they taste bad.

"Come along now," Mrs. Ali says, so I follow her back to the Unit. As my feet automatically step along the path, I can't stop the images that appear in my mind: a bus stuck in London traffic, explosions, flames. Screaming; bloody hands banging against windows; a final explosion. Then, silence.

A stone memorial, thorny roses, and all those names.

Mrs. Ali leaves me in a chair outside an office. "Wait until she calls you," she says, and disappears down a hall. The door says DR. WINSTON, EDUCATIONAL PSYCHOLOGIST. Soon it opens; another student comes out.

A woman's voice calls from inside. "Next!"

Does she mean me? There is no one else about.

"Next!" the voice says again, louder, and I get out of my seat, peek uncertainly through the door.

"Hello, is that Kyla Davis? Don't be shy, come in."

She smiles—or does she? Her face has bright red lipstick painted on in a turned-up crescent. She has so much makeup caked on that if she smiled properly, her face might crack.

"You've got your school ID done, I see: good. See that, by the door? You put your card along it when you come in. It says who you are."

I turn back: There is a card-sized slot set in a small boxlike machine attached to the wall by the door.

I look uncertainly at my ID, take it in one hand and look back at her.

"You don't have to take it out of the holder, just hold it, facedown, on the slot."

I do so, and it beeps.

"Good girl, now have a seat. You do that whenever you go in or out of any classroom or office at our school; also at the Unit from now on. So we always know where everyone is." She beams that lipstick smile.

I perch on the edge of a seat in front of her desk.

"Now listen up, and I'll just explain the rest of your day." And she tells me that I'll be doing tests all afternoon, to see whether I will go to mainstream classes, start with classes in the Unit, or have some mixture of both. And I'll get a schedule of my assigned classes tomorrow morning.

"Any questions?" she says, but she is already folding her computer shut.

"Well, yes; one."

"Oh?" She pauses, surprised.

"Can I take art? I can draw really well. My nurse said that I should be able to, and . . ." My words trail off. Her eyes are looking impatiently at the clock. She is not interested.

"Tell you what: How about I put a note on your file." She smiles brightly again, and taps at the screen. "There: 'Kyla expresses an interest in art.' All right? Now scoot off to lunch downstairs, there's a good girl."

I stand, and head for the door.

"Wait."

I pause in the doorway.

"You have to scan out, of course! Or the computer will think you are still here."

Oh. I hold the card in the slot; it beeps.

Downstairs I find the room I had lunch in yesterday, and this time notice the card scanner by the door. I scan in; it beeps.

As promised, the afternoon is filled with hours of tests. All on a computer, multiple choice. Mrs. Ali stays and watches as I endlessly press *A, B, C,* or *D.* The questions are mostly easy, and cover many subjects: math, English, basic history, geography, biology.

When I'm finally done, my eyes are tired and shoulders stiff, but I think I did all right. They'll tell me tomorrow, Mrs. Ali says, and then sees me out the door as the final school bell rings.

I get on the bus with Ben, having persuaded Amy to go with Jazz alone. That I'd be all right.

Drifting down the aisle after him, now that my mind is free from all those tests, it is back to the memorial, and the AGT killing a whole busload of students. A bus like this.

I catch the movement too late.

My foot is caught on another that flicks out in front and I trip, fall forward. I try to reach my hands out to stop myself, but my backpack is yanked from behind, pulling my arms backward. My face smashes on the back of a seat and I sprawl on the ground.

Laughter rings out.

I get to my knees and touch my lip; my fingers come away red.

I pull myself up, spin around.

It's her: the girl who blocked the empty seat yesterday, so I couldn't sit next to her.

"Enjoy your trip?" She smiles.

My muscles tense, and I step toward her. The smile falls off her face. Her eyes widen.

"Kyla? Kyla!" Ben takes my arm, yanks me around. Pushes me in front of him toward the back of the bus.

The bus driver gets out of his seat and starts down the aisle.

"Everything all right?" he says.

No one answers. He doesn't see me behind Ben. He goes back to his seat, and soon the bus pulls away from school.

Ben slips a warm arm around my shoulder, guides me into a seat.

"You have to watch your step, Kyla," he says, but his face is unreadable. His eyes show concern, not outrage, yet he must know she tripped me. That this was no accident.

He finds a tissue in his pocket and holds it out. I press it against my lip. Pull it away and look at it. Bright red, though not much of it.

I've had worse.

Have I?

"I'M ALL RIGHT."

"You don't look all right." Mum dabs at my lip with antiseptic. "What happened?"

"I tripped on the bus, and banged my face on a seat."

I don't mention the foot that tripped me, or the laughter that followed when I hauled myself up. Or how I'd turned and was ready to smash that girl in the face. And she knew it, too: A look of uncertain fear crossed her eyes before Ben pulled me away.

"Where was Amy when this was happening?"

And I don't know what to say. I know Jazz being her boyfriend is a secret; is Amy being in his car also a secret? And Mum isn't even meant to be home yet; she left work early. She must have some sort of dragon radar.

"She couldn't catch me," I say, finally. Which is true enough, since she wasn't there.

"Where is she now?"

"At a friend's house, I think," I say, trying to be vague.

"She didn't come home with you after you hurt yourself?"

"Uh . . ."

Her mouth sets in a thin line. "Go up and change."

I stay in my room, holding ice to my lip.

I was going to hit that girl on the bus; I know I was. There was no conscious thought or plan; it was in my muscles tensing up, my hand curling into a fist. My body reacting.

I'm not supposed to be able to do that. My Levo should stop me. Any trace of violence, and it is supposed to knock me out.

But nothing. Somehow I stayed near enough to 5 through the whole thing. How can this be?

After it happened, Ben and the others just sat smiling together as usual, even though they all knew one of them had been deliberately hurt. And it's not like they don't care. Ben came and helped me, didn't he? More like in their happy little Slated brains it is not enough to create a ripple.

I'm nothing like them.

I don't understand.

The front door opens below; I hear voices.

Heated voices.

Minutes tick past, then there are footsteps on the stairs. The door opens: Amy.

"Are you all right?" She crosses the room, tilts my chin up to look at my lip. "That's got to hurt."

I shrug. "A little."

"Good."

She picks up her book by the spare bed, her robe on the back of the door. All her stuff that has spilled into my room the last week of her staying with me so I won't be alone at night. She crosses the hall and goes into her room, shutting the door behind her with a slam.

Like he knows by some feline empathy trick that he is needed, Sebastian peeks into the room, meows and jumps up next to me.

Rubs his head against my arm until I pet him. A tear rolls down my cheek and hits my lip. It stings, and I lick it off.

Green trees blue sky white clouds green trees blue sky white clouds . . .

"Dinner!" Mum yells up the stairs.

I ease sleeping Sebastian from my lap onto the bed, and go down to the kitchen.

"I made soup for you; easier to eat with that lip."

"Thanks."

I sit.

Mum puts my bowl and two plates of pasta onto the table, then goes back to the bottom of the stairs.

"Dinner, Amy," she yells, then walks back into the kitchen. "Well, if Miss Amy can't be bothered to join us, she can go hungry." She plonks down at the table.

I look at my soup.

"Well, try it. I made it just for you."

I pick up the spoon.

"Are you all right, Kyla?" She grabs my wrist just as my Levo vibrates: 4.3. She sighs. "You didn't just trip on the bus, did you."

A mind-reading Dragon.

"Tell me."

"It's not that."

"What, then?"

I don't say anything; just stir the soup.

"It's Amy, isn't it. What did she say?"

I let go of the spoon, slump in my chair. "She's angry with me, and I don't understand."

"Teenage girls: What a nightmare! Boys are so much easier. Wait here."

She stomps up the stairs; moments later returns with Amy, and yanks her into the kitchen.

"Sit!"

Amy sits.

"Listen up, miss. Kyla didn't tell me anything, all right? About your silly little boyfriend, or driving in his insane car, or anything. I put it together all by myself. Now: You two sort yourselves out. I'm going to eat by the TV." And she picks up her plate and stomps off into the other room, shutting the door with her foot.

Amy looks at me guiltily. "I'm sorry. I thought you must have told her."

"She's like a mind reader," I say.

"Somehow she tricked me into confessing. And you can't keep secrets; your face is an open book no matter how you try. I should know that. I'm sorry."

She starts on her dinner, doesn't say much else. But I can see it in her eyes: She won't tell me any more secrets.

I can't be trusted.

And that night, she stays in her own room, leaving me to sleep alone.

The driver is honking the horn. Why, I don't know. They aren't going anyplace; it is gridlock. The road has become a parking lot, right in front of heavy brick buildings with a sign hanging in front: LONDON LORDER OFFICES. *Trapped like rats in a nest.*

I scream at the driver. "Do something! Open the doors! Let them out!"

But he doesn't know what is about to happen. He can't hear me.

First there is a whistling noise, a flash of light, a concussive BANG that rips through my skull and makes my ears ring. And then the screaming starts.

Choking smoke; bloody hands beating at windows that don't open; more screaming. Another whistle; a flash; an explosion. There is a gaping hole in the side of the bus, but most are silent, now.

I cough in the smoke, choke on acrid burning fuel, metal, and worse. Stuff my hands in my ears, but the screaming just goes on and on.

Then, it stops.

And I'm not there anymore. I'm somewhere—someone—else. Terror and smoke and blood, all gone. Not a memory of a past event, not anything . . . just gone. A dream. No more.

No less.

I'm laughing and playing hide-and-seek with other children in my green place. High trees above long grasses, bright dots of purple and yellow wildflowers. I scrunch down behind some bushes, and I see: my hands, my feet. They are small. I am small. My heart thuds a pleasant thump-thump, thump-thump, *from the game. Will they find me?*

When my eyes snap open I can't see anything. I open them wide and then wider, stand and feel my way along the wall to the window, pull the curtains aside and look out. There is no moon tonight.

It worked. Going to my Happy Place in the midst of a nightmare: it actually worked. No screaming the house down, no blackouts. A nearly acceptable 4.8 on my Levo.

But my Happy Place changed in my sleep. The trees, grass, and clouds were still there. But I wasn't alone, this time; I was playing hide-and-seek with children. I was younger, much younger, in that place.

The horror of the first dream is fading, the details starting to disperse like smoke drifting in the sky. Yet it still feels so real; like I was there, watching, that day, when all those students died.

Madness.

17

MY STOMACH IS CHURNING WHEN I GET ON THE BUS THE NEXT morning. But Amy has my back.

And there she is, in her usual seat: the Slater Hater who tripped me yesterday. Sitting upright and staring out the window. I watch her carefully as we go past. She won't catch me unawares again.

Amy follows my eyes. "That the one?" she whispers, but I don't say anything.

When I sit next to Ben at the back of the bus, his eyes widen. "Poor you," he says, and touches my face with fingertips, a featherlight touch around my lip. It bruised up overnight and looks worse today than yesterday. "Does it hurt?"

"Only if I smile," I say.

He slips my cold hand in his warm one. "No smiling today, then," he says sternly, and wipes his off.

His face, serious for once, looks different. The happy expression all Slateds wear, is gone. His eyes still smile, though. I'm struck again by a feeling, one that says I know him and have always known him; that close to him, I am safe. My stomach lurches. Not in a bad way.

Mrs. Ali is waiting for me at the Unit. She takes one look at me, and frowns. "What happened to your face?"

"I fell on the bus."

"Really."

"Yes."

"Listen to me, Kyla: If anyone is hassling you, *tell me*. It will be dealt with. What really happened?"

I look into her eyes, and see only concern. But just when I think I might tell her everything, some voice inside says *bad idea*.

"I tripped, and fell."

She frowns. "Well. If you *remember* anything else about it, tell me. Anyhow, we've got your test results. A clever girl, you are: It is straight into mainstream classes from today. Year eleven, so you're just a little older than the other students. Not that anyone will know if you don't tell them; most of them will be taller than you, anyhow."

She hands me my schedule. "Come on. Your homeroom is in English block."

I open the schedule and scan it, quickly at first; then again, taking more care. English, math, history, biology, study hall, general science, agriculture, and Unit, whatever that means. Most classes are three times a week, different times, different days. But no art.

"What about art?"

"What's that, Kyla?"

"Art. It isn't on my schedule."

"No. You don't get to take an option like the other students. We have to fit extra classes in at the Unit. There's no room."

I stare back at her. This can't be happening. It is the only thing I actually want to take; part of the reason I wanted to come to school. We even had art classes at the hospital.

"But—"

"No buts; there's no time. You'll be late for homeroom. If you have a problem with it, talk to Dr. Winston," she says, and she sweeps out of the Unit. I follow along, numb. This can't be right. Even Nurse

Penny said I could take art as long as they thought I was good enough, didn't she? And that doctor had no interest in me or what I wanted, that was obvious enough. There'd be no point talking to her.

Mrs. Ali drags me along paths and through buildings, dodging through students rushing in all directions. At the class she reminds me to swipe my card, then introduces me to Mr. Goodman, my home-room and English teacher. Other students begin to arrive, to take their seats. And she leaves, saying she'll be back to take me to my first class.

I stand uncertainly by the desk at the front, not sure what to do.

Mr. Goodman smiles. "Wait here with me for a moment, Kyla," he says.

Other students come in, swipe their cards, and sit down, one after another; the final bell goes. One last girl comes in and crosses from the door.

"Late again, Phoebe?"

"Sorry, sir," she says, but she doesn't look sorry. She sits, at the last double desk, the only empty chair left in the room right next to her: the girl who tripped me on the bus.

She looks at my swollen lip and smiles, and I look back at her, not smiling. Whispers start around the room. Do they know?

"Quiet now, 11C," he says. "This is Kyla; she is joining our home-room. I want you to make her feel welcome."

I stand next to him and look across a room full of eyes; some merely curious, some hostile, some uncertain. But all staring. At me, and at the Levo on my wrist.

"Have a seat there next to Phoebe," he says.

I walk, eyes digging into me and dragging my steps, making it hard to move. I pull the chair away from Phoebe as much as I can and still be at the desk, and sit. Mr. Goodman turns to write on the board. Everyone watches Phoebe.

My Levo vibrates. I glance down: 4.4. Phoebe smirks; it vibrates harder. 4.2.

She raises her hand. "Sir? I think our new student is about to blow up."

Everyone titters, and stares. So many eyes; eyes everywhere. 3.9 . . .

I close mine. *Green trees blue sky white clouds green trees blue sky white clouds . . .*

I hear heavy steps, and feel a hand on my shoulder. "All right, Kyla?" Mr. Goodman says.

Green trees blue sky white clouds green trees blue sky white clouds . . .

I open my eyes. "Yes."

"Good girl. Now copy down your citizenship pledge from the board, please."

I open my notebook.

Last lesson of the morning brings a pleasant surprise: Ben. He is in my biology class.

He waves when I swipe my card at the door, whispers to a few other boys who grumble and shift across, leaving an empty seat next to him.

"How's it going?"

I shrug, don't say anything, but it must be on my face.

"It gets better," he says. "Really it does. My first day in classes sucked, too."

And I stare up at Ben, and wonder. Sometimes he seems like every other blank-brained grinning-like-a-lunatic Slated boy I've ever met.

Yet I can see he has thoughts of his own, too. Maybe, just maybe, I'm not as different from the rest of them as it seems sometimes. Or perhaps it is just Ben, making me feel like I'm not in this alone.

He pulls a face. "Remember: no smiling. It hurts."

"Oh, yeah. Right." I banish the ghost of a grin that had been lurking, and smile at him with my eyes, instead.

Our biology teacher, Miss Fern, is loopy and fun. She has us picking birds we'd most like to be and looking up details in books and on websites, then making a poster.

I flick through a book to start, no idea what bird to choose. Until I see black eyes, white feathers, a solemn, heart-shaped face so flat it is like a mask with dark slits. *The barn owl.* Something about the owl says *this is me.*

I soon dispense with taxonomic description and dietary habits and begin drawing: sketching my owl in different positions to start, then settling on in flight, wings stretched wide. Absorbed in sketching, I remember not to use my left hand. It takes away from the experience, but it is still good.

Miss Fern stands over my shoulder. "Kyla, that is awesome," she says. "You have a gift."

Other students crowd around and say nice things about it, too. This class seems much more okay with me being in it; perhaps because Ben was here, first. He draws the eyes of the girls, seems to have an easy friendship with the boys. He is just one of them; they accept him, so they accept me. How does he do that?

The bell rings; I can see Mrs. Ali through the door, waiting in the hall.

"Come for lunch?" Ben asks.

I smile. "All right, just give me a minute." Then I take my time to pack up, until most of the students are gone. Ben waits, a question in his eyes. Will I dare? I walk up to the teacher's desk.

"Miss Fern? I wonder if . . . I mean, I hope maybe, you can help . . ."

"What is it, Kyla? Spit it out."

"I want to take art, but they won't let me. They say I can't do an option."

"Is that a fact. Well. We'll see if we can do something about that," she says. "Can I borrow this?" She gestures to my owl poster, and I give it to her.

I turn, and jump: Mrs. Ali is standing right behind me, lips in a thin line. I didn't hear her come in; didn't even hear the door.

"Can I go for lunch with Ben?" I ask her.

"No. You are scheduled to have lunch in the Unit, and you must stick to your schedule." She turns to Ben, who waits by the door.

"Sorry, Ben. Kyla has Unit now."

He waves and is gone.

Back at the Unit Mrs. Ali gestures for me to follow her into an office, not the lunchroom.

"Lunch is on my schedule," I dare to say.

She shuts the door.

"Kyla, listen very carefully. You are on a short string, dangling. If the string gets too short, it is a long drop."

Is this a threat? Yet she smiles, her warm, gentle smile. It doesn't go with her words.

"I don't understand."

"Kyla, I am here to help you as much as I can, to become a useful, happy, integrated member of our society. To do this, you must learn to follow rules. Your class schedule is just one form rules can take.

You signed a contract when you left the hospital, promising to follow them all: your family's rules, the school, your Group, the wider community." She touches my cheek, her hand warm like her eyes, but her words are cold. "If you break the rules, try to get around the rules, or even just give them a little bend, there will be consequences."

18

"GOOD EVENING, EVERYONE." NURSE PENNY IS IN ANOTHER bright cardigan to go with her voice; this time, it is orange. Thursday night, seven P.M.: time for Group. No sign of Ben, or Tori either, for that matter. The others are all smiling in their seats, and I try to imitate them. A day later and my lip is still impressively bruised, but not nearly as sore.

"Now, perhaps we could start by going around the room, and everyone saying a little of what they've been doing since we last met?"

She starts on the other side of the room, glancing at the clock now and then while tales are related. One tried horseback riding; another had his eyes tested; a third got a puppy. Riveting stuff.

It is about to be my turn when the door flies open at the back, and Ben dashes in, dripping wet. Long-sleeved T-shirt and shorts cling to him, outlining his body in an interesting way.

"Really sorry I'm late," he says, and grabs a chair. He pushes it next to mine and I try not to stare.

Penny pretends to frown at her favorite, but it doesn't quite work. "You haven't been running in this weather, Ben."

He shrugs. "Just a little water, it won't kill me."

"Kyla was about to tell us what she's been up to this week."

All eyes are on me.

"Uh, I started school on Monday. And I'm in classes, as of yesterday. Ben is in my biology class."

Penny looks surprised. "In mainstream classes already? Is it all right?"

I shrug. "Mostly. But . . ." And I stop. Is talking about no art classes some vague rule infringement?

"But what?" she says.

"Nothing. It's fine," I say.

"Don't forget to tell about Sunday," Ben says.

Penny looks at him and he explains. "We met at the Thame Show." And he launches into a description of the Sheep Show that has everyone in giggles. Even Tori had laughed at their silly names, and the way the sheep were paraded across the stage.

"Wait a minute," I say. "Where is Tori?"

Ben looks at me, then back at Penny, a question mark on his face.

"Tori isn't in our Group anymore," she says, and moves on to the next in the circle, who learned how to make chocolate chip cookies. A box of cookies is produced, and conversation ceases as they are passed around.

Ben munches on a handful, crumbs getting stuck on his wet shirt. I resist the impulse to brush them away.

"Ben," I say, in a low voice, "why isn't Tori in our Group anymore? Did she tell you? Why hasn't she been in school this week?"

He shrugs. "She didn't say anything; I don't know."

"Aren't you worried? Maybe something happened to her."

He pauses. "Maybe she's got the flu or something; I didn't really think about it," he says, but I can tell by his face that he is, now. "Tell you what: I'll stop by her place later, and make sure she is all right."

I nod, and Group carries on. I wonder about Tori, and Ben's reaction to her vanishing with no explanation. She was his girlfriend, or so I thought. Yet I get the feeling if I hadn't asked, he wouldn't have thought to. And it isn't like he doesn't care; he just didn't think about it. I wasn't much better as I'd noticed she wasn't in school, but never said anything. There were so many other things to worry about.

I wonder if he'd notice if one day I wasn't here anymore. Would he sit next to some other girl in biology, and not give it a second thought?

Penny has me wait at the end.

"What happened to your face, dear?" she says, concerned.

"I tripped and fell on the bus."

"I see. Was it an accident?"

I hesitate.

"Tell me, Kyla. I won't say anything about it if you don't want me to."

I shake my head. "It wasn't an accident. Someone tripped me."

"Oh, how dreadful. I'm sorry that happened. You have to take care. Some people aren't very nice, are they? How are things going now?"

"All right. I know who to watch out for."

"Sweetie, understanding that you have to look out for some people is a big step. Let me know if there is anything I can do to help," she says, and squeezes my hand.

I stare back at her, thinking I had things muddled up. Mrs. Ali had seemed so nice, and then wasn't, at all. And Penny was so annoying when I first met her, but now I feel like she is on my side.

"Thanks," I say, and give her a real smile.

I get up to go.

"Wait, Kyla," she says. "I asked your mum to come in to chat for a minute."

Moments later Mum appears at the back of the hall, shaking an umbrella. "What dire weather!" she says, scowling and stomping across the floor.

Mum: another one who is puzzling. Is she on my side, or not? Is she the Dragon, or someone who makes me soup when I am hurt? I don't know.

Mum has a chat with Penny about me, but this time I let them get on with it and don't interrupt. Penny is saying I'm ready to have a little more freedom, and do some things on my own to develop independence. Mum disagrees. But eventually says, all right.

A night full of surprises.

19

I TILT MY FACE TO THE SKY. TO TINY DROPLETS, SO SMALL they aren't felt as individuals, but rather just a general sense of wetness. More like mist than rain. But they gather together; a few little trickles form and run cold down my face. Not like tears which are hot.

"You're supposed to put your hood up to stay dry, not spread it out like a rain catcher," Ben scolds. He reaches a hand on either side of my face, pulls up the hood of my jacket, then tucks my hair in on both sides. His hands are warm.

Our eyes meet and he pauses, his hands still on either side of my face. The rain and the woods fade away. His gold-flecked eyes with more depths than first seen hold mine, still, in place.

But then his hands drop; he looks both ways. No one is in sight, but we can hear our classmates' voices not far behind.

"Come on," he says, and starts to walk in the other direction, away from the others. Then turns back to where I stand, my feet uncertain. Should I follow? He holds up his right hand, his little finger curved up, the others tucked in.

I look at his hand, unsure, until he glances down to my left hand, then back to my eyes. I hold up my hand. He hooks my little finger in his and gives it a tug, turns and walks through the trees, pulling me along. His hand held up still, tugging mine with our little fingers linked together. It is so silly, I start to giggle.

I hadn't noticed at first that Ben was leading us away from the others, bit by bit. Why? Despite the cold, I feel flushed. Our biology class is spread out in the woods. We're meant to be collecting water samples from a creek and leaves from undergrowth or trees to identify later. Their voices are distant and becoming more so.

He stops, turns to face me. Suddenly nervous, I step back. "Should we get some leaves? How about those—"

"I need to talk to you," Ben says, and his smile fades away. He didn't seem himself on the bus this morning, either, now that I think of it. I'd asked a question with my eyes, and he'd said *later*.

So now is later. He just wanted to get me alone to talk. Bits inside are jumbled up; relieved, then annoyed. Confused.

"What about?"

"Tori."

I turn my head so he won't see the sudden flash of hurt when he says her name. I should have known.

"You got me worrying something happened to her, and I went to her house after Group last night." He hesitates. The droplets of mist are becoming more the heavy *plop, plop* of bigger raindrops that start working their way through the leaves still on the trees above us. He takes my hand and pulls me closer under a thick tree bough.

"She's not there anymore." He almost whispers, as if the trees are spies.

"What do you mean?"

"I spoke to her mum, and it was really weird. At first she just said that Tori doesn't live there anymore. And I said why, is she with her dad in London? And she went a bit funny. Said things weren't working out, so Tori was returned. She had an odd look on her face and said I shouldn't be there, shouldn't be asking questions. She almost threw me out the door."

"She was *returned*?" My eyes feel round in shock as I struggle to take it in. "They can do that?"

"That was the word she used. Like she was talking about a pair of boots that didn't fit, or a package sent back to the post office."

"But returned to where?" I say, and realization starts to make horror take over from shock. Tori was seventeen, and you can only be Slated if you are under sixteen, so they couldn't just do her again. Did they assign her to another family? If not, what happened to her?

There is a sound, a small vibration, muffled by Ben's coat.

"Let me see," I say, and he holds out his hand. I push up his sleeve to see his Levo: 4.3. "What can I do?"

He shrugs a bit helplessly. "I should run," he says, but he doesn't move. His other hand tightens on my shoulder, and his Levo vibrates again. 4.1.

I slip my arms around him; his go around my shoulders. He moves closer. The rain is falling harder, but he is so much taller, leaning over, that I am sheltered. And even through my jacket I can feel the *thump-thump, thump-thump* of his heart. Mine is beating faster, warmth is sliding through me as I bury my face in his damp jacket. But he is upset because of Tori. It isn't me he wants to hold.

A whistle sounds; we both jump and pull apart.

"That's Miss Fern, calling everyone in. She must have decided it is raining too hard," he says.

"Run?" I ask.

And we do, slipping and sliding on wet leaves down the path, until a few minutes later we reach the group just as Miss Fern starts counting heads.

Today's prac abandoned due to weather, Miss Fern gives us questions to answer.

But I can't concentrate. What happened to Tori? I have a sick feeling in my stomach that says *nothing nice*. I didn't know her for long. She had a knack for saying things out loud that were in my head. Mum had snapped at her at the show, telling her to mind her words. Maybe she wasn't being nasty like it seemed at the time. Maybe, Mum was trying to warn her.

Ben's levels are so up and down that Miss Fern finally excuses him from class and sends him to the track with a TA to run laps.

When the bell is finally about to go, Miss Fern comes around and looks over my shoulder and sees how little work I've done. "Is this the thanks I get?" she scolds. But then she smiles and I see she doesn't really mean it.

"For what?"

She sits in Ben's empty seat. "I've spoken to Mr. Gianelli, head of the art department, and showed him your drawing of the owl." She winks.

"And?"

"He's doing battle to get you in his class. We'll see what happens, but I expect he'll win. He is too annoying to say no to for long."

I don't see Ben again until assembly.

He's sitting with his homeroom, a few rows up and across. His hair is plastered to his head—from rain, or sweat?—but his color is better. He turns when we file in, spots me.

Okay? I mouth. And he nods yes, with a small smile.

Every grade has assembly once a week; year eleven is on Friday afternoons, so this is my first. I'm at the end of the row, Phoebe enough seats away to ignore. The girl next to me is Julie, a girl I sit next to in English. While not entirely friendly, she has been okay, showing me where we are in *Romeo and Juliet* and explaining stuff. Everyone shuffles in their seats, and there is a low hum of voices that abruptly ceases when a door opens at the front.

"*That* is the head of school, Rickson," Julie hisses in my ear. So she is still explaining.

He wears a blue suit that doesn't quite fit against his gut, and stands very straight like he is trying to compensate. His eyes are cold as they sweep around the room, stopping here and there as if to say *I'm keeping an eye on you.* Though I'm not sure if it is him that has everyone still and quiet like stone, or the two men and one woman who file in behind.

Their faces are neutral, their suits identical gray jackets and pants.

"Lorders," Julie says in the quietest whisper, so faint I'm not sure if I heard or imagined the word.

They are like the ones we saw at the Thame Show, when just by being there they silenced the crowd, as they do now. And just like that day, my stomach twists in a cold knot of dread.

Who, or what, are Lorders? Somehow I know but don't know at the same time. And then I remember my dream: the school bus blown up, so many students dying, and the sign hanging on the building next to the bus that said LONDON LORDER OFFICES. But if it was just a dream, something my mind made up after seeing the memorial, how did I put Lorders in it when I didn't know what they are? Maybe it wasn't just a dream. Perhaps Lorders were the target of the bombs that killed those students. But if it wasn't a dream . . . why was I there? Six years ago: I was just ten years old. It doesn't make sense.

The Lorders move off to the side, taking no obvious part; just listening, watching.

Rickson addresses the assembly, and I carefully force my eyes away from the three of them to him, doing my best to listen with part of my brain while the rest still whirls in shock. He goes on about academic and sporting achievements of students. He mentions that the cross-country team open training continues Sunday; he hopes many of us will go along, and names students from our school who placed in the county finals last year. Team tryouts will be next month. Then he says with great sadness that some students are still not fulfilling their potential, and suggests we all try harder.

Everyone stands, and Julie nudges me to do the same. We start filing out, past the Lorders. I almost can't breathe, but somehow put one foot in front of the other, carefully keeping my eyes straight ahead. All the while expecting a cold hand to reach out and clamp on my shoulder.

They stop a few students at the exit and take them to one side. The students go pale, and everyone avoids their eyes. Maybe they weren't fulfilling their potential.

Maybe Tori wasn't, either.

20

THE MAN SPREADS WHITE STUFF—CEMENT?—WITH A METAL thing like a pie spatula across the top row, then, one at a time, plonks bricks on top. Wipes cement that oozes out between the bricks, smooths it around between them. Then starts on another row.

I stare. He glances up a few times, keeps working, placing the bricks one after another.

I know I'm staring, and that you shouldn't stare at people; they generally don't like it. But I can't help myself.

Brick after brick. It is five rows off the ground now.

If I stand here much longer, there will be trouble. Mum is probably timing how long it should take me to mail the letter still clutched in my hand at the mailbox on the corner of the next street. The first time I've been allowed to go anywhere on my own. It may also be the last time if I don't get on with it.

He looks up again, sits back on his haunches. About thirty years old, in blue overalls covered in streaks of paint, cement, grime. Greasy hair. He spits on the ground.

"Well?" he says.

I jump.

"You want something, darling?" He grins as his eyes focus on my wrist, my Levo, then slide back up to my face.

"Sorry," I say, and dash across the street and around the corner, hearing him laugh behind me.

I mail the letter and cross back again. There is a white van parked where he works, with BEST BUILDERS painted across it. He is still placing bricks one after another, building a garden wall.

He whistles when he sees me and I keep walking, cheeks burning, home.

"What took you so long?" Mum says, perched on the front step. Watching, she'd waved as soon as I turned the corner onto our street.

"Nothing; just walking."

"Is everything all right?"

"Yes, fine." I head for the stairs.

"Where are you going?"

I turn. "To do some homework," I lie.

"Well, all right. Diligent little student, aren't you? Dinner will be in an hour."

In my room I shut the door and grab my sketch pad, hands shaking. My Levo starts to drop: 4.4 . . . 4.2 . . .

And I start drawing a wall. Brick after brick from the ground up. My pencil moves fast and then faster; my Levo stops falling, then creeps back up to 5.0. I must finish the wall, and I must draw it with my right hand for it to be correct. After everything today: Tori returned, Lorders in assembly, Lorders in my dream. Somehow I know that as long as I build the wall, everything will be fine.

Green trees blue sky white clouds green trees blue sky white clouds . . .

I almost forget about the wall during dinner. The surprise announcement from Mum that she and Dad have decided, Slated or not, Amy is old enough to see Jazz if she wants.

But before I go to sleep I pull out the drawing, checking to make sure there are no gaps in the wall, no imperfections that can be gotten through. By what, I do not know.

Pain fills my legs, my chest. There is no going on, not for me. I collapse on the sand.

It doesn't matter how he shouts or threatens or pleads, nothing he can do to me will matter soon.

It's getting closer.

He kneels and holds me and looks in my eyes. "Never forget who you are. It's time. Quick, now! Put up the wall."

Closer.

So I build it, brick by brick, row by row. A high tower all around.

"Never forget who you are," he shouts, and shakes me, hard, as I put the last brick—clink—into place. It cuts out all light.

All there is now, is blackness, and sound.

Horrible screams split my skull. Terror and pain, like an animal backed in a corner. Facing death.

Or something worse.

It is a while before I realize.

It is me.

Then, it is as if I step through a kaleidoscope; everything shifts and changes. Grasses tickle my bare feet. Children's voices sound through trees, but I lie down, hidden in the long grass, and watch clouds drift across the sky. I don't want to play today.

Gradually the clouds and the grass drift away. I open my eyes, dreaming over for tonight. I won't shut them again.

It worked, once again—going to my Happy Place in the middle of a nightmare.

But this time, I hadn't wanted to leave it, no matter how horrible. I was sure I was about to find out something, something important. As if seeing bricks cemented into place today, one after another to form a wall, somehow triggered something deep inside. Some recognition, a trail that if followed may help me finally understand who or what I am, what is wrong with me.

What was chasing me? Who was the man? *Never forget who you are,* he said.

But I have.

Most of all: Why—and how—was I building a wall?

21

IT FEELS STRANGE TO BE HEADING BACK TO THE HOSPITAL, the first time since I left. That day I was so scared to leave its walls and venture into the wider world; it feels like eons ago, a whole other lifetime, yet is more like days.

But we might not make it in time for my eleven A.M. appointment with Dr. Lysander. In fact, we might not make it at all. Amy has the map out looking for alternatives, and Mum is cursing under her breath and flicking between radio stations for traffic reports.

"Twenty minutes it has taken us to go the last mile. We might as well turn around," Mum says.

"What if we get off at the next exit?" Amy suggests. She'd been so keen to come today, hoping she might be able to meet Dr. Lysander. She didn't want to lose her chance now.

Mum turns off the radio. "No reports." She frowns. "I don't like this. Something is going on. Amy, find my phone and call Dad."

Amy finds it in Mum's bag and pushes buttons on it as I watch, surprised. Mobile telephones are forbidden to anyone under the age of twenty-one. Maybe it is all right because Mum is next to her and told her to do it?

"There's no answer. Should I leave a message?"

"Yes. Tell him where we're stuck, and ask him to call."

We crawl along, up a gradual incline. A few helicopters fly

overhead. We get close to the top of the hill, then stop. Sirens sound, and black vans dash past on the highway's shoulder.

The phone rings; Mum answers.

"I see . . . All right. . . . Fine. Bye."

She hangs up. "There are some road checks up ahead. Nothing to worry us, I should think."

The traffic starts moving again, slowly. We reach the top of the hill. On the other side, the traffic is stationary. We inch along and stop again. There is a swarm of men dressed in black like hospital guards, stopping and searching cars on both sides, but we get waved on.

"Who are they?"

"Lorders," Amy says.

I snap around to look again: They are not in gray suits like other Lorders I've seen, but black pants and long black shirts with some sort of vest on top. All the hospital guards dress just the same; does this mean they are Lorders, too?

I feel ill, and finally ask the question I have been avoiding.

"What are Lorders?"

Mum turns, eyebrows raised. "You know, Law and Order Agents. They track gangs and terrorists. They're looking for someone."

They must really want to find them to be stopping and searching every car on a motorway.

"But are they the same as the ones in gray suits at the Thame Show, and at school?" I ask.

"Yes, they were at the show; I can't imagine why. They usually wear gray suits, but dress in black when they are in operations; counterterrorism mostly, these days. Used to be gangs. But are there Lorders at school?" Mum says, frowning a little. "Amy, is that so?"

Amy nods. "Sometimes they come to assemblies. They're not always there; just now and then. More so lately."

There are fields sloping up to our left, trees above. I catch a movement: a slight flash, as if the sun caught something glass or metal.

"There's someone up there," I say.

"Where?" Mum asks.

"In those woods," I say, and point. "I saw a flash."

"Are you sure?"

"Yes."

She takes out her phone again, but then a helicopter appears where I'd pointed, and men run from below up to the trees. She puts it down.

Rat-a-tat-tat sounds loud in the air.

"What are they doing?" My eyes open wide. "Are they shooting at someone?"

"Flashing Fodders," Amy says, and sniffs. "Freedom or die they want? Die it is."

The traffic soon starts moving again, and Mum calls the hospital to tell them we'll be late.

We approach New London Hospital the same way we left it, almost two weeks ago; it unwinds in reverse before my eyes. Outlying areas are again bustling with people and traffic; offices and apartment buildings teem with activity. Closer to our destination there are more guards on corners, dressed in black: Lorders. The crowds seem to open around them, as if they are surrounded by an invisible bubble that must not be crossed.

Just as the guard towers of the hospital come into view, there is another roadblock: more Lorders. We sit in traffic between a truck and a bus, and I can't stop thinking of my dream: a whistle, a flash, an explosion. My eyes hunt side to side but find nothing suspicious. They are searching vehicles; we inch forward. But then, just like on the motorway, they wave us through without stopping. This time I notice the Lorders focus on Mum, touch their left shoulder with their right hand, then hold their palms forward.

"Why don't they stop us like everybody else?" I ask.

"Sometimes being my father's daughter comes in handy," Mum says, and I remember *Wam the Man,* who crushed the gangs that terrorized the country nearly thirty years ago. "Sometimes, it doesn't," she adds, so quietly I almost don't hear.

"What do you mean?"

"Must you ask so many questions?" she snaps. Then sighs. "Sorry, Kyla. We can talk about this another time, all right?"

"Why do you play hide-and-seek in your dreams?" Dr. Lysander leans back, hands crossed in front. Observes and waits.

I'd worked out early on with Dr. Lysander that I had to give her something real. I have never told her about the beach, the fear, the running; in various forms, it is a recurring dream I've had ever since I first became aware at the hospital. But if I don't tell her something true, she knows.

It's not just that she is good at reading facial expressions, involuntary gestures, eye movement, blinking, all the usual things you can learn to observe. But with this Levo on my wrist monitoring emotions, it is plain and logged. All she would have to do is scan it to see if I am telling the truth or lying. Though Dr. Lysander is confident she can see everything without resorting to such devices. Her confidence is justified.

Even so, deception isn't impossible, just difficult. Like being a magician and attracting attention away from the very thing she would like to examine, if it is noticed. Trying not to give the trick away.

"May I ask you a question?" I say.

Dr. Lysander sits back. She will often answer questions, if you dare to ask them. But it is best to check first as she isn't always in the mood.

She tilts her head forward. Permission granted.

"Why the fascination with hide-and-seek? It's a happy dream; I'm just playing. Nothing *wrong* is happening."

"What could it represent?"

"I don't understand."

"You hide from others; it is a game you are playing, you see? Why do you hide? What do you hide?"

Oh. I think about it for a moment. Am I hiding something? Not that I know.

Leaving the hospital is much like the last time, the day I met my family. We spiral up out of the underground parking lot to a gate; Amy's and my Levos are scanned, guards have a quick look in the car and finally raise the barrier. Relief washes over me as we leave the fences and guards behind. The whole hospital complex felt heavy and dense around me today, as if it were crushing the air out of my lungs. How did I live there for so long?

And the guards: They are Lorders, too. When I lived behind those walls, I just accepted the towers with their guns, the barred windows, the guards that patrolled outside with dogs. The high fences.

Is it all to keep people in, or out?

I stare out the window all the way back from the hospital, Mum driving and busy with her own thoughts, while Amy sulks, upset that her hero, Dr. Lysander, wouldn't take time to speak to her and just brushed her off.

We are going *home*. Is it mine? It is becoming familiar; comfortable, most of the time. I no longer wake in the morning unsure where I am, and can find my way around in the dark. Going back to the hospital today felt not comforting, but claustrophobic: It made me want to jump out of the car and run all the way back to the country.

At least Dr. Lysander agreed with Nurse Penny and told Mum to let me do more stuff on my own now; she said I can explore, go walking alone if I want. But Mum was less than pleased when Dr. Lysander said she wants to see me not once a fortnight, but every single week. Every Saturday we'll have to make this trek.

We are nearly home before I remember: Why did Mum call to ask Dad about what was happening on the road? It wasn't on the radio news, then or now.

Why would he know?

SUNDAY MORNING THE SKY IS A BRILLIANT BLUE, BUT SO cold my breath is a white shroud about my face. I shiver and wrap my arms around myself as I wait at school for the bus that will take us for cross-country training. More students arrive, and a teacher with a clipboard.

The bus pulls into the school, followed by a car behind: Ben. I wait for him while the others climb on the bus.

Ben's smile is surprised. "I didn't know you run," he says.

It was that horrible closed-in feeling at the hospital yesterday that made me decide to come. I know why Ben runs; I used to, too, on the treadmills in the hospital gym. *Endorphins,* they are called: chemicals released in your brain when you run and run, past the point of exhaustion, past the point of aching muscles. Into a zone where you don't feel what you are doing to your body anymore, just exhilaration coursing through and you never want to stop; everything inside becomes calm and clear, in icy focus. And maybe I want to run because of my dream, where I can't run anymore and collapse. I want to be able to run away from that.

Mum took a little convincing that I was serious and wanted to go, and had to be reminded that Dr. Lysander said to let me do things on my own. Amy just smirked and teased me about Ben when Mum wasn't listening.

The cross-country coach, Mr. Ferguson, gives me a funny look as

Ben and I climb onto the bus. "Not another groupie," he says, and rolls his eyes at Ben. Some of the other boys smirk and I start to get what he means.

"I can run," I say, and scowl at the pink rising in my cheeks.

"Well, we'll see, little lass," he says, and laughs.

There are a dozen or so boys and almost as many girls. They all seem to know one another, and "little" I am, smaller than any of the others.

I slip into a bus seat by the window; Ben sits next to me. As the bus pulls away from school, he leans down and whispers in my ear, "Is it true?"

"What?"

"Are you just here because I am?"

"No!" I say, indignant, and punch him in the arm.

"Ow!" He rubs it. "I was kind of hoping you were."

I look away, confused. Does he mean it? What about Tori? I don't know what to say, so I say nothing.

The ten-kilometer course is multiterrain: footpaths over fields and woodland, with a few hills, ditches, and creeks to scramble across. Not exactly a treadmill, and I start to wonder how I'll be. They've all done this course before. Ferguson shows me a map and says there are course markers—small orange flags—all the way. I scan the map, several times; it only takes moments to commit the route to memory.

The boys start first. I watch them take off across the field. We must wait ten minutes. I do stretches and warm up. Ferguson walks over.

"You haven't been to any of the other training sessions," he says.

"No. I just joined the school a week ago; I couldn't."

"Fair enough. Just watch your step, and pace yourself, all right?

Ten kilometers is a long way to go. I get hell every time I have to call an ambulance."

"Your concern is touching," I say.

Surprise crosses his face, and he laughs. "Ha! You're all right. Let's see what you can do, eh?"

A few of the girls look less than pleased.

He starts us off.

We run across fields at the beginning. Unused to the uneven ground, I take it easy, getting into a rhythm. We're spread out with me somewhere toward the back of the middle, the boys well out of sight.

The sun, the *thud-thud* of my feet on the ground, the faster *thump-thump* of my heart: It all feels good. Time to go faster. I turn up the pace as we follow a path through woodlands.

Around a bend, a branch on the ground suddenly lifts up. There is no time to jump it or divert, nothing to do but catch my foot against it and fall over. I go flying through the air, hands out. As I land heavily, two girls off to the side drop the branch and run off. Laughing.

I can't breathe, and lie on the ground, gasping like a fish flipped on a beach. Gradually normal breathing comes back, and I start to sit up.

A few girls pass, and another; one pauses. "Are you all right?" she says. I just wave a hand, and she keeps going.

They're all past me now.

There are scratches on my arm and a cut on one knee. I stand carefully and test my legs; everything seems all right. At least Ferguson won't need to call an ambulance today. Anger surges through me. Stuff them! I was loving running; why did they have to do that? And I breathe in deep, again and again, to calm down, and check my Levo: 5.8. Must still be up from running.

It is a long race, a little voice inside reminds me. A *very* long race.

I start again.

I go fast, then faster. There are trail markers as Ferguson said, little orange flags every now and then that show the path. But then, as the path forks into two, the flag is on the left, not the right: the wrong side? I pause and close my eyes, consider the map I'd memorized before setting off. *Definitely* on the wrong side.

Is someone playing another game? No matter. The map is firmly in my mind. I ignore the misplaced flag and keep running.

Soon I pass the girl who had asked if I was all right, and the others who didn't. I'm *there,* in that place where running and breathing are everything, and everything is each foot thudding on the ground, flying along. I'm covered in mud from splashing along a creek, my arm and knee are bleeding, and I don't care.

I smile as I pass the two girls who tripped me with the branch, giving them a wide berth. I can see the surprise, then effort as they try to speed up, but can't. They disappear behind me.

And so I pass another, a few more. I've lost count—was that the last girl? Not content with doing *all right* anymore, I want to be first. I go faster.

I pass a few of the boys, too, then a few more, before the finish line appears in the distance—the place we started.

Ferguson, Ben, and half a dozen boys who have finished start cheering when they see me appear over the hill.

When I run over the line, Ferguson squints at his stopwatch. "Flipping heck. Did you sprint the whole way?"

I stop and try to answer, but can't speak. The world starts spinning sickeningly.

"Don't answer me! Run it off," Ferguson says.

Gasping, nauseous, I run circles around the parking lot, again and again, slower each time, until I can finally stop without wanting to throw up.

More of the boys finish, and a while later, the girls.

"What happened to you?" Ferguson says when he sees the blood on my arm and leg.

I shrug. "I tripped," I say. "It's all right; I won't need an ambulance."

He laughs, gets the first aid kit, and puts a bandage on my knee.

"We're a good pair, you and I," Ben says when we get on the bus.

"Oh?"

"I was first of the boys; you were first of the girls."

"How much before me did you get there?"

Ben shrugs. "Five minutes or so. Why?"

"Well, we started ten minutes after you. That means I was faster than you."

Understanding then surprise cross his face, and he grins. "Good. I needed a reason to train harder."

He peeks at my Levo, 8.1, and shows me his, 7.9. "You beat me there, too," he says. The bus pulls away and he leans in close. "So now is a good time for this," he says, his voice low so I have to lean in, and am glad of it. His body radiates heat, and mine is getting cold, colder by the second.

"A good time for what?"

His smile falls away. "I've been checking around a bit, asking a few questions."

"About?"

"Tori isn't the first to disappear. There have been others at our school, Slateds, that one day just aren't there anymore. No explanation."

"Returned," I whisper, and a cold shiver passes through me. Ben slips an arm over my shoulder.

"That's not all. Others, too: not Slateds. Like those three pulled out of assembly on Friday. They're gone, too, and it isn't the first time it has happened."

Naturals going missing, too? The ones at assembly were taken aside by Lorders; they must have taken them. My stomach twists.

"But why?"

"The boys I can understand. I heard one got caught with a mobile phone. And the other was a jerk, always getting in fights and stuff. Maybe he was in a gang?"

"And the girl?"

Ben shrugs. "She never did a thing wrong. But she was very smart, always asking teachers awkward questions, like in history. About why things were done, or not done."

Asking awkward questions. Like Ben.

"Ben! You've got to stop trying to find out stuff; you might be next."

"But what about Tori? If no one asks, no one cares. Don't you see? It could be you, it could be me. I have to know what happened to her."

"I don't want you to disappear," I whisper, and he pulls me closer. Mud and sweat in a hug, his heart beating under my ear.

A few of the boys make smooching noises at us, and Ferguson turns around. "No canoodling on the bus," he yells, and I sit up straight. Ben still clings tight to my hand.

Just as he clings tight to Tori.

A surprise: Not just Mum but also Dad is waiting for me when the bus gets back to the school. I wave good-bye to Ben and the others and walk over to the car, muddy and exhausted, with a bandaged knee. Everything is stiffening up so much now, it is an effort just to put one foot in front of the other.

Mum jumps out of the car. "What in hell happened to you?" she says, horror on her face.

"I'm fine. And look." I show her my Levo: 6.6. Even with the distress of our whispers on the bus, running is obviously the way to keep my levels up.

"But the state of you!" And she marches off to have a word with Ferguson. Dad gets out of the car as well, looks me up and down.

"It was good fun, then?" He grins.

"Oh, yes." I smile back and lean against the car, feeling like I'll fall over if I don't. I haven't seen Dad since he scared me in the dark in the kitchen—he's been away for work—but now he looks happy, relaxed, nothing like the grim one who questioned me for nearly screaming when he startled me in the middle of the night.

"How'd it go?"

"I came in first."

He whoops, holds up his hand. "High five?"

"What?"

"Hold up your hand, like this." I do, and he claps his hand against mine. Then he gestures at Mum and winks. "She's not going to like it if you keep this up. She has a low tolerance for dirt and blood."

That night, Jazz comes for dinner. Amy smiles great dopey grins at him all evening, Mum does her best dragon impression, and Dad tells bad jokes. Jazz even answers to Jason, looks resigned to his fate, and doesn't talk much beyond saying "yes, please" and "thank you." I just concentrate on eating.

"Hungry today?" Mum says, surprised as I go for seconds of roast beef, potatoes, and gravy.

I shrug. "I did run ten K's this morning."

"Don't forget to have some greens as well," she says. On my plate are a few green spriggy bits, like little trees. So far I'd managed to avoid them.

"What is it?"

"Broccoli. Haven't you had it?" she says, looking surprised.

"I don't think so." With all eyes on me there is nothing for it. I spear some with a fork, chew, and keep on chewing. It's springy and horrible. I try to swallow it down, but my throat rebels: It won't go. I gag and start to choke.

"Are you all right?" Mum half gets up, but I hold up a hand and she sits down again, and somehow I manage to swallow. When no one is looking I shove the rest of my broccoli into a napkin, and then later, into the garbage bin. *That* was disgusting. But beyond the nauseating taste and feel of the stuff . . . is something else. Some importance wrapped up in it, but when I reach for what it is, it twists and is gone.

23

"**You're to skip homeroom and go see Dr. Winston**,"
Mrs. Ali says. "Now."

"What? Why?" I stare back at her, but her face is unreadable.

"I expect she'll tell you. Go upstairs and wait." She smiles, but it
doesn't make me feel better.

What is this about? I climb the stairs and sit down, hands clenched.
Maybe, somehow, they know Ben and I have been talking about people disappearing. Maybe the bus was bugged, and the Lorders are
pulling him out of his class, right now. Maybe, they will—

Her door opens; a boy steps out.

"Next!" a voice yells.

I stand and walk into the psychologist's office. Scan my card, shut
the door and sit down.

"Good morning, Kyla!" She is smiling her painted-on lipstick
smile.

"Hi."

"A teacher has been talking to me about you. Do you know what
about?" She purses her lips. I scan my mind—a teacher? Have I done
something wrong?

"One of my teachers? I . . . I don't know."

"Don't look so panicked. It is one of your teachers, but you don't
know him yet. Mr. Gianelli, head of the art department. It seems he

saw a drawing of yours, and has been most *persistent* in insisting you be moved into his class."

"Really?" I can feel the smile taking over my face.

She frowns. "He was *most* annoying."

"I'm very sorry about that, but . . . um, so can I take his class?"

"Yes. Here's your new schedule." She thrusts it at me. "We had to move your math class also to make it fit. You'll have Unit at lunch twice a week to make that up, and can do as you will the other days from now on."

"Thank you so much, thank you, I—"

"Just *go*."

I dash out of the seat, scan my card at the door.

"Oh, and Kyla?"

I turn. "Yes?"

"Don't look so pleased with yourself. I don't want to be bothered by you, or by anyone about you, again, anytime soon. Is that clear?"

She smiles brightly as she says the words, which somehow makes them worse.

I wipe the grin off my face. "Yes," I say, and bolt out of the room and down the stairs.

Mr. Gianelli, my champion, isn't what I expect at all.

"Who are you?" he demands, scowling, when I slip in just after the bell.

"Kyla Davis."

"Who?"

"A new student. You arranged it with Dr. Winston?"

At the mention of her name, his scowl deepens. "Aha! You are the owl girl. I had to endure three meetings with that insufferable woman on your behalf."

I look nervously behind me, but the door is shut; Mrs. Ali is gone. As I turn back and glance over the students, my heart sinks: Phoebe. *Oh great.* She is in my art class, too.

He whips my owl sketch out of a pile on his desk, holds it up to the class and, before he lets me sit down, proceeds to tell everyone exactly how I could make it better. And he's right.

But today, we are painting.

What to paint?

My Happy Place; maybe it will help me go there. I start on the sky. Soon I am absorbed in the blues, mixing them on a palette, adding wisps of cloud, white swirls with a palette knife. So lost in the sky that I almost don't register low voices behind me.

"Wonder what she did to get Slated."

"Bet it was bad."

"Couldn't have been much; she's a scrawny little wuss."

"Maybe she tortured little children 'cos they were the only ones smaller than her."

"Maybe she set fire to her house and roasted her parents alive. Sort of a mum and dad barbecue. Bet they screamed."

I spin around.

"Maybe I slit someone's throat with a palette knife." I balance it on one hand as if checking the weight.

Her friend backs off, but Phoebe laughs. "You know she can't hurt anyone now, no matter what she did before. She'll die if she tries. Her brain will fry: zap!"

I turn back to my painting.

Green trees blue sky white clouds green trees blue sky white clouds . . .

"Happy with your new schedule?" Mrs. Ali asks, smiling pleasantly at break.

And I don't know whether to say the obvious yes, because with or without Phoebe and trying not to think about what they said, I love it. Or will she feel I've been getting around things, and I'm in trouble if I'm happy about it?

She laughs. "Your face—you should see it sometimes."

So she is in a good mood today.

I smile hesitantly. "I love my art class. It will really help me"—I scan my brain for what the head said at assembly—"reach my full potential."

She looks amused. "Don't just parrot the words, Kyla. You must do your best at all times to fulfill your contract."

"Can I ask a question?"

"Sure."

"What happens if someone like me doesn't fulfill their contract? Can they be . . . returned?"

She stares back at my eyes. Something crosses her face, so fast I'm not sure what it is; then it is gone. She smiles. "Just keep your head down for a while, Kyla, until Dr. Winston forgets how you annoyed her."

She walks me to my next class, and I think about what she said. She didn't answer the question. And that, in itself, is an answer.

24

Thud-thud; thud-thud. My feet thump along the track.

Maybe she tortured little children . . . maybe she set fire to her house and burned her parents alive . . . or slit someone's throat with a palette knife.

I run fast, and faster.

I can see my hands with a knife. Maybe a sharp one from the kitchen, not a palette knife: too blunt. Or setting a fire: spraying petrol and throwing a match. Or, instead, flammable liquid in a glass bottle, a cloth in the end set alight and the whole thing smashed through a window. Would I have stayed to listen to the screams? No. How could you be sure to get away?

But I didn't get away. Here I am.

The track blurs past and I run to keep my levels up, but can't stop the thoughts and images jumbling in my mind.

What about torturing little children? I couldn't have done that. Could I? Then I remember my dream: students blown to bits on the bus. They weren't much more than children.

Could I have done any of these things?

Someone is getting close, behind me; I speed up, but still they gain. I glance to my right: Ben.

"Hey," he says. "You can go."

I nod, unable to speak, my lungs full of the effort of keeping up the oxygen supply for my body.

A few more laps, and a few more, Ben beside me now. Once the paintbrush was out of my hand and art class over, Phoebe's words kept repeating over and over in my head. I'd come straight to the school track at the end of my last morning class, today the first day I didn't have to go to the Unit for lunch. Ben's presence is comforting, though he gives up trying to speak when I don't answer. Gradually, he lowers his pace. Reluctant to leave him behind, I slow down with him, bit by bit.

"Enough?" he finally says, and I nod. We slow and stop. He links his arm into mine and leads me away, and we walk around the school grounds, along the paths. Other students mill about but ignore us.

"Want to tell me what is wrong?"

I shrug.

"Something had you running like a lunatic."

"Just a few things some girls said, that's all. It's stupid."

"What?"

I don't answer, but I tug his hand to change direction. We walk alongside the administration building until we get to the memorial, and I stop in front of it.

So many names, carved in stone: all dead. Six years ago. What an imagination I have. I give myself a shake. I was only ten years old then; I couldn't have been there.

"Kyla, what is it?"

"Don't you ever wonder? What you did to get Slated. What if I was a terrorist? What if I killed people, like these students; threw a bomb on their bus."

Ben shakes his head. "I don't know what I could have done. I can't think I could have ever done anything as horrible as that; you, either. But we'll never know. All we can do is live our lives as they are now; be who we are now."

I consider his words. The thing is, I can't imagine Ben ever having done anything dreadful; Amy, either. But somehow I am less sure of myself.

"But how can I know who I am now, if I don't know who I was?"

"I know who you are: Kyla, lunatic runner, and my friend." He slips his arms around my shoulders. "Kyla with the shy smile, and the face that shows every feeling inside. What else is there to know?"

I look up into Ben's warm eyes, like melted chocolate, just now asking a question: *Who are you, Kyla?*

"I like to draw, and paint," I say slowly. "I'm good at it, too."

"Kyla the artist. Good. What else?"

I rack my brains for answers. "I hate broccoli. I like cats." It's a start, I guess.

Ben smiles and his arms tighten. My stomach flips. *Sweet sixteen and never been kissed.* There is something in his eyes that says it will be *now,* me with clothes stuck to my skin and hair limp from running, out in the open where anyone might see. Tori's presence still hangs between us, but just now he doesn't seem to care, and neither do I.

But something draws my eyes, makes me turn to look at the memorial and all the carved names. The one at the top suddenly jumps out as if someone had shouted it out loud.

Robert Armstrong.

I gasp and pull away. Ben lets go.

"What is it?" he says.

I step up to the memorial and feel along the letters. Amy told me Mum had a son named Robert, who died. Before she married Dad, her name was Armstrong.

Robert Armstrong.

Is it her son? My . . . brother?

"Kyla, what's wrong?"

But I shake my head; I can't tell him, though I see the disappointment. His face says *Don't you trust me?* Amy made me promise to never mention Robert, so how can I?

The afternoon passes in a blur. My levels manage to stay up in the 5s still from running, but my thoughts are in turmoil. How could Mum have me—Amy, too—if her son was killed by terrorists? And years before, her parents were murdered, as well. To get Slated you had to have done something really bad. What if I was a terrorist?

Dinner is weird that night. Mum seems to keep staring at me, catching me out. To sit up straighter; to eat my broccoli, which no matter how I try gives a gag reflex; to answer inane questions about school. Maybe she is watching for me to slip up enough so she can send me back. *Return* me, like Tori.

Amy has to study for a math test; I jump to wash up. I will do everything exactly right. I concentrate: stack the plates, wipe the counters. Wash each dish with extreme care, and—

"What is with you tonight?"

I spin around and knock a glass off the counter; it smashes on the floor. Splinters fly everywhere. Mum sighs, and I scamper for the dustpan and brush in the cupboard.

"I'm sorry," I say, and kneel down to brush the shards into the pan.

"Kyla, it is just a glass. It's no big deal. Now, are you going to tell me what is wrong?" And I look at Mum, really look at her, and she isn't the Dragon, at least not for now. Her face is troubled, not angry, and she reaches out a hand to help me stand up. "What is it, hmmm?"

I can feel pricking at the back of my eyes and blink furiously, but it's no good.

"Well?"

"I hate broccoli," I say, and burst into tears. But that isn't why I am crying, is it? It is more that I hated broccoli the first time I tasted it, here, just days ago. As soon as it was in my mouth, I gagged: My body recognized it. If I always hated it—even before I was Slated—I'm not a new person, no matter that they say that I am. If I'm not a new person, whatever I may have done is still there, still part of me, hidden someplace inside. And while my brain is turning these thoughts over the rest of me is busy crying, in great gulping, hiccupy sobs—like my body and my brain aren't connected, they don't go together. And I don't understand why.

My Levo starts to vibrate; Mum curses under her breath. Drags me into the lounge and onto the sofa. Fetches Sebastian and makes me hot chocolate. Sits next to me, rubs my shoulder while Sebastian purrs on my lap. Her face a question that does not understand, but says nothing.

"I'm too much trouble; you're going to want to send me back," I finally say into the silence.

"What? Of course not. What do you mean?"

And I tell her about Tori being returned. And there is no surprise on her face.

"Tori was the pretty girl with Ben at the show, right?"

I nod. "What happened to her?"

She hesitates.

"Please tell me."

"I honestly don't know," she says, but some part of me can see she agrees with Ben's and my conclusion: *nothing good.* "But her mum might not have had anything to do with it."

"What do you mean?"

"She was pretty lippy. Somebody else might have heard stuff she said, decided she wasn't fulfilling her contract, you see? She wasn't *grateful* enough for being given a second chance."

"Somebody, like who? Is everyone around me spying on me all the time?" I look side to side as if unseen eyes and ears are behind the furniture.

"It's not as bad as that, Kyla," she says gently. "A few will make regular reports: your teachers, your nurse. Dr. Lysander, I suppose."

"Do you report on me? Does Dad?"

"Of course. It is part of what we agreed to when we took you and Amy. But don't worry: I would never say anything that would cause them concern. Understand?"

Was it my imagination, or did she stress the *I* of that sentence?

"Kyla, listen to me: I'm not going to send you back. All right? I wouldn't do that."

"No matter what?"

"No matter what. And I won't make you eat broccoli again, either."

Later that night, lying in bed, Sebastian a long band of warmth stretched out against my back, purring, it is hard to remember what had me so upset I cried. But I could tell—like with hating broccoli, like being able to drive. Like drawing better with my left hand. And the way I cried, in great gulpy sobs. I didn't know how to cry, I wasn't good at it; it wasn't something I *did*.

Whoever Kyla is, there is another person hiding away. And it is her I am afraid of, most of all.

First, there is the sound.

Scrape, thump; scrape, thump. *Like something metallic drawn across a coarse surface, or a shovel pushed into sand, lifted and dumped, again and again.*

I open my eyes.

Not a shovel but a trowel: scooping rough mortar, slapping it down on the top row of bricks, high above me.

Scrape, thump; scrape, thump.

Bricks form a circle pattern, a wall, all around. If I reach out my hands mere inches, side to side, front to back, all I can touch are roughly built, round walls. And it is getting higher, row by row. The only light is a dim circle high above, and getting dimmer.

I'm in a tower, with no windows, no doors. The top of the wall is high above me, and—scrape, thump; scrape, thump—*getting farther away by the second.*

Abruptly the circle of light disappears. The sound ceases.

Panic turns to anger. I strike at the walls, kicking and punching, again and again; I collapse against it, unable to sit down in the confined space, bare feet, hands and knees bruised and bloody.

Let me out! I howl.

My eyes snap open. Staring back at me are two circles of reflected light. They blink: Sebastian?

I sit up, switch on the bedside light. Sebastian is next to me on the bed, his fur standing on end, his tail puffed out; on my arm is a neat row of even scratches, welling up red.

"Did you wake me up?" I whisper, and reach out a tentative hand, lightly stroke him. He may have saved me a blackout. Did he somehow know, or did he just scratch because I flailed at him in my dream?

Soon his fur settles down, and he flops beside me and purrs. My heart rate slows; my Levo eases up from mid 3s to almost 5 over time, but I don't close my eyes. The light is staying on.

I am afraid of the dark.

25

"YOUR CHARIOT?" JAZZ SAYS, AND BOWS.

Since the deal with Amy seeing Jazz involves her not being alone with him, it looks like I won't be taking the bus with Ben after school so much anymore. I climb into the back.

No seat belt. Amy and Jazz get in the front, and I sigh and brace myself as Jazz lurches out of the school grounds and along the main road, then exits down a lane. Not going straight home?

"I've got a surprise for you, Kyla," Jazz says, looking more in the mirror at me in the backseat than at the road.

"Watch it!" Amy says, and he brakes hard, just in time to avoid sheep crossing the road. A farmer glares; even his dog seems to glare. The sheep amble across with blank expressions.

"Whoops." Jazz waves, mouths *sorry* at the farmer.

"What's the surprise?" Amy says when we start off again.

"Mac's found a reclaimed seat belt to fix up in the back."

"Hurrah!" I say, with real enthusiasm. *Try to stay on the road in the meantime,* I think, but don't say out loud.

Jazz does pay a little more attention to where he is going after the nearly hitting sheep incident, and I relax, just a little. My eyelids start to close on their own, so tired after last night's dream and the effort of staying awake after it. Every time my eyes drifted closed, I felt brick walls settle around me. Now my head droops forward against the seat in front, and images jumble around in my mind: the monument, Robert Armstrong carved on it, the tower . . .

"Try to stay awake," Amy says, and my eyes snap open again.

"See? My driving's not so bad if passengers can actually nap," Jazz says.

Mac pulls the backseat out of the car.

"Shall we go for a walk?" Jazz says, and winks at Amy. "But perhaps you are too tired," Jazz says to me, pointedly.

"Yes, you look tired," Amy says. "We won't be long." They start walking away, heading for a footpath sign down the road.

"If you don't want me to come, why don't you just say so?" I say at their retreating heads.

Mac looks out from the back of the car and laughs. "Get yourself a drink if you want."

"No, thanks," I say, remembering his homemade beer from the last time.

"There are soft drinks in the fridge," he says, with a smirk that says he knows what I'm thinking. "Go on, have a snack if you want, whatever. Put the TV on. They'll probably be a while." He laughs again.

Translation: Don't stand there and watch me work on this pile of junk car.

Fine. I wander back into his house. Sure enough, in the fridge are drinks that look more innocuous than the brown bottles in the cupboard. I *am* hungry, after running a few thousand laps at lunch today to keep my levels up. Ben came along and didn't ask why I ran. Maybe he's given up asking me things when I don't answer.

I find cheese and thick-cut, uneven bread: homemade? I stick my head out the door and yell, "You want a sandwich?"

"Sure," comes back. "I'll be in in a bit."

So I make a few sandwiches. I'm not big on TV, but I put it on and flick through all three channels. BBC1 is some stupid comedy show with a laugh track that makes little sense to me; BBC2 is a gardening program about increasing allotment production; BBC3 is news and weather. I watch it while I eat. Rain is coming the next few days. This autumn's harvest figures are up. Some bit on neighborhoods in London. They show footage of roads I've seen on the way to and from the hospital, but they don't look the same. The burned-out buildings— they're not there. No guards, either.

"You look thoughtful." Mac stands in the doorway.

"Well, it's just that I've been down that road, and it looks different on TV. It is cleaner, neater. Different."

Mac raises an eyebrow, sits down. "They mostly only put happy places and people on the news."

I frown. "Well, that isn't really news, then, is it. People aren't always happy. That building—look, there: It was a shell when we drove past, a week ago. It hasn't been fixed up that quick."

Mac picks up a sandwich. "Ah, but it looks prettier this way, don't it."

"That's stupid."

"It certainly is." He laughs again.

And I look back at Mac, chewing his sandwich. He doesn't look or talk like adults usually do. Well, he isn't that old, I suppose.

"What? Ask whatever is in that brain of yours," he says, an amused look on his face.

"Did you bake this bread?"

"Yes."

"Do you cut your own hair?"

"Yes."

"How old are you?"

"Twenty-two."

Not that old, then, younger than I guessed. Six years older than me. And a thought grabs me: *six years older than me*. The memorial at school was from six years ago.

"Did you go to Lord Williams's School?" I say, the words coming out without thought. It must be the lack of sleep.

"I did."

"Did you know Robert Armstrong?"

He looks levelly back at me, and something passes over his face. The laughing leaves his eyes. He gets up and grabs one of those brown bottles out of the cupboard and sits down again.

"Yes, I did. He was a friend of mine," he says quietly as he flicks off the cap with an opener.

"Was he my . . . brother?"

He shrugs, takes a drink from the bottle. "Depends how you look at things, I guess. He was the son of the mum you've got now."

The mum I've got now. Not my original. Interesting way to put it, but everyone insists she is *Mum* to me.

I open my mouth to ask about Robert, but he puts up a hand. "Enough questions out of you for a minute; you answer a few of mine. Why'd you ask about Robby?"

And I stare back at him, not sleepy anymore, and a bit scared. Robby, not Robert; he was *real,* an actual person. Somehow I know these are dangerous topics. Why did I start?

"It's all right," he says. "Tell me."

And there is something about Mac that makes me think *I trust you,* so I do tell him, surprised that I dare. About how I'd been fascinated with the memorial; couldn't stop thinking about all those students, just fifteen and sixteen, who died on that bus. And that I had a nightmare about it, then saw the name: Robert Armstrong. But didn't know for sure who he was.

"You, young lady, are an interesting creature," he says.

"I'm not a creature!"

He laughs. "Sorry. You've been Slated, yet unlike that brainless imp young Jazz is currently trying to defile on a field someplace, you seem to still have an actual mind of your own."

"Amy's not brainless! And she's not . . . er . . ." And I don't know what to say, as I have no idea what she and Jazz are getting up to. And I have an uncomfortable feeling I'm supposed to be minding them and am failing in my duties.

He laughs again. "All right, she's not *stupid;* that isn't what I mean. She just doesn't question anything."

Oh. So we're back to *Kyla is different.*

He leans forward in his chair, laughter gone again and dead serious. "But there is a very important question I have for you."

"What?"

"It is one thing to ask questions; what do you do with the answers?"

I can see he means this seriously, so I think a moment. What do I do with the answers . . .

"I suppose, I'm trying to figure things out; to understand them. Just for myself."

He nods. "Just for yourself: That is the important thing, Kyla. You must keep your questions inside most of the time, take care who you ask. And the answers, keep them inside all of the time. Can you do that? Can you keep things to yourself?"

"Yes."

He leans back in his chair, has a drink of his beer. "Well, fire away. What do you want to know?"

I swallow. I want to know what happened that day. But do I? I deflect.

"What was he like, then, your Robby."

"Just a guy like the rest of us, I guess. Serious, a bit shy. And smart: He was into science and stuff. Quite the most amazing thing about him was that he had the most beautiful girl in school as his girlfriend. Couldn't work that one out."

"Did they report what happened on the news? It wouldn't have been *pretty.*"

"True. But they do report stuff like that; they just say how the in-human evil Antigovernment Terrorists casually slaughtered innocent schoolchildren as part of their ongoing campaign of terror."

"Is that what happened?"

"Not exactly. The AGT tried to bomb Lorder offices; the bus got in the way. They died. Don't imagine they meant for it to happen."

"But it still happened. They still killed Robert, and all those other students," I say, outraged. It doesn't matter what they were *trying* to do. They may have been trying to kill other people, who may or may not have deserved it, not a busload of kids. But they still did it.

"Yes, and no."

"What do you mean?"

"Robby didn't die on the bus."

"What? But he is on the memorial; it says he did. How do you know?"

"I was there."

I stare back at Mac, horrified. I hadn't asked the most important question, as it turned out; I didn't know to ask it. Though maybe I should have worked it out for myself.

My Levo vibrates.

"Are you all right, Kyla?"

I look down; 4.3. I shrug. "At the moment. Got any chocolate?"

"Is that all it takes?"

He finds some and I eat it, focus on the sweetness, on breathing, and think myself out of it. My levels climb back up to near 5.

"I'm sorry," I say. "I can't help it."

"That must really suck."

"If I get angry about it, it just makes things worse."

"I can relate to that."

I breathe in deep. "Please. Can you tell me what really happened?"

"Can you take it?"

"I think so."

So he does. He was near the front of the bus; it was the back that got hit. He remembers the sounds, the smoke, people screaming, much like my dream. He says he just had a slight head injury and got hauled out. Robert was standing there, too, being restrained, screaming *Cassie, Cassie,* over and over again: his girlfriend's name. He looked unhurt. Then Mac passed out.

Later in the hospital they questioned him about what he'd seen that day. He just said he couldn't remember anything. That he got knocked out, even though he didn't lose consciousness until later. They seemed to believe him. He got out of the hospital and was told who died: Cassie and Robert were on the list.

"But if Robert wasn't hurt, what happened to him?"

"I don't know for sure. I was too scared to ask."

And in the way he looks away, the shadows that cross his face, I see the shame that never goes away. That he lives. That he never told the world about Robert. And something else: he *knows*. There is some part of this story he is keeping back.

He gets up and opens a drawer, hands me a photo.

"There they are: Robby and Cassie."

I can see Mum in him: the same square jaw, curly hair. An average boy with his arm around a girl who was something else: *beautiful*. Perfect skin, heart-shaped face, silky honey hair. Perfect, that is, until she was on the wrong bus, on the wrong day.

"But what happened to him? Tell me."

"I tried to find him on missing persons websites a while back, but never did. Guess no one reports you missing if they think you are dead."

"You think you know what happened to him."

"Probably."

"What?"

He hesitates. "I think he was Slated."

I stare back, unable to take it in. "Slated? He couldn't have been. That is only for criminals."

"Think about it: Why are so many kids missing? There are websites full of them. What happens to them, really? Look: Robert was so traumatized by what happened, they probably thought to make him a useful citizen he had to be Slated. That he wouldn't get over it any other way. They were trying to help him."

Though I can tell by Mac's face he thinks this is wrong. I don't know what to think. Missing kids? I can't process what he is saying. Could Slating really be used on children who aren't criminals?

"What are these missing persons websites? I've never heard of them before."

"Listen, Kyla, this is very important. Very high on the Cannot Be Mentioned List. This must be a secret."

"What?"

"Come on."

I follow him to a back room. It's a mess, with clothes and junk everywhere, but then I see when he moves some stuff it is all just hiding a computer.

"This is a bit—a lot—illegal," he says. "Not government gear: hush-hush."

"Oh."

And he shows me. There are all sorts of underground websites that the Lorders can't control, run from outside the UK: in Europe and the US. Missing persons are just one type of website, and there are so many missing, of all ages. But especially children.

"How old are you?" he asks.

"Sixteen."

He starts tapping away. Sixteen—female—blond—green eyes.

"What are you doing?"

"I'm just going to show you the scale of it."

Images flash up on the page: dates when last seen, names, ages. Thirty-six hits all up. And I start scanning down the page. So many girls, most in their teens when they disappeared. What could have happened to all of them?

"Holy crap," Mac says.

"What?"

"Look at number thirty-one," he says, and I scan down. He clicks on the photo, and it enlarges: a pretty child, gap-toothed grin. Big green eyes, fine palest blond hair; in jeans and a pink T-shirt, holding a gray kitten in her arms. Underneath it says *Lucy Connor, disappeared from school in Keswick, Cumbria, age ten.*

"She looks a little like me," I say slowly.

"She looks a lot like you," Mac says. He clicks on a link that says *predict appearance now.*

The screen changes to a teenage version of Lucy. That face; those eyes. *No.* It can't be. I look at Mac, then back to the screen, half expecting her to be gone, that I imagined what I saw. But she is still there, staring back at me. I'm skinnier, maybe; her hair is longer. Otherwise it is like looking into a mirror.

"She doesn't just look like you. She *is* you."

It's the shock, I suppose. My levels don't go down, they stay at about 5, but I stare at the image on the screen. Stare and try to take it in, but cannot. I start to shake.

Missing?

Where've I been since I was ten?

Vaguely I'm aware of Mac shutting the computer down, taking my hand and leading me into the front room.

"Sit," he says. A moment later, "Drink this." And he puts a small glass in my hand. I drink it back; it burns.

I cough. "What is that?"

"Whiskey. It's good for shock."

It starts to send warmth out through my body. We hear voices coming up the path.

He kneels in front of me and holds a finger to his lips. "Not a word, Kyla. We'll talk about this another time. Promise?"

"Not a word. I promise."

"Good girl," he says, and takes the glass.

Amy and Jazz come in through the front door. She looks happy enough, not defiled as far as I can tell. No grass in her hair or anything; they're just holding hands.

"Sorry we were gone for so long," she says as we head for the car. "Hope you weren't bored."

"Belt up?" Jazz says, and I do up the new—reclaimed from a wreck—seat belt.

Mac comes out and waves; the car lurches up the lane, and he is soon out of sight behind us.

Green trees blue sky white clouds green trees blue sky white clouds . . .

That evening I plead homework and hole up in my room.

Sebastian usually comes up with me after dinner, but there is no sign of him tonight, and I miss his company.

Lucy had a kitten.

There is pain inside if I look at her too close in my mind. She looked so happy in that photograph, arms full of squirming kitten. What happened to take her away from that life?

Lucy is a *she,* not an *I;* I can only think about her in the third person, as something separate and distinct from myself. Anyhow, maybe it is all some stupid coincidence. She can't be me; she just looks like me. That computer-generated version of Lucy at sixteen is all guessing, anyhow. She might look completely different by now.

But still, her laughing eyes are imprinted on my mind and won't go away; they need *out.* I jump up, grab a sketch pad. Pencil in my left hand. And I start to draw, only half paying attention to the scratch across the page as my mind whirls with the possibility of *Lucy.*

Maybe Lucy hated broccoli and liked cats.

She was reported missing. Somebody out there wants to know where she is, what happened to her. Maybe her parents; maybe they love her, and are desperate to know that she is okay.

In which case, if I am—if I was—Lucy, there'd be no point in contacting them, would there? Lucy isn't okay; she is as good as dead. She doesn't exist anymore. She's been Slated.

She stares back at me from my drawing. I'd done her without the kitten, a different backdrop, but her eyes are the same. I get up to look in the mirror, then back at the drawing. *My eyes.* Though apart from younger, hers look happier, too; even without the kitten.

This drawing I'd done with my left hand, paying almost no attention. It's good; it is better than good. She looks like she could step off the page and into my room, or turn around and climb that . . . mountain?

A cold prickle of goose bumps walks up my back. Behind her I've drawn a long ridge that slopes down on her left, something I've never seen in person: mountains. They weren't in the photograph.

26

THE NEXT MORNING, SEBASTIAN IS STILL MISSING.

Every morning he is on my bed when I wake up. But that is two mornings now that when half-awake I reached out in all directions but couldn't find him, or a warm place he had recently been.

No sign when Amy and I go down for breakfast, either. Surprised to find Dad behind some papers in the front room while Mum tears through the kitchen making lunches. Sebastian's dinner from last night is still untouched in his bowl.

"Where's Sebastian?" I ask Mum.

"I don't know. I'm busy enough without hunting for a stupid cat. He's probably off stalking a mouse or visiting a friend."

Amy looks up from her cereal. "I haven't seen him for a few days, either. Dad, have you been in the shed?"

He looks over whatever he is reading. "Last night. I'll check after breakfast," he says, and disappears back behind it.

"Sometimes Sebastian hides there and gets locked in," Amy explains.

But I can't help but worry. If children go missing and nothing is done, what about a cat?

I race to get ready, then check the garden. The shed in the back is locked and has no windows, but I call Sebastian's name and listen at the door: no response.

A *toot toot* sounds out front: Jazz. Now that he is official and has a full complement of seat belts, he is collecting us for school.

I come around the side of the house to see Amy already there.

"Come *on*. If we're late for school, bet we'll be back on the bus."

We lurch up the road, and I keep my eyes searching the gardens and footpaths for Sebastian. And the road. So many cars like Jazz's up and down every day at full speed.

But see nothing.

Amy catches me looking. "Don't worry! I'm sure he'll be home when we get back later."

"Worry 'bout what?" Jazz asks.

"Our cat is missing," I say.

"Cats are explorers, like me; they like to wander the world, see what there is to see."

Amy rolls her eyes. "Sure, Mr. Columbus, whatever you say."

"What's with the shed out back?" I ask.

"What do you mean?" Amy says.

"There's no key for it. It's not on the house keys that hang inside; I checked."

She shrugs, disinterested. "I don't know. Only Dad uses it."

"Probably full of man stuff," Jazz says. "Like rakes and lawn mowers."

"No. Those are in the little shed on the side of the house," I say, having raked leaves a few days ago while Sebastian chased the rake. I feel uneasy. He has been my shadow since I arrived. Where is he?

With Jazz driving we beat the bus by enough to be early. I slip off to the school learning resources unit before class to do a search of the other thing playing on my mind: Keswick, where Lucy lived before she disappeared. I just have to know: Are those mountains in my drawing a real place?

As I log in, I find myself comparing the school computer to Mac's. This one is like every computer I have ever seen, until yesterday. We have the same at home; Dad installs and maintains computer systems, and I bet they are the same, too. The search screen has the interlocking *C*'s as always at the top left. I've never really focused on them before: *CC* for *Central Coalition*. The government. Mac's screen had no trace of this logo.

My fingers are reaching to the keyboard, about to type *Keswick,* when it hits me. Yesterday, Mac cautioned against searching for missing persons or anything touchy on other computers: They are all monitored, he said. I log off, search undone. Suddenly queasy that Kyla Davis searching *Keswick* where one Lucy Connor disappeared six years ago might set off an alarm in some faceless place.

Minutes later I am staring at a dusty old illustrated atlas of the UK from the reference shelf. I guess I was wrong. I did still draw Lucy with a cat: *Catbells: a popular ridge with walkers, a few miles' walk from Keswick along the shores of Derwentwater.* The spitting image of the drawing I did last night.

Maybe I've seen a picture of Catbells somewhere before and just put it in my drawing. Or maybe some part of me remembers; some part of *Lucy.* I squint at the photograph in the book, then close my eyes. Trying to *be there* in my mind. But it is no good. If I think about it directly, I remember nothing. Yet my left hand seems to know a thing or two.

A librarian is looking at me curiously across the room. She puts her cup of tea down on the desk. I hurriedly shut the book, shove it back on the shelf, and make an exit.

• • •

Mr. Gianelli leads us out into the sunshine with our sketchbooks. They had that wrong, the weather report on Mac's TV: There is no sign of the *rain, rain, rain* they said would start today.

He marches us the short walk to the woods around Cuttle Brook and plonks himself down on a bench with a flask of tea. "Go! Shoo! Draw something, come back in an hour and amaze me with your work."

Everyone scatters, most in twos and threes. Paths lead off in all directions. I watch which way Phoebe goes and head the opposite way.

Paths crisscross around, and I head into the densest part of the woods; I run for a while, anxious to put space between me and the others. I find a rock to sit on and start sketching trees, almost bare now. Grasses are dying back along the brook, leaves rotting underfoot.

No one is around. I switch to my left hand. What happens if I draw, pay no attention, let my mind wander?

I think of Lucy's kitten. Gray with tabby stripes, short hair. Chubby or thick fur or both. A squirmy, wriggly ball of fur. Pounce: I draw her pouncing on a bit of string. She'd wobble on her back legs, rear up, wiggle and jump. She? Yes, somehow I am sure this kitten is a *she*.

But I can't get lost in my drawing today. Instead of a gray kitten, Sebastian starts to appear on my page. Worried and restless, I shut my sketchbook and wander down the trail.

These trees were planted as a nature reserve more than fifty years ago; our biology teacher told us. Part of it burned out during the riots in the twenties, but it has grown back now. Not regulated anymore, it is left to go wild. Birds flit about; there are scurrying rustlings in the bushes. I stray off the main trail to a spindly, barely there path, and wander. It winds in a random way, gradually leading me back in the direction I came.

When I come around the bend, she is so still I don't notice her at first: Phoebe. Sitting alone on the ground, leaning against a tree with a sketchbook on her knees, absorbed. A robin is hopping near her feet: her subject? He is chirping, and she seems to be holding a conversation with him, making little murmuring noises, and he hops closer and closer, until he finally jumps up on her foot.

And she smiles. Phoebe's face transforms with it: Her eyes are small and wide-set, her hair hasn't seen a brush in a while, and she is covered in freckles. But somehow, smiling at the robin, she looks different; gentle, sweet; *not-Phoebe.*

She wouldn't smile to see me here, I realize. I step back quietly, but she must have caught the movement, and starts; the robin flies away.

"Dammit," she says. She turns to see who interrupted, finds me and scowls. "How did you sneak up on me?"

I pause, torn between answering and running.

"Sneak? I didn't sneak," I hear myself say. "I was walking and saw you talking to the robin. How do you do that?" Curiosity drags the words out.

"I wasn't talking to any bird," she says, defensive. "And you *did* sneak, or I would have heard you."

And I realize she is right. I didn't *sneak,* like how she means—not on purpose, anyhow—but without considering what I was doing had avoided stepping on any twigs that would snap, moved with care about the undergrowth to avoid noise.

"Can you talk to robins?"

"Shhh," she says. And I see he is back. She smiles again, not at me. If I move and he flies off, I'll catch it; if I stay, I annoy her. What to do?

She draws and I crane my head to see. It is pretty good. I'm surprised. Stuff she's done in class is average.

Eventually he tips his head to one side and flies away. She shuts her book.

"Listen, you. Don't tell anyone I was talking to a robin, understand? Or you'll regret it."

I shrug. Why would I, and who'd care if I did? I turn to start back the way I came, but something needles inside, and I find myself turning back. It is just her and me, no crowd about on her side, and I'm bugged.

"What is your problem with me? I've never done anything to you."

"Don't you *know*? Are you really that stupid, spy-head?"

I can feel my fists clenching but force them to relax, and breathe deep. Glance at my Levo: 4.8; okay at the moment.

"No one is here to help you if you blow up." She laughs.

"Why'd you call me that?"

"Because a spy-head is what you are. Whatever you used to be, you're not a real person anymore. You're a walking talking government spy, with that chip in your head tracking everything you do and say. *You* can't be trusted. The rest of us—we'd never say anything to anybody older—but you can't help yourself. Can you? You and others like you report on people, and next thing you know, they vanish. *Your* fault."

She gets up and stalks toward me. I'm frozen, and she pushes me hard in the shoulder to get past and up the narrow path.

My Levo vibrates. I'm not a *spy*. I'm not.

Am I?

I get back to Mr. Gianelli just in time to avoid being late. He is taking in the best sketches, holding them up for all to see. Phoebe's robin is one of those chosen. I haven't done much and try to hide at the back, but it is no good. He gets my book out of my hands; finds half-drawn trees, grasses; Lucy's kitten and Sebastian.

He snorts and hands it back. "I'm guessing you didn't find your feline friends under a tree."

"No, I—"

"The whole point of taking you young *artists* out of the classroom is to draw what you see around you. It's usually Phoebe I have to call up about drawing her menagerie of pets."

"Sorry," I say.

Gianelli starts back for the school, others follow. I start packing my stuff in my bag when a hand reaches out and grabs my sketchbook: Phoebe.

"Give it back!"

She dances out of arm's reach and opens it. A look—something—passes over her face when she sees Sebastian. She smooths the page and hands it back.

The phone rings at dinner that night. Mum scowls. "Let them leave a message," she says, but Dad goes to answer it.

I pick at my dinner, not hungry. Still no sign of Sebastian; after two days, even Mum is starting to worry.

Dad comes back in, coat in his hand. "Who wants to go with me to pick up the cat?"

He tells me in the car: Sebastian was brought in to the vet a few miles away. He's been injured in a scrap, with a fox maybe? But he is fine.

"How'd they know to call us?"

"He's chipped. They scan the chip to find out who he is, where he lives."

Oh. So Sebastian has a chip in his head, like me. "If someone hadn't brought him in, could we track him? With the chip?"

"Depends on the type of chip," Dad says, looking at me sideways as he drives. "Not with Sebastian's. Though they can do tracker chips, and do with police dogs and the like. Why do you ask?"

I shrug.

"Tell me," he says. And there is something about Dad, the note in his voice, that makes you answer him when he asks questions.

"Just something someone said at school. She said that I'm like a spy for the government 'cos I've got a chip in my head. That I can't be trusted."

He laughs. "A spy? Well, well. I best mind what I say in front of you, then."

"Is it true? Does it record stuff I do and say?"

"Of course not," he says, but I get the feeling that isn't the whole answer.

At the vet it says CLOSED on the door, but we are let in.

"Hey, Double D, how's business?" the vet says to Dad. Double D? Oh. *David Davis.*

"You know, same as always." They exchange a look.

The vet pushes a swing door behind the counter. "Miss Best. Bring that cat out, will you?" he calls.

"Is he all right?" I say. "Where did you find him?"

"It wasn't me. The girl who helps out here had him at home and brought him in today. And he's fine. Gave him a few stitches and a shot to be on the safe side."

"What do I owe you?" Dad says.

"On the house," he says. "Come have a look at this a minute," he says, and they head into an office.

Behind the counter, the door swings open and out comes Phoebe, carrying Sebastian. Even from the other side of the waiting room I can hear he is purring, though he is shaved down one side, and stitches are sticking out. Poor Sebastian.

But what is Phoebe doing here? My eyes widen, and my mouth hangs open as I start to realize what must have happened.

"Don't catch flies, Slater," she says.

"You knew. You had him, and you saw my drawing and knew he's my cat, so you brought him in."

She shrugged. "Someone found him hurt yesterday and gave him to me to look after. Then I brought him around here today and told the vet whose cat it was. Though he scanned him to check, anyhow."

"Thank you so much."

She eases Sebastian into my arms.

"Don't be stupid enough to think this makes us friends. This don't change anything, chip-head," she says, scowls, and goes back through the door.

I turn; Dad is back in the room, raising an eyebrow. A thoughtful look on his face.

He holds the door open. "Come on. Home time."

158

We get in the car and are almost home before Dad says it. "That was her, wasn't it." A statement, not a question.

"Who?"

"The girl who said you were a spy."

I say nothing. If I say yes, then I *am* a spy, after all.

27

THE FIRST THING I HEAR THE NEXT MORNING IS A DEEP rumbling purr: Sebastian. He seems to have decided that my pillow is the place to sleep and is curled across it. I, for one, am going to let him sleep wherever he likes.

He seems unfazed by his experiences: scrapping with foxes or whatever creature it was, rescued and given to Phoebe, stitched by the vet. He accepted special tidbits of dinner from Mum when we got in last night, then went straight to sleep on my bed.

Phoebe: I can't figure her out. She is so nasty, yet that robin trusted her. Sebastian purred in her arms, and she brought him back to me. I saw her face when she handed him across; she didn't want to give him back, yet she did. She must like animals and birds better than people.

Well, I like Sebastian better than most people, so who am I to judge?

It's the bus for Amy and me today, as Jazz has a class trip.

As we get on, I wonder: Should I stop and tell Phoebe that Sebastian is all right? I try to catch her eye and she scowls, gives a slight shake of her head. So the answer to that is *no*.

I sit with Ben at the back.

"Hey," he says. "All right?"

"Sebastian's back home," I say. And I lower my voice and tell him about what Phoebe had done.

"Just goes to show you," he says.

"What?"

"That people aren't always how you think they are. That was a nice thing she did for you. Who would have guessed?" He smiles.

Though I am sure she did it for Sebastian, not me. *Nothing's changed,* she said last night.

Mrs. Ali waits for me outside my first class.

"Can we have a quick word?" she says, and draws me into an empty office across the hall, not waiting for an answer. She shuts the door behind us.

"Is something wrong?" I say.

"Don't look so worried, Kyla. You haven't done anything. But you know that I am here to help you, don't you?"

"Uh, of course."

"Listen to me, Kyla. If anyone is hassling you at school or causing you problems, you have to tell me. I don't like hearing about things from other sources. It makes me look like I'm not doing my job."

I stare back at her, confused. The only one who fits that category is Phoebe, yet no one knows about that: We were alone in the woods when she said those things. "I don't understand. What have you heard?"

Mrs. Ali smiles and shakes her head slightly. "Poor Kyla. This world must be so confusing for you; that is why I am here to help you work things out. But I can't help you if you don't help me. So is there anything you want to tell me, dear?"

"No. I don't know what you mean," I say, yet I am convinced: Somehow, she knows something about Phoebe and wants me to tell her about it.

But no matter what Phoebe said, I'm no spy. Anyhow, how could I say anything against her when if it weren't for her, we wouldn't have Sebastian back? We wouldn't even know if he was alive or dead.

Mrs. Ali stares back at me, and I can see it in her eyes: She knows there is something I'm not telling her. She shakes her head. "I'm sorry, Kyla. You might not know that you need my help, but you do. I'm all that is between you and . . . most unpleasant possibilities. Do look after yourself. Now, go to class."

And she turns, opens the door, and marches out.

My knees turn to jelly. That was a threat, wasn't it? What *unpleasant possibilities*?

And I stay in the office, pull the door shut and try to draw myself together. Picturing my Happy Place, floating on the clouds. But more and more I get a sense that something is *wrong,* that I've done something. And I'm going to pay.

At the very least I'll get told off for being late to class. I shake my head. *Right, Kyla, pull yourself together.* I take a deep breath and reach for the doorknob, but hear footsteps. Clipped, precise footsteps. I hesitate; my hand drops back to my side. The office light is off, the hall is lit and there is a window in the door. I step back into the shadows and watch. The footsteps get closer; two men appear, in gray suits. *Lorders.*

They open the opposite door to my English class, where I should be right now.

Is this an *unpleasant possibility*? Have they come to take me?

They disappear inside and return moments later. And between them is a white-faced Phoebe.

At the end of the day when I get on the bus, there are whispers; whispers and pale faces. Eyes walk up my spine as I go down the aisle and sit with Ben, but when I turn to look around, no one meets my eyes. They think I've done something. They know she was nasty to me, so somehow, Lorders taking her out of class is my fault.

Phoebe's usual seat stays empty; she doesn't come late. The bus pulls away. So they didn't just *talk* to her, then let her go, did they?

I shiver.

Ben takes my hand. "Are you all right?" he says, and watches my eyes looking around the bus, from face to face. Sees the eyes that slide away. "What is going on?"

I shake my head. What can I say with so many hostile ears listening in?

I want to run tonight, I want to run *now,* but am hemmed in on the bus, bodies all around. I concentrate on Ben's warm hand, close my eyes, wish myself anywhere but here.

"Tell me what is wrong," he says. "Maybe I can help."

I open my eyes and shake my head. "Not now. Are you training before Group tonight?" I ask. He nods. "Can I come?"

He grins. "Of course."

"We can talk then," I add.

And his hand tightens on mine. He knows it is something serious, if I have to run to be able to talk about it.

28

IT TAKES SOME CONVINCING. MUM WOULD NEVER HAVE LET me go, but Dad is still home, just on his way again, bag in hand, for a work trip.

"Please. I need to run," I say, and he seems to understand. Somehow talks Mum around.

He is gone by the time Ben knocks at the door.

"Are you sure about this, Kyla? It feels like rain," Mum says, anxiously scanning the dark sky.

"I'll be fine," I say. "This is waterproof, isn't it?" I tug at my jacket sleeve. And I'm not in any danger from cars; it's not like anyone could miss seeing me in this fluorescent vest she made me wear over the jacket.

"You will stick to main roads?"

Ben promises to look after me and stares levelly back at Mum. She seems satisfied and off we go.

We start out slow and speed up. We've got an hour until Group, five miles to go: easy.

Ben looks at me curiously now and then as we run. I can tell he is waiting for me to talk, but suddenly, I am unsure what to say.

Fact: Phoebe was mean to me. Fact: She was taken from school by Lorders, and wasn't on the bus home. But that is all I know, isn't it?

I run flat out. Ben keeps up, matching my speed. His much longer legs don't have to work as hard.

"We'll be there early at this rate," he says. "Slow down?"

So we do; first to a light jog, then a walk.

"Is this about Phoebe?" he asks.

"What do you know?"

"I heard about it when I got off the bus this afternoon. Someone said someone saw her getting pushed into a Lorder van this morning. But it was all he-said-she-said; none of them actually saw anything themselves. Though she wasn't on the bus home."

"It's true: I saw them. Two Lorders went into the class, and a minute later came out. One was holding her arm; they marched her down the hall and out the building."

"Does anyone know why?"

"I was going to ask you that."

He hesitates. "Some people think you might have said something. Got her into trouble."

"I didn't! I wouldn't."

"I know that. Especially after she got your cat back," he says, and I can see he means it. But I'm not so sure. I might have had something to do with it, whether I meant to or not.

"Is there more?" he asks.

I shrug. "Just stuff Phoebe said: that we are spies for the government, because of the chips in our brains."

"That's not true."

"But what if it is, and we don't know? Maybe I gave her away without even knowing that I did. Maybe somebody just scanned my brain, and *pow!* She's gone. Because she said stuff the government didn't like."

Ben shakes his head. "That can't be true."

"Why? How do you know?"

"Because if it was, we'd have been the first to go."

I stare back at him in shock. Out of habit I check my Levo, but it is all right—still up from running, at nearly 7—but my skin is reacting to what he said, crawling like little spiders. I shiver. He's right. We've talked about Tori being returned, and those others taken from assembly, and questioned what is going on. Much worse than anything Phoebe would do or say.

And no matter what, I still have the horrible feeling that somehow, it must be my fault. Because of Mrs. Ali: She said she didn't like hearing things from other sources. She must have heard something about Phoebe, and somehow, it is connected with me.

"I found out something else," Ben says. "Why someone took your cat to Phoebe. She looks after loads of animals, injured ones; for people who can't pay the vet. She has a way with them."

Who will care for them now?

"Let's run," I say, and take off again.

We overshoot the village hall where Group is starting soon and keep going. And as my feet pound again and again on the ground and my body pushes past tired and into exhaustion, I think of all the things I didn't tell Ben. About Lucy Connor, the girl reported missing; about Robert—Robby—who survived the bombs, but is still on the memorial.

We finally turn back for Group. "We're going to be late," I say.

"Are we?" Ben shrugs. He's always late. But somehow I'm not sure Nurse Penny's special dispensation for his timekeeping will spill over to me.

• • •

We race into the hall fifteen minutes late.

"I was just about to call your mum," Nurse Penny says to me, a hand on each hip. No word to Ben.

"Sorry! It's all my fault," Ben says. "I took us around the long way; we didn't have enough time to get back."

She thaws and smiles at Ben. "Oh all right then, sit down, you two. We were just beginning to go through everyone's goals for the next few months, all right?"

I tune out while she goes around the group. My goals: Keep as far as possible from Lorders and stay out of trouble. *And find out what happened to Phoebe,* an insistent voice whispers in my mind.

When she gets to me I'm so preoccupied I don't notice until Ben nudges my shoulder.

Penny frowns. "Try to stay with us, Kyla. Perhaps the running is too much for you. Now, do you have any goals you'd like to share?"

Not many; not out loud. But what I finally say has echoes of my thoughts: *Do well at school and stay out of trouble.*

Group is finally over.

"Take care," Ben says, squeezes my hand, and leaves to run home. I watch him go and wish I could follow.

The others trickle out. I head for the door, but Penny calls out: "Wait, Kyla. I want a word with you."

So I turn back. "Yes?"

"Is everything all right?"

"It would be good if people didn't constantly ask me if everything is all right!" I snap, without thinking. I blush. "I'm sorry. I shouldn't have said that." She might be one of the ones keeping tabs on my every word, my every thought.

She sighs. "Sit down, Kyla."

I sit.

She shuts her netbook, sits next to me.

"I'm on your side," she says. And her words are so much like Mrs. Ali's, I draw back. But she looks distressed. "Don't, Kyla. Don't look frightened of me like that. Off the record, we can talk off the record. Do you understand? I'm not running back to somebody with everything you say. You can trust me."

Despite everything, I believe she means what she says. But who knows what she might do for my own good?

"So tell me. It is all over your face; something is wrong. What is it?" she asks.

Though maybe I can get information. "It's just this girl was taken from school today. By Lorders. I knew her, that's all."

"Oh dear. What happened?"

"Two of them went into class and marched her out. She was seen getting pushed into a black van."

"Do you know why?"

"I'm not sure. It might be some things she said."

"There is more to this story, isn't there," she says, then holds up a hand. "But don't tell me! This girl: How old was she?"

"I don't know. She was in my class at school."

"Year eleven?"

I nod.

"Listen, Kyla. This is very important. Don't ask questions; keep out of it." She grips my shoulders tight between her hands and stares into my eyes. "This is for your own good. Do you understand me?"

"Y-y-yes," I say.

All at once she lets go. Smiles brightly. "See you again next Thursday! Have a good week, my dear."

She marches out; I turn, and Mum is at the back of the hall. I walk over to her and she raises an eyebrow.

"Is everything all right?"

"Yes, fine," I say. Then, with sudden inspiration, add, "We were a little late from running. She was just telling me off."

Mum frowns. "Punctuality is important, Kyla." And she carries on a lecture all the way home.

The next afternoon, year eleven students file in for assembly, just like every Friday afternoon. But it feels different this week.

Everyone is carefully putting their feet one in front of the other. There is little conversation, no jostling, no weekend plans made. The head isn't even here yet. But everyone knows about Phoebe, and they are scared.

No one talked if they knew I was listening, of course, but I'd heard snatches and whispers all day. Somehow her disappearance was more troubling than Tori's, or those others from assembly last week. Everyone could see why they went. But Phoebe mostly kept her unpleasant self to herself; she didn't congregate illegally, or mouth off to authority, not like the others who disappeared.

When Rickson walks through the door, two Lorders behind him, the room is already hushed. He scans the crowd: Every eye is forward, every back straight.

"Good afternoon, year eleven," he says, and smiles, clearly pleased.

The assembly is short. When it is over, the Lorders once again stand by the exit at the back. They watch, staring at each face in turn as we file out.

No shoulders are grabbed, no one pulled aside.

This time.

Jazz is driving today; I reach his car before Amy. She appears around the side of the building. Jazz spots her and waves, then turns to me.

"A quick word before Amy gets here," he says, his voice low.

"What?"

"Mac wants to see you; he said he'll let me know when next week sometime. And not to say anything, to *anybody*. All right?"

Amy is there before I can respond; he turns, hugs her and yanks the car door open. I try not to shake while I climb in the backseat.

Mac and his very illegal computer; his missing persons website, with Lucy—me?—on it. He trusts me to keep quiet, as he said. To say nothing. Mac has done well and beyond what Phoebe and other students have *disappeared* for, and he is too old to Slate. What would happen to him if he is found out?

I wish he wouldn't trust me. Whatever he wants to see me about, I don't want to know.

29

I WANT TO RUN.

Waves of panic rise up inside, increasing the closer we get to the hospital. The traffic isn't so bad today; Mum is trying a different way. She said it is farther to drive but might be quicker. *In, out; in, out.* I concentrate on breathing and the roads. Memorizing the grid, laying it out in my mind to distract myself from thinking about Dr. Lysander.

She sees all. If I don't volunteer something of interest, she will probe until she finds a scab I'd rather wasn't picked. But today it isn't just my concerns I need to protect, but more: Mac. Ben. Lucy, too: me/Lucy a separate being inside I want to shelter from inquisition, but she is *here*. A shadow, a ghost, following along next to me, matching my steps.

Soon we're approaching from the other side, new to my eyes, but the hospital looks much the same: high fences, guard towers at regular intervals. I automatically chart the dimensions, the numbers. The exits and gates. A delivery van is waved through one as we pass; we carry on around the perimeter to the same gate we've used before.

We wait our turn as they look under cars with mirrors, having everyone get out and be scanned while cars are searched.

"There must be an alert," Mum says, and I jump. She's been silent most of the way today, leaving my thoughts to fester as they will. I study her: There are shadows under her eyes. She looks tired and drawn. The phone rang last night, I remember now. Very late but I'd been awake; heard her steps over the ceiling, the murmur of her voice.

"Is everything all right?" I ask.

She half smiles. "I should be asking you that, shouldn't I?"

We move up another space as a car ahead gets through; two more to go.

"I asked first," I say.

"You did. But this isn't the place to discuss it. On the way home, all right?"

Another space forward. So something *is* wrong, and she is going to tell me about it, but in front of Lorders isn't the place.

"Don't tell me any secrets," I say in a rush. "I'm not sure I can keep them."

She laughs. "I'll keep that in mind."

Forward, again. We're not waved through this time; now it is our turn. There is a swarm of Lorders about, more than I've seen in one place before. In black for operations, not gray suits, with vests and weapons. Tense. Not that they ever look relaxed, exactly, but today, tension radiates off them.

We get out of the car and are scanned, head to toe, while a few others quickly go over the car. Again I can't help the reaction, the *fear* that floods through me with their proximity. But they don't seem to notice. We get pushed back into the car and are through.

"What is all that about?" I ask.

"Don't worry, Kyla. There is probably some concern about an attack, but they'll handle things. They always do."

I study her face. The way she said that didn't sound right. Like Lorders always handling things isn't good, but something else entirely.

Imagination, Kyla. Get a grip.

• • •

"Come!" Dr. Lysander calls out. Her voice is familiar, clear without being loud. She doesn't have to raise her voice; she is used to being obeyed without question.

As usual mine is the only occupied seat in her waiting area, with Mum off for tea with a nurse she knows. I stand and go through the door, glad to escape: Two Lorders are standing in the hall.

"Good morning, Kyla," she says. Dr. Lysander, unlike Mum and the Lorders—me too, for that matter—looks unruffled. Calm. Her usual self as she always is and always will be. Her dark eyes are analytical, but not unkind; she is detached, yet in the moment.

I find myself smiling back at her, feeling strangely reassured. *Danger, take care,* a voice whispers inside.

"You look happy to see me today."

"I am," I find myself answering, as I sit opposite her desk.

She half smiles. "Well, that is nice, I suppose, but why?"

I shrug. "You are always *you*. The same."

She raises an eyebrow. "I'm not sure if I should be pleased with that observation. Though it is mostly accurate." She glances at her computer, taps at the screen. "So. If you are finding continuity a comfort today, are there changes or potential changes that are troubling you?" She fixes her eyes on me.

There is nowhere to hide. *Tell the truth, just not too much of it,* a voice whispers again. I blink.

"I was scared coming into the hospital today," I admit.

"Of?"

"All the security. Last time we came there were roadblocks, and today they were searching cars."

She tilts her head to one side a moment, as if listening to her thoughts. "It is perhaps a reasonable thing to fear. You understand about the AGT—the Antigovernment Terrorists? There was some intelligence that an attack is planned on the hospital. They are being careful."

My eyes widen. "You're not scared."

"No. I've been through too many alerts for them to hold fear." She leans back in her chair. "Yet I'm curious why they would trouble you."

Terrorists; bombs. Explosions, screaming, and . . .

"Tell me, Kyla," she says.

"There is a memorial at my school. Six years ago a busload of students got in the way of an AGT attack, and most of them died."

"Ah, I see. So you start to understand the cause and effect: the terrorist, the death."

"How could they do that? They were just kids. They didn't *do* anything."

"Wrong place, wrong time." She shrugs.

"They were real people!"

The eyebrow goes up again. "Of course. Real people get hurt every day, and it causes pain to those who care for them."

"You sound as if you are separating yourself from it," I say slowly. Looking at her and realizing I can see things, too.

Real surprise registers in her eyes. "Very good, Kyla. I am, and I do."

"Why?"

"Part of it is just being a doctor. I can't fix every hurt; I just concentrate on those that I can."

Part of it she said. There is more she is not saying. But I'm not dumb enough to try to pick at her scabs; it is her job to poke at mine.

She looks at her screen again. "I see you are doing well in school and at Group, that you have made a few friends. That you haven't had any more blackouts. This is all good. Any nightmares?" Her eyes are back on mine.

Bricked into a tower, trapped and beating on the walls . . .

"Well?"

I switch. I don't know why, I just do. I tell her about my dream of the bus bombing. She listens as I describe the screaming and the blood on the windows. The smell of burning fuel and flesh.

She flinches, a slight involuntary movement. Not so controlled, then. She raises a hand, and I stop.

"You have too much imagination for your own good. But now I see why the alert has worried you. You are safe here, Kyla. This is one of the safest places to be."

Safe, closed in, trapped: She is trapped in as much of a tower as I could ever imagine in my dreams.

"Do you ever get out?" I ask.

"What do you mean?"

"Do you take time out? Go to the country, take a walk in the woods or something."

"You are full of surprising questions today! And I do. Once every few weeks—tomorrow, it will be—but I don't walk. I have Heathcliff, my horse: I go on trails, and—"

She suddenly stops, shakes herself. "I don't know *how* you get me to talk like this." She smiles to herself. "You should be the doctor. Now, listen to me. Stop worrying about the terrorists. Let the Lorders handle them; it is their job. Here is what *you* need to do. You need your one thing, your goal, your love. A focus. What is yours?"

"Art," I answer. There is no other contender, after all.

She smiles. "I knew you would say that. See, you have your

predictable moments, as well. Concentrate on your drawing, your painting. Make this your reason for being, and the rest won't be so important."

"Like your horse?" I say.

"Just so." She answers straightaway, and I wonder as I leave, shouldn't her patients be her answer?

On the way home, Mum either forgets she said she'd tell me what is bothering her, or she decides not to. Either way, I don't ask.

My mind is busy with the things Dr. Lysander said, and didn't say. There was no mention of Mrs. Ali or Phoebe, and she isn't one to shy from difficult subjects. The only answer is that she doesn't know about it. At least that probably means that Mrs. Ali hasn't filed a nasty report about me. And I don't think I said anything I shouldn't, anything that could get anybody else in trouble.

Maybe I can keep secrets, after all.

Help me.

Lucy holds out her hands. The right is perfect, five white fingers, even nails. My fingers, but smaller. The left is bleeding, fingers bent at wrong angles.

I back away.

Green eyes, my eyes, shine until a fat tear spills over each lid.

Please. Help me . . .

"Wake up, Kyla."

I jump, open my eyes; confused. Mum is undoing her seat belt. The car has stopped. We're home.

30

IT IS COLD, AND THE RAIN THE WEATHER REPORT PROMISED last week has finally arrived. It is incessant, steady rather than a deluge, but has gone on long enough now that it is starting to get through the leaf canopy overhead in great, soaking drops.

We run together, Ben and I. We've pulled away from the rest. So fast that I'm not cold, despite the soaking, but still. "Crap weather," I gasp out.

"Yeah. Typical October," Ben answers.

How would I know? It's the first October I remember.

When we arrived for cross-country training this morning, instead of having the boys before the girls, Ferguson had us start a minute apart in finishing time order from last week. So Ben and I set off first as we were fastest last time. We hit the pace hard, knowing the others will be keen to catch us up.

We clear the woods and start up a hill. No cover now, and it is raining harder, unsteady underfoot with mud and leaves. The path is cut into the hill so the water channels down it. We have to slow down to keep our feet.

"Isn't this great?" Ben says, soaked and spattered head to toe with mud.

"Wonderful," I say, sarcastic. But then laugh. It is *wonderful,* running past feeling, into the zone where all I am is *alive.* I feel every drop that lands on my head, as if I can follow each one as it falls from the sky, slowing them down with my eyes to watch their progress. Every sense, every feeling, is on overdrive. If I push hard I can almost forget about Tori and Phoebe. And being haunted by Lucy. She is there when I close my eyes, holding out her hands, pleading for help. It makes no sense for so many reasons.

"Stop a sec," Ben says when we get to the top of the hill. We huddle under a huge oak tree. He squats down to sort a twisted shoelace, does it up again and leans against the tree.

We can see all across the valley from here; the sky is rolling in blacker. None of the others are in sight.

"Bet they turned back," Ben says. "Wimps!" He laughs.

"Should we?"

"Nah. We're past halfway now; no point."

"Let's go," I say. Anxious to keep going, faster. To make running *all there is.*

"What's up?"

I shrug, hold my arms around myself.

"Tell me, Kyla," he says, and I look up into his soft brown eyes, and I *trust,* I really do—but should I?

I shiver and he wraps his arms around me.

"Want to run," I say.

"Not until you talk."

And Ben's eyes are worse than Dr. Lysander's: They are pinning me against this tree. As my breathing and heart rate slow, I start to shake, but not with the cold. I bury my face against his chest so his eyes can't hold mine anymore.

"Maybe I can help," he says.

There are so many reasons to say nothing. I promised Mac.

Knowing dangerous things could put Ben at risk. I don't know if Ben can keep secrets, really keep them; I don't even know if I can.

Ben draws away, turns, sits on a rock in the pouring rain. Pulls me onto his knee.

"We're not going anywhere until you tell me what is wrong."

I sigh, close my eyes, and settle against him. To stay *here,* in this moment, doesn't sound so bad. His arms tighten around me, he shifts and puts a hand under my chin, tilts my face up. And I open my eyes; his are closer now, he leans forward. My heart flutters, beating faster once again even though I've stopped running. His eyes intent on mine like that other day when I thought he was going to kiss me, but all he wanted to do was talk about Tori.

Tori, Phoebe, and Lucy: So many ghosts between us. But I can exorcize at least one of them with the truth. I pull away a little, choose *words.*

"Do you ever wonder why you were Slated?"

"Are we back to that?" He shrugs. "Sometimes. It's hard not to. But we can't know who we were, and—"

"But I do know."

There is a pause where all I can hear is the rain, and all I see is doubt in Ben's eyes.

"What do you mean?" he finally says, his face carefully neutral.

I swallow. There is no point in ignoring her, is there? She won't go away.

"My name was Lucy Connor. I went missing when I was ten years old. I had a gray kitten. Someone b-b-broke my fingers. And somebody misses me." And with each whispered sentence, I shudder. Something is twisting inside, shaking, trying to break. Instead, I cry.

Burrowing into Ben's arms, and he just holds me, strokes my hair, with the rain pounding down all the while, the wind picking up. The storm outside and in.

"How could you know these things?" Ben finally says.

And once the tears stop enough to speak, I tell him about the illegal computer, missing persons websites, and Lucy. And gradually, I see: He starts to believe.

"I don't understand," he says. "Missing persons?"

"Lots of people go missing. They're not arrested and tried; they just go missing. Maybe we're not even criminals."

Ben shakes his head. "They can't do that, it's illegal. How can the government break its own laws?"

"Maybe we didn't do anything wrong, and the government just decided they didn't like something we did, or said. Do you want to find out? If you were reported missing, too."

A complex play acts on Ben's face. He starts to speak, but I hold up a hand. "Wait," I say, and turn my head. It is hard to hear over the wind and rain, but is someone coming?

A figure appears over the edge of the hill. I try to jump up, but Ben holds me tight. It is one of the boys from training; he smirks at us sitting there and runs past.

Ben releases me; I spring up. "What did you do that for?" I scowl.

"He was going to see us, anyhow. Might as well let him think we were having a cuddle, not a dangerous conversation."

Having a *cuddle*. Is that what we were doing, or was it just a cover story? My face burns despite the cold. I turn once again at a sound; is someone else about to overtake?

"Let's run," Ben says, and without waiting for an answer, he sprints ahead at full speed.

Well. I follow after him and try to catch up, but can't; he must have been holding back before. His stride lengthens, and soon he is out of sight. It is almost like something is chasing him, something he doesn't want to face.

It is only me.

31

PHOEBE'S ROBIN IS ON THE FRONT WALL IN THE ART STUDIO.
No other pictures hang there. Many are displayed on the sides, the
back, but never the front. She hasn't signed her sketch; no one but us
would know whose it is. Instead of barking at us to hurry, Mr. Gianelli
is silent as we file in and scan our cards, for this, our first class since
Phoebe was taken. Everyone sees her sketch of the robin and falls silent also.

He must know. I glance toward the door; Mrs. Ali stands there.
She still shadows me between classes most of the time, though it is
obvious I know how to get around. She is keeping tabs on me. Will she
always? Ben and Amy don't have anyone in their footsteps.

Mrs. Ali glances around the room; she can sense something is up,
looks from face to face. She stays.

"Class, today I want you to think about something: the importance
of connecting with what you put on paper. Take our friend Mr. Red
Breast here. See the care, the connection; it takes an ordinary moment and moves it beyond, makes you be better than you are, finds
the artist within. The *communication* between you and your subject,
yes? Give and take. How you see your subject, in a way nobody
else can."

And he stands back, so he is with us: All eyes are on Phoebe's
sketch. Everyone, together, studying the drawing. The robin that

trusted her, hopped closer and closer. Phoebe's smile as she sketched, murmuring at the robin, him chirping back. Seconds tick by, to a minute of silence, then two.

He shakes his head sadly and returns to the front of the class.

"Today, draw something or someone you care about, that makes you *feel* something; feel anything. Good or bad, I don't care. Go! Get started."

He slumps at his desk. Movements begin around the room; small, unhurried. Paper smoothed. Pencils, charcoals selected. All as if waking from a dream, a trance.

I lean over crisp, white sheets. Out of the corner of my eye I track Mrs. Ali. Hers are thoughtful, puzzled; she departs.

Gianelli looks older today, the lines about his eyes more pronounced, his skin as gray as his hair. A silent protest at one of his students being taken, but we all know what he did just now, the risk he took. I see him slip a flask out of his pocket, tilt it into his tea. Then start a sketch of his own.

Without thought or question, I use my left hand. Turned in my seat a little so I can see the door, in case Mrs. Ali comes back.

Draw someone I care about; someone who makes me feel *something . . .*

Quick and smooth strokes. A subject I haven't tried before, but there is no trial and error with my left hand; it is right the first time. His thoughtful eyes. Strong chin, dark hair that is more wavy than curly, just below his ears: Ben.

Where are you? He wasn't in biology this morning. Worry makes me chew my lip so hard it hurts. He hasn't done something stupid? I asked Miss Fern, but she didn't know; she wasn't hiding anything, though; there was no worry or remoteness in her. I'm starting to understand that there are different types of teachers. Fern, Gianelli, and the running coach, Ferguson: They are real. They might tell me off on occasion, they're not always nice, exactly, but they talk to me like I exist, like I matter. Then there are ones like the head, Rickson, Dr. Winston, the ed psych, and Mrs. Ali, who for all their smiles and "I'm just here to help you" chat are really just watching for mistakes, for anything outside the rules.

I jump when the bell goes. Time passed unnoticed. I lay down my pencil as Mrs. Ali appears in the door. Gianelli starts to gather up drawings and pin them up around the robin. When he gets to me, I say, "Wait. It's not finished." He looks at it and sees that it is, but doesn't comment, moves on to the next one as I pack it away.

I look up at the sketches. It is a sea of faces, important to each of us. Some probably a mum or dad, brother or sister, friends. One of a dog.

Mrs. Ali appears at my shoulder. "Let me see," she demands, and opens my folder. Stares at my drawing of Ben and raises an eyebrow. I flush.

She studies it. "It is a good likeness of Ben," she says finally.

It is better than good. It isn't just that it looks like him: It is his eyes. They are *him,* a him that I don't want to share. The way he looked at me yesterday, just before I thought he might kiss me and I pulled away. Before I told him about missing persons and Lucy. Before he *ran.*

We walk across the class to the door just as Gianelli pins up his own drawing. He's never done that before, showed us something he did himself. Everyone still left in the room looks up and catches their breath: It is Phoebe. He has captured a side of her I didn't know. The anger is gone; her face, the way she stands, everything about her is so very sad. She stands alone. Mrs. Ali's eyes grow cold as she stares at Gianelli.

I go to the track at lunch, afraid to look; afraid of what it might mean if I can't find Ben. He always comes here at lunch. Is he here?

I scan the track. There are a few runners scattered along it today, now that the rain has stopped. Most I recognize from training, but not the one I am looking for. I hug my arms around myself, watch them a few moments. Trying not to think. Where could he be?

I turn to go and crash straight into Ben.

"Careful," he says, and puts out both hands, one on each of my shoulders, to steady me.

"Where've you been?" I demand.

He shrugs. "Here. Where else?"

"You weren't in biology."

"No, I was late. Had a doctor's appointment, then Mum got a flat tire on the way back," he says, his eyebrows raised in a puzzle.

"You could have told me!" I say, and push my hands into his chest to shove him away, then start to walk off. I'd been so worried and he just had a stupid appointment.

"Well, I hardly knew we were going to get a flat tire," he says, in a reasonable tone that just makes me madder. He follows and catches my hand, hooks his little finger in with mine and holds it tight. "What's wrong?"

The anger fizzes out and my eyes are filling. I blink. "I thought something happened to you."

"You were worried about me?" And he smiles, looking very pleased about it. But before I can decide whether I want to punch him or hug him, it happens.

Bzzzz on my wrist. I sigh in exasperation.

He grabs my hand, and we look at it together: 3.9. "Come on." He pulls me back toward the track. "See if you can keep up today. You were a bit slow yesterday."

Slow?! I hit the track before Ben, pour everything into my legs, my feet. Ben gradually catches up but doesn't pass me. Though maybe he holds back? I go faster, until there is nothing left. Bit by bit I pull ahead, and I feel a cold sense of satisfaction. *This is the way it should be . . .*

As the running takes over, some small part of me is amused. Why did I get so angry with Ben? It wasn't reasonable, was it. I was confused about yesterday—about why he took off when I told him about Lucy and wouldn't talk about it afterward—but if he is anything like me, he needed time to take it in. And he expected to make it back in time for biology, so there was no reason to tell me he wouldn't be there. I can almost laugh at myself.

But I can't. Because the problem here is a serious one. One I don't want to face.

What is Ben to me?

When we stop I see Ferguson. Standing by the gym, stopwatch in hand, shaking his head a little. We walk past him as we leave.

"A flipping record. What a shame," he mutters to himself, shaking his head.

"What does he mean?" I say, stalling, before Ben can ask me . . . well, anything.

"Not sure, but I'm guessing we broke the track record."

"But that's good, right?" No matter the motivation for running like that, no matter that it might be difficult to repeat the frame of mind that made me do it.

Ben shrugs. "Sure. If you like breaking records."

"But he said it was a shame."

"Of course. Since we can't compete."

I stop short. "What do you mean?"

"Slateds can't be on school teams; you know that."

And as he says the words, I realize: I do know. I've been told some variant of it, anyhow. But I hadn't connected the dots together to apply it to cross-country running.

"But why let us train, then? What is the point?" Anger courses through me, but my levels are still safely up from running.

Ben shrugs. "I asked last year if I could train with them. Once he saw how I can run, he said yes; suppose same applied to letting you come along. I train with the team—helps spur them on to do better."

"Doesn't that make you angry? You are the best—or maybe, I am—and we can't compete. That isn't fair."

"Maybe I am, maybe you are; maybe I just let you beat me today," Ben teases. He's not really bothered by any of this, I see.

But instead of getting more angry, I crumple inside myself. I feel like Phoebe in Gianelli's drawing: isolated and alone. Even Ben, for all his wanting to find out what happened to Tori, doesn't seem to notice how things are run, how unfair it all is.

Ben asks if I want to train before Group again on Thursday. Train for what? But I say yes just as the bell rings for the next class. I'm a sight: My hair is soaked to my head, my clothes stuck to my back, and no time to use the gym showers. No one will want to sit next to me in English.

No change there, then.

Mrs. Ali corners me at the end of the day.

She smiles her gentle smile, her eyes are warm. A cold shiver goes up my spine.

"Kyla, dear, we need to have a talk." We stay in the classroom after the other students leave. My teacher spots Mrs. Ali and, muttering something about a cup of tea, makes an exit.

"How are things, dear?"

"Fine," I say, shifting miserably in my damp clothes, cold now that the warmth of the run is long gone.

"I see. Are you having problems coping with anything?"

"No," I lie.

"Well, listen a moment. I see a potential problem. That is you, and your friend Ben."

I shift, uncomfortable in my seat. "What do you mean?"

"Now, dear, you've only been out of the hospital, for what, three weeks?"

"Twenty-two days."

"Just over three weeks, then. Now I know Ben is a good-looking boy, and a decent one, too, by all accounts."

I flush, beginning to see where this is going.

"But you know, dear, that you need to concentrate on school, on your family, on integrating into your community. Not on a boy."

"Sure," I say. "Can I go now?"

She sighs. "Kyla, I am also well aware that excessive exercise is a

188

way to overcome the monitoring effects of your Levo. In the future, you are not to run the school track with Ben at lunch. Is that clear?"

"Perfectly," I say.

"You may go."

Stunned, I head for Jazz's car. More confused than anything else. *Ben.* I feel a pang. I can see that I won't be seeing much of him at school anymore. As far as the running goes, if I can't get on school teams anyhow, why bother? Though she didn't mention Sunday training. Maybe she doesn't know about it.

Is it me being with Ben that is Mrs. Ali's problem? Or the "excessive exercising." At the hospital, the nurses told me to run on the treadmills as a coping strategy, to keep my levels up. Does she want me to crash?

Jazz's car isn't parked in the usual place, but I spot it up ahead. He has pulled out of the student parking lot to line up near the exit, but the cars aren't moving. What is going on? He and Amy get out when they see me approach.

"Where've you been?" she asks.

"I got cornered by Mrs. Ali."

She shudders. "Is everything all right?"

"Peachy," I say, about to add more, but then get distracted by Jazz.

He isn't listening, I can tell. His eyes are fixed on something behind us, the smile has fallen from his face, and as I start to turn to look, he puts an arm on both of our shoulders to push us toward the car.

"Get in. Now," he says, and yanks the door open.

I climb in and twist to see out the window. Gianelli is walking past us, flanked on either side by Lorders. Another walks behind.

They are heading toward a black van double-parked by the school buses, blocking the exit. Gianelli stumbles; a Lorder yanks on his arm and pulls him to his feet, and they continue on.

None of the buses have left, even though I was late getting out. Students are waiting, but the bus doors are shut.

There are Lorders scattered about the bus bays. In black vests. Armed. A dozen or so of them, maybe a thousand students.

We all watch, as Gianelli—one old man, an artist, who stood up and protested in his own way—is shoved toward the van side door. His head bangs on the roof, he falls and the Lorder plants a boot to get him through the door. It is slammed shut.

No one does anything; no one says anything. I don't, either.

32

"I WONDER WHAT HE DID. IT MUST HAVE BEEN BAD." AMY seems fascinated and not remotely upset. "Wasn't he your art teacher?"

"He *is* my art teacher," I say.

"Well, I don't think he is anymore. They've never marched someone off in front of everyone like that before, have they?"

"I don't want to talk about it!" I say, but Amy persists.

"Come on, you must have heard something. *Tell* us."

"That's enough, Amy," Jazz says.

Amy looks startled. "What's it to you?" she says.

I take off. I'd been roped into going for a walk with them when we got home, never mind that I want to be alone in my room. But Mum said they couldn't go on their own, and here I am.

But no one said we couldn't walk some distance apart, did they? I race ahead, needing the speed, needing to run. It is the same footpath I went on that first walk with Amy and Jazz, three weeks ago today. Is that really all? It seems *much* longer ago than that. That day it was all a wonder: the woods, the trees, the fresh green smells. *Then,* I didn't know about Lorders, didn't know Ben. Didn't know about *missing persons*. The list of things of which I was ignorant was *so* long. Is it still?

I can't stop seeing Gianelli's head hit the roof of the van, him slumping to the ground. That Lorder kicking him like a sack of potatoes into the van. All because he drew a picture of Phoebe. Now he is missing, like she is; like Tori, too. Where is he now? Where are all of them?

I run up to the lookout at the top of the path, run back halfway, then start walking back to the top. Despite the dark thoughts, my Levo is safely masked by excessive exercise up and down a hill.

I can't understand why they took Gianelli. All he did was draw Phoebe. It's not like it is a secret that the Lorders took her; they yanked her out of a class, didn't they?

And there couldn't have been any more public way to take Gianelli; there's no hiding what happened to him.

Inside, a whisper: *Maybe that is the point.*

Gianelli's minute of silence for Phoebe, his "draw something you care about," then drawing her himself. These things all said that her being taken was wrong. He had to be punished for disagreeing with the government's actions. Doing what they did in front of all the students shouted loud and clear, without using words: *We are in control. We can do as we will.* If they did it as a secret, what would be the point?

"Hello, Slater."

I jump, so absorbed in my thoughts that I paid no attention to my surroundings. My feet had me at the lookout point again, but this time, I wasn't alone.

A man leans on a tree overlooking the path. Standing in shadows but visible enough if I'd been using my eyes outward instead of in. I flush, realizing he could have been watching my ascent for ages, that I'd just walked past him with no notice. That he was now between me, and Jazz and Amy.

"Aren't you going to say hello?" He smiles, and it isn't a nice smile.

Greasy hair, an unhealthy complexion, both too pale and blotchy red on his cheeks and nose. He doesn't look like the type to be walking footpaths. His face is somehow familiar, but who is he? Ah, yes: the bricklayer. I stared at him building a garden wall in the village, then had nightmares of brick towers.

"Isn't this a lucky coincidence?" he says. "I've been wanting to talk to you. Come and sit down." The way he says *coincidence* makes me think it is nothing of the sort. Has he been watching, following?

He walks across to sit on the log where Amy and Jazz rested the last time I came up here. I don't move, and look back down the path. Shouldn't they be here by now?

"I won't bite," he says, and smiles again. "I just want to talk to you about my niece. I think you knew her: Phoebe Best."

"Phoebe? Do you know where she is?" I say, and step toward him.

"Come on. Sit down, and I'll tell you." He pats the log with his hand.

I hesitate, then perch on one end of the log, leaving as much space between us as possible.

"Now, you know you have to get closer to talk about these things. I can't shout, can I? The trees may have ears, eh?" He laughs and spits on the ground.

I shift a little closer.

"That's better."

"Is Phoebe all right?"

"In a minute. I want to talk to you about something else first."

"What?"

"That was your cat, wasn't it."

"What do you mean?"

"Day 'fore she disappeared, I dropped Phoebe at the vet's with some cat she picked up. She was always picking up strays or forest creatures to look after. Daft girl."

I don't say anything, and look back down the path again. Where are they?

"Now Phoebe told me the cat belonged to some Slater, one she had words with even though I told her that was dangerous. And for some crazy reason, she wanted to give her back the cat. Then, the very next day, Phoebe doesn't come home from school. Now, what do you know about that?"

I jump to my feet.

"Where are you going? Don't you want to talk about Phoebe?"

Every instinct screams *run*. But some calm part inside waits, stands there. Needs to hear what he has to say. "Well?"

"Nice to me, Phoebe was. She's gone now. It's your fault. You said something to the Lorders, and they—"

"No! I didn't!" I shout. *Run*. I turn and bolt down the path, hearing and feeling the movement behind that says he chases.

But I just reach the first bend in the path when voices float up: Amy and Jazz are close by. *At last.*

They emerge around the corner, arms entwined. Obviously over whatever argument they had. I almost crash straight into them. Jazz steadies me with a hand on my arm. My eyes are wide.

Jazz frowns. "Is everything all right, Kyla?" he says, and looks up the way I came.

I spin around, but no one is there.

Amy links her arm in mine. "I'm sorry I went on about Gianelli. Jazz explained to me that you were upset about him." She says the words, but I see she doesn't really get it.

Jazz looks at me curiously. I can tell he knows something is up, but he doesn't ask, just lets Amy prattle on. We walk down the path back to the village.

A van is parked at the side where the footpath joins the road, BEST BUILDERS painted down the side. And it's him, in the front seat: Phoebe's uncle. The window is down; he winks, then whistles as we walk past.

Jazz scowls, and we carry on up the road; laughter follows behind us.

"Who is he?" I ask.

"That waste of space is Wayne Best," Jazz says. "Keep clear, he's a freak." Advice I plan to follow.

Home, at last. Amy runs inside the house when we return to ask if Jazz can stay for dinner; when I try to follow, Jazz tugs at my shoulder.

"What?" I say, expecting questions about what spooked me at the lookout, and not sure what to say.

He waits for the door to shut. "Mac wants to see you," he says in a low voice. "Next Monday. We'll go up after school, and I'll take Amy off for a walk again. All right?"

But before I have a chance to even think what to say, let alone to say it, Amy opens the door. She shakes her head. "Mum says not tonight; another time?"

Jazz looks relieved to get off staying for dinner; Amy is oblivious. How does she not see things for what they are, right in front of her eyes? I go in so they can say good-bye.

"So, how was school today?" Mum asks the room at large while she ladles food onto plates. Since Dad doesn't go to school, I'm assuming she expects Amy or me to answer.

I look at Amy, hoping she'll fill the space. But she just shrugs; annoyed, most likely, that Jazz wasn't invited to stay for dinner.

Dad gets up to carry plates to the table. "No stories to tell? Was it a good day, a bad day? Did anything interesting happen, anything unusual?"

He puts a plate in front of me, and I get a strange feeling that somehow, he knows at least some of what happened this afternoon.

I look at Amy, plead with my eyes for her to say something, anything. But nothing.

I sigh. "My art teacher got taken by Lorders."

Mum gasps, sits down. "Bruno Gianelli?" she says.

"Yes." I look at her, surprised. "Do you know him?"

"He's been at the school a long time. He was my art teacher when I went there. He was a great painter, and a good . . ." She stops in midsentence. "Well, that was a long time ago. Who knows who he is now."

"What will happen to him?" I ask.

Mum and Dad exchange a glance. Mum gets up and fusses over stirring something on the stove.

"That depends what he did, I guess. Don't worry yourself over it," Dad says.

Later that night, in my room at last, door shut, I am curled up on the bed around Sebastian. He purrs. I try to process everything that happened today in a way that makes sense, but I can't, and I can't stop thinking about it, either.

Only solution? Pencil, paper. *Draw something that makes you feel something, good or bad.*

Left hand. Feverish sketches, over and over again, into the small hours. The missing: Tori. Phoebe. Lucy. Gianelli. And Robert—my almost brother, that I never met—from all those years ago.

The bus driver lays on the horn, for all the good it will do. They aren't going anyplace: It is gridlock.

A pretty blond girl near the back of the bus rests her head on a boy's shoulder. He slips his arm around her. They don't mind the delay. Others are restless. A few read books; some older boys torment a smaller one; girls talk about boys, boys talk about girls, and friendless ones stare out the window.

I scream at the driver. "Do something! Open the doors! Let them out!"

But he doesn't know what is about to happen. He can't hear me.

The pretty girl feels cold. The boy stands, up out of his seat to get her his jacket from the overhead.

That is when it happens: a whistling noise, a flash of light, a bang. And the screaming starts.

Choking smoke; bloody hands beating at windows that don't open; more screaming. The boy with the girl who used to be pretty is quiet, though. He wraps his arms around her, but it is too late to tell her he loves her. She is dead.

Another whistle; a flash; an explosion. There is a gaping hole in the side of the bus, but most are silent now. The boy is pulled to safety away from the girl, and that is when he joins the few survivors. In screaming.

I stuff my hands in my ears, but the screaming just goes on and on.

It is a while before I realize.

It is me.

• • •

"Hush. It's just a dream."

I struggle, then realize where I am. In bed, at home—the current version of it, anyway—and these are not Amy's but Mum's arms that hold me. Amy appears in the door, yawning, then leaves again. Mum must have been awake to get here before her.

My Levo vibrates: 4.4. Not so low, yet I can feel the fear, taste the blood. It is all still in my eyes. That was Robert, and Cassie—the pretty one. My subconscious must have plucked their faces from that photo Mac showed me.

Sheets of paper, my drawings, are all over the bed. Mum smooths them out without comment and starts putting them together in a pile. Until she gets to the one of Gianelli.

I'd drawn him as he was in the classroom, standing defiant under his sketch of Phoebe, and so it is a drawing within a drawing. Phoebe is his Phoebe, the lonely girl I never knew.

Mum's face is so sad as she looks at Gianelli. I have just enough presence of mind to scoop the other drawings together before she sees the one I drew of Robert and Cassie. She touches Gianelli's face. "What did you do?" she whispers to the drawing. She turns to me. "We're on our own now; this is just between us. What happened to Gianelli? You do know, I can see you do. Your face is so transparent. You need to learn to hide things, like the rest of us. But please tell me."

So I do: about Phoebe's robin, and what Gianelli said. That we stood in silence, then he drew her as I had done.

"Stupid, dear man. To think things have got so bad, they'd take him just for that," she says. "Now listen to me, Kyla. I know, believe me I do, how upsetting all this is to you. How hard to understand. But you must learn to hide things away inside. Or you won't last. I don't want you taken away. Promise me that you will try?"

So I promise. What else can I do? I mean it as I say the words.

"I'm going to destroy this," she says, and holds up the sketch of Gianelli. "Are there others like it?" She turns her eyes to the pile of drawings. But if she sees Robert's face, what will she do? As "between us" as she says this is, I'm unsure how she'd feel about Mac.

"Let me see," she demands, and reaches her hands toward them.

But then there are footsteps on the stairs; heavy steps, coming down from above. She shoves Gianelli and the other drawings together under my blankets. The door opens.

Dad smiles. "Is everything all right in here?"

Mum turns. "Just fine. A little nightmare, that's all. Isn't that so, Kyla?"

"Yes, I'm fine now," I say. Dad stands there, still; waiting for Mum?

Sebastian wanders in and jumps up on the bed, turns round and round on the blanket over the hidden sheets of paper. They make faint crinkly noises. Then he flops down. I pet him and he starts to purr. *Where were you when I needed you, cat?* Mum turns out the bedside light, gets up and leaves. Turns at the door.

"Try to get some sleep now," she says. But her eyes say something else: *Destroy those drawings.*

I think about it for a while. Then I hide them. The carpet lifts up under the window. I tease it up and slip them underneath.

33

"THAT'S NOT FAIR." AMY STANDS HER GROUND, A HAND ON each hip.

I do up my laces; Ben will be here soon.

"I suppose you're right. It isn't fair," Mum says, and a feeling of dread fills me. *Shut up,* I say to Amy with my eyes, but she isn't receiving.

"You won't let Jazz and me go for a walk alone; why should Kyla be allowed to go out with Ben on her own?"

"We're not going out, we're *running,* and going to Group," I point out. "And he is just my friend." *Is he,* I wonder inside.

"Well, Amy makes a good point," Mum says, but then turns away from Amy and winks at me, mischief in her eyes, then faces Amy. "Tell you what: How about you go running with them?"

Amy recoils. "Running? Are you *serious*?" And she flounces up the stairs.

"You'll be careful?" Mum says, and zips up my jacket a little more.

"Of course."

"There is a question on your face."

"Is there?"

"One day soon, Kyla, you should practice a poker face in front of a mirror."

"What is a poker face?" I say, asking one question to avoid her looking too closely at another.

"Poker is a card game. You try to keep your face neutral, so other players can't tell if you have a good hand."

I pull the curtain aside to look out the window. Come on, Ben; be on time for once.

"And to answer your unspoken question, you are different from Amy. It's a strange thing, but I trust you to go running alone with Ben. I don't trust her judgment with Jazz. Understand?" The phone rings and she goes to answer it.

Mum sees more than I think sometimes; more than Amy understands. It is true that Amy and Jazz are constantly touching each other, arms linked, kissing, and Ben and I don't do that. But they don't do it in front of her, so how can she tell?

Mrs. Ali sees things different. Since she banned me from running with Ben at lunch, I've barely spoken to him all week, and any day we don't have a moment together doesn't feel right. Of course, Mrs. Ali saw my drawing of Ben. Mum did not, and won't, since I've hidden it away with the others under the carpet.

I peek through the curtains again, and this time, Ben is running up the road: at last.

"Bye, Mum!" I yell, and slip out the door.

As usual we run flat out to start. Say nothing beyond hello. Excessive exercising: Is that what this is? I love the *thump-thump* of my feet on the tarmac, the escape into another place where all that matters is going fast and then faster. Ben's longer legs run a slower rhythm to match my speed, so his *thud-thud* and my *thump-thump* blend to a familiar skittering sort of music that soothes after the last few days.

It has been strange at school with Gianelli gone. Not even whispers I've heard, not like when Phoebe went and everyone buzzed about it. This time there is a silence on the subject. Perhaps that is because everyone saw what happened to him, so there is no need to spread half-truths and gossip. Gianelli has not been replaced; art classes have been canceled until further notice. That lesson slot for me has been moved to Unit where the only acceptable activity is homework.

I start to slow down; usually Ben is the one to do this, to talk. But today I have a few things on my mind.

Ben makes no comment; he drops his pace along with mine, and doesn't ask any questions like he usually does. In fact, he has barely said a word all week. I'd thought of what to say and how to say it, but when I look up at him as we drop to a walk, it all goes.

"Are you angry with me?" I ask.

"What?"

"You heard me. You haven't been right all week. Not since Sunday, really."

"Don't be silly. Of course I'm not angry," he says, but he looks angry.

I stop. "What is it? Have I done something?"

He runs his hand through his hair. "Kyla, not everything is about you all the time, all right?"

I recoil, step back: That felt like a slap. "What is it, then?"

"Shhh," he says, and I realize I raised my voice. He grabs my hand, laces his fingers between mine. A car goes past; he looks both ways. None in sight. "Come on," he says, and pulls me into the shadows of trees at the side of the road.

There is a path, hard to see in the darkness; it leads to a fence with a metal gate that gleams faintly in the moonlight, fields on the other side. The road is barely a few minutes' walk away; there are faint sounds and lights now and then as a car passes.

Ben stops and leans against the fence, his face in shadows. "Quiet words in the night," he whispers. He puts his hands about my waist and lifts me up so I'm sitting on the top of the wooden fence and we are eye to eye, keeping one arm steady around me. My eyes start to adjust more to the darkness, and I can see he has that look on his face. Like he did in the rain when I thought he might kiss me; the one I drew in Gianelli's last art class, then hid away.

He leans in quick, so fast I don't react, and kisses my cheek lightly.

"I'm not mad at you, Kyla," he says in my ear, and his words send shivers down my neck. My stomach flips, and as if on its own my hand starts to reach up to his face, to touch his lips, to . . .

He shakes his head, regret in his eyes, and pulls away. "We need to talk," he says. "We haven't got much time."

My hand drops back down again.

But then he half leans back on the fence, into shadow, and doesn't say anything. Leaves rustle in the breeze, the fence feels icy underneath me; now that I've stopped running, goose bumps rise on my arms and legs, and I shiver.

He moves closer and takes my hands in his.

"I've missed running with you at lunch," he says. I'd managed to tell him that I'd been banned from the school track.

"Me, too."

"You've missed me?"

"I've missed running!" I say, and he raises an eyebrow. "And you," I admit. He grins, and it is there: He knew it all along. Just wanted to make me say it.

"Well. I can understand about the running. It's only when I'm going flat out that I seem to be able to focus on things, to think them through." He frowns. "But all that stuff you told me on Sunday; even when I run, it won't go away."

And I hear Mrs. Ali's words echo in my ears: *Excessive exercise is a way to overcome the monitoring effects of your Levo.* And I realize that the only time I see Ben as he is now, not just the smiling Slated boy from when we first met, is when he has been running. It is like it *lets him out.*

He lets go of my hands, leaving them cold and empty, and leans against the fence. "And I can't stop thinking about what happened to Tori."

I fold my arms in on myself to hold the pain inside. Tori is the ghost that always comes between us. Then I shake my head to banish the thought. No, not a ghost! She couldn't be. Could she?

"And Phoebe, and your art teacher, and everyone else who disappeared. And all the missing persons on those websites you told me about. From everything I've been able to find out, it is getting worse. More and more disappearances."

"Then come with me. After school on Monday, and you can see it for yourself. See if you are on the website." A broken promise to tell no one. This isn't just anyone; it is Ben, and I trust him. But guilt hangs uneasy on my head just the same.

"The thing is, Kyla, I don't want to! I don't want to know."

"I don't understand."

"*You've* been reported missing. Somebody cares about you; they want you back. What if no one wants me, and that is why I'm here? Like what happened to Tori: Her new mother decided she didn't want her anymore. What if my real parents just dumped me?"

"But it doesn't work like that. You have to have been arrested and tried for something, done something, to have been Slated." But as I hear myself say the words, they sound false. I begin to understand the implications of those missing children, like Lucy: Where did she go when she went missing? That is the way it is supposed to be, but it isn't always that way—not if those websites are for real. It's not like you can complain that you shouldn't have been Slated; once it happens, you don't remember a thing. And anyone who has been properly convicted isn't missing, after all. Their parents would know what happened to them.

"You get it now, don't you," Ben says.

I nod. "I didn't think it through that way."

"So why should I find out? What good will it do? I don't remember anything from before, anyhow; I'm not the same person. And my family now is all right; better than all right, really."

And I realize I don't really know anything about them. "Tell me," I say. And we start back for the road to get to Group, and Ben tells me about his dad, a primary school teacher who loves playing piano, and his mum, who runs the dairy workshop, makes art out of metal, and can't carry a tune. And they couldn't have children of their own. After three years with them now, he cares for them. Why upset things?

And while he talks I listen, but part of me is thinking of what he said to start with: *What if no one wants me?*

And I think, *I do.*

But I don't say it out loud.

34

THE LORDERS ARE SEARCHING CARS AT THE HOSPITAL GATES again today. Another two of them stand guard in the hall outside Dr. Lysander's office, and my skin crawls when I walk past. I watch them, unable to stop myself, from my seat in the waiting room. They are alert, you can tell, to every sound and movement throughout the hospital. But they pay less attention to me than if a tiny spider sat on the wall. Slated: unworthy of notice. Not a threat.

"Come in," Dr. Lysander calls at last, and I scurry away from them, glad to put a closed door between us.

"Is something chasing you?" She smiles.

"Of course not."

She raises an eyebrow.

I sigh. "If you must know, those Lorders give me the creeps."

"I'll tell you a secret, Kyla. They give me the creeps, too."

My eyes widen. "Really?"

"Really. But I just ignore them, pretend they're not there. If I don't acknowledge them, then they don't exist."

She says that calm and certain, as if her lack of attention can make entire people disappear. Go missing.

I shudder involuntarily, then glance up quickly to see if she noticed, but she is busy tapping at her screen. She looks up again.

"Last week you decided to focus on your art. How is that going?"

"Not very well."

"Oh? And why is that?"

"Art lessons have been canceled. The art teacher got taken by Lorders in front of the entire school."

Shock travels across her face so quick it would have been easy to miss—eyes that widen, an intake of breath—then her face is back to detached, neutral.

"How do you feel about that?"

"I've been drawing at home, but it isn't the same."

"You misconstrue. How do you feel about your art teacher?"

This is interesting. I know from everyone's reactions that it is taboo to talk about what Lorders have done, and to whom. Yet here she is, asking me straight out what I think. *Be careful, Kyla: They are just in the hall. Who knows what they can hear?*

"I'm sure they had their reasons."

"Now, Kyla: It is obvious you have strong feelings on this subject."

"It is?"

"Your eyes are the window to your soul."

How annoying. I've been practicing at home, in front of a mirror, to keep a poker face, like Mum said I needed. But as soon as I thought of anything I had feeling about, good or bad, I could see it reflected in the mirror. *Think about Sebastian.* That seemed to help.

"Do I have a soul?"

"You are getting too good at trying to deflect me. It is merely an old saying, a proverb."

"But can someone who has been Slated have a soul?"

She sits back in her chair, an amused half smile on her face. "Well, if one believes in the existence of souls, I cannot see any relevance of the Slating procedure to the presence or absence of one."

"Do you believe in them?"

She half shakes her head. "You forget who asks the questions here, Kyla. Answer mine," she says with a warning note in her voice.

So I try to come up with something I can say about Gianelli that isn't dangerous, but then think: *No. He deserves better. He deserves the truth.*

"He was a good person. He cared about us, and now he's gone. How do you think I feel?"

She frowns. "Answering a question with a question? You know better than—"

BANG!

A wave of sound ripples through the office. The building shakes, a shudder rumbles through the floor under my feet as fear rips through my body. Screams, distant and faint, but not distant enough.

Terrorists?

The door springs open behind me, and I spin around in my chair: the Lorders from the hall. For the first time I am happy to see them. One talks in a headphone linked to his ear. "Come with us now," the other says, looking at Dr. Lysander, but she doesn't move, seems frozen, face blank, behind her desk. "Now!" he yells, and she starts, gets up, and they flank her, start marching her to the door. Do I follow?

She half turns. "Kyla, go to the nurses' station. Don't worry, you'll be—"

Then the Lorder grabs her shoulder and pushes her through the door. The look of shock returns.

She can't make them disappear anymore.

There are distant bangs, screams, *rat-a-tat-tat* noises like guns in old movies. Guns: where? I tilt my head: somewhere below, or outside. I cross Dr. Lysander's office to the window.

It doesn't have bars; it overlooks an internal courtyard, several floors down. With plants and trees, benches. There are nurses huddled there; no signs of guns or who may be wielding them.

Dr. Lysander said *Go to the nurses' station.* I start for the door, then stop. Her computer is on her desk. Still open.

BANG!

The whole building shakes; that was closer, this time.

I pause. Panic says *run,* but is doing battle with curiosity. *When will you get another chance like this?*

And I'm trembling, my stomach twists like breakfast might be on its way up. What do I do? I stare at the door, my feet take one step toward it, one back again. *Who says it is any safer out there than it is in here?*

I drop into her chair.

My photo is to the right of the screen: Kyla 19418. That is the number on my Levo. Left of the photograph are Dr. Lysander's notes: some brief ones from today, though no mention of Gianelli. A list of dates runs down the side; last week is at the top. I hesitate, then click on it. And there it is: all we discussed that day. Her observations.

There is a menu bar across the top under my name, with headings: Admission; Surgical; Follow Up; Recommendations.

I click on Admission. And there I am, in full color. Me, but not me. On a hospital bed, but it is different: There are straps on the sides of it. My hands are tied, my feet. My hair is longer, a tangled mess. I'm even thinner than I am now. My face is blank, my eyes vacant: not windows to my soul or to anything else.

And while I stare at the computer screen, some part of me still hears: shouts, gunshots, a scream that chokes off. But I am mesmerized. I scan quickly through my admission and surgical notes.

Searching for any clue as to why I am here, but find nothing. Just mumbo jumbo about scans, complete with visuals of my brain.

Footsteps, shouts. They are closer now.

But what is this? I clink on a link marked Recommendations.

And *louder*. I look up at the door.

Move, hide, now! A voice in my head again. Where? I look around the room, glance down at the computer to close the windows I opened, but then the last link I clicked comes up on the screen: Recommendations. A table with actions and dates.

Board recommends termination. Dr. Lysander overrules. Retreatment undertaken. Monitor for signs of regression after retreatment. Extra Watchers recommended. Board recommends termination if recur. The last is dated the week before I left the hospital.

Move, hide, now!

The door springs open.

Too late.

A man stares at me. He isn't a Lorder: His hair is straggly, his eyes wild, and his black clothes are meant to look like their operations gear, perhaps, but fall short close up. Some part of me still gathers these details while the rest focuses clearly on just one thing. A gun, in his hand, which he raises and points at me.

Another face appears over his shoulder.

"Leave her! She's got a Levo. She's been Slated."

Still he points the gun at me. "It would be kinder, wouldn't it?" he says.

I shake my head, backing up against the wall. Trying to speak, *no, please no,* but the words just form in my mind, get stuck in my throat, and don't come out.

"Don't waste the bullet!" the other one yells, and yanks his arm. They take off down the hall.

I slip to the floor, shaking violently. My Levo says 5.1. *Explain that one.*

I can't.

Before long, self-preservation takes over, goads me to get up. I shut all the computer windows I opened, leave the computer on the desk as it was, and peer out the door. The hall is empty; there are screams to the right where those men ran. I run the other way.

The lights flicker several times, then go out. It is pitch-black. My eyes open wide and wider, but can see nothing in the windowless hall. A scream starts trembling deep in my gut, trying to work its way out. *Get a grip; you know the way. Remember!* I breathe in slow and deep, force the grid of the hospital into my mind. Eighth floor. Go to the nurses' station like Dr. Lysander said.

One hand on the wall, light on my feet, trembling but careful to make no sound, I walk to the end of the hall. Double doors, turn left: You have reached your destination.

All is silence. I walk forward, hands out to find the edge of the desk, but I slip on something on the floor and sprawl on the ground.

The floor is wet. Sticky. There is a funny metallic smell that catches at the back of my throat and makes me gag. *Blood.*

I back up blindly, on hands and knees, and smack into something—no, someone—on the floor: a hand, an arm. A whole person, a woman, in a nurse's dress. No sound, no movement, a great sticky pool . . . I force myself to follow her arm up to her neck. She is still warm, just, but quite clearly dead. That last scream I heard, before those two men came. With the gun. They shot her; they must have.

Dead.

I scramble back to my feet and run, blind, back down the dark hall.

Stop; too much noise! Hide.

Some instinct forces me to slow down, take careful steps. Quiet ones. I try to think if I noticed the nurse at the desk earlier, when I got off the elevator. I walked right past her on my way in, but I can't think what she looked like. If I knew her, I would have noticed, wouldn't I? But I was distracted, saying good-bye to Mum, and then . . .

Mum! She went to have tea with her friend like she always does. Where do they go? I don't know! Mum, where are you?

Take control. Calm down, NOW.

I breathe in and out until my heart rate slows and the wave of panic is retreating, walled in. Contained. *Stand still and listen.* But I can't hear anything, not a sound. The hospital is eerily quiet like it never has been before.

Without consultation my feet take me to the emergency exit stairs, automatically heading for the place they know best: the tenth floor. My old room. Careful and quiet, one hand on the wall, I climb, one step at a time. Stopping to listen now and then, but hearing nothing. Finally I reach for the door to the tenth, suddenly afraid it will be locked. It opens: perhaps because of the power failure? I step through the door and into the hall; there are dim emergency lights on this floor. Voices and people moving about, calm voices, no shouts or screams. I step forward.

Then a light shines in my face.

"Is that Kyla!? Oh, it is." The light is lowered, and it is Nurse Sally, one of the tenth-floor nurses who was on my wing when I stayed here. I'm absurdly happy to see a face, a living face, one I know. I smile, and she clasps my shoulder. "It *is* you. Oh, darling, here for a checkup, were you? Come on. We must all go to the cafeteria. Help us, will you, with some of the newbies. They're confused."

And she has me take the hands of two Slateds. New ones. Unsteady on their feet, but smiling great beatific grins as if this is the most wonderful day of their lives.

She pushes a wheelchair: a very new one. Not trusted to walk.

Down the hall we go; soon it is crowded with nurses and patients.

"Hurry!" An impatient voice at the back. One of several Lorders, herding us along.

We shuffle to the tenth-floor cafeteria—the only place big enough to get everyone in. They push the last of us in and barricade the door.

There is natural light here from high barred windows, bright after the dim emergency lights, and I blink.

"Kyla, you're hurt! What happened?" And Nurse Sally is pushing me into a chair, checking my arm, my shoulder.

"Hurt? I'm not . . . Oh. I see. This isn't my blood," I say. "I tripped on someone, who . . ." And I can't think about that, or even finish the sentence, so switch to another. "What's happening?"

"Don't worry. I'm sure everything will be fine."

"They're shooting people; killing them. They're not fine."

Her mouth drops open. She shakes her head. "I forgot how direct you can be. There was an AGT attack. It's over. They're just tracking the last few down, so they're keeping everyone under wraps until they do."

"Are you okay, honey?" Another nurse beams at me, with a handful of syringes of Happy Juice. Making the rounds of the room.

"Fine," I say, and think of Sebastian. It must work, my poker face;

she moves along. Sally goes with her; they start checking everyone as they go.

I back up and sit on a chair at one of the tables. There is a girl strapped in a wheelchair next to me, brown hair cascading forward over her face. Her Levo vibrates. I look about for a nurse, wave at Sally to come over, but she doesn't see. The girl is slumped down in her wheelchair, trying to reach for something . . .

Ah. There, on the floor. I pick up the soft toy she must have dropped: a floppy-eared bunny.

"There you go," I say, and put it in her hands. She looks up and smiles. A beautiful wide smile of perfect joy.

I recoil. No; it can't be. That smile doesn't belong on that face. She is gorgeous with it, it suits her, but it is all *wrong*.

"Phoebe?" I whisper.

35

SOMETHING SHARP JABS MY SHOULDER.

Warmth slides through my veins. Almost instant: My heart rate slows, my fists uncurl. Ah . . . not just Happy Juice. Something stronger.

I fade in and out.

At some level I am aware, but not.

The lights are back on. I'm in a wheelchair going down a hall, but I don't know where; all I see is the floor. I can't lift my head to look.

There is the warmth of a shower. A nurse holds me upright while another scrubs my skin. Blood washes away so easily when it belongs to someone else. I watch as my skin is perfect and white again. Pretty.

Fluffy towels, clean clothes.

Hospital-issue clothes. This is wrong. I fight to focus on why, but cannot.

I'm tucked into a bed, but it isn't my bed. The sheets are cool, my skin feels feverish against them. Not my bed? I try to keep my eyes open. They flutter, then shut.

"Kyla, come on, now. Wake up. Kyla . . ."

I'm warm and happy; floating; unconnected to my body. I don't want to go back. *Leave me alone.* I slip through layers of darkness, the voice fades away . . .

Bricks are all around me. Above, too, as far as I can see. I scratch at the mortar. It is starting to crumble. Bit by bit. It won't be long now . . .

Soon, I'll be free.

Another voice. "Come on, Kyla. It's time to go home."

Mum?

My eyes snap open.

We spiral out of the hospital parking lot to the exit.

Mum seems completely unruffled. She told me on the way to the car that she'd been in her friend's office when the first blast hit. They locked themselves in and hid under a desk.

When it was over, she couldn't find me. No one knew where I was. The floor where I'd been, and the one below—doctors' offices, meeting rooms—had been targeted. No key personnel were hurt, though. They were all whisked away like Dr. Lysander. But when I pressed her, she admitted that some nurses and a few Lorders died. And all the AGT.

Eventually I was tracked down, away in la-la land by the time she found me. Delayed reaction and shock, they thought, had caused my levels to plunge. They just caught me with an injection before I blacked out. And since I'd been sedated, they didn't want to release me without a full going-over and scans.

Mum said she pulled strings. Called a few friends in high places to get me out and take me home. Said everyone at the hospital was in so much of a tizzy that they went along with it to make her go away.

Home.

I sleep some in the car, but the injection is wearing off. Things are starting to come back; in pieces at first, then all in a rush.

I am unable to even believe that the terrorists got into the hospital, let alone what they did, the people they killed. *Don't waste the bullet.* If they had more bullets, maybe I'd be dead now, too. All that blood; the nurse whose face I cannot remember . . .

I force my mind away from her, and it slips back to Dr. Lysander's office. On her computer, it said *Board recommends termination. Dr. Lysander overrules.* What does it mean?

Strangest of all: Somehow, through everything that happened, I'd stayed level, or near enough. It makes no sense.

It was seeing Phoebe that finally pushed me over the edge.

With some sort of serious delayed reaction of her own, Mum's iron nerves wait until we get home and through the front door, then collapse. She rolls into a ball on the sofa and dissolves in tears.

"What should we do?" I say.

"Call Dad," Amy suggests. Mum shakes her head no from the sofa.

"How about Aunt Stacey?" And she seems okay with that, so Amy calls her.

Soon Amy is playing with baby Robert while telling me how to make dinner, and Stacey and Mum are well into a bottle of red wine.

By now Amy has gleaned a little of the story: that terrorists attacked the hospital. I haven't told her—or anyone—that I saw two of them in Dr. Lysander's office, or that one nearly shot me. Or about the nurse who died. Amy is fascinated and wants every detail, but something stops the words from coming out.

• • •

On the news that night there is a five-second mention: *Earlier today, armed AGT attempted to mount a vicious attack on dedicated medical staff at a major London hospital. They failed.*

Tell that to the nurse whose blood was all over the floor.

36

"**Quite an adventure you had yesterday,**" **Dad says, one** eye on me and one on the road.

"I guess so."

"Were you scared?"

"Yes."

"Good."

I look at him in surprise.

"You'd have to be completely mad not to be scared," he says. He stops at a red light. "Did you sleep all right?"

"Yes."

"No nightmares?"

"No." I'd been afraid to close my eyes, but if I dreamed, I remembered nothing.

"Interesting. There you have something *real* to be scared of for a change, and you sleep like a baby." He looks quite fascinated, like I'm a puzzle he is trying to figure out. I get the feeling he doesn't like not understanding things, people—anything.

"Maybe the injection I had at the hospital hadn't worn off yet," I suggest.

"Perhaps," he says, but I get the feeling he knows they don't last that long. "What did you think of the terrorists?"

Does he somehow know that I saw two of them face-to-face? No.

How could he? His eyes are on the road now as he navigates a twisty narrow stretch.

"Well?"

What do I think about the terrorists . . . I haven't been able to stop thinking about them. Blowing up busloads of students and killing nurses. "They're evil," I say.

"Some people think they have a point. That the Lorders go too far; that they are the evil ones. That what happens in that hospital and others like it is wrong."

My eyes widen, shocked he'd dare say that, even as something that *some people*—unidentified and faceless—may think. "But the AGTs kill people, innocent people, who don't have anything to do with *anything*. It doesn't matter why, it is still wrong."

He tilts his head side to side, as if considering what I said. "So, it isn't so much their point of view as their methods to which you take exception? Interesting."

He pulls into the school. I was going to ask him to wait a moment, unsure if Ferguson has been told by Mrs. Ali to exclude me from Sunday training as well as keeping me off the track at lunchtime. But suddenly I just want out of the car, away from Dad, his questions. His saying *interesting* in a way that says so much more is hidden in every word.

And this time Ferguson is already here. He tilts his head in a hello as I get out of the car, doesn't register surprise that I am there. Dad gives a half wave and pulls away.

Mum had been adamant I should stay home today, but Dad said she couldn't keep us under her eye all the time and might as well let me go. She was back to being herself this morning; last night, too. By the time Aunt Stacey left and we had dinner, she was all contained.

When Dad got in hours later, you wouldn't have known she'd ever been upset.

Dad certainly says the strangest things.

"I know what happened to Phoebe."

"What? I mean, how could you?" Ben leans back against a tree, breathing heavily. I'd run as if Lorders were after me, from the course beginning to the top of this hill; he barely kept up. Until I was exhausted enough to stop, to be able to talk, and know our levels would be in check.

"I saw her."

"Where?"

"At the hospital. She's been Slated."

Quickly I tell Ben the events of yesterday. I skip the worst bits—not so much not wanting to tell him, as not wanting to think about it enough to describe it—like they are hidden behind a little door, slammed shut, in my head. Some things want to stay in a dark corner and never come out, and that is just fine with me. I'd visualized this in my mind before I went to sleep last night: pushing the memories behind a door and locking it with a key. Maybe that is the real reason for no nightmares?

"Terrorists actually got into the hospital? I can't get my head around this," he says, looking very like he wants to dash up the path. I grab his hand to hold him there, and he holds mine tight.

"And don't forget about Phoebe," I say.

"Are you certain it was her?"

"Yes." It was her. Despite her smiling a grin of joy I've never seen on her face before, I had no doubt.

"So, she's been Slated. But she was just taken by Lorders, what, a week and a few days ago? There couldn't have been a trial or any-thing."

"No."

We walk along the path. We should have ages before anyone catches up to us; there was no rain to slow things down today, and with last week's mud mostly dried up, we went at full speed. When we reach the rock where I first told Ben about Lucy, Ben stops, sits, pulls me onto his knee. Wraps his arms around me tight. Says in my hair, "I'm so glad you're okay. I don't know what I would do if you disappeared, too."

Disappeared, too . . . *like Tori.* Though being blown up by terrorists isn't quite the same as Lorders taking you. At least if you are splat-tered, your fate is obvious. *Not if no one knows about it.*

We just sit like we are, not moving. It's a frosty October morning, but the sun is warm on my back, the rest of me warmed by Ben, so close. My face is against his chest, breathing in damp, and sweat, and something else that is just *Ben.* His breath is on my hair; his heart thuds along with mine, and I want to stay here, in this moment, forever.

Finally he pulls away a little. Face serious.

"Listen. Phoebe was fifteen—I checked with a friend of hers. So when they took her, they Slated her. But what about Tori? She was seventeen: too old. And Gianelli. What happened to them?"

"I don't know."

"We have to do something about this," Ben says, and fear swirls through my guts.

"Like what?" I say.

"Tell people—about Phoebe, at least, since we know what hap-pened to her. What they did to her can't be legal."

I shake my head. "You can't say anything! Or you'll be the next to go."

"But how will things change if no one knows?"

"No," I say.

"But—"

"No!" I jump up, start stalking down the path.

Ben follows. "Kyla, I—"

"No. Promise me you won't."

We argue back and forth, and, in the end, the only promise I get from Ben is that he won't do anything without talking to me first. Then we take off running once again before anyone can catch up to us. Thudding along the trail, to the place where all I am is running, and I can think about anything or nothing and both are okay. When the end is in sight—our bus and Ferguson ahead—I pull Ben's hand.

"Listen. Come with me after school tomorrow," I say. "Come see the websites I told you about. People are telling about stuff there."

He grins.

37

JAZZ LOOKS SERIOUSLY ANNOYED.

"Which part of *tell no one* didn't you get?" he says, and scowls.

"Ben is all right."

He shrugs. "He probably is, but that isn't the point."

"I'm sorry."

"Now I'm not sure whether to take you to Mac's, or not."

I shrug. For my part, I don't really want to go. Now that I've had a chance to think things through more carefully, anything Mac wants to talk to me about over his illegal computer I can do without. Despite practicing, my poker face still isn't up to scratch if anyone asks questions, and who knows if Ben even has one?

Amy appears in one direction, Ben in another. I'd run full tilt to get here first and asked Ben to take his time so I'd have a chance to explain.

"Well, you decide," I say.

Jazz sighs. "All right. He can come. Mac can always choose not to talk to you about whatever the hell it is, or not."

I wave at Ben to let him know it is all right to come over; he gets there as Amy does.

She raises an eyebrow. "Well, if it isn't Ben."

He grins, she grins back. Jazz slips an arm around Amy and kisses her cheek.

"All in!" he says, opens the door, and pushes Ben toward the backseat. He clambers in, and I get in after him. I get the side with the seat belt.

"Hang on tight," I say as I do it up. "There's only the one."

When we get to Mac's and out of the car, Mac raises an eyebrow at Ben, but once he spots his Levo seems less bothered by him being there than Jazz was.

Jazz introduces them, looks at me, and shrugs: universal male language?

"Shall we go for a walk, Amy?" Jazz says, and holds out his hand. Looks at Ben, then Mac. More unspoken words: The question on his face says *Do we have to take him with us?*

Mac shakes his head. "Go on, you two lovey-doves. Enjoy the sunshine. Won't be many more nice days like this until spring."

They disappear down the footpath.

"Come on in. Drinks?" Mac says.

I shake my head, as does Ben.

"So, to what do I owe the pleasure?" Mac says.

"I thought you wanted me to come," I say, confused.

He raises an eyebrow, and I realize he means Ben.

"Oh." I blush. "Ben's all right. You won't tell anyone, will you?"

"Of course not," Ben says. "We're both worried about people who've gone missing, and—"

Mac holds up a hand. "Not my problem. In fact, I don't know a thing about it."

Ben and I exchange a look.

"How about you two watch TV, or do whatever takes your fancy on the sofa. I've got a car to work on." And he goes out the back door; it swings, and slams shut with a bang.

I look at Ben and shrug, about to say some variation of *I have no idea what is going on,* when the door to the hall opens behind us.

We both spin around. In the door stands some guy: twenty or so, red hair, freckles; a serious face. One I've never seen before.

"Hello, Lucy," he says, and smiles.

He walks toward us.

"I'm Aiden," he says, then looks at Ben, one eyebrow raised.

"This is Ben. But don't call me Lucy; I'm Kyla."

"You *were* Lucy. I've seen the photos, and now that I see you in person, Mac is definitely right. You are she; she is you."

"Maybe I was. But I'm not anymore. And what has it got to do with you?"

"Yeah, who the hell are you?" Ben says.

Exactly what I was thinking, but my eyes widen in surprise when Ben says it.

Aiden laughs. "Ben, I can see you are someone I need to talk to. Glad you came."

We both still look at Aiden, not speaking.

"Ah, sorry. Who am I, or who am I supposed to be?" He laughs, but there is no happiness in the sound; it is hollow. "Officially, a telephone technician by day, but I also work for MIA."

"MIA?" Ben asks, puzzlement on his face, but the letters mean something to me.

"MIA: Missing in Action, right?" I say. "Like on the website. Trying to find out what has happened to people like . . . like me," I say, finding the nerve to say the words out loud.

"That's it," he says, and grins. "Come on; let's show Ben."

We go down the hall to Mac's spare room, where the computer is already out from its hiding place and turned on.

"Show me Lucy," Ben says. Aiden searches her name, and there she is. I can see Ben assessing the happy face on the screen: Lucy Connor, age ten. Then looking back and forth between the two of us. "Yes, it is definitely you," he finally says. My heart sinks. It's not like I wasn't already pretty sure, but if somebody I know as well as Ben is convinced it is so, there can be no arguing with the conclusion. It changes from *maybe* to fact.

Aiden grins. "So, what is next for Lucy?" He spins my chair around, a hand on each arm, and stares straight in my eyes. His are blue, deep blue, and unwavering. "The question I have for you, Lucy, or Kyla— whatever you want to be called—is this: What are *you* going to do about it?"

"What do you mean?"

He takes the computer mouse and moves the cursor over a button marked *Found* on the screen, underneath Lucy's photograph. "Should I press it?"

"I don't understand. What does it mean?"

"Simple: It will tell whoever reported you as missing that you are okay. Then you enter information to get in contact."

"No," I say.

Aiden's eyes are back to mine. Disappointment reflected in his.

"Think of them, always worrying, wondering what happened to you. Maybe it's your mum, or your dad, who has never been able to get over losing you. Maybe you've got sisters and brothers who miss you, too. Maybe that kitten you are holding is now a cat, sitting on the doorstep of your house right now, waiting for you to walk up the street."

"*No*. This is crazy. I don't know anything about *Lucy*, or where she comes from. I'm not her anymore."

Aiden's hand is poised over the mouse still, and I yank it away from him.

He sighs. "Think about this, Lucy."

I start to protest the name again; he interrupts.

"I will call you *Lucy*. No matter what you think *now* because of what was done to you, it is who you are," he says, and leans back against the desk, a thoughtful look behind his careful smile. "What do you think MIA is about?"

"Trying to find out what happened to people, I guess."

"That is important, but it is just a small part of what we are trying to achieve. We are finding people who were taken illegally so we can hold the government to account for it: expose them to the world. Without anyone standing up and saying this is wrong, nothing will ever be done to stop it. It is happening more and more all the time. They must be stopped."

I gasp. "You're with the terrorists, aren't you."

"No."

"It sounds like it to me."

He shakes his head. "No, I'm not. We're not with the government; we're not with the terrorists. We're trying to find a better way. *Without* violence."

Ben takes my hand. "Kyla, listen. This sounds just like what we were talking about yesterday. Maybe there *is* something we can do?"

I am starting to tremble; my Levo is dropping. It vibrates: 4.3.

"Leave us alone a minute," Ben says. Aiden goes, shuts the door behind him.

"You know he is right, don't you?" he says.

I shake my head. I feel sick with a certain fear that the more we find out, the worse everything will be; that nothing will be right from now on. Ben wraps his arms around me tight, rocks me back and forth, until eventually I stop shaking. My Levo starts a slow climb up to 5, and Ben calls Aiden back in.

His face is concerned. "Are your levels all right now?"

"I think so."

"It's a bitch, isn't it. Being hooked up to one of those. But there may be a way to get rid of your Levos before you are twenty-one."

"How?" Ben says.

"One of the things we found out when we started to look into missing people is that some of the ones who go missing are Slateds."

"Like Tori," Ben says, and then explains. "She was a friend of ours; seventeen years old. We think she was taken by Lorders."

"Sometimes they are taken by Lorders. Now and then there are problems with the Slating process that aren't picked up before you leave the hospital, some memory traces that aren't eliminated." *Regression,* my mind whispers. "They are taken back to the hospital, retreated, or . . ." He hesitates.

"Terminated," I say, then realize I said it out loud, not just in my head, and wish I hadn't.

Aiden looks startled. "Yes, just so."

These words were on my records on Dr. Lysander's computer. He looks about to ask how I know, but no matter how far from the Lorders' side Aiden appears to be, I'm not saying.

"You said that sometimes they are taken by Lorders," I say quickly, before he can ask. "What about the others?"

"Some are taken by terrorists."

"Why? What would AGT want with them?" Ben asks.

"They've been working on how to disable or remove Levos. We don't know all the details, but they have had some success."

"Really?" Ben says, eager curiosity all over his face.

But any damage or interference with a Levo results in seizures and death to the wearer. We were warned of this repeatedly before leaving the hospital. What happened to the Slateds while they were working it out? "Some success?" I say. "Probably more failure."

Aiden looks grim. "True. They've tried different types of pain-killers and physical removal; induced comas, Happy Juice and related medications." He drones on about endorphins and synthetic brain chemicals, and I tune out.

I look at my Levo. Even slight pressure on it causes an extreme headache, makes my levels drop. It isn't tight, but because of the pain I can barely turn it. The grip it has on my life is absolute.

"The pain . . . the deaths they would have caused," I whisper.

Aiden doesn't deny what I say, and I know I'm right.

"But think of the possibility of being free of it," Ben says, his voice excited. "It's worth taking a risk."

"Not if those taking it aren't given the choice!" I snap. "And you just wait until you're twenty-one. Not long to go to be sure of living, is it?"

But Ben looks enthralled. My stomach twists, my Levo vibrates: 3.9 this time.

"Dammit," Aiden says. Ben hugs me, rocks me back and forth.

3.7.

"Kyla, it's all right; everything will be fine," Ben whispers in my ear, strokes my hair, but all I can think of is the *pain* . . .

3.4.

Vaguely I'm aware of Aiden leaving, returning seconds later.

"Take one of these," he says, and holds out a pill, a glass of water.

I shake my head no as my Levo buzzes again, loud; levels still dropping, my head is spinning, vision going funny . . .

He grabs my face between his hands, and before Ben or I can react, tilts it back with one hand and chucks the pill to the back of my throat with the other. I choke and cough, but it starts to go down.

"Why'd you do that?" I yell.

"Didn't want to have to get an ambulance out here. Think of Mac," he says.

I cough again, still almost choking on the pill painfully stuck partway down.

"Drink this, it'll help," he says, and holds out the glass. I take it and swallow the water, but before the pill has even gone down properly my levels are coming back up. Nothing to do with a small white tablet; all to do with the anger coursing through my veins.

"What is it? What did you make me take?"

Aiden looks at me curiously. I can see his brain trying to connect the dots: Girl is Slated; levels were dropping; now she is angry, which should make levels drop further. Why isn't she unconscious?

Kyla is different.

"What did you give her?" Ben asks.

"It's just a Happy Pill," Aiden says. "Similar to the injections they use at the hospital. The AGT have been developing them in pill form."

And I fill in the rest in my mind: developing them for their experiments on kidnapped Slateds. They're just as bad as the government. And despite what Aiden says, that he isn't with the terrorists, has nothing to do with them and their wicked ways, here he has their tablets in his possession.

"Keep these. In case you need them," Aiden says, and holds out a bottle of pills.

"I don't want them," I say. "And I don't want anything to do with you."

Aiden sighs. "Listen, Kyla—if that is who you want to be—I can't make you help us if you don't want to. I think, for now, you just need to think about things some more. All right? Mac can always get in touch with me if you want to see me again."

He turns to go.

"Wait a minute," Ben says. "Maybe I can help. Am I on this website of yours?"

"Want to find out?" Aiden asks.

And as I stare at Ben, he nods.

"Are you sure?" I ask. "I thought you said you—"

He catches my hand in his. "Yes," he says, though he doesn't look sure.

Aiden sits back down at the keyboard. Enters male—age seventeen—brown hair—brown eyes. They scan pages and pages of hits that come up; none match. Not even close.

"Shame," Aiden says. Ben's eyes are a mix of relief and disappointment: because he can't help MIA find another missing person? Or, maybe, because nobody is missing *him*.

Aiden turns to go; Ben follows him out to say good-bye.

I stare at the screen, hit the back button until Lucy's face returns, fills the screen with a toothy grin. All it would take is one click on *Found* to change everything, forever.

But there are so many things tied up with *no*. There is fear, strong and certain, that this can only lead to the Lorders throwing me in the back of one of their black vans, disappearing in a way that will make being Slated seem kind. Fear, also, that whoever is looking for Lucy will find me wanting, or I won't want to know them, or both.

But under all these reasonable things is something dark, something buried. Deep in the pit of my stomach is a cold conviction: I don't know *why* I was reported missing, because I'm pretty sure the government was right to Slate me. There is something wrong with me, deep inside, and I don't want to know what it is.

Hush.

Things I can't know seem just out of reach, just past my understanding. This must be what they are watching me for at the hospital: regression. Dr. Lysander saved me once; but this time, if anyone notices, it will be termination.

Be still. Be patient.

If Aiden is looking for someone who wants to jump up and down and be noticed, he couldn't be more wrong than to consider me a candidate.

Stay silent as the grave.

Later, before we say good-bye, Ben holds my hands in his. Looks at me with eyes I always want to agree with, that I never want to show disappointment in me or my actions. Just now they are trying to persuade. "I know this is scary, Kyla. But we could really do something, make a difference. Think of Tori and Phoebe. Gianelli, too. Promise me you'll think about it?"

And I make the promise, because, after all, it's not like I'll be able to think about anything else. He hugs me, holds me close, and I wish so many things. That we could stay this way. That we could be alone someplace in a world with no Lorders, no Slating, no Levos. Or at the very least that I could do what he wants.

But I just can't.

38

AND THINK ABOUT THINGS, I DO: LATE THAT NIGHT. ALL through school the next day, wandering to classes, unaware of my surroundings.

The thing Aiden said that stuck the most is that whoever reported me to MIA may be missing me, right now. A mum, a dad, brothers and sisters? Even that gray kitten.

But unlike Lucy, this imaginary family is faceless. They are unreal; their feelings abstract and removed. I could walk past them in the street and not know it; they are part of my life that is gone forever. Yet, just the same, I can imagine the agony of not knowing what happened to someone you care about. Even with Tori and Phoebe, who I barely knew and, in the latter's case, didn't particularly like, I feel this way; it is the uncertainty, the not knowing. Or with Phoebe I *did* feel that way, before. Because now I know what happened to her.

Maybe that is one place I *can* do something.

"I'm going running," I announce in the car on the way home from school.

"But we're doing homework together," Amy protests, looks at Jazz.

"So what? Do it. I'll be home before Mum," I say. And they soon agree, though it is against the rules for them to be in the house alone. Though Jazz asks where I am going and says to stay off the back ways on my own. And I almost tell him the truth when I say I will stick to main roads, as I will: until I get to the lane that leads to Phoebe's house.

Earlier today, our English teacher gave back our marked books. They were taken in when Phoebe was still here, and I spotted hers in the pile and slipped it inside mine. Written on the inside front cover was all I needed to know: Phoebe Best, Old Mill Farm. A library map has it just a few miles from our house.

Thump, thump. My feet on the road lull me along, though not at my usual breakneck speed. I need time to think what to say. "Hello, your daughter has been Slated" seems harsh. *Be careful.* Last thing I want is for them to storm the hospital and demand her back; bet it wouldn't take long for the Lorders to pin the problem on me. And then there is her creepy uncle, Wayne. I haven't run into him since that day on the footpath. I shudder. If his van is parked out front, the whole thing is off.

I almost run past the turn without seeing the faded sign. OLD MILL FARM points to a narrow lane, more an overgrown rutted track than a road. Walking now, I set out along it. Thick brambles line the sides of the lane and trees reach together above, making it closed in, a green tunnel. *Nowhere to hide.* Unease rises inside my gut. I slip off the track and push into the woods alongside.

According to the map it is half a mile to their house, but picking my way with no path through dense undergrowth and trees, it soon seems longer. Branches pull at my hair, twigs and thorns catch my clothes, and I look longingly at the lane.

Just as I stand, one foot forward and one back in indecision, engine sounds come from the direction of the house. A vehicle, going fast: I duck in shadows next to a tree. Wheels spin on the lane as a white van goes past. I catch a glimpse of the driver as it rattles along: Wayne Best.

My heart sounds *thump-thump* in my ears. That was close. What would he have done if I'd been on the lane, and he'd spotted me scrambling out of the way? I must be mad. *Just be careful.*

Another bend, and buildings are in sight. Though they look more like a collection of sprawling barns and outbuildings than a house, some of them half falling down. A fence surrounds the lot. Out front is a metal graveyard, littered with shells and bits of rusted-out cars, tractors, and other machinery. It looks dead. Quiet. Maybe no one is home? I consider turning around. *You're here now.*

One building to the right of the cluster looks to be falling down less than the others. There are a few straggly bushes in front of it and an actual door rather than a hinged bit of wood.

I hesitate, then cross to the lane and open the gate. The lane becomes a track that leads off to the left behind the buildings; fields slope up beyond. Uneven chunks of concrete are spaced through mud at even intervals to lead a path through bits of machinery to the door. *Listen first.* There are rustlings in the trees behind me; no voices, no radio.

I step out onto the first concrete step and hop along to the next. They are soon so far apart I almost have to jump between them. The house is just a few steps away when there is a small noise, a movement, to my left. I turn.

Two eyes. Teeth, sharp teeth. A low rumbling growl. A big dog, maybe a mix of German shepherd and something else, and he doesn't look happy.

I start to shake. Do I back up slowly, do I run, what? I eye the distance between me and the gate. Somehow I think if I run, he will chase. I'm fast, but not that fast; the gate is too far. I'm closer to the house. *Hold your ground.*

He takes a few steps closer, growling still, then starts to bark.

I tremble with the effort not to run, and my stomach starts heaving. Sure, barf on the dog. That will improve his mood. I swallow and back up slowly, one step at a time, toward the house. Maybe someone is home. Maybe the door is open.

He growls deep in his throat, stalks toward me.

Run.

I bolt for the house. Jump at the step and scrabble at the handle. But it won't turn: It is locked.

Maybe this is it.

He launches at me, so big a paw hits each shoulder and knocks me off the step and onto my back in the dirt. My head thunks hard against the ground, my eyes fill with tears. Pinned down. Frozen in fear I stare up at bared, sharp teeth; waves of hot, rank breath on my face; his eyes on mine. He growls.

"Hold!" A man's voice.

The teeth go back inside the dog's mouth but he doesn't move, still heavy on my chest, growling rumbling through his paws into my shoulders.

Footsteps.

"Well now, Brute, what have you caught there? Up! So I can take a look."

The dog—*Brute, huh*—jumps back. I sit up, start to stand.

"Stay put," he says, scowling.

I sit back in the muck and stare up at his face: close-set eyes and greasy hair, so like Wayne he must be his brother. Phoebe's dad?

"Who in hell are you?"

"I'm Kyla. A f-f-f-friend of Phoebe's," I manage to get out. Brute's ears perk up when I say her name.

"That worthless brat didn't have any friends without four legs."

"We were in school together."

"So? You must know she ain't here, then. What do you want?"

"To see her mum."

"She ain't here, either. Get lost."

I stare back at him, and at Brute.

"Go! Get up and get out of here before I change my mind."

I scramble up, and Brute growls louder. Hoping he'll hold him, I dash for the gate. I'm nearly there when I hear thumping sounds, running, behind. Without turning I run the last few steps, rip the gate open and slam it shut. The latch clicks just as Brute slams against it; it shudders, but holds. Phoebe's dad is laughing by the house. "Don't come back!" he yells.

No bloody chance. *See what happens when you try to do the right thing?* That is enough of that. Phoebe is a closed book to me from now on.

My Levo says 4.8. How? Just like when I was at the hospital, scared and running. Both times you'd expect my levels to plummet. I walk along the lane, too shaky to go through the woods this time, or to run. All at once it is too much; I stop, and lunch heaves up out of my stomach.

Lovely. As if mud or worse all over me and a powerful headache aren't enough.

Headache? I touch my hand to the back of my head and wince. My fingers come away red. I must have hit the ground harder than I realized. Since I was distracted by a snarling monster with bad breath and big teeth at the time.

I want to collapse on the ground, right here. Not caring where I am, or who might come along. *Get going.*

Nothing for it but a few miles' walk home. I start back up the lane when I hear something coming up behind me and spin around, terrified. Perhaps I'm not going away fast enough; has he sent Brute to hurry me along?

But it is a woman, half running toward me. She raises a hand. "Wait," she calls out, and reaches me, breathless, moments later. "Did you want to see me? I'm Phoebe's mum."

I stare back at her: thin, straggly hair tied up, lines etched around eyes full of care and worry. My resolve to have nothing more to do with Phoebe and her family wavers.

"Do you know something about what happened to her? Please tell me, please."

She grips on my arm, tight.

I nod, and wince with the movement.

"Are you hurt? Let me see." And she gets out a hanky and dabs at the back of my head. "It's just a small cut, maybe could use a stitch. I'm sorry about Brute. He's been a monster since Phoebe went. He loved her."

"That dog was her pet?"

"Oh yes. He used to follow her around, tail wagging, like an overgrown puppy. Made Bob so angry; he is a guard dog, after all." And when she says *Bob,* a trace of fear crosses her face. Imagine being married to that man; imagine him being your *father.* She looks nervously back the way she came, as if he might appear, and I start walking fast in the other direction.

She follows, her hand on my arm. A silent plea. And I hear Aiden in my head: Imagine not knowing what happened; the worry. Imagine.

"I saw Phoebe last weekend," I finally say. "Just by chance."

"Where is she?"

"In the hospital in London."

"Oh, God. Is she hurt?"

"No, no! She's fine."

"I don't understand. Why is she in the hospital?"

"She's been Slated."

She stops in shock, and I forget about pursuit and stand with her.

"Oh, Phoebe," she whispers to herself. "You are lost to me." Her eyes start to fill with tears.

"I'm sorry," I say.

"Is she happy, is she well?"

"Yes."

"Thank you for coming, and for telling me."

I start walking away; she turns the other way to the house. Words drift back, faint on the air: "Maybe she is better off."

Maybe she is.

"What on earth happened to you?" Amy says.

"I fell over."

"Get those things off here so you don't trail mud through the house. You don't smell too good, either."

"Thanks."

Amy bundles Jazz into the kitchen and strips me off in the hall, dumps my stuff in the washing machine while I have a shower. The cut on the back of my head isn't bleeding anymore, and is hidden by my hair.

By the time Mum gets home the three of us are sitting at the kitchen table with cups of tea, doing homework.

"You lot look industrious," she says, an eyebrow raised as if somehow she knows there is more than meets her eyes.

That night Sebastian purrs and I try to sleep. My head still aches, but more of a dull throb now than a sharp pain.

Despite the encounter with Brute, I'm glad I told Phoebe's mum; at least she knows. And I can see they won't storm the hospital or raise a fuss: Her dad couldn't care less that she is gone, and her mum wouldn't dare.

Maybe Phoebe *is* better off; her own mother said it. Any family Phoebe gets assigned to in months to come has got to be better than where she came from. No wonder she was so miserable to everyone; everyone, that is, except animals like that horrible dog. At the hospital her face was full of joy. What they did to her was a kindness, wasn't it?

Maybe my family was just as bad.

The voice won't go away though I shut my eyes tight. It says things I don't believe, don't want to hear. Now that it is night and all is quiet, it is even louder inside my head.

"Mummy and Daddy aren't coming for you, Lucy. They don't want you. They gave you away, and you will never see them again."

Cold, I pull the covers tight around myself. The sheets feel wrong, all scratchy. Nothing is as it should be. Even the air is wrong; it smells funny. Salty from the sea that I never saw before today.

I wrap the pillow tight around my ears, but it is still there.

"They gave you away, and you will never see them again . . ."

39

"HEY, HOW'RE THINGS?" BEN SMILES HIS KILLER SMILE, AND I want to answer him, tell him everything. That I actually *did* something, in talking to Phoebe's mum. And even about the dream that woke me again and again last night. He is the only one I could even think about telling any of this, but what would he think of my dream? If my parents gave me away and didn't want me then, why would they have reported me missing now? It doesn't make sense.

"Is everything all right?" he asks.

I just shrug and swipe my card as we file into biology class. What can I say, surrounded by so many ears?

We take our usual seats on the back middle bench. And there, at the front of the room, is a surprise: no Miss Fern.

Instead there is a man, one I've never seen before. He is half sitting on the desk and facing the class, watching everyone as they take their seats. Whispering soon starts between some of the girls, and it is easy to see why: He is gorgeous. And it isn't just the attractive bits—wavy streaked blond hair, the height of him, the way his clothes fit and hug his body—but how they are all put together. He draws the eye.

He scans across the room, casually, bench by bench. His eyes reach mine, and something happens. I can't work it out. It is like something passes between us. Nothing stupid and mushy, but something else. Some recognition in his, some answer in mine . . . but it isn't *me*. I feel all flustered, and heat rises in my cheeks as he holds my gaze, unsmiling, for too long to be reasonable. When he finally looks away it feels like I've been dropped from a height. My head spins; my stomach twists.

"Good morning, class," he says. "Miss Fern won't be in today, or for some time. She has had an unfortunate accident. I am Mr. Hatten." He turns to write his name on the board.

Was there a pause in his words between *unfortunate* and *accident*? *No accident.* Not Lorders, like Gianelli; not again. I bite my tongue to focus on *that* pain instead. Have they taken her, and if so, why? I can't think of a single reason. She was a good teacher, but in other ways under the radar. Anyway, there was no secret about it when they took Gianelli, so why would there be now?

Maybe there was some other reason to replace her. Maybe Hatten is one of *them.*

I study him as he goes through the class from the front, getting everyone to introduce themselves while he makes a seating plan. He doesn't look like a Lorder. For a start, they always wear a gray suit or dress in black on operations. But it is more than that. Lorders, however alert and vigilant they may be for trouble, don't acknowledge anyone under the age of twenty or so; we are beneath notice. Hatten is different: He is *here,* present, interested, and aware of every person in the room. He is something else.

"And you are?"

Ben smiles. "I'm Ben Nix. But is Miss Fern all right? What happened to her?" he asks.

Heads swivel; ears perk up. It isn't always the right thing to do, asking questions.

But Hatten smiles. "She'll be fine. She was involved in a car accident and is in the hospital. Next?" Hatten says. And his eyes are on me again. Even across the room they are a strange color. Blue, but a pale, barely there shade of blue. If not for a darker rim on the edge of the iris they would almost blend into the white.

"My name is . . . Kyla," I say. What is wrong with me? I'd been on the edge of saying something else, a name that had winked into existence and then vanished before I even knew what it was. He raises an amused eyebrow, like he felt the slip I nearly made. *Get a grip.* This time I manage to look away before he does. My hands I clasp tight together to stop them from trembling.

Hatten begins the class. He borrows one of the students' notebooks to see which modules we have studied; we just started a section on biological classification.

He shuts it.

"We're going to do something different today," he says. "A practical on the brain." He points at Ben and me. "You two, help me out. Get the brain models and pass them around, one per pair." Ben jumps up and I follow him to a cupboard; inside we find three-dimensional models of the brain, each bit numbered and fitting together, interlocking like a puzzle.

The minutes tick past with us taking the brain apart and putting it back together, writing the names of each structure by number on a work sheet. Cerebellum, brain stem, frontal cortex, left and right hemispheres . . . The diagram reminds me of the cross sections of my brain I saw on Dr. Lysander's computer. That wasn't a sketch, though; it was a scan through my living brain.

"Listen up," Hatten says. "One last thing. Everyone, hold your hands together to make a small circle between them you can look through." He draws an *X* on the whiteboard. "Hold your arms out;

with both eyes open, stare at the X through the circle in your hands. Now, close one eye at a time without moving your hands. When you close one, the X should disappear; when you close the other, it should still be there in the center."

So we do: I hold my hands up and look at the X. Sure enough, when I close my left eye and look with my right, the X is blocked by my hand. When I close my right eye and look with my left, it is dead center.

Hatten scans the room, then his eyes settle on me. "Kyla? Which eye saw the X?"

"Left," I answer.

He smiles. "Interesting. You must be a biological anomaly."

I say nothing. He goes on. "Dominant eye is generally the same as dominant hand. If you saw the X with your left eye, you should be left-handed. Yet there you are, holding your pen in the right hand.

"How about the rest of you? Did everyone else find their dominant eye and hand are the same?" Voices concur. I shift uncomfortably in my chair.

"I see we're nearly out of time," Hatten says. "But you might be wondering why we did this last experiment in connection with our work on the brain model." Still his eyes are on me, not looking around the room at anyone else; just on me.

"It was a key discovery in the study of the brain: the influence of handedness on the development and organization of memory storage and access. If you are left-handed, in certain key respects, memory access is right hemisphere dominant; if you are right-handed, the left is dominant. Though in rare individuals this doesn't hold; often those with artistic abilities seem to be able to use their brain differently." He finally looks away, gazes about the room, then straight back at me. "This is all very important in surgery and treatment of brain conditions."

Surgery. *Like being Slated.*

The bell rings. End of class.

"Hand your sheets in on your way out!" he says.

Everyone shuffles about, putting books away.

Right-handed . . . left-handed. My left forms a fist of its own accord; my left fingers smashed with a brick. But that was only a dream. *Was it?*

"Kyla?" Ben nudges me. "Come on." I shake myself internally and make myself get up, walk closer and closer to the front desk with feet like lead, so slow that I'm last after Ben. Mrs. Ali stands waiting at the door.

I put my sheet on top of the pile in Hatten's hands.

"Did you find that . . . interesting?" he asks, and winks.

I jump, don't answer, and bolt for the door and Mrs. Ali.

She frowns. "I want a quick word before your next class, Kyla. Come on."

She pulls me into the empty classroom next door.

"There have been some concerns raised about you, my dear." She smiles her gentle smile. *That is when she is most dangerous.* "And by what I just witnessed, I must echo them."

What she just witnessed? I frantically scan the last moments of class: Was she there when Hatten said I was a biological anomaly? No, I'm sure she wasn't. She arrived at the end. And she couldn't have seen him wink; his back was to her.

"What do you mean?"

She frowns. "That lovely new teacher asked you if the class was interesting, and you didn't even answer him."

That lovely new teacher, huh. There is more to him, and I'm guessing it isn't all lovely. But I get the impression she doesn't know a thing about it.

"And a number of your other teachers say you have been distant, inattentive, and not ready to learn."

"I'm sorry. I'll try to do better."

"Don't just try; do it. This is a warning, Kyla. We've talked about this before. Don't forget you are being punished until you are twenty-one. Your contract requires you to do your best to integrate and do well at school, with your family and community. You are over sixteen now; if you fail, other treatment options are available." She smiles warmly. "Now, run along to your next class, dear. Have a nice day."

She disappears out the door, down the hall. Ben: I need Ben. Everything is tumbling inside: confusion about Hatten, who he is, what he said; shock and fear at Mrs. Ali's threats. My levels are on the way down.

When I step into the hall, Hatten is just coming out of the biology lab. He pulls a face at Mrs. Ali's retreating back, crosses his eyes. "What a bitch," he whispers, winks again, and smiles a cheeky grin. He looks younger, more natural like that—as if his teacher face earlier was a mask—and I can't help but smile back. He leans in close and holds a finger to his lips: "Shhh, our little secret." Then goes in the other direction.

Well. I could swear he heard every word Mrs. Ali said. How? And what is "our little secret"?

Time will tell.

Ben is out front, waiting. "I saw Mrs. Ali leading you off for a chat. Is everything all right?"

"Things could be better," I say. Though I check my Levo and am surprised it has gone up to 5.1. Did Hatten's pulling silly faces stop its descent? Or, more, was it him standing *close*. My heart still beats faster.

"Can you come for a run before Group tomorrow?" Ben says, face worried.

"Of course. We'll talk then." The first bell for the next class goes, and we rush in opposite directions.

Time to be attentive and ready to learn. Or to get better at faking it, at least.

40

I PULL ASIDE THE CURTAIN NEXT TO THE FRONT DOOR AND scan up the road: no sign. *Hurry up, Ben.*

"Kyla?" Dad calls out from the front room. I go to the door. "Come talk to me a moment while you wait."

I hesitate, look down at my feet: running shoes on.

"Don't worry about that, she'll never know," he says.

Mum may be out, but I'm sure she has some sort of radar that keeps tabs on whether shoes are worn on the carpet. I wipe them carefully on the mat and stand uncertainly in the doorway.

"Have a seat," he says, and smiles.

I perch on the edge of an armchair.

"Your boy isn't very punctual, is he?"

"No," I admit.

"So he is your boy, then."

"What?"

"*Your boy.* You know, your boyfriend."

I color. "No."

"Or maybe you'd like him to be."

"No! I don't know. We're just friends."

He raises an eyebrow and it feels like he can see, he can understand my mixed-up feelings better than I can.

"Be careful, Kyla. Just because we've allowed Amy to see Jazz doesn't mean that you are ready for a boyfriend. You're not long out of the hospital. And you know that until you are released at twenty-one you have to listen to your mum and me on everything, including this."

"Yes."

"I'm not sure I like you going off running with this Ben on your own."

I don't say anything. Any protest I could make would just make him sound more right. But I need to see Ben, need to talk to him, so much. After everything this week I just want to hold his hand. *Oh.*

"Your mum seems to think it's all right, so I'm going along with her on this. For now. But see that you keep things *just friends,* as you said. You do understand why?"

"Um, I'm not sure."

"There is real concern that you can't handle those sorts of feelings so soon after Slating. That you could end up with your levels so messed up, you can't control them."

This echoes warnings I heard in the hospital. But how? Ben helps my levels stay up, not down. Unless . . .

"You want me to stay under control." I say the words slowly, my surprise at the realization making them come out before I have a chance to censor them.

Some amusement crosses his eyes.

There is a knock at the door: Ben. I spring to my feet, but Dad raises a hand. "Stay here a minute," he says. He goes to the door, answers it, and I wait; listen to Dad introducing himself to Ben, a little chat about running and school. Ben, as always, is open, polite. Pleasant. The sort of boy adults like.

Dad sticks his head through the front room doorway. "Go on, then," he says. "But remember what we spoke about."

"Sorry about that," I say after the door is safely shut behind us.

"About what?"

"Dad."

"What about him? He seems all right."

"Never mind."

We race up the road, fast and faster, and soon I am lost in the cold air, the night, the familiar rhythm of our feet on the road. The *thud-thud* of Ben's long legs beat a different tempo than mine, but we are matched in speed. Side by side.

We slow as we reach the place with the footpath off the road.

"Talk?" I say.

Ben takes my hand, leads me into the shadows under the trees. The night is clear, and the nearly full moon casts enough light to see the way. As we walk to the gate I think about what Dad said, what the hospital said. Avoid boys: They mess up your levels. But mine are the highest now they've been all week. What do they know?

Like before, Ben swings me up to sit on the top of the fence. He stands in front of me, wraps his arm around my waist. He brushes my hair away from one side of my face, leans in. "What did you want to talk about?" he whispers into my ear, and his breath sends goose bumps up and down my neck.

I don't say anything, my mind suddenly blank. My blood still thudding through my veins from running. *From something else.*

"I made a promise to myself," Ben says.

"What?"

"That if we came here again, I would do this." He slips one hand under my chin, a light touch, and everything is mixed up, swirling inside, in panic, but not the kind that makes you want to run. The cold fence under me, warm arm around my side, the hand on my chin—every sense hyperaware. Ben leans forward and lightly touches his lips to mine. Sweet and gentle: Ben. He pulls away, smiles. And all I want to do is pull him close, kiss him again and again. *Calm down.* What if Dad is right, and this will destabilize my levels?

"Now. What did you want to talk about?" he asks.

"Hmmm?" I say, staring into his eyes. And I reach up, trace his lips with my finger. Mine are tingling.

He grins, amused, and takes my hands in his, links our fingers together. "You *said* you wanted to talk about something. But if you'd rather . . ." And he bends to kiss me again. Once. Twice . . .

Everything is spinning and swirling inside, but then somehow I remember and push him away a little.

"Talk?"

"If we must," he says, his voice husky, a little shaky, and this time it is my turn to smile.

And I tell him about going to see Phoebe's mum, and that I told her Phoebe had been Slated.

Ben's eyes shine in the moonlight. He hugs me. "I knew you'd see, after you thought about things. That we should help Aiden and MIA."

I shake my head. "No. You're wrong. I wanted to tell Phoebe's family what happened to her so they'd know, but I don't want to go public about me."

"What about Lucy? What about *her* parents?"

"Think things through, Ben," I say. "How old was Phoebe?"

"Fifteen."

"So, when she stepped out of line, she was Slated. But what would happen to me?"

And I tell him about what Mrs. Ali said, what she threatened. *Other treatment options* for over-sixteens. I'm on a warning; being watched. Any step out of line and I'll be gone like Tori.

Ben pales. "I don't want anything to happen to you."

But this reminds me of something else. "Did you used to kiss Tori like you just kissed me?" The words are out before thought, and I wish I could grab them back.

He raises an eyebrow. "Would it matter?"

Before I can say something else to regret, he laughs. "No. I never kissed Tori. She was just a friend."

"But I thought—"

"You thought wrong. Tori had a hard time of it with her family. She needed someone to talk to, and I'm a good listener."

I noticed. But I also noticed that Tori didn't think Ben was just a friend. But this time, I do manage to keep it to myself.

He smiles. "Kyla, believe me: You're the only one I want to kiss. And I don't want anything to ever happen to you." He shakes his head, rubs his temple. "I don't understand how my brain works."

"What do you mean?"

"When teachers and nurses at the hospital talk to me, everything they say is right, and reasonable, and I listen to them. But when Aiden spoke to us the other day, I saw they were wrong and he was right, that the government should be called to account for what they are doing. Now you explain dangers that should be obvious, but I hadn't worked it through. It is like sometimes I can't think straight. The only time my brain seems to function is when I've been running, like now."

It's Slating.

And I think back to what Aiden said, and how he said it. He has his own agenda. He wasn't worried what might happen to us if we went along with his plans, was he? And he knew just what to say to push Ben to his way of thinking: He knew how suggestible Ben is. How I should be, too. *Kyla is different.*

"What do you think we should do now?" I ask.

"I don't want anything to happen to you. What do you think?"

"It's Slating. It makes you want to go along, do the right thing, do what is expected."

"That just makes it more wrong. More something we should do something about." His face is troubled; he is thinking for himself, and this is what he thinks.

No. Stay silent as the grave.

"Ben, listen. We need to keep clear of Aiden and do what we are supposed to do at school and at home. Think of your family: What would it do to them if something happens to you? Wait until we get our Levos off. Doing anything before then to draw attention to ourselves is too dangerous. When we are twenty-one, *then* we can look at things again and see what we can do."

Ben listens and I see again how *suggestible* he is. State anything strongly enough and he'll go along with it. What a dangerous world for someone like him. An overwhelming urge to *protect* Ben washes over me, shakes through me. Someone like Ben . . . should be someone like me, too. But somehow, it isn't, not in the same way. A Slated, but not like the rest of them. *Kyla is different.*

"You're right, Kyla," he says. Wraps his arms tight around me once again. Kisses my cheek, and it could have led to more, and I wanted it to, so much. But maybe kissing me is just something else I've suggested to him.

"Come on. Let's get to Group," I say.

As we walk back to the road, I ask Ben what he thought of Hatten saying I was a biological anomaly, and about handedness and brain surgery. But Ben brushes it off, doesn't seem to want to talk about him.

We run the rest of the way, and as we do my mind spins around. Before, being with Ben had made me feel safe, but I see I had it wrong. I need to keep him safe. I need to look out for both of us.

Why can I think for myself in ways that Ben can't? I don't understand at all.

41

MUM'S FACE IS GRIM, CONCENTRATING; HANDS SO TIGHT ON the wheel her knuckles are white. We were notified yesterday that we were to use a different hospital entrance. Was the usual one damaged in the bombing last week? Soon the traffic comes to a complete stop.

"Are you all right?" I ask.

She jumps. Half smiles. "Shouldn't I be asking you that?"

"I asked you first."

"Fair enough. I'm just feeling tense about going back to the hospital after last week. Aren't you?"

Strangely, no; at least, not the way she means. I've no doubt that the Lorders will have everything so locked down now that a terrorist wouldn't stand a chance of getting within a mile. But Mum looks like she wants to jump in the opposite lane and race as far away as she can.

"I think they won't let anything happen after last week, so it is safer than it ever has been."

Mum tilts her head to one side. "You're probably right. I still don't want to go there."

Me either, though for different reasons. I'm not sure my poker face is ready for Dr. Lysander today. It is one thing to decide to go along and do as expected and be the perfect little Slated; it is another thing to do it.

"I know. Let's dash off and go out for lunch instead," I say.

Mum laughs. "Funny girl. Wouldn't it be great if we could?"

"Well, *you* could. Dump me and go off for the day. You must be sick of spending every Saturday taking me to the hospital."

"Too true. But I can't just go wherever I like. You see up the pole at each corner? Like to your left there." I look out the window. There is a traffic light and a pole next to it. Up top of it is a small black box, a device of some sort. *A camera.*

"They monitor the identity and position of every car in London. If I start wandering around beyond expectation, who knows what might happen? Though maybe I'd get away with it."

"Is that because of who your dad was?"

"And my mum. She was important, too."

"So even adults can't go where they want."

"No. Not these days."

"Could they before?"

"Things have changed, Kyla. When I was your age it was very different."

"Was that when everything kicked off, in the twenties?"

She winces. "Do I look that old? I was your age in 2031."

"But you'd remember the twenties, then. When there were all the riots, and gangs, and everyone cowered in their homes in fear and never went out."

She laughs again. "That is one version of events. That was also when mobile phones were banned for under-twenty-ones. They used them to organize demonstrations, you see? But it wasn't as bad as all that. Not to start with. Though it *was* different from today; you had to be careful where you went at night, that sort of thing." Her eyes track to the side, to Lorders at the corner. In black with machine guns.

"Now you just have to watch out for *them*."

She nods slightly, and I'm surprised.

"You said it wasn't so bad to start with. What about later on?"

"Don't you take history in school? After the crash—you know, from the credit crunch and economic collapse throughout Europe—when the UK withdrew from the rest of Europe and closed its borders, there was a period where things did go pretty crazy."

"I've seen films of the riots."

"They show the worst of it. Most of the student demonstrations were peaceful, in the early days. But frustration and anger grew."

In history lessons it is all out-of-control mobs, wild-eyed teenagers destroying property and killing people. Stunned that Mum would tell me this, I say nothing. She is talking, maybe, to distract herself from where we are going and what happened there last week.

"Mum and Dad used to fight about it late at night; I'd creep down the stairs and listen in."

"Your dad was the prime minister. So he won the argument."

"Not to start with. Early on he was just another candidate; there was an election on the way. Mum was a lawyer, big on civil liberty."

"What is that?"

She shakes her head. "To think you need to ask that question. What do you think it means?"

"Liberty means something like freedom, doesn't it?"

She nods. "Freedom of speech, freedom of action, freedom of assembly. So Mum had very different ideas from Dad about how things should be sorted out. She ended up campaigning for a new political party: the Freedom UK."

"So they were on opposite sides?"

"Yes."

"But your dad won."

"Not exactly. It wasn't a clear result. The two parties had to form a coalition, though Dad's party had the stronger position. It made for interesting breakfast times, believe me. So the thing is, Kyla, neither of them won. They compromised. And that gave us you."

"I don't understand."

She turns the radio up slightly and faces me. Speaks in a low voice. "You have to keep secrets for me to talk about this anymore. You told me once that you can't; I think you probably can. But do you want me to go on?"

The good little Slated should say no and avoid dangerous knowledge. *But she isn't in control just now.* "Tell me."

"Well, on the one side you had my dad and the beginning of the Law and Order movement that gave us Lorders. Zero tolerance on violence and civil disobedience; harsh punishments for lawbreakers. On the other side was the Freedom UK view that the young—the student demonstrators, the gangs—should be rehabilitated. That often what they have done isn't their fault; it is where they came from, how they were raised—they might have been mistreated. They deserve consideration and respect as human beings; help, not punishment."

"How does this lead to me?"

"There were these discoveries—I don't understand the science much—about memories in the brain. They were trying to help people with autism and so on. But they found a bit by accident that a certain procedure took a person's memories away."

"Slating."

"Exactly. So it was the perfect solution for the Coalition government. Instead of harshly punishing criminals, they could be given a clean slate—that is where the popular term, Slating, came from—and start over. A second chance."

I think about what she said. "So both sides could say they got what they wanted. Is that what compromise is?"

Mum laughs, but it isn't the sort of laugh at anything funny, and her face isn't amused. "More like neither got what they want, and both blamed the other for anything and everything. They did it then, and they still do it now in the Central Coalition we have today. And that is also where Levos came from."

I look at the circle around my wrist that runs my life; 5.2 just now. I give it a twist and pain stabs through my temples. I know it will do this, yet can't stop myself now and then from pulling at the chain of my prison. "How does them compromising give me a Levo?"

"Well, the Freedom UK said we must make sure the poor Slateds are happy; the Lorders said we must make sure they don't slip back to their evil ways. Answer? A Levo. You have to stay happy; you can't do anything wrong. Both sides are pleased as they got what they said they wanted."

"Huh. Obviously, they've never had to wear one."

Mum laughs again. "Just so."

"Did you take sides? Between your mum and dad."

"Mostly I tried to keep peace at home and sat on the fence. Then."

"Then?"

She doesn't answer for so long that I think she won't. Then turns to me, her eyes glistening. "You could say when they died, I got off the fence."

We are nearly at the search point. Neither of us says anything else. Her parents died when a terrorist bomb hit their car. Whatever she might have thought before that, there is no doubt in my mind which side of the fence she ran to: the Lorders. She must have, after terrorists killed her parents. How could she not?

Yet, while our car is searched, I watch Mum's face. There are things going on inside her that go beyond her words. As before, the Lorders acknowledge who she is; there is some deference in them around her that I don't see in their interactions with other people. She accepts it. But she doesn't like it.

I wonder what she left unsaid.

Dr. Lysander taps at her screen, then looks up.

"I see that during the attack last week, you went to the tenth floor. Then your levels dropped so much, you had to be sedated. Tell me about it."

Straight to the chase.

"I tried to go to the nurses' station like you said. The lights went out. The nurse . . ."

And I stop. I don't want to think about that.

"I know about the nurse," Dr. Lysander says. "That must have been shocking for you to deal with. But you didn't black out then."

"No. I went to the stairs, to the tenth floor. I'm not sure why."

"It was your place here, the one you knew best; it makes perfect sense for you to go there. But why do you think you got through it all, and then, just when things were safe, your levels dropped?"

Because of Phoebe. But I can't say that.

I shrug. "Maybe once I stopped running, it all crowded in on me."

She tilts her head to one side, considering. "Perhaps." She doesn't look convinced, like she knows something else is behind it.

"Were you all right?" I ask. "I was worried about you." And the words are true as I say them. There is no doubt that she would have been a target for the terrorists.

Her eyes open a little wider, her face softens. "Thank you, Kyla; I appreciate that. I was fine. They took me to a safe place with some other people to look after us."

"Why didn't they take that nurse, as well? Did you know her?"

"I did: Angela was her name." She looks sad. "But sometimes choices have to be made."

"But—"

"Enough, Kyla. I have something to ask you. Did you find out everything?"

"What?"

"Did you learn what you wanted to know."

My stomach twists. She knows; somehow she knows. That I looked at her computer. I stay silent, guts twisting in fear. Imagine what the Lorders will make of *that*.

"Yes, Kyla, I'm afraid I saw what you did. There is a little camera, you see? In my office, one that I monitor. Also the computer tracks what files are opened and shut again. So I saw just what you did." She sits back in her chair calmly. "But I've turned the camera off now and deleted that sequence. No one else knows. Come on. Pull your chair around, and we will look together."

My jaw drops.

"Now, Kyla," she says.

I pull my chair to the other side of the desk next to hers. And she goes through the files I looked at, one by one, and explains: the admissions process, my brain scans, the surgery. Then to the Recommendations section that I couldn't get out of my mind.

"This bit here: Board recommends termination. Dr. Lysander overrules. What does it mean?" I ask.

"The hospital board was concerned about your nightmares and control, generally. They felt letting you out of the hospital environment represented a risk to yourself and those around you."

"You overruled. You didn't agree with them."

"That is what I said. But they were right. At the very least you were a risk to yourself."

"I don't understand. Why did you let me out?"

She half shrugs. "I convinced myself you deserved the chance; I was curious, certainly, how you would do. But mostly I wanted to study you and see what would happen."

"Like a rat in a cage."

She half smiles. "More like a rat released from a cage."

"But why would you want to study me?"

"There is something different about you, Kyla. I want to know what it is. Did something go wrong in the procedure? No; every test and scan says it was successful. Yet there is something . . . This is just you and me, here. No one else. Can you tell me?"

"I don't know what you mean."

She raises an eyebrow. "Is there anything else you want to know? Can I satisfy your curiosity; then perhaps, you can satisfy mine."

I squirm. There are so many questions I could ask, but I should ask none of them.

Ask.

But it is dangerous. I am supposed to be being the perfect Slated girl; I told Ben, I agreed within myself to follow this course of action.

Ask.

"Who is Slated? I mean, I know convicted criminals are Slated. But who else?"

"What makes you think anyone else would be Slated? That would be illegal."

I stare back at her, don't answer.

She nods her head a few times, amusement crossing her face. "You are perceptive. And that is an interesting choice of question. Surprising, even. Why do you ask it?"

"It is just some people I know who have been Slated I can't imagine ever having done anything wrong."

"Sometimes life is very painful, Kyla. At times people need help to get through it, and we provide that help."

"I don't understand."

She hesitates. "An example, then: your sister. What is her name again? I recognized her that day she waited with you."

"Amy? Why would you remember her?"

"It is breaking a few dozen laws talking to you about this, Kyla." She taps at her screen. Amy's face fills it: Amy 9612. She goes to the admission screen. Again there is a photo, but it is very different from mine. Amy is years younger, but there is no mistaking her smile: She is full of joy on her way to being Slated. Dr. Lysander enters a password to get further; so that is why I couldn't find out why I was Slated. I needed a password.

"See, here: *Patient 9612 presented herself at the hospital begging to be Slated. She was evaluated and deemed a suitable candidate for VS.*"

I shake my head. "That can't be right. Why would anybody *want* to be Slated? Why would anybody want one of these?" I tug at my Levo, harder this time, and pain slams into my temples so intense that tears come to my eyes.

"*VS* is *Victim Slating.* Some young people are so damaged by their early lives that the only way to make them useful members of society is to take the pain away. Make it as if it never happened."

"What was so bad she would want to be Slated to forget about it?"

"I remember her; I evaluated her. Such a sad story. You see, she was meant to be minding her little brother one day, but lost attention. He chased a football into traffic and was killed in front of her. She couldn't deal with the guilt and later tried to take her own life, but couldn't go through with it. Then she came to see me."

Oh, poor Amy. I can't take this in; I can't believe this happened to her. Dr. Lysander stated the facts in her usual voice, calm and precise. Yet I can see in her eyes her own sadness at what happened to Amy.

"When Amy came in it was the year before we started systematically checking potential suicide cases like hers for Slating. It is a kindness."

"Why tell me about Amy?" I whisper.

"Because I know you can take it. It will help you understand what we do, and I know you will keep this information to yourself."

"If Amy knew . . ." I trail off. She chose not to remember; why tell her now?

"She can find out. If she wants to," Dr. Lysander says.

"What? Can we just ask what the reason is, and be told?"

"Not now. But when you are twenty-one and your Levo is removed, you have the right to know. If you want to. Not names and places or anything specific; just the facts. Why you were Slated, what you did or didn't do. But the truth is, at that point, almost nobody wants to know. They just want to get on with their lives and put it behind them. Do you, even now?"

"Do I what?" I say, though I know what she means.

"Do you want to know? Do you want me to go to your file, enter the password, and see what it says."

I back away, shaking my head. I don't want to know.

Yes, you do.

"Kyla, that is enough for today. But over the next week I hope you will think things through. I hope you will repay me for answering your questions, and answer some of mine. Now go."

There has been too much to take in today. First Mum and all that stuff about her parents, the government, and their compromises.

Then Dr. Lysander: She wants something from me. *Kyla is different.* But why? I can't answer her questions when I can't find the answers for myself. What is going on? And most of all, why did she tell me about Amy? I don't want to know; I don't. I can't stop thinking about it. Even though it shows that I was right; she never did anything wrong to get Slated, not really. She asked for it.

It is all I can do to stop myself from running to her and holding her when we get home. But she'd think I was nuts.

She wanted to be Slated; she wanted to forget. She is better off as she is, without that pain. Isn't she? *But it was her choice.*

What about me? *What about Lucy?* Did she make that choice?

I don't want to know, but whispers of the past echo in my mind. They won't go away.

42

CROSS-COUNTRY TRAINING ISN'T ON THIS WEEK; THEY ARE
holding team tryouts. Since Slateds are not allowed on school teams,
Ben and I are excluded. Never mind that we are the fastest in the
school, or that every muscle fiber in my body is screaming for release.
But I can't say anything; I'm a good little Slated. *Yeah, right.*

To add to the general wonderfulness of the day, Amy has come
up with a plan for my Sunday afternoon, and after what I found out
about her yesterday, I couldn't say no to her. Even though I
wanted to.

"Kyla? Come on." Amy and Jazz stand by the door while I hunt
through the cupboard for my jacket. My official chaperone duties
await.

Amy peers at the sky. "I'm not so sure about this weather."

I think it is perfect. The sky is a uniform dull gray; it is cold and
damp. There is no rain now, but the air feels heavy and wet, as if it carries myriad tiny drops that are too wishy-washy to get together and
become rain. A general miserable state of weather that suits my mood.

"Have no fear; I have come prepared for all eventualities," Jazz
says. "En garde!" He bows and has a mock sword fight between his
oversize umbrella and a tree branch.

We continue through the village to the footpath sign, then stop.
Amy and Jazz lean on the stone wall next to the path. "Aren't we
going on?" I ask.

"Soon," Amy says, and looks at her watch. She goes on about the internship she'll be starting on Tuesday at the medical center, and "soon" becomes a few minutes, and a few more.

"There he is," Jazz says. I turn, and Ben is running toward us. He waves.

"Surprise!" Amy says, and grins.

Last night at dinner Mum said that Dad had raised the issue of me running alone with Ben, and they decided it wasn't going to happen anymore. I didn't say anything. What could I? Any argument I might make would just make them seem more right, as if there was something going on between us deemed unsuitable for a sixteen-year-old newly released Slated. *There is, isn't there?*

"Do they know he is coming with us?" I ask before Ben reaches us.

"No. You want to run? Go ahead and run. We'll walk behind."

"Thanks," I say, and hug Amy. She looks surprised, hugs back.

"I've been there, done that. I know what it is like," she says. And I know what she means; she thinks as soon as they are out of sight, Ben and I will be like her and Jazz. All lovey-dovey. But today, more than anything, I just want—*need*—to run.

Ben and I take off up the footpath. "Not so fast today," I say. Though my feet are itching to pull me along with as much speed as they can find, I can't get home all plastered in sweat, or it will be obvious that Amy and I haven't stayed together.

"Why?" he asks. "Usually you can't wait to take off."

I hesitate. "I can't look like I've been running. I'm supposed to stay with Amy," I say, and don't mention that they've decided I can't run with him anymore. If I don't say it out loud, it seems less real.

So Ben and I jog lightly up the path. Along the hedge, the holly bushes, and the fields, until we are dodging tree roots through the woodland. Ben hasn't been this way before. The gray skies seem to come down to meet us as we go higher; droplets of mist cling to my skin, my hair. Moisture and cold penetrate into my bones as tendrils of white creep closer and gather around us.

I stop by the log at the top. "This is the lookout," I say, and grin. "You can see the whole village."

Ben stops. "You'll have to help me out. Which way is it?"

I turn him in the right direction and he peers down the hill. A few of the taller trees almost poke out of the low fog, ghostlike and indistinct. The fields and houses below are invisible.

"Ah, yes. Impressive view."

I hit him on the arm. "Well, usually it is all right. You can even see our back garden."

"What now?" he says, and he smiles a slow smile that says he has a few ideas, ones that make my stomach flip.

"Uh, we wait. For Amy and Jazz to catch up. Or maybe we should go back down? They might want to call it quits in this weather."

"Let's wait a little," he says, and smiles again. Steps closer.

I'm not sitting on a fence this time, and Ben is so much taller. He leans down, but instead of looking up I bury my face in his chest. His arms close around me and banish the cold.

"This is why Mum and Dad don't want me to be alone with you anymore," I say, and sigh.

"No. Really?"

"Yep."

"But they're not watching right now."

"I thought we agreed to do what we're told and be good. Until we are twenty-one."

"Five whole years without a kiss? I don't think so."

Ben the rebel. At least as far as kisses go.

I relent. "All right. Just one."

With the mist all around us, the world is muted, has receded, disappeared. *What you cannot see is more dangerous.*

But as I tilt my face up, and Ben smiles, and leans down, there is a small noise. A snap.

"Well well, what have we here."

We spin around. And standing there is Wayne Best.

"Kyla, isn't it?" he says, and grins.

I take a step back. "How do you know my name?"

"Well now, you went and visited my brother. Met his dog Brute up close and personal, I hear." He laughs. "Aren't you going to introduce me to your friend?"

"I'm Ben," Ben says, and smiles. Unaware of the undercurrents.

"Hi there, Ben," he says, and holds out his hand. *No, Ben.* But it is too late. Ben holds his out, and Wayne sees his Levo. Drops his hand back without a handshake.

"Another Slated! You must grow on trees." He spits on the ground. "And here I was about to warn you off hanging around with a Slater like that."

"Now just a minute," Ben says, finally getting that Wayne isn't Mr. Nice.

"Shut up!" Wayne snarls, and shoves Ben backward onto the log. "Sit there and be quiet. I want to . . . *chat* with Kyla."

And Ben starts to stand again, his face alternating between confusion and anger. I shake my head slightly. "Stay there. It's all right."

I turn to Wayne. "What about?"

"Well, I think my brother chased you off too quick. Why'd you want to talk to Phoebe's mum?"

So they don't know I spoke to her. *They don't know Phoebe has been Slated.*

I stare back at him, mind blank, yet convinced I shouldn't tell him. If Phoebe's mum thought they shouldn't know, I'm sure she had good reason, and I'll not say. *Ben, keep quiet,* I plead silently.

"I got *ways* to make you talk." He steps closer.

Ben stands, pushes between us. His Levo vibrates, loud. "Back off," he says. But his face is white, contorted with pain. *No, Ben!*

Wayne laughs. "What are you going to do about it, Slater?" He pushes Ben, who tries to take a swing at him, but his Levo vibrates louder and he shudders, slumps to the ground.

"Leave him alone!" I scream, and kick at Wayne, hard, but he twists, and I miss my target and just get him in the leg.

And he moves forward but I can't run, I can't leave Ben, and I'm scared, but more I'm *angry*. Something inside is shaking and kicking, screaming to get out.

But then Wayne looks over my shoulder, backs away and runs.

"Kyla? Kyla!"

Jazz bursts up the path, Amy on his heels.

"We thought we heard you scream. What's wrong?" he says.

Don't tell them.

"It's Ben," I say, already on the ground next to him. "His levels. Ben, Ben, are you all right?" His Levo vibrates again.

"What is he?" Amy says, breathing hard from running.

I hold his hand, look at his wrist. "3.2," I answer, terror twisting in my stomach.

"Oh, God," she says.

Ben groans. "In my backpack. Hurry. Pills," he mutters.

Pills? I fumble in his pack through a water bottle and spare socks, and my hand finds a small bottle, pulls it out. But the label says headache tablets?

I look at Amy; she shrugs. "Can't hurt," she says.

"Now. Give me one now," he gasps.

I do and he swallows it dry, not waiting for the water. I wrap my arms around him, pleading inside for him to be all right; Amy sits on the ground with us, alternately stroking my hand and Ben's, and Jazz is on standby to run for paramedics. But Ben soon stops shuddering, the color starts to come back to his cheeks bit by bit. His levels start to rise.

He whispers to me the pills were from Aiden.

Aiden's Happy Pills.

It is a while before Ben can walk. He nearly blacked out. *My fault.* Somehow I convince Jazz and Amy to go ahead, just a little, so we can talk. But I make sure to keep them in sight.

Ben's arm is over my shoulders, leaning a little, walking slowly. "I'm sorry," he whispers.

"Why?"

"I wanted to protect you. I was useless."

"It's not your fault."

"But I don't understand." There is an uneasy pull in my stomach; I knew he'd get there eventually. "How come *your* levels were all right?"

I shrug. "Honestly? I don't know. They shouldn't have been. Don't tell anybody, whatever you do. Or I'll be gone."

Ben pauses, digests this and finally nods.

"Why didn't you tell Amy and Jazz what happened? We have to tell someone about that man. He's dangerous."

"No. We can't. It would lead back to Phoebe, that I told her mum that she's been Slated."

"So?"

"These are not the actions of a good little Slated. I'm being monitored and watched, remember? If they start chipping away at what happened, they might find out something about me that they don't like."

"All right," Ben says at last. "But promise me you will never walk up here on your own. Ever. Promise?"

And I do.

Jazz drives Ben home, just a few miles away from us. His house is detached, brick, with a big garden. Bicycles lean against the side, and there is a dog in the front. But she is nothing like Brute. Skye is a beautiful, bouncy golden retriever who leaps about Ben and the rest of us, tail wagging. Ben's parents gave her to him as a puppy when he first came to live with them.

Ben's mum comes out of the garage in overalls. Younger and prettier than I expected, thirty or so maybe, long dark hair tied back.

When Ben introduces us her eyes light with recognition. "This is Kyla? Oh, pleased to meet you." She takes Jazz, Amy, and me into her garage workshop, full of shiny machinery, scrap metal, sculptures. She is finishing one of an owl: loops of twisted metal for talons, nuts for eyes, salvaged interlocking fan blades for feathers. Metal scraps discarded as worthless have become a wild creature that looks as if it could take off in flight. "Like my drawing," I say, and that is when I see it: my owl drawing that Ben asked if he could have, pinned to the wall. She was copying it.

We leave Ben there and I watch out the car window as he waves, then disappears back inside the garage.

Ben's life used to be happy, uncomplicated. The easy affection between Ben, his mum, even that overgrown puppy, is so in evidence. No MIA, no Happy Pills, no deranged footpath attackers.

No me.

That night Amy comes to my room for a chat. I knew she would.

"Look, Kyla. I've been thinking. Maybe Mum and Dad are right."

"About what?"

"About you and Ben. I'm guessing you had some sort of argument or something, and that is why he nearly blacked out. Whatever it was, if he can't handle it—if you can't—then maybe it is too soon. I don't think you should see him anymore. At least not for a while."

"It's not that!" I protest.

"Then what is it?"

I don't want to lie to her, so what can I say? "It's not that," I repeat.

"Well. We're not going to help you see Ben anymore. So whatever you do or don't do, that is up to you. Good night," she says, and goes back to her room.

Sebastian jumps up. "Looks like it's just you and me, cat," I say, and he flops down and purrs, evidently happy with his lot.

No more kisses until you're twenty-one.

Huh.

Though I can't deny Amy's conclusion, even if her reasoning is faulty. Ben would be better off without me.

Ben *will* be better off without me. No matter how much it hurts inside, I'm getting out of his life before I do any more damage.

43

THE NEXT MORNING I GET TO BIOLOGY BEFORE BEN AND consider changing seats to sit with someone else. But Hatten is still there as our substitute teacher; I don't want to get any closer to him. So the usual back row with Ben it is.

"I need to talk to you at lunch," Ben whispers when he arrives.

"Can't."

His eyebrows rise. "Why not?"

"Busy."

"You want to hear this. And there is something I need to tell you, about Miss Fern. Meet you by the library, all right?"

"But—"

"Quiet, everyone," Hatten says. "Hope you all had as good a weekend as I did." He grins in a way that suggests he spent it up to no good, and a few of the girls giggle. He leans against the front bench. No tie today; was that just a first-day thing? Tight black pants, a dark shirt, unbuttoned more than most teachers. It drapes on his body. Is it silk?

Ben needles me in the ribs. "Quit staring at him," he says. I jump, then look around the room instead. Every girl in the class—a few of the guys, as well—seems transfixed by our replacement teacher. Me, I'm just nervous.

"Today, class, we will carry on with our study of the brain," he says, and I'm even more nervous.

But he goes through our work sheets from last time, corrects errors. Puts up endless slides of brain scans and drawings, and the class passes, minute by minute. Nothing happens at all until he winks at me as we leave.

But this time a few of the girls see him do it. The jealous looks they give me suggest I'll pay for that later.

Curiosity won't let me stay away. Ben waits, outside the library.

"Well, what is it?"

Ben looks at me; something crosses his face. "Not here. Come on, let's go for a walk."

I follow him across the school grounds. We look both ways and duck out the gate to Cuttle Brook Woods. Where Phoebe drew her robin; it seems a long time ago, but it isn't really. Not quite three weeks. We walk in silence along the main path, then branch off into denser woods on a faint trail. Still Ben does not speak. Whatever he wants to say has deserted him. His face is dark and unreadable.

"What about Miss Fern?" I prompt him finally.

He sighs. "All right, her first. I told you my dad is a primary school teacher? Another teacher he works with went to college with Ferny— that's what they called her—and they went to visit her in the hospital yesterday afternoon."

"Is she all right?"

"She will be. Multiple fractures: She's trussed up in some traction thing."

"Was it a car accident like they said?"

"It happened in a car. But it was no accident. She says someone forced her off the road."

I gasp. "Was it Lorders?" I whisper.

He shakes his head. "No. They're investigating it."

"But if it's not them, who else would do something like that?"

Ben shrugs. "I've no idea. I just thought you'd like to know."

"Is that it? Because I need to get back, and—"

"Kyla, listen. I promised you I wouldn't do anything without talking to you first, so here I am. Talking to you."

"What about?" I say, uneasy. *Something is wrong.*

"This," he says. He pulls up his sleeve, exposing his Levo. A bright circlet of metal, digital numbers in the green at 7.8. Why so high? He doesn't look that happy. He reaches with his other hand and savagely twists his Levo. His face contorts with pain.

"Stop it! What are you doing?"

"Look," he says, and holds his Levo in front of me, but it is still in the green: 7.6. Twisting it like that should have made his levels plummet.

"I don't understand. How did you do that?"

"I've taken another one of Aiden's pills, and no matter what I do, my levels won't drop. I've tried all sorts of things; they stay up."

"So?"

"Don't you see? The link between Levo and brain is blocked by the pills. It can be removed *without* blacking out, without any effects." Ben's face is shining, his eyes bright and overexcited. Like someone with a fever. *Or on drugs.*

"You don't know that," I say, but my mind is scrambling with the possibility. Is he right? The Levo reads emotions by communicating with chips surgically implanted in the brain. Too low and this activates a cascade that briefly interrupts blood flow to the brain, giving a blackout or, lower still, the interruption is permanent, causing seizures and death. Yet if there's a way to keep levels unaffected . . .

"Yes! It all adds together: what Aiden said, about the AGT removing Levos. The pills block the link between brain and Levo. They must." He catches my hands in his; his eyes search mine. "Think about it, Kyla: What it would be like to just be ourselves. Feeling what we want."

He gathers me in, holds me. His closeness makes my heart beat faster, my skin tingle, my body want things it doesn't even know. All the things I'm told to avoid because of my Levo. What would it be like without it? We could be whoever we want to be; stay together. No one could say we were destabilizing our levels. We could be as happy or as sad as we like.

But this is a fairy tale. There would be no place for us, here, in this world.

I pull away. "What are you planning, Ben," I whisper.

"I'm going to take a few of these pills, then cut off my Levo and destroy it."

Fear twists inside. *No, Ben, no.* "What? Are you insane?"

"No. I have been insane, buying into what I was told. Now I'm saner than I've ever been. Aiden was right, though he didn't go far enough. This is wrong, what they've done to us. Look at what happened yesterday. I couldn't protect you. If Jazz and Amy hadn't been there, then . . ."

And he doesn't finish the sentence. My mind shies away, also. Last night I escorted that particular memory to a little door in my brain, kicked it in and locked it up tight. I don't want to think about it, in case it finds a way out.

"No, Ben, you mustn't!"

"Aiden said the AGT have done it; it has worked."

"But he also said they had a lot of failures. You don't know how they did it. And the pain, Ben: You still felt it when you twisted your Levo. I saw it on your face. Not all the links are cut."

He shrugs. "I'll get through it."

"If you get it wrong, you could die."

"What is the point in being alive like this?"

"You don't mean that. And you can't just cut a Levo off with a pair of scissors. They are almost impossible to damage."

"Mum's workshop has stuff that can cut through anything metal. I help her all the time; I know how to use it all."

My mind casts about, desperate for an argument he will hear. "Wait. What about after? If you can get it off, what then? You can't stay with your family, or at school. Everyone would look at your wrist and know what you've done. The Lorders would come for you."

"I have a plan," he says, but when I question him, he says nothing.

He said Aiden's way wasn't far enough.

He wants to join the terrorists.

"You're not thinking . . . no. You wouldn't. Not the AGT."

And there, in his beautiful eyes, is admission, confirmation. He wants to be a terrorist. My throat clenches. He doesn't know the things they do; he couldn't and still be thinking of this.

"It's the only way to make the government listen, to change things. We have to make them do it! Don't you see?"

I shake my head, back away. Is this Ben, or is it the pills? Have they made him think like this?

"Look at you," he says. "After yesterday, you didn't even want to look at me. You didn't want to talk to me, nothing. I was six feet of *useless.*"

"That wasn't your fault, and it's not that!"

"What is it, then?"

"You're just proving it all over again."

"What?"

"You'd be better off if you never met me."

"How can you say that? Kyla, don't you know how I feel about you?"

But I don't want to hear. If how he feels makes him kill himself, what good is it? Nothing.

"No. No! You mustn't do this. Promise me you won't."

He shakes his head. "I have to think for myself; you can't do it for me. As much as you might like to."

And I stare back at Ben in shock. Smiling, uncomplicated Ben, who I thought needed my protection. He's not smiling now, and he doesn't want it. He doesn't want to know what I think, or the impact his actions might have on me. Nothing.

What else is there to say?

I turn away and head back toward the school. My Levo vibrates; great. I glance down. 4.2.

Ben follows behind. "Here. Take one of these." He holds out his bottle of "headache tablets."

"No, thanks. I've seen what they can do."

Instead, I run.

The rest of the day passes in a blur. My levels hover around 4; I wrap a scarf around my wrist so no one will hear it vibrate. All I can think about is Ben. I have to stop him, but how?

At the end of the day I get to the car before Amy and ask Jazz to tell Mac I want to see him, hoping he'll get Aiden along as well. I'd vowed I wouldn't speak to Aiden again, but maybe he can help talk Ben out of something so crazy, or, at the very least, tell him how the AGT did it. If he isn't there, maybe Mac can help me persuade Ben to wait until he tracks him down. It is the only thing I can think of to try to stop Ben.

Late that night, blank paper and pencil lie idle in my hands. Even my drawing has deserted me.

"The question we are considering is how to deal with pain. Pain can kill, all on its own; the body goes into shock and shuts down. If it is severe enough."

The boy smiles, even less idea what is coming than I have. He is nothing like me. He sits where he is told, speaks when spoken to, and smiles great dopey grins all the while. Even more so now with that drip in his arm, the empty whiskey glass in his hand. His pupils are dilated and a thin sheen of sweat glistens on his skin, though the shop is so cold I can see my breath.

"It doesn't work under general anesthetic; they must be conscious. I haven't worked out why. Yet." Still the boy smiles, either not listening or not understanding. He is older than me: fifteen or sixteen, perhaps. "This time, in addition to the usual concoction, we're trying cocaine: an oldie but a goody. Hard to source these days, but we tracked some down.

"Hold out your hand," he orders, and the boy complies. He straps his arm onto a table. That is when I see the saw: It is lined up with the boy's wrist.

"You're not . . ." I start to protest. I hate blood. Hate it! The metallic smell, the color, the slippery feel of it, and I start to spin inside, holding on to the table with one hand, my stomach on its way up.

He shakes me, hard. "Who are you?" he shouts. Abruptly the spinning is gone. I am calm, observant. "You have to work on your control. You don't want to let her out, do you?" he says, his voice dangerous.

"No! Sniveling wimp." I stand straight.

"Good girl. And no, I'm not cutting off his hand. Though that would be an interesting experiment on pain, in itself."

He pulls up the boy's sleeve, exposes a metal circle. Like a bracelet, with numbers like a clock, but it isn't telling the time.

"Is that . . . is he . . ."

"This is a Levo, and he has been Slated." He twists the boy's wrist and adjusts the straps so the Levo is lined up at right angles to a split in the metal table. In line with the saw. "This saw is diamond-tipped, and is the only thing that will get through the metal they use in these devices; believe me, we've tried everything. Cold, heat, chemicals, all sorts of cutting devices. But an old-fashioned diamond-edged saw works best."

He slips on goggles. "Stand back a little, there may be some spatter if I go too far." He flicks a switch, the saw spins, whines. He pushes it toward the boy's hand. His Levo.

The boy watches, eyes wide, uncertain now. He looks at me. The saw reaches the Levo, strikes against it and a loud grinding noise begins, sparks fly. And then he starts to scream . . .

Pain twists through my arm; I struggle, but soon realize it is just tangled blankets that hold me. The only things glowing in the dark are Sebastian's eyes.

I switch on the bedside light. Sebastian's fur is on end, standing straight up his spine, down the length of his tail. A row of scratches trails down my arm: This is the pain that woke me. It wasn't part of my dream at all. The second time Sebastian has woken me in the middle of a nightmare.

"Thanks for the wake-up call, cat," I whisper. Soon he settles as I pet him, smooth his fur. He curls up to sleep, but I leave the light on, unwilling to find darkness all around me again.

Imagination, cruel and horrible, or traces of memory I should not have? Where do I go in my dreams?

Some instinct says it is both. My dream self didn't know what Levos were, other than in an abstract way; she didn't recognize that boy as Slated, though it was obvious. But there is one inescapable conclusion.

Ben must be stopped.

44

"TIME TO GO!" MUM HOLLERS UP THE STAIRS.

But when I get to the bottom of them, instead of marching through the front door, she turns and leans on it.

"Is everything all right?"

Everything is so far from all right that even if I could tell her, I wouldn't know where to begin. Instead I glance at the clock by the door. "I'm going to be late for Group if we don't go."

She pauses a moment longer, then opens the door. "You know, Kyla, maybe I could help if you tell me what is wrong. The way you've been mooning about the last few days, there is obviously something."

There is a part of me that longs to tell her everything. She might see a way out of this box that I can't.

Danger.

"Is it Ben?" she asks as we pull away from the house.

I nod. That much I can admit.

"Did you two have some sort of fight?"

I scowl. "Did Amy tell you that?"

"Don't be angry with her. She was worried about you, and about Ben."

I stare out the window. Amy's good intentions are causing so much trouble.

"Kyla, you do understand why your dad and I thought it best if you don't go running with Ben alone?"

I look back at her. "Toeing the line," I snap before I can stop myself.

Mum half laughs. "I do remember what it is like, you know. To be young and want to be with somebody."

"Then why can't I run to Group with Ben?"

"Because you can't right now. But just so you know, I don't always agree with your dad. I went along because, officially, he is right, and we can't do things that will get you in trouble, can we? But keep things as they are for a little while, and we'll see if we can get Ben around now and then. Chaperoned, I'm afraid." She smiles, and I know she is trying to help, thinks she is on my side. But it is so much more complicated than she can imagine. Ben might not be around long enough for "a little while," or any other sort of while.

If only I could talk to Ben alone, make him see sense.

Wait a minute.

"Maybe there is something you could do to help."

"What's that?"

"Could you maybe pick me up a little late tonight? Not long. Just so we can talk for a few minutes, sort things out."

"Your dad would have my head if he knew."

"I won't tell him!"

She sighs. "All right; neither will I. I'll give you twenty minutes. Good enough?"

"Thanks," I say.

"Oh good, a smile. Try to have one on later when I pick you up, all right?"

Group begins as usual. Penny wears a bright cardigan and is too cheerful to be normal; Ben runs in late. He doesn't sit next to me, and

I try to stuff down the hurt. Is he still angry about the way I left him, walking off like that?

In Group everyone talks inanely about things that don't really matter. I eye the clock as each minute ticks down. We go a few minutes over, and I almost have to bite my tongue to stop myself from objecting. When Penny finally says we can go, Ben stands and heads for the door.

But I am out of my seat and get there just as he does.

"Wait," I say.

He turns, looks at my eyes for the first time this evening. Says nothing, and it is like a dagger inside. I almost slink away. But I have to talk to him. I have to find the words that will put an end to his plans.

"Ben, please. Can we talk? Mum is coming late. We've got a little time."

He glances across the room; Penny is looking the other way, talking to the parents of one of the others.

"Come on, then," he says, and I follow him outside, along the parking lot in the shadow of the hall.

"Are you angry with me?" I say, and then want to bite it back. There are so many things that need saying; that could wait.

He shakes his head. "Of course not. But I am trying to keep away from you. I don't want you to associate with me in public, so when things go down . . ." He pauses. "I don't want you to get in trouble."

I sigh. "Does this mean you haven't come to your senses? Are you still planning to go through with it?"

"You didn't really think I'd just change my mind, did you?"

"I didn't, I just hoped. But at least wait until we can see Aiden again. He can tell you how they did it, give you a better chance." *Talk you out of it.*

Ben shakes his head. "Listen to me: I'm not going to change my mind," he says in a quiet voice, determination threaded through it. "And I don't think from what he said that Aiden really knows what they did, anyhow."

"Please, Ben. I don't want anything to happen to you."

His eyes soften. "What I'd really like to do now is drag you off into the woods and kiss you."

But around us cars are pulling in, collecting children. There are eyes everywhere. He takes my hand and links our fingers. "This will do for now."

"Ben, you have to listen to reason. Don't do it."

"We've gone over this already, haven't we?"

"But how exactly are you planning to do it?"

"I've started going through equipment in Mum's workshop. I'll figure something out this weekend."

"So soon?"

"Yes. Mum is going away to Dad's sister, who had a baby; Dad is already there. I convinced them I could stay here on my own."

I stare at him miserably. "Please, Ben—"

"Kyla, listen. If this works, we can cut yours off, too. We can run away someplace, together. Without our Levos no one could keep us apart."

"What about the AGT?" I whisper as quietly as I can. "Have you given up that idea?"

He shakes his head.

"So, just you, me, and a major terrorist organization. Sounds like heaven."

"Think about it. We could change the world."

Mum pulls in, waves.

"I have to go."

"No smiles, Kyla?"

I slump back in the seat.

"I'm sorry," she says.

Once we get home I escape tea and sympathy as soon as I can, but I can't escape my thoughts. Ben, cutting off his Levo, screaming in pain. If he somehow survives, Ben in the AGT.

I have to stop him.

Everything is misty, unclear. I straighten the goggles.

"Here: This is the switch. You push the saw along this track. The diamond wheel should make quick work of his Levo. The key is to cut it off as quickly as possible before the pain and shock cause death, but not so quickly the hand goes as well. Where most attempts fail is in stopping when the pain hits instead of pushing through it. Understand?"

"Yes." I am calm, observant. Interested in the experiment.

The subject is sweating, eyes dilated. His hand immobilized on the table. He reeks of whiskey.

I flick the switch. The wheel spins, whining as it hits speed.

Pushing it closer and closer, I glance up and see the subject's eyes. Blue, wide: not scared. Not yet.

"Watch what you're doing!"

I look back to the saw as it touches the Levo. Sparks fly in an arc.

The screaming begins.

I pull the saw back.

"No! He'll die now if you don't cut it off and do it fast."

But I'm spinning, faster than the saw. Screams of agony rip through my skull. I clench my eyes shut, and with them shut I see more clearly. He changes: The screaming boy is gone. And in his place is Ben.

"No! Ben, no!" I lunge for the machine, to stop the saw before it reaches him, to release the straps, but arms grab tight around me and hold me firm.

"You must stay in control. You know the rules."

"No!"

"You're next."

I fight, kick. Struggle, scratch, and scream. But it is no good. I'm strapped into a chair, my arm to the table.

The saw whines . . .

Bzzzz . . .

My eyes snap open, desperate to escape the horror. A dream, but I can still hear the saw?

Bzzzz . . .

I reach for the light and when it happens again, I feel it on my wrist: My Levo is vibrating, a dangerous 3.2. I'm nauseous and shaking. This time, to begin with at least, I was the one wielding the saw. Could I ever really have done something like that?

Slowly, so slowly, my heart stops racing, my levels coming up, but I can't let go of the images. They replay again and again in my mind. A diamond-edged blade. Whiskey. A quick cut.

Was I really there, in that place, torturing that boy?

Somewhere inside there is a crack, a glint of light.

I don't want to know, but I can't escape it. In my dream, when I was put in place to have my Levo cut off, I was terrified: not of the pain, or that I might die. But of being without my Levo. I hate it, what it means and represents, what it does to my life. Yet for some reason I needed to keep it so much that the mere thought of losing it filled me with terror.

Why?

45

FRIDAY MORNING WHEN I REACH THE BACK OF THE BUS,
Ben's usual seat is empty. I half stand as the bus pulls away and look
at every head. No; he's not sitting elsewhere. He's simply not here.

I panic inside. He didn't. No. He said his parents were away this
weekend; that was when he was going to try to cut off his Levo. He
wouldn't have jumped ahead, would he?

Numb, I go through morning classes as if back in a nightmare. I
even consider asking Mrs. Ali for help. If I tell her what Ben is thinking, they'll stop him. They won't let him do it. But then what would
the Lorders do to him?

If it's not too late already.

I wander the grounds at lunch, alone. Can anyone help? *Try Jazz.*

Final-year students have their own study hall in the main building,
and Amy says they go there at lunch. I head there now. With Amy out
on her internship, I won't need to dodge her. Some instinct through
all of this has said to tell her nothing. She thinks I shouldn't see Ben
anymore; how would she react if she finds out he is planning to cut off
his Levo?

I stand, uncertain, in the door. *Please be here, Jazz.* The room is
crowded, full of students chatting in groups, on benches eating lunch,
at tables and study carrels doing homework. I scan the room and can't
spot him anywhere. But I can't quite see around the desks and shelves
into the far corner; I crane my head around.

"Out of the way, please," a voice says behind me. I move to one side and two older girls walk in and look at me pointedly.

"Wait. I'm looking for Jazz MacKenzie?"

They ignore me and keep going.

"Jazz?" I say, louder. He peeks around the corner of a desk halfway across the room.

He smiles, walks over. "Hi, Kyla, how're things?"

"Can we talk a minute? I mean, away from everyone."

"Of course," he says. "Hang on a sec." He comes back with his jacket on. "Let's go for a walk."

We head down the hall and out of the building. The sky is gray, and a light drizzle is falling. Enough for the benches and paths to be mostly deserted.

"What's up?" he says when we clear the last of potential eavesdroppers.

"I'm really worried about Ben. He wasn't on the bus today."

"Well, he might have slept in, or have a cold, or be at the dentist. Any number of reasons why he wasn't there."

I don't say anything else; he looks at my face. "But you don't think it is any of those things."

"No," I whisper. I hesitate; better for Jazz if he doesn't know details. "It's just that Ben was thinking of doing something really stupid. Now I'm afraid he's done it."

"I see."

"I don't know what to do," I say miserably. The drizzle increases to rain. My Levo vibrates, but I keep my hands buried deep inside my pockets so Jazz won't hear.

"Amy thinks you shouldn't see him anymore. She agrees with your parents."

"What do you think?"

He shrugs. "I think Ben is all right. You're really worried?"

I nod.

Jazz tilts his head to the side, thinking. "Tell you what: Let's bunk off school for the afternoon and swing by his place, yeah? See if he's okay."

I find myself agreeing; Jazz goes back for his bag, says he'll meet me by his car in a few minutes.

This is a bad idea.

I shrug off that thought as I cross the grounds to the student parking area, keeping a lookout for teachers. True, skipping class this afternoon will be hard to explain, and Mrs. Ali is already on my case. It's not like no one will notice. *A very bad idea.*

Jazz is longer than a few minutes, and I start to worry. Did he change his mind? No. He would have told me.

But then he bursts around the corner, a big grin on his face. "Ben is on a class trip."

"Really?"

"I checked: They post them up on a bulletin board by the office. His agriculture class is spending the day at a farm. I'm surprised he didn't tell you."

My knees go weak with relief, and I feel dizzy, almost like I'm going to throw up.

"Hey, you all right?" Jazz looks at me curiously.

"I will be. I just really need to talk to Ben."

"Well, we could go to his place after school. Ditch the bus and I'll take you, get you home before Amy or the Dragon knows a thing about it."

"Really?"

"Sure. Why not?"

"Thanks."

Jazz shrugs, grins. "No big drama," he says, winks. "Meet you here end of day, all right?"

"Deal."

I hug the relief to myself all afternoon. Why didn't Ben tell me about his class trip? Though we had other things to talk about. *More like argue about.*

The sky clears through the afternoon. By the time I meet Jazz at his car, the clouds have gone. The sun is shining.

I sit in the front seat for the first time. Uneasy, suddenly, what Amy will make of this if she hears about it from anyone.

"I'll tell Amy someone was hassling you on the bus, so I gave you a lift home. All right?" Jazz says, as if reading my mind.

"Sure."

I sit back in the car, late afternoon sun shining in my face, seat belt on. One hand holds tight to the door, but I've gotten used to Jazz's driving a bit more now and don't really register when he slams on the brakes at a light, then takes off way too fast, and repeats the same at the next intersection. He whistles along to the radio.

Last night's dream runs through my mind, a replay on a loop with no end. My head is full of screaming; of the smell of salty fear, whiskey, and blood, all mingled together, so real I have to fight not to gag.

Ben must be stopped. But what if he won't listen?

Jazz pulls in to a house four doors down from Ben's.

"My pal Ian lives in this one. I'll be here when you want to go."

When I get to Ben's house, Skye is in the front garden. She runs over to me, full of excitement. Half knocks me over in her eagerness to lick my face. Ben said she is always so happy, it's like she has been dog-Slated.

"Settle down, dog!" I admonish, pet her.

I knock on the front door and wait. No answer.

Maybe he's not back from the school trip yet?

Skye was by the garage door when I got here, so I head over. Knock.

No answer. I listen; *there*. Was that a slight noise inside?

I try the door: locked. And knock again. "Ben?" I call out.

This time there are footsteps, a clink of a lock turning in the door. It opens.

"Kyla?" Ben grins. "What are you doing here?" He looks both ways, pulls my arm and draws me in. Skye tries to follow, and he pushes her out, then shuts the door and turns the key in the lock once again.

He's not in his school uniform. His eyes are unnaturally bright.

"Weren't you on a class trip today?"

"I was supposed to be. I decided to take the day off."

"You're going to get in so much trouble for that."

"It will hardly matter. I won't be there next week." He smiles. "I'm glad you are here. So I can say good-bye."

And I see grinding equipment laid out, safety glasses. Towels. His backpack packed full of stuff like he has somewhere to go.

Dread runs through my body, turns it to ice. I pull my hands away from his. "No, Ben, no! You're not going to do it now?"

"Why wait? Everyone's gone for the weekend. Perfect timing."

I shake my head, trembling, tears pricking the backs of my eyes. "Please don't do this. Don't leave me."

"Shhh, Kyla. It'll be all right. One day soon I'll come back for you."

"Not if you're dead."

He laughs. "I'll find a way." He links his little finger in mine, holds them up between us. "You can't break a pinky promise." He holds it tight. "Kyla, I promise. We'll be together again."

He bends and kisses me lightly, starts to pull away, but I slip my hand around the back of his neck and hold him close, kiss him again and again, desperate to stay here, in this one moment. His arms wrap tight around me and I close my eyes, lean into him. Why is everything so hard? Why can't we just stay like this?

He loosens his arms. "Go, Kyla. Go now."

I shake my head. I have to stop him, make him see. "No. Wait. Please. At least talk to Aiden. Maybe he can tell you how, so it has a better chance of working?"

"No, Kyla. We've been through this."

Think. I have to show him how stupid this is, that it can't work. "Tell me what you are planning to do."

Ben shows me his mum's fancy new cutter. Some new engineered metal that is meant to be stronger than any other.

I shake my head. "No. It won't work. Diamonds are stronger."

He tilts his head to one side. Goes to another bench. "There is this." He holds up an old one-handed angle grinder. "It's got a diamond-edged disc."

"It still won't work, Ben. You can't just hold your hand up in the air and grind your Levo off. You'll never hold it still enough, not when the pain hits."

He finds a C-clamp. "Should do the trick," he says. "I'll clamp it to the bench. Please leave now, Kyla."

"I'm staying. You can't stop me," I say, desperate to find the words that will make him see. Make him give up this crazy plan. But I stare back at him, his eyes, and slump in defeat. Nothing I say makes any difference. He's made up his mind.

My head drops to my hands, almost dizzy with shock when it hits me: I have to help him. I have to. It has to be a quick cut. He'll start and not be able to finish, and die in horrible pain. If I can't stop him, I have to help him.

I look up, wipe the tears away. Forcing calm, control outside while inside I'm screaming *NO NO NO NO* . . .

"I'll do it," I say. "I'll cut off your Levo."

"No. No way, Kyla. Go."

"Listen. I know how to use one of these," I say, and pick up the angle grinder. It feels comfortable, natural in my hands. Harder to do this with a handheld grinder than the special fixed grinder set up in my dream, but the principle is the same. "It will be much safer if I do it instead of you. You won't be able to control it with the pain."

"I can't put you through that. No, Kyla."

"Look. I can do it." I clamp some scrap metal into the C-clamp, put on safety glasses. Turn the grinder on and the sound, so like my dream, makes me want to scream, but I cut a straight line through.

"Steady hands; I'm impressed. But—"

"No buts. I'm helping you, or you're not doing it. I won't let you do it alone. I won't let you die alone."

He stares back into my eyes, shakes his head softly.

"Let me help you," I say. "You know it makes sense."

"That doesn't make it right."

"Then don't do it at all!" I start to say, ready for one last try, one final attempt to make him see, but he shakes his head and my words fall away.

His face is reluctant. "It makes sense," he admits. "But are you sure you can do it? Are you sure you want to."

"Yes."

He hesitates. "All right," he says finally. He holds up Aiden's Happy Pills. "But at least take one of these."

"No way."

"I can't have you blacking out halfway through."

I hesitate, but he is right. What if my levels drop and the grinder with them? "Fine," I say, and down one pill with a glass of water. Ben takes a handful. "Is it safe to take so many?"

He shrugs. "Too many is better than too few, I reckon." Soon there is a thin film of sweat on his skin, his pupils are dilated. Like the boy in my dream.

My dream . . .

"Whiskey. Have you got any?"

"I think so. Why?"

"It helps cushion shock."

There is a door between the garage and house; Ben goes through, then returns with a bottle. Drinks some back. Coughs and pulls a face. "This is vile."

"Please don't do this. Please. It's not too late to change your mind."

"You don't have to help me; I'll do it alone. Go home, Kyla."

"No! If you are going ahead with it, I'll help you. But Ben, listen. I think that once it starts to cut into the Levo, there is no going back. It has to come off all the way to stop the pain."

"Yep. No matter what I say, keep going."

"If you scream, people will come."

"I won't make a sound."

"Who do you think you are, Superman or something?"

"Super Ben!" He laughs and sits in the chair next to the bench, clamps his Levo to it. As it compresses, his face contorts with pain.

"Kyla, hold on for a minute. In case things go wrong, we need to make it look like I did this all by myself. No matter what happens, you have to get out of here. Promise me you will. And if you get caught here, say you found me like this. Promise!"

"Okay. I promise."

"Put on some gloves," he says. "Over there. Wipe off the controls, the handle, everything you've touched." I put the gloves on and do as he asked.

"Ready?" I whisper.

"Wait."

"Yes?" Hoping against all hope that he will say: *Stop this. I've changed my mind.*

"Kyla, whatever happens to me: I love you. I'll always love you." And okay, he has had enough Happy Pills to make a Lorder friendly, and whiskey on top of it. He barely knows where he is, let alone what he is saying, but he looks like he means it.

I stare back at him and I want to say the words, that I love him, too, but they are caught inside my tightening throat and won't come out.

"Do it!" he says.

And it is like I am in my dream, that horrible dream. I am not myself. I am this nightmare girl: calm, collected, able to do things like this. Where does she come from?

I pick up the angle grinder, release the safety, and hit the on switch. A quick cut. It must be fast.

The wheel spins and whines.

I look at Ben. He nods. *Do it,* he mouths.

The spinning blade connects with his Levo. Sparks arc and fly all around.

Unlike the boy in my dream, Ben doesn't scream. But his face contorts, sweat pours out and I try not to look, to not watch his face. I must focus on the blade, hold it steady.

Skye must know, through some canine link with Ben whom she has adored and been adored by since she was a puppy, and she starts to howl and scratch at the door, then the door thuds as if she is throwing herself against it.

Sparks continue to fly and I've started so now I can't stop. The blade bucks and kicks, chatters, and the grinder is getting so hot that even with gloves I can hardly hold it anymore. There is a trickle of blood coming out of Ben's mouth and his body is convulsing, but somehow he is still silent, isn't trying to pull away.

The last bit of the Levo is putting up resistance. It pulls and bucks and then . . . *Snap!* It is off. I release the switch and pull the grinder back, but not before Ben's arm jerks. His wrist touches the blade as it slows. There is blood and I throw the grinder down, rush to release the clamp and grab a towel to wrap tight around his wrist.

"Ben? Ben!" I shake him; his body is limp, he is unconscious, there's more blood trickling from his mouth—did he bite his tongue? He slides off the chair. I pull the gloves off and throw them to the corner, and feel at his neck. His pulse is erratic.

Dimly I hear Skye howling. A car. The garage door rattles, then opens.

Ben's mum.

"I forgot the baby's . . ." she starts to say, then takes in Ben on the floor in my arms. "What happened?"

And tears are running down my face, I'm shaking my head, and can't speak.

Tell her what Ben said.

"I c-c-c-came to see him and found him like this."

And she is pushing me away and checking the towel which has blood soaked through now, then sees. Color drains from her face. "His Levo is gone." She looks up at me. "What happened?"

I shrug helplessly. *Lie.*

"I don't know. He must have cut it off."

Ben's limp body arcs. And again. He is convulsing. Seizures? Oh, God, no. Damaging your Levo leads to seizures and death. That is what they always told us!

She pulls a phone out of her pocket and calls an ambulance.

"Get out of here, Kyla. Go."

And I am shaking, limp; Happy Pill or no my levels are dropping fast. It vibrates.

"Go! I don't know what *really* happened here. But for now, go. Get out of here before they come!"

I can't leave him, I can't.

"Get out. It is what he would want."

Yes. That is what he said to do.

I stagger for the door just as sirens sound in the distance.

"Not that way," she says. "Use the back door and the canal path. Go!"

And I stumble out the back door. Across their yard, through the gate at the bottom. There is the canal path, like she said. Somehow I drag myself down it behind the houses. Count them along to four. Jazz's friend?

There is music pouring out the back so loud the ground is vibrating. I pound at the back door, but there is no answer. I let myself in.

Jazz takes one look at me and turns off the stereo. Then they hear the sirens.

Tears are pouring down my face.

Jazz puts an arm around my shoulders. "Kyla? What's wrong? What happened?"

Another siren joins in, as if attempting two-part harmony, but the sound is discordant, harsh, loud—and heading this way.

Lie.

"B-b-b-ben. He cut off his Levo," I whisper.

"But I thought that was impossible."

"It's supposed to be. Even if you don't black out, any damage to your Levo, and the pain kills you." Or the seizures. I try to blank it out of my mind, but cannot. Ben . . .

Out the front window there are now not one but two ambulances in Ben's driveway. What does it mean? If Ben . . . I swallow. Even my thoughts falter, can't grasp the worst of what might have happened, can't find words for the images I cannot banish. All I can see is Ben's body lying on the floor, convulsing, his face contorted with pain.

Another siren begins to wail in the distance, but this one is different. The pitch, the tone, are not the same as the ambulance vehicles, and the sound resonates in my head, makes my heart beat faster, my skin crawl. *Hide! Do it now.*

But I hold my ground at the window. The source of the noise appears around the corner: a long black van. Unmarked, but with a flashing blue light in the front. I jump away from the window and push back Jazz and Ian, who were coming up behind me.

"What is it?" Jazz asks.

"Lorders," I say, feeling faint, sick. *The paramedics called Lorders. They can't be trusted.*

"We've got to get you out of here," Jazz says. "Now."

So cold: I'm trapped in ice from head to toe. My Levo buzzes, and Jazz grabs my wrist to look.

4.4.

One Happy Pill is not enough.

"Dammit, Kyla, what can I do to help?" Jazz says, real worry in his eyes.

"Nothing. It's too late," I say.

4.1.

I wrap my arms around myself, shaking. I should have stopped him. It's all my fault.

3.8.

I left him, just left him there . . .

3.5.

Bleeding, dying, and I just ran away. Ben . . .

Jazz curses. "No, Kyla; not here, not now. Come on." He drags me to the back door, swearing Ian to secrecy that we were here.

"That who was here?" Ian says. "I'll let you know if I find out anything about Ben."

Jazz half carries me to the fence, through the gate to the path.

3.2.

"Run!" Jazz says.

". . . What?"

"Run as if your life depends on it." *Maybe it does.*

Run? Now? I look at my feet, will them to start, and stumble into a walk, a jog. Then the rhythm starts to take over.

"Faster!" Jazz says, following behind. "I know you can go faster."

Run like Lorders are after you. Full tilt, flat out, as if every Lorder that ever was is right on my tail; as if Wayne Best is about to catch me. I focus on Wayne's ugly face and some flicker of energy finds my feet.

Jazz grabs my wrist: 3.9. "Not good enough. Keep going." We run and run. He breathes hard, not used to it. I keep going, but still the images flood my mind: Ben. Hurt, or worse. If hurt and taken by Lorders, worse might be better. What has happened? What could I have done to stop it? Not knowing what happened to Ben is grinding through my core. I want to collapse and cry, but whenever I slow down, Jazz prods me from behind and makes me go on.

Ben's beautiful, gentle eyes; and this. They don't go together. What has happened to you?

Ian will find out for us.

Yes.

Keep running.

The light is going by the time we head back for the car.

"Levels?" Jazz asks.

I check. "5.2. How'd you know to make me run?"

Jazz shrugs. "Something Ben said once."

Ben.

"Come on. Let's get you home." Jazz peeks out on the road, standing in the shadows. No signs of ambulances or Lorders. "Looks clear."

Ben.

By the time Jazz pulls up in front of my house, my Levo is vibrating again.

"Hang in there, Kyla. Come on, you can do it."

I just shake my head helplessly; it is dropping too fast.

"Time to face the Dragon?" Jazz says. "Come on."

He half carries me to the door. It opens before we get there.

"Where the hell have you—" Mum starts to say, then she sees my face. "In, in," she says. Jazz helps me to the sofa.

Bzzzz . . .

3.1.

Ben . . .

46

AGONY. MY WORLD IS FILLED WITH PAIN; THERE IS NOTHING else. Pulsing, dripping red pain, a vise clenched tight around all that I am, all that I was, all that I may be.

Slowly, other things become tangible. The floor: I'm lying on the floor. Voices. *Ben . . .*

A jab in my arm. Warmth drifts through my veins, all over my body. It doesn't take the pain away; nothing can take this pain away. It just makes me care less about it. I open my eyes.

"Hello there," Mum says, and smiles. "You're back."

"Hmmm?" I say. Then everything goes black.

"Ben! You came."

He smiles. "I couldn't leave without saying good-bye." He kneels down.

"Don't leave me. Don't go, please . . ." My eyes run with tears.

"I can't stay, it's too late." He smiles again. It is on his lips, but his eyes are sad.

"Be strong, Kyla." He leans down, his lips brush mine, gently: our third kiss.

He pulls away, insubstantial. Light shines through him.

"Good-bye, Kyla," he says, voice soft, words drifting away into silence. Then he is gone.

Our last kiss.

"Ben!" I shout his name, try to sit up, but fall back. I'm in bed. My bed. Sebastian is at my feet; faint light leaks in from the open door to the hall.

"Kyla?" Mum says. She's sitting in the chair next to me. "Hello there." Her face is tired, pale. I try to sit up again, but the movement sends waves of agony through my skull. I gasp.

"Stay still," she says.

"What happened to Ben?"

"Don't worry about it now."

I try to concentrate; it makes the pain worse. But there is something, just out of reach, I need to know.

"Tell me," I plead, and feel wetness on my cheeks.

"Hush. Jazz brought you home; you blacked out as you came through the door. That is all I know."

"Paramedics were here?" I whisper.

"Of course. They gave you an injection, and then another; you came to for a second and then passed out."

Danger. I close my eyes. They'll know. The Lorders: They'll know I was there, at Ben's. The paramedics will tell them I blacked out, and Ben is my friend. They'll put it together.

I slip back to black.

When I open my eyes again the sun is peeking through the curtains, and I am alone. This time I manage to sit up, the throb in my skull dull and insistent, the nausea in my stomach urgent. *Not now.* I swallow and breathe deep until it passes.

There is a murmur downstairs. Voices? Mum and someone else.

I slip out from under the covers, somehow manage to stand, and walk on rubbery legs to the window. Down below a black van is parked in our driveway.

Lorders.

Adrenaline rushes through my body, says *run*. But it is all I can do to stand up. I ease myself back into bed. The best I can do is play dead. Moments later there are footsteps on the stairs, and the door opens.

"Kyla?" Mum says, voice soft. I stay still. "I told you, she is asleep. Can't this wait?"

"No. Wake her, or I will do it for you." A cold male voice.

There are footsteps across the room, Mum's hand on my cheek.

I flutter my eyes half open, whimper. Mum is staring into mine, her eyes an urgent message: saying what? Two gray-suited men tower in the door behind her, making the room seem small. *Close your eyes.* They flutter closed once again, while my insides swirl. What has she told them; what do they know? If our stories aren't the same . . . *danger.*

"I can't see why you need to speak to her, poor thing. She's been through enough. I've told you what happened: that she was worried about that Ben not being in school, they went—"

That Ben: said in a certain tone, disapproving.

"Quiet!" one of them says. "Wake her."

"Kyla, love, wake up now. There's a good girl."

More messages: She is telling me how to play it. I'm young and daft; they know we went to Ben's, she doesn't like Ben. *Thanks, Mum.*

I stir this time. Open my eyes. Smile a sleepy Slated smile at Mum, then wince. "My stomach hurts," I say plaintively.

"Poor darling. These gentlemen just want to ask you a few questions now, all right? Let me help you sit up a little." Mum fusses with my pillows. "You tell them exactly what you told me happened," she says. Another message? *Tell the truth as she knows it.* And I scramble in my brain to remember what she knows, what she doesn't.

Poker face, you're on. I hold Sebastian in my mind and imitate Phoebe's face: open, blissful. Smiling with an occasional wince of pain when I move my head.

"Yes, Mum," I say, and turn to the impatient men in the doorway. They look unused to waiting. Is it Mum, being her father's daughter, that has them behaving as they are? A cold certainty says if she were anyone else I'd have been yanked away for questions, not answering them here.

The younger of the two men consults a netbook. "You are Kyla Davis?"

"Yes."

"Why did you black out yesterday?"

Not asking what happened? I banish surprise from my face. "I was very upset. My friend Ben wasn't in school, and my other friend took me to his house to see if he was all right."

"Your other friend?" Still it is the younger man who speaks, who takes the lead; he glances at Mum now and then with a look of awe. But it is the other one to worry about. He stands in a certain way that says he is in charge.

Do I answer, don't I? *Mum knew.*

"Jazz MacKenzie; Jason. He's my sister's friend, really. But he looks out for me."

"And then . . . ?"

"Ben wasn't all right, at all." I allow distress into my voice. "There were ambulances, and Jazz said we shouldn't get in the way, and I had to go home. But I was worried about Ben, and I guess I blacked out."

Mum snorts. "That Ben, the cause of so much trouble."

"Mum and Dad told me not to run alone with Ben anymore," I say. "I like running." I smile a great Slated grin.

"Did Ben ever show you any pills?"

"Pills? I don't think so." *Amy saw his pills.* "No, wait. He had some headache tablets in his bag. He took one when he wasn't feeling well on Sunday."

"Surely that is enough questions," Mum says. "The poor girl isn't well at all."

On cue my stomach starts spinning again, but this time I don't calm it and breathe deep. I can feel what little color is there draining from my cheeks.

"Mum, I think I'm going to be sick." She grabs the garbage bin just in time. Waves of nausea tear through me, and each shudder slams into the pain in my skull. My stomach is mostly empty, but the Lorders back away with looks of disgust.

"That is enough for today," Mum says.

The younger man starts to back out of the room; the older tilts his head to one side. Raises his hand and the other stops. "Not quite," he says. He looks at the other Lorder. "Search this room."

Mum raises her shoulders. "Is that really necessary, Agent Coulson?" she says, ice in her voice. Emphasis on his name that says she knows who he is if he steps out of line.

He raises one eyebrow, amused. "Oh, I think it is. Get her out first." He nods at me dismissively.

I'm still retching over the garbage bin; dry retching now.

"She can't walk. You'll have to help," Mum says, and with a nod from the other, the younger man approaches. Lifts me up with a face like he is cradling a sewer rat, and deposits me next door on Amy's bed.

Searching my room, looking for Happy Pills, no doubt. They won't find any. I droop back on Amy's pillows now, too exhausted to think, to move. *Your drawings,* a voice hisses inside, and my eyes snap open.

Under the loose carpet by the window: my hidden drawings. Of Gianelli after the Lorders took him: Mum told me to destroy it. How I wish I had. And the one of Ben. If they see how I drew him, they won't buy the innocent little Kyla and her "friend." They'll see how I feel about him. I force my eyes closed. Minutes pass. I hear Mum admonishing them not to make a mess. There is no outcry, no "look what I found." I start to hope they won't find them, even though I can't believe it.

Finally there are heavy steps in the hall, down the stairs. Moments later, their van starts out front. They are leaving, as easy as that? Somehow I don't think that is the end of their interest in me.

Mum painted an image of Ben they wanted to see: Ben the dangerous boy, the one warned to stay away. And I backed her up. It felt disloyal, wrong. "I'm sorry, Ben," I whisper. Tears well up. *Ben would want you safe.*

I drift, not asleep or awake; my thoughts jumble around out of order and make no sense. Flat images like still photographs flit in and out of my mind, wash over me. Ben, running. His mum's owl with wings stretched wide. Ben in the moonlight of my dream, light shining through him. There are footsteps up the stairs, and the door opens. I struggle to open my eyes, to move at all, but my body feels full of lead. The door shuts again. Vaguely I hear movements across the hall, in my room, then Amy's door opens once again.

"Kyla? I've put your room to rights. Come on, Amy will be home soon."

She helps me up and across to my room. It smells all fresh and clean; the sheets, new and crisp. I can almost forget the Lorders were here, pawing through my things. "Thanks," I whisper. For this; for everything.

Suddenly unable to stay awake another second, everything goes black.

"Kyla?" Mum says. "I've brought you some soup." She looks herself. No signs of stress from a Lorder visit.

"I'm not hungry."

"Eat it anyhow."

She helps me sit up, tries to feed me, but I take the spoon from her and do it myself. I don't want it, but as I taste tomato and orange and something else spicy, it is all good, and I am hungry. I shouldn't be. How can I eat after what happened?

I finish the soup.

"We have to talk," she says. "I'm sorry to do this. You should be resting, but this can't wait."

"Okay."

"Why did you black out?"

The Lorders' question, but she deserves more of an answer.

I sag into my pillows. What do I say, what don't I? It is all too much to handle. Tears leak out between my lids again, and my Levo vibrates. Then Mum is there, sitting next to me, her hand light on my head, smoothing my hair.

I open my eyes and see her through the blurry tears. "What do you know?"

"Jazz didn't say much. Just that you were worried about Ben. He took you to his house, but you didn't go in because there were ambulances and Lorders there, and then he brought you home."

I nod, then wince. So I'd guessed right: Jazz didn't say I was with Ben. "What happened to Ben? Please tell me."

"I don't know for sure."

"I have to know. Please . . ."

"If I can find out, I'll tell you. But you mustn't ask anyone else about it, do you hear me, Kyla? This is important. Don't talk about Ben, don't look upset, don't do or say anything about him. Not at school, or at home, or anywhere else."

I stare back at her, head throbbing unbearably, but not as bad as the pain inside when I think about Ben. How can I pretend like nothing is wrong? *Because you must.*

"What you've told the Lorders today is your story, the only story. Keep it just the same to *anyone* who asks: at Group, school, here at home." Home? She means Amy and Dad. And her choice of words: What I am to say is a *story.* My story, not the truth. *She knows more than she lets on.*

She gets up and goes to the door, then turns back.

"Oh, Kyla? That was such a beautiful drawing of Ben. I found it and the others last night. I'm truly sorry I had to destroy them." She shuts the door.

Eyes wide, I stare at the space she just left. *Thanks, Mum.* Again. They would have found them, I'm sure. Somehow she knew they would come, and she searched my room last night while I slept. And I realize she would have found the one of her son, Robert, too; she must wonder how I know what he looks like. How I know about him at all.

Is she protecting me? Or, maybe, she doesn't trust me. She wanted to make sure there was nothing that made me guilty of anything beyond a few ill-advised drawings.

How would she feel if she knew that it was because of me taking Ben to see Mac and Aiden that he got the pills, that he got the idea, even, to try what he did? How would she feel if she knew I was the one who wielded the grinder that cut off his Levo?

Late that night I hear a car and wonder if the Lorders are back. But when I slip out of bed to look, it is Dad. He's not due back for days. There are voices below; he sounds cross. Very.

But when I wake up the next morning, he is gone.

47

MUM KEEPS ME HOME FROM SCHOOL FOR DAYS. UNTIL I DON'T want any more time between four walls, with nothing to do but be crowded in by my thoughts, and cry, with her and Sebastian smothering me with hugs and feline kindness. Amy joins in when she is home. They form a united front, a concerted effort to keep my levels from taking me under.

And physically, I am fine; almost normal, just a dull throb behind my temples. I could go to school if it weren't for the Ben-shaped ache inside that leaves me cold, unable to move. But all their *niceness* doesn't help. The only thing that does is thinking of Aiden.

The more thought I put into it, the more I put the blame for this whole mess on his red-haired head. And on Mac for introducing Aiden to us. And Jazz, too, because Mac is his cousin. And I wouldn't know Jazz if not for Amy. Amy and I wouldn't be here if it weren't for Mum. Bit by bit my anger grows, and I nurse it, like a toothache, no dentist in sight. I need it.

It gets me out of bed and dressed. I emerge downstairs in time to escape.

"Kyla? What are you doing?"

I look up from lacing my sneakers. "What does it look like? It's Group tonight, isn't it?"

"I'm not sure you should be out of bed."

"Don't you think it would be better all around if I put in an appearance there tonight?"

She looks back at me, measuring something in her mind. Nods slightly. "If you can be like your normal self, you should be there. I'll drive you."

"No. I want to run."

"You're not well enough to run; it's been less than a week since your blackout." Her arms are crossed and her face set.

Explain or you won't be going anywhere.

I breathe in and out slow; release. Turn and face her. "Physically, I'm fine; not a hundred percent maybe, but it isn't far, and running makes me more *myself*. Helps my levels. It isn't that I want to run; I *need* to run. Can you understand?"

She bites her lip, uncertain. "But by yourself?"

"I'll be fine. Really. It is all major roads; nothing will happen to me. I promise."

She relents. "All right. But I'll pick you up. Deal?"

"Deal."

She scoops me up for a hug. I open the door, and I'm off.

It would be sensible to start with a slow jog, work up speed slowly and see how I go. My head pounds with every jar of foot on the ground, and I haven't eaten much lately. But I pour everything I have into my muscles, my legs and feet, go fast and faster until it takes over. I stop noticing the pain in my skull. The night, the road, the *thump-thump* of my feet are all there is.

But the sound is hollow. The last time on this run, Ben's rhythm combined with mine. My feet falter when I pass the path that leads off the road, where Ben lifted me up onto the fence. Where we were alone and he kissed me that first time.

Now that I am running, I can think about my dream where he came to say good-bye. I couldn't think about it before; it was like a wound that, if touched, screamed in pain.

Dr. Lysander says my dreams are made up of random thoughts and images stolen from my subconscious mind. That they aren't real. That sometimes people do incorporate memories into their dreams, but if you've been Slated you need to build up your banks of memories before this can happen, and in the meantime, the mind makes things up to fill the void. The long and short of it, according to her, is that my dreams are made up; they are not real. *Sometimes they are.*

Some of my dreams come from memory, just as my drawings do; I'm sure of it. Like the drawing I made of Lucy: I put mountains behind her from where she lived. How could that not be a memory? But with some of my dreams, I am less sure. Like the one where my fingers are smashed with a brick. It felt real, at the time; now, if I think of it, it feels like a memory of a true event. But is it just a memory of my dream? Then there are dreams like the one I had of the Slated boy strapped down and having his Levo cut off: That felt more than real. But then Ben was superimposed on the dream, and it could never have happened that way. My fear put him there. And the ones of me running on the beach, being chased: Those ones are more insubstantial. There is less detail to ground them, to make them feel as if they hold any reality.

But what of Ben's good-bye kiss? Did his spirit visit my dream? *Ghosts are fairy tales for children.* No. I refuse to believe it. Anyhow, Ben isn't dead; he can't be. *He may be.*

Aiden: I conjure him up in my mind. Red hair. I run past the hall; keep going. Blue eyes? Yes, they were dark blue, thoughtful eyes. I start to reduce my pace. A dusting of freckles across his nose and cheeks. I turn around, walking now. His smile I remember, too. Not like a Slated smile; a real one. Or was it? He wanted to use me for his own reasons. And Ben, too. He gave Ben the pills, put the idea in his brain. Nearly there now.

I glance down at my Levo: 8.1. Really? Even with the running I can't believe it. When I ran with Jazz the other day I was so distressed I could only manage a 5.

It's the anger.

I don't understand. My levels fall when I am distressed, but anger brings them up. There have been other times like this, I realize, like when Wayne threatened me, and with Phoebe. But it makes no sense. Levos are designed to be sensitive to any extremes of emotion, true, so the misery I've felt the last few days has, as expected, kept them down, sometimes dangerously so. But the Levo's main purpose is to stop any possibility of violence, any harm to self or others. Yet anger seems to prop up my levels. *Kyla is different.*

I face the door to the hall; it is time to be the same as everybody else. Deep breath, square shoulders, smile. You're on.

I grab a chair.

Two bright spots of unnatural red shine on Penny's cheeks. Her smile seems stretched. Then I see him, in the corner of the hall, sitting in a chair and looking like he'd rather be just about anywhere else.

A Lorder. And not just any Lorder: the younger one who carried me and searched my room. Though not in his gray suit or black operations gear. In jeans and a shirt. He looks almost normal.

"Hello, Kyla. That is everyone now. Shall we begin? Have you all had a good week?"

Everyone. She knows Ben isn't coming. There is an ache inside. Maybe some part of me was crazy enough to hope that he'd be here somehow. That either it was all a blackout-induced nightmare, or the paramedics just patched him up and shipped him home again.

"To start with today, we have a special guest who is going to say a few words. Everyone, this is Mr. Fletcher." Mr. Fletcher, not Agent Fletcher.

He stands and walks over, next to Penny. The others remember their training and all obediently call out hellos; I remember in time to do the same. To not stand out. He squirms under the weight of our smiles. Penny sits down.

"Today I want to talk to you about drugs."

He carries on into a long lecture on the dangers and evils of drugs, and to never, ever take pills or anything else unless they are from your doctor. And if anyone ever tries to give you something, tell a parent or teacher about it immediately. His eyes are traveling around the group, one by one. He's not here to make a public service announcement; he's looking for someone, anyone, whose reactions aren't what he expects. He's looking for anyone who knows where Ben got his Happy Pills. I can see he is, for a change, trying not to be scary, but he isn't doing a very good job. Many of the others' smiles falter when he describes horrible things drugs can do.

Ben said the Happy Pills let him think for himself, without the Levo getting in the way. *They did.* Is that such a horrible thing?

Fletcher leaves when he is finished, relief clear on his face as he heads for the door. It is like he thinks we are contagious. After he's gone Penny's brow softens and her natural smile returns, but her eyes are sad. She knows something about Ben. She must.

When Group ends, I linger until others are gone. Walk over to Penny. "Can I talk to you?"

"Of course you can, dear," she says, but her eyes are urgent, she shakes her head no, side to side. "And I need to check your Levo; I hear you had a blackout last week."

She gets out her scanner, chatting relentlessly about the weather. Something is wrong.

She plugs the scanner into her netbook and gasps. "Kyla, look at the graph. You went down to 2.1 the other day. Dangerous." I look at it with her and also see what she doesn't say out loud: The last two days, my levels have been in the 3's and 4's most of the time. 7.1 just now: a side effect from the run.

She holds my hand, shakes her head sadly.

"What happened?" she asks. But she cups a hand around her ear, shakes her head again.

Someone is listening in.

I nod, mouth *I understand.* And tell her the Lorder-approved story: that Ben wasn't in school, Jazz took me around and there were ambulances, but I don't know what happened to him.

"Kyla, dear. Forget about Ben. He won't be back; just put him out of your mind. Concentrate on your family, and getting on with your schoolwork." She says the words, but her eyes are sad, and she slips an arm around my shoulders. I can feel the tears start again in the back of my eyes. *Find the anger.*

A movement of air—a cool breeze that lifts the hairs on my arms—makes me turn toward the door, uneasy, half expecting Fletcher to be back. Instead it is a surprise of another sort.

"Dad?"

"Hi, Kyla; hi, Penny. Ready to go?" He smiles, but I am not reassured. I haven't seen him since spotting him out the window late the other night; he was not in a good mood then from what I overheard and was gone by morning. I get up and head for the door.

"Take care, Kyla," Penny says.

"Thanks."

We get in Dad's car, but instead of turning left for home, he goes right. "Thought we could go for a little drive, have some time for a chat."

"Okay," I say, uneasy. *He wants to talk without Mum listening.* "Is everything all right? I thought you weren't back until Sunday."

"I should be asking you if everything is all right. I've been hearing things about you, Kyla. You and your friend Ben."

"Oh."

"*Oh.* Is that all you have to say for yourself?"

His tone is conversational, his smile and open face are present and accounted for; his words say something else. *Be careful.*

"I'm sorry. What do you mean?"

"I'm not buying it."

"What?"

"The wide-eyed innocent look, the whole act. You're involved, somehow, in what happened. Now listen to me. Your mum has convinced me—this time—to let things lie. That it is in my best interests for it not to come to light that you've been up to something under my nose. And frankly, I don't care whatever you may have got away with this time. But no more. Not in my house. Not everything is your mum's decision; there are things she cannot control. Do you get it?"

There are a million things I could say. I could deny all the accusations hidden behind his words; I could repeat the authorized story of events; I could cry and pretend I don't understand.

"Yes. I get it," I say. I hold my hands together to stop them from shaking. *Use the fear; feed the anger.*

Dad nods. "That was the only answer you could have given to stop me from returning you right now."

He drives on in silence. We do a loop around to the other side of our village, and he pulls into our driveway. "You're too clever by far. Take care you keep out of trouble."

48

A SLEEPLESS NIGHT FOLLOWS; TOO MANY MISERIES SWIRL through my mind, wanting attention. The morning alarm for school comes early, but there is no question of taking another day off. A good little Slated wouldn't, and I've been told: I'm keeping out of trouble. But how can I get through today, be ordinary, pretend like nothing is wrong? How? *Put one foot in front of the other; take one step at a time.*

So I get out of bed. School uniform on; brush hair. Pretend to eat breakfast. And wait for the bus in gray drizzle, arms folded tight around myself, shivering against cold that falls from the sky and sinks deep in my bones.

When the bus comes I can't bring myself to sit at the back, in Ben's seat, so I pick the only other empty one. We're halfway to school before I remember this was Phoebe's seat. I catch a few barbed glances; they don't like that I sat here. But does anyone even notice one Slated boy less in the back row?

Through classes and breaks, there are no whispers of "where is Ben" like after Phoebe was taken. Not that I could answer the question, but the lack of it digs at me. Is it because they don't notice his absence, or are afraid to ask?

Then, the moment comes: I drag my feet to biology. I'd been dreading this class. No Ben next to me on the back bench, and Hatten, with his knowing eyes, peeling away at the layers I've been throwing up around myself.

After we all scan our cards in and sit down, he stands at the front. A deep blue shirt today. It emphasizes the lack of color in his pale blue eyes. He smiles his slow smile; girls sigh. He starts the lesson, then stops a moment later. Looks around the room.

"Are we missing someone today?"

Students exchange glances, and that is when I see: They know. They have noticed there is no Ben, but it is taboo. A subject of no discussion. No one answers.

"Come on," Hatten says. "I've only had this class a few times; don't think I know everyone's names yet. Who is missing?"

Stay still. Be quiet.

"Ben. Ben Nix isn't here," I say, the words bursting out of me, some compulsion making me say his name out loud. To make him real, not like someone who never even existed, who doesn't matter.

"Where is he?" he asks, his eyes on mine, and there is something in them. A flicker of amusement, like a cat playing with a mouse trapped under one paw. *He knows.*

"I have no idea," I answer, quite truthfully.

"Does anyone else know?" he asks the room in general. Silence. "No? Perhaps he isn't well."

Then he carries on with the lesson.

"Kyla? Wait. I want a word, please." Hatten smiles and holds open the classroom door for the last girls who were dragging their feet to leave his presence. They flash me a look of pure dislike and flounce out of the room.

He steps out, looks down the hall both ways, then comes back in and shuts the door. Leans on it.

I say nothing.

He smiles, and it is a maniac grin: a wide smile of pure delight. "It's you," he says.

"What? What do you mean?"

"You're the one. I was sure you'd make it."

"I don't know what you're talking about."

He walks toward me and I back away. He stalks closer and grins; I'm trapped. He puts a hand on the wall over my shoulder. Not touching, but so close the heat of his body prickles my skin.

He leans in. "Do you hear the voices, Kyla, or whatever your name is? Voices in your head," he whispers.

My heart pounds, *th-thump, th-thump,* loud in my ears.

"Listen to the voices. What are they telling you now?"

Run!

I squirm away, bolt for the door.

"How does it feel?" he asks.

I turn back to look at him; I can't help myself. "How does what feel?"

"Knowing that you killed Ben. That he is dead, and it is all your fault."

"I didn't! I . . ." What color is left drains from my face. "Is he really dead?" I whisper.

He smiles. "What do you think?"

Run!

I dash through the door and down the hall, then race across the school. *Go to the track.*

My feet pound twenty times around before I remember: Mrs. Ali banned me from the track at lunch. I concentrate. No; that isn't quite right. She banned me from running with Ben at lunch, and Ben isn't here, is he? But I leave enough time for a shower at the end.

I have somewhere to go after school.

49

I'M WAITING BY JAZZ'S CAR AT THE END OF THE DAY.

"Hi," he says. "I didn't think you'd still want to go."

I force a smile. "Is it okay?" Forcing myself to sound casual, like still going to Mac's as planned isn't a big deal. But it is the biggest deal. Holding on to confronting Aiden—focusing the anger—is the only thing that has kept me from dissolving into a puddle. *He is dead, and it is all your fault.* No! If he is, it is Aiden's fault: Aiden and Mac.

"Of course," Jazz says. "I was hoping you'd come. Let's go."

We're well away from the school before I dare ask.

"Jazz, did Ian find out anything about what happened to Ben?"

He tilts his head side to side. He looks like he doesn't want to answer.

"Tell me! Whatever you know. Please, I need to know."

"There isn't much to tell. Nothing we didn't already know, or guess."

"Tell me anyhow."

"Ian's mum is a friend of Ben's mum. She told her that when the paramedics got there, they seemed to revive Ben, but he wasn't breathing on his own. Once the Lorders arrived, they kicked her out. When the ambulances left, the Lorder van followed, and they weren't in a hurry to get to the hospital—no lights or siren—so she was afraid of the worst. But they won't tell her where they took him, or what happened."

I say nothing. Blink hard and stare out the window. Alive or dead, the Lorders took him away. What is there to say?

Jazz takes the last turn, and soon we're pulling up to Mac's. He parks the car out front.

"Kyla, there is something else. Ben's mum gave Ian something to give to you."

"What?"

"It's in the trunk."

We get out of the car, and he kicks the trunk, hard, until it pops open. "Better than a key," he says.

There is a cardboard box inside, a big box.

"Go on," Jazz says, and I open the lid. There is paper wrapped around something, and I tug at the top pieces and see metal. Metal feathers! It is the owl. She must have finished it. I run my fingers along a wing.

"She said Ben asked her to make it for you, so she wants you to have it," Jazz says.

"I didn't know that," I whisper. She brought this creature to life, based on my drawing. It's so beautiful, and it is from Ben. She still gave it to me, even though she must wonder if I had anything to do with what happened. She never would have if she knew what I did. Tears prickle behind my eyes, and I blink them back. *You can't keep it.* My face falls. "I can't take it home. How can I explain where it came from?"

"I figured as much. That's why I brought it today. I bet Mac can keep it for you here. Let's ask him," he says, and grabs the box. "Come on."

I follow him to the house. Ben's mum wouldn't have given it to me if she knew where Ben got the pills. If she knew the part I played. *He is dead, and it is all your fault.*

Jazz opens the door. "Hello?" he calls out.

Mac appears from the kitchen. "Hello. How are you, Kyla?" he says. He half smiles, but his eyes are sad. He knows about Ben. "Want some tea?"

"Tea?" Jazz says, in mock outrage. And heads for the cupboard with the beer. Mac fills the kettle, and while it boils sends Jazz out back to look at some new car he is working on.

I lean against a cupboard. "Is Aiden here?"

Mac nods. "In the back room," he says. "I'm so sorry about Ben. He was a nice guy." His face is full of sadness, but if it weren't for him, Ben would never have met Aiden and gotten those pills. *If it weren't for me.*

"Is there anything . . ." Mac starts to say, and puts a hand on my shoulder, but I shrug him off. I want to rage at him, but I hold it in for now and back away.

"I want to talk to Aiden."

"All right. I'll keep Jazz out back awhile. I'll tell him you wanted some time alone."

"Sure. Whatever."

I stalk down the hall to the computer room and open the door.

Aiden is at the desk, head in hands.

He looks up. "Hi," he says, his eyes wide, round, dark blue startling against pale skin. "Mac just told me about Ben. I can't believe it." He gets up and reaches out a hand toward me, but I turn to shut the door, and it drops.

"What do you know?" I ask.

"Just what I heard from Mac, which I guess he got from his cousin. That Ben cut off his Levo." He shakes his head. "Why would he do that?"

"You mean you really don't know?" I say, disgusted.

"What do you mean?"

"You gave him those pills; they did something to him. And you told him about the AGT cutting Levos off and that it worked. You did this to him!" I say. My voice is getting louder, shrill.

"Not so loud," he says, glancing at the window.

"I've been hushed for days, not able to say anything. I will say what I want now, and you will listen."

"I'm listening," he says, his voice quiet, drawn in.

"Those pills weren't just Happy Pills, were they? They didn't just make his levels go up. They did something else."

Aiden inclines his head forward. "That is true," he says. "They help stop the Levo from dominating how you think."

"They made him do it!"

He shakes his head. "They don't work like that. All they do is stop your levels from dropping so you can think for yourself."

I shake my head, denying his words. But it sounds so much like what Ben said. Like running: The pills let him think and feel what he wanted without threat of a blackout. *It set him free.*

"I understand your anger about what happened. But it's not my fault. I don't understand why he would have done that. Just thinking for himself wouldn't do it. Something must have happened, something that pushed him. Made him feel it was the only option."

I stare back at him in horror. The something that happened . . . was Wayne, and Ben being unable to protect me.

I wrap my arms around myself, the anger and the misery getting mixed up in themselves. "No," I say. "That's wrong. If you hadn't given him the pills it would never have happened."

Aiden flinches. "I'm sorry, Kyla. So sorry. But think this through. It's not my fault for giving him the pills, or Mac's for bringing me here, or Jazz's for bringing you here."

I stare at him, freaked out. It is almost like he is reading my thought processes through, following where my mind is going. But he *can't* take away my anger. I need it. And the only one left to blame if they are all taken out of it is *me*.

"Then whose fault is it?" I whisper.

"Think about it. Who Slated Ben? Who gave him a Levo in the first place, and booby-trapped it against removal. Who did these things?"

"The Lorders. They did it."

"Now you see why what we are doing is so important. We have to expose what they do. Help me with MIA."

Danger. I shake my head, back away. No. After everything that has happened, he is still twisting things around, manipulating me to try and make me do what he wants. Everything he says sounds so reasonable, but it is wrong. Without Aiden, nothing would have ever happened to Ben. And what would happen to me if I help him? Any step out of line and Dad will return me; he said so. He, Coulson and his Lorders, and Mrs. Ali: They are all watching my every move. And Dr. Lysander and her "tell me what is different about you, Kyla." They and Aiden are all crowding in on me. This is the hunt; I am the prey.

"Are you all right, Kyla?" Aiden says, finally realizing what he has missed. That my Levo hasn't vibrated once through all of this. He looks curiously at my wrist, but I cover it with my hand. *Hold the anger.*

I head for the door.

"If there is ever anything I can do, anything . . ." His voice trails off.

I pause. "There is one thing. Find out what happened to Ben."

He says nothing. I turn back.

His face is sad. "Kyla, I'm sorry. It is unlikely Ben survived. But if he did, the Lorders had him. It wouldn't have been for long."

"Find out," I repeat.

"If I learn anything, I'll pass it along to Mac." But he stresses *if*, like it is a closed book.

I leave him and shut the door.

Mac and Jazz are out back still, but I don't join them. Not yet. Sadness is threatening the anger; it won't focus, wobbles, and my levels are on the way down. I wander into the kitchen, and there, on the table, is the box with the owl. *This won't help.*

I pull the rest of the paper away and pull it out onto the table.

It is magnificent. The last time I saw it the wings weren't finished; they are now, and span several feet across. It is amazing how all the disparate bits of metal have been joined together to form something greater than the sum of its parts. I lightly touch the wings, the sharp talons, beak. A beautiful, lonely creature, but deadly if you happen to be a mouse. I run my fingers across the back of the owl's body. What was that? A slight noise, a rustle, as if something is loose. I turn the owl around for a closer look.

It is hard to see. One very tiny corner of white. I just manage to trap it between two fingernails, and pull; out comes a small square of paper.

A note?

My hands start to shake as I unfold it.

Dear Kyla,

*If you have found this, it means things have gone very wrong.
I'm sorry to cause you pain. But know that this was my decision,
and mine alone. No one else is to blame.*

Love, Ben

That night, sleep eludes me again. My levels hover around 4, and my stupid Levo keeps vibrating every time I nearly drift away. I want blackness, dark, silence; no feeling or thought or anything. But it won't come. I'm alone in the night; not even Sebastian is here to keep the demons away.

Finally I can't stand being still any longer and head for the stairs and a drink. But there is a light on in the front room. I peek through the door; Mum is there, a book in her hands, Sebastian on her knee.

"How do you live with things?" I say.

Mum jumps a little, looks around and sees me in the door. She puts down her book. "Things?"

"Bad things happening to people you care about. Like your parents. And your son."

"Come here," she says, holds out her hand, and I walk over, sit next to her on the sofa. She links her arm in mine.

"I should be able to answer that, but I can't. There isn't an answer. You just go on, one day at a time. It does get easier after a while."

Mum makes us hot chocolate, finds a blanket and we stay on the sofa. She reads, Sebastian purrs, and, eventually, I sleep.

50

TODAY I MUST ACT LIKE I HAVE NEVER DONE BEFORE. AND IT isn't just the official story about Ben I need to stick to, the people and events surrounding what happened to him that I need to hide. Last time, Dr. Lysander said she wants an answer: Why am I different from other Slateds?

And I know. I have finally worked it out: how I am different that is, though not why. When I woke up in the morning, groggy and stiff from sleeping on the sofa, the answer was in my mind.

It all relates to anger.

My Levo does its job if I am sad, upset, or distressed for any number of reasons; my levels drop as expected. They can even drop so far I black out. But when I get scared or angry, they don't. It seems to almost protect my levels. Yet the main purpose of a Levo is to stop the Slated from acting in anger, to prevent violence against self and others.

Mine doesn't work.

There is no doubt in my mind that if anyone else figures this out, I'm history. Dr. Lysander might be curious and want to fiddle about in my brain to determine how or why this happened, but even she can't keep the hospital board away, the Lorders. *No more Kyla.*

My poker face is much improved, but it isn't enough. No matter what happens, I can't get angry. Not here at the hospital, not at school where eyes are watching. Not at all. *Good luck with that.*

Huh.

The only way I know to do this is to let in the pain, the misery, the loss. All the things I've been trying to block, ever since Ben . . . I swallow.

Bzzzz.

I look down at my Levo: 4.4.

Too much.

"Come in!" Dr. Lysander calls, and I go through the door.

"Have a seat, Kyla." She half smiles and taps at her screen. I sit.

She finally looks up. "I won't ask how you've been; I see on your records: not very good."

"No."

"Tell me about Ben," she says, her voice soft, encouraging. A strange set to her familiar features: sympathy.

"Ben was my friend at school. And he was in my Group also. My only friend, really."

"And what happened?"

"He didn't come to school one day, and I was worried about him. I got Amy's boyfriend to take me to his house, but there were ambulances and Lorders there. He took me home, and I blacked out. And Ben hasn't been back to school, or to Group, and nobody said anything about him! It's like he never existed; no one even cares." My blood quickens, my hands involuntarily start to form fists, but I make them relax, force my breathing to stay even.

"I care, Kyla."

"Then can you tell me what happened to him? Please."

"Honestly, I don't know. It doesn't concern me unless he becomes a patient at this hospital; otherwise, I have no idea."

"Can you find out?"

"No, I cannot," she says gently. "But Kyla, you know what you were taught about your Levos. They can't be removed without causing pain, seizures, and death; levels would plummet too fast for the Levo to be destroyed in time to stop it from causing death to the wearer."

"Always?" I whisper. "There's no chance . . . ?"

"There is always a small chance of equipment failure. That things can go wrong with surgery or with the implanted chip. Nothing is fail-safe. It is my job to minimize these chances, and if anything goes wrong, to determine why." She tilts her head. Is she thinking of the question she asked me last time?

Danger! Let in the pain.

But I can't bear it . . .

You must.

I hold Ben's face in my mind. How he looked when he laughed. Running like the wind. Holding my hand. *Love, Ben,* he said on his note. But overlaid on it all, the last time I saw him, convulsing, in pain, and I left him. I left him and ran to save myself. Hot tears sting my eyes.

Bzzzz . . . 4.2.

Bzzzz . . . 3.7.

Dr. Lysander pushes an intercom, speaks into it. A nurse appears. They talk over my head and the nurse jabs me in the arm. Welcome warmth slips through me, and my levels start a slow climb up.

The nurse leaves and Dr. Lysander taps at her screen, glances at me a few times, then sits back in her chair.

"That is enough for today," she says. "But, Kyla, believe me when I say: It is best to forget him. But if you can't, it does get easier."

The way she says the words . . . so like Mum.

"Do you know?" I whisper.

"What do you mean?"

"You do, don't you: You've lost someone; something horrible happened."

She twitches in her seat; a nerve has been touched. For an instant there is pain in her eyes, a flash of something real, then it is gone. Her face is blank. *She has a poker face, too.*

"Go home now, Kyla," she says. Subject closed.

I get out of my seat and head for the door.

"Oh, and, Kyla? I haven't forgotten what we were talking about last time. But we'll leave it for today."

A brief reprieve, then. Not an escape.

It's not until late that night, lying in bed, hoping for sleep, that I realize my mistake. I'm not supposed to know that Ben tried to cut off his Levo. But when Dr. Lysander started talking about it, I didn't ask her why, or act surprised, or anything.

Oops. *A mighty big oops.*

Then I realize something else. If she truly knows nothing about Ben and what happened to him, she wouldn't know about that, either.

She was lying, too.

Absolute darkness surrounds me. I open my eyes wide and wider, but it is inky, and black. I can see nothing. I hate it! I lash out at the brick walls, the tight circle that surrounds this space where I stand. There isn't enough room to stretch my arms side to side or to sit down. No finger-holds to climb up.

There must be a way out.

Rapunzel's tower had a window; she had long hair. All I have is dark-ness, fingernails, fists, and feet.

And anger. I hammer and kick at the walls, again and again: nothing. Until finally, exhausted, I slump against the wall. That is when I feel it with my hand.

A little mortar is loose! One spot, just below waist high. I scratch and claw, again and again, not worrying about fingernails or blood or skin. Hands heal, as I know too well.

Finally there is a tiny glint of light. I almost cry with relief. It tantalizes, but is too far down for me to look through, to see what is out there. No matter how I try, I can't squish down low enough in this confined space.

Enough! I howl in rage.

Let me out!

51

I SLEEP LATE, AND WHEN I FINALLY OPEN MY EYES I'M surprised Mum has let me alone, Sunday or not. After my dream woke me last night I'd had to leave the light on, darkness too thick and heavy to tolerate, and lay there, thinking, then finally got out my sketch pad and drew for hours. Only letting myself drift back to sleep once the sun was up.

What does my dream mean?

If my anger is in a prison, it needs to stay there. It won't take away the pain, just delay it. I can't stop feeling what I feel about Ben or anything else. Any more than I can stop being who I am. Or deny who I once was.

All these dream fragments: wispy truths and half-truths, real or imagined events. How can I tell them apart? I can't.

I also couldn't tell Dr. Lysander was lying. How can I even be sure that what Ben wanted to do was really wrong?

Aiden is right. If Ben died, the blame lies square and certain on the Lorders and their hospitals. The government, and doctors like mine. They are the enemy. Not Aiden.

Yes! Focus your anger on them instead.

No. That is where Ben was wrong. He wanted to join the terrorists. He was careful what he said, he didn't want me to know anything that could get me in trouble. There was nothing there to link me with anything he had done or was planning to do, but I knew: That is where he was heading.

Not me.

Aiden's answers are dangerous. But the way he wants to do things is right.

I take out my sketches from the dark hours, and there they are, the missing: Ben, Tori, Phoebe, even Lucy. I can't turn my back on them. The world needs to know. And most of all, I need to know: What happened to Ben?

Downstairs, Amy is in the kitchen doing homework; Dad is still away; Mum is making soup.

She smiles when I come in. "Awake, at last. I can see the extra sleep has done you some good."

I smile back at her. It wasn't many hours of sleep. It is more that instead of fighting within myself, I think I know what I want to do now. What I need to do. That makes me look rested in a way I haven't since I first met Aiden.

"I'm going for a walk," I announce.

Mum peers out the window. The sun is shining, but heavy black clouds are creeping in from the west, covering half the sky. "Better make it a quick one, then."

"Shall I come along?" Amy asks.

"No. I want to go alone."

"Stick to main roads, Kyla," Mum calls out.

I walk through the village, past the footpath Amy and Jazz always take. Where Ben and I walked—no, ran—ahead of them, and so many things followed.

I continue, to the end of the village: past a few farmers' fields, up to some woods. I'm just thinking of going back when movement catches my eye.

I turn. Unable to see anything at first, I scan along the field, the woods. Then I see him. On a fence post between the field and the woods: an owl. Snowy white and looking back at me, surveying the world like he owns it. But it is daytime, not night, and even I know owls are night creatures.

But no one has told him about it.

Fascinated, I stare.

He stares back, and I step closer, off the road and along a faint path between the fence and the woods. I get near enough to see his eyes, the definition of his feathers. Then he flies off. Flapping great white wings, so like the metal sculpture. He swoops, lands again. On a gate at the end of the field this time. He looks back, eyes fixed on mine.

Waiting?

And so I step toward him. We repeat this dance, again and again. Each time I halve the distance between us he flies on, then waits until I follow.

This goes on until we are well into the woods, and I begin to realize that I am hopelessly lost. My usual map sense is gone. I haven't been paying attention to where my feet travel as I follow the owl's flight above. The sky rolls in, black and furious now, covering the sun. Rain will soon follow. He rests on a tree branch, this time, high enough up that he doesn't fly away when I draw close.

"Thanks," I say to him. "You got me, what do you want to do now?"

He stares intently, turns his head to one side. Looks behind me and then launches into flight, high above the trees. He vanishes from sight.

"What do I want to do with you now? Well, well."

I spin around.

It's him: Wayne. The bricklayer.

I blink, unbelieving.

"Did you follow me?" I say, and start backing away.

"Well, yes; I did." He smiles, but it is all lips baring teeth, not in his eyes. He steps toward me.

I step back again, turn to run, but stumble as my foot catches against a tree root.

He moves faster than I expect. Hands grab and twist my arm. Push me into a tree.

"No one is here to help you this time," he says as I struggle. "You've got to pay for what you did. Phoebe was family: blood for blood."

"I didn't do anything to her, I—"

"Shut up!" He lets go of my arm, yanks me around. Smiles into my eyes with huge hands on my shoulders, pinning me into the tree. "We can do this the easy way or the hard way. Either is fine with me."

And something . . . *snaps.* Inside me.

Almost audible, a crack, a split. A glint of light shines through where none could reach before.

The wall.

I twist slightly and jam my knee, hard, between his.

He curses and falls, pulling me down with him.

"You'll pay for that," he snarls.

I don't think so.

He is a foot taller. Maybe twice my weight. But my arms and legs and muscles all know what to do.

I lash out.

It is over soon.

I stand back. This man who dared to touch me now lies still, bleeding on the ground. Jaw smashed; blood pours from a cut on the back of his head. Is he . . . is he dead?

I step closer, afraid to know, afraid not to know. I lean over him, not wanting to touch him, but trying to force my hand to his neck, to feel for a pulse.

His eyes snap open. I jump back, but his hand grabs my ankle. A scream works its way up my throat and I pull away, hard. I kick my foot again and again, but his hand is a vise, clamped tight. I reach down and peel his fingers off one at a time, and *run*.

Headlong through the woods. Branches snap in my face and my feet trip on roots, but I push as fast as I can through trees and tangled bushes until they suddenly give way to a path. *The* path; yes. I came this way. I remember now. The logical, planned part of me takes charge of my feet, slows them down.

My Levo says 6.

How can this be?

My head begins to pound wildly, my hands shake, my feet stumble.

"What have I done?" I whisper to the trees. "How?"

Hush.

"Who said that?"

I spin around, but no one is there. I am alone.

Somewhere inside I am calm. A new wall is being built, blocking that which connects my Levo to my thoughts and feelings, and it is strong.

"What have I done?"

But my questions are quashed as soon as they form.

Let it be.

I spin around once again; no one is there. The voice is in my head. The voice that has always been in my head.

"Who are you? Are you Lucy?"

No! That sniveling weakling is gone forever. I am . . . you. The you that was.

"What do you want?"

I want us to be together.

"No."

You have no choice.

"No!"

I fall to the ground.

And this intruder inside me pulls a brick. The crack widens, cement crumbles and bricks shatter and fall. The whole tower collapses.

A kaleidoscope floods my mind, images first slow and then flashing fast through my brain, whirling and spinning. I'm dizzy, my head will explode, but I can't stop it. My guts twist and I vomit, again and again, until there is nothing left in my stomach, but still I heave on the ground.

How can this be? My memories should be gone. What has happened; what is happening now?

I stare at the darkening sky, heart thudding wildly behind my ribs. Gradually my head stops spinning; the memories stop screaming for attention and settle down. Scurry away and slot themselves in where they fit, where they don't.

How can this be? What does it mean?

Pale, ice-blue eyes; they know. They always know. Hatten's face appears in my mind: angelic when he smiles, when I do as I should. I shy away from thinking about when I do not.

I gasp out loud as I remember his name. *Nico.* That is how I knew him then, back when he was the center of my life. He controlled it; pain, pleasure, how one can become the other. Much like love and hate. He taught me how to be two people at once: pathetic Lucy and her alter ego. The wimp and the warrior. Lucy is gone; only the other remains. Nico is the one who smashed Lucy's fingers with a brick when she resisted the separation. But he did it for me, to protect me: to make me safe if Lorders got their hands on my brain. And they did. I was Slated. So everything he did to Lucy saved me in the end.

How did he find me?

Not as Nico. But even in different clothes and a new role as teacher, his smile is the same. Just for me and me alone, ignoring the other girls in the room, finding his special one with his eyes. His slow wink. *What a bitch,* he'd said that day, about Mrs. Ali. Still on my side. No matter that I couldn't remember who he was then. He tried to push me, I see now, being so horrible about Ben. He was trying to make my memories come out from where they were hiding.

However he found me, he or some terrorist friend of his must have put Miss Fern in the hospital so he could take her place at my school. Nico—or Hatten, as he is now—has gone to a lot of trouble, and there could only be one reason. To be in Kyla's world. My world. But why?

My eyes widen.

What does he want with me?

The question barely forms before the images begin, tumbling through my mind one after another, faster and faster. Death and instruments of death: explosives and blasting agents, guns and incendiaries, where best to aim a hidden blade. Nico taught me so many ways to end life. Even with my bare hands.

No!

Yes. Just ask Wayne.

I spring up and start to run through the trees, away from Wayne's body and back toward the road. *NO, NO, NO, NO, NO* screaming through my brain, pounding with my feet. I won't! I can't. I'm not that person, not anymore.

What about Ben?

Ben. My steps falter. I look down at my Levo, so like the one we cut out of his life—perhaps taking his life along with it. 6.2? I twist it, hard, on my wrist: nothing. It should at least cause pain. With what I did this afternoon, I should be dead, zapped in my brain by this *thing* that has ruled my life ever since I was Slated. It is still on my wrist, but somehow blocked by new barriers in my mind.

What Ben tried to do was be free of his Levo, so he could make a difference. Do something.

And here I am. Free of my Levo.

Goose bumps tingle up my arms.

I lean against a tree and close my eyes. There are his: warm and brown. The ones that cared for me, no matter who or what I once was. Would he feel the same if he knew the truth?

I can't believe he is stopped, has gone forever. Still and silent, like the metal owl.

I WON'T believe it.

Nico might think I'm here to do what he wants, but he is in for a surprise. There is a price he must pay. He will help me find Ben, or I'll have nothing to do with him or his schemes.

I whisper a promise to the trees and the wind, to the rain starting to fall from the sky, to the owl whose flight brought me to this place.

"Ben, I'm going to find you."

READ ON TO FIND OUT WHAT HAPPENS NEXT IN

FRACTURED

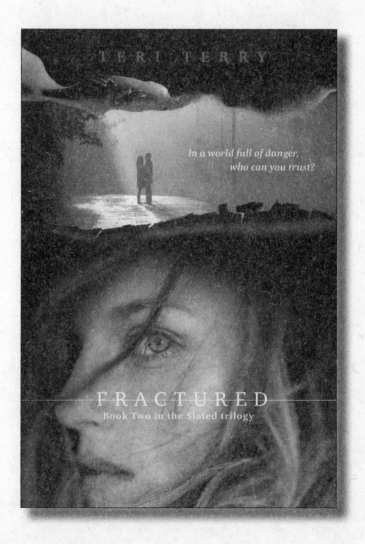

TERI TERRY

In a world full of danger,
who can you trust?

FRACTURED
Book Two in the Slated trilogy

RAIN HAS MANY USES.

Holly and beech trees like those around me need it to live and grow.

It washes away tracks, obscures footprints. Makes trails harder to follow, and that is a good thing today.

But most of all, it washes blood from my skin, my clothes. I stand, shivering, as the heavens open. Hold out my hands and arms, rub them again and again in the freezing rain, traces of scarlet long gone from my skin but I can't stop. Red still stains my mind. That will take longer to cleanse, but I remember how, now. Memories can be parceled up, wrapped in fear and denial, and locked behind a wall. Brick walls, like Wayne built.

Is he dead? Is he dying? I shake, and not just from the cold. Did I leave him suffering? Should I go back, see if I can help him. No matter what he is, or what he has done, does he deserve to lie there alone and in pain?

But if anyone finds out what I've done, I'm finished. I'm not supposed to be able to hurt anyone. Even though Wayne attacked me and all I did was defend myself. Slateds are unable to commit acts of violence, yet I did; Slateds are unable to remember any of their pasts, yet I do. The Lorders would take me. Probably they'd want to dissect my brain to find out what went wrong, why my Levo failed to control my actions. Maybe they'd do it while I still lived.

No one must ever know. I should have made sure he was dead, but it is too late now. I can't risk going back. *You couldn't do it then; what makes you think you can now?* A voice that mocks, inside.

Numbness spreads through skin, into muscle, bone. So cold. I lean against a tree, knees bending, sinking to the ground. Wanting to stop. Just stop, not move. Not think or feel or hurt, ever again.

Until the Lorders come.

Run!

I get up. My feet stumble into a walk, then a jog, and finally they fly through the trees to the path, along the fields. To the road, where a white van marks the place Wayne disappeared, BEST BUILDERS painted down the side. I panic that someone will see me coming out of the woods here, by his van, the place they will eventually look when his absence is noted. But the road is empty under an angry sky, raindrops pounding so hard against the tarmac, they bounce back up again as I run.

Rain. It has some other use, some other meaning, but it trickles and runs through my mind like rivulets down my body. It is gone.

The door opens before I get to it: a worried Mum pulls me inside.

She mustn't know. Just hours ago I wouldn't have been able to hide my feelings; I didn't know how. I school my face, take the panic out of my eyes. Blank like a Slated should be.

"Kyla, you're soaked." A warm hand on my cheek. Concerned eyes. "Are your levels all right?" she says, grabbing my wrist to see my Levo, and I look at it with interest. I should be low, even dangerously so. But things have changed.

6.3. It thinks I'm happy. Huh!

· · ·

In the bath I get sent to have, I try again. To think. The water is steaming hot and I ease in, still numb. Still shaking. As the heat begins to soothe my body, my mind is a jumbled mess.

What happened?

Everything before Wayne seems hazy, like looking through smudged glass. As if watching a different person, one who looks the same outside: Kyla, five foot nothing, green eyes, blond hair. Slated. A little different than most, maybe, a bit more aware and with some control issues, but I *was* Slated: Lorders wiped my mind as punishment for crimes I can no longer remember. My memories and past should be gone forever. So what happened?

This afternoon, I went for a walk. That's it. I wanted to think about Ben. Waves of fresh pain roll through with his name, worse than before, so much so that I almost cry out.

Focus. Then what happened?

That lowlife, Wayne: He followed me into the woods. I force myself to think of what he did, what he tried to do, his hands grabbing at me, and the fear and rage rise up again. Somehow he made me angry, so full of insane fury that I lashed out without thought. And something inside *changed.* Shifted, fell, realigned. His bloody body flashes in my mind, and I flinch: I did *that*? Somehow, a Slated—me—was violent. And it wasn't just that: I could remember things, feelings and images from my past. From before I was Slated. Impossible!

Not impossible. It happened.

Now I'm not just Kyla, the name given me at the hospital when I was Slated, less than a year ago. I am something—someone—else. And I'm not sure I like it.

Rat-a-tat-tat!

I half spin out of the bath, sloshing water on the floor.

"Kyla, is everything all right?"

The door. Someone—Mum—just knocked on the door. That is all. I force my fists to relax.

Calm down.

"Fine," I manage to say.

"You'll turn into a prune if you stay in there any longer. Dinner is ready."

Downstairs, along with Mum, are my sister, Amy, and her boyfriend, Jazz. Amy: Slated and assigned to this family like me, but different in so many ways. Always sunny, full of life and chatter, tall, her skin a warm chocolate where I am small, quiet, a pale shadow. And Jazz is a natural, not Slated. Quite sensible apart from when he stares at gorgeous Amy all moonily. That Dad is away is a relief. I can do without his careful eyes tonight, measuring, assessing, making sure no foot is put wrong.

Sunday roast.

Talk of Amy's coursework, Jazz's new camera. Amy babbles excitedly about getting asked to work after school at the local doctor's office where she interned.

Mum glances at me. "We'll see," she says. And I see something else: She doesn't want me alone after school.

"I don't need a babysitter," I say, though unsure as I say it if it's true.

Gradually the evening fades into night, and I go upstairs. Brush my teeth and stare in the mirror. Green eyes stare back, wide and familiar, but seeing things they didn't before.

Ordinary things, but nothing is ordinary.

Sharp pain in my ankle insists I stop running, demands it. Pursuit is faint in the distance, but soon will be closer. He won't rest.

Hide!

I dive through trees and splash along a freezing creek to cover my steps. Then crawl on my belly deep under brambles, ignoring pulls on my hair, clothes. Sudden pain as one catches my arm.

I must not be found. Not again.

I scrabble at the ground, pulling leaves, cold and rotting, from the forest floor over my arms and legs. Light sweeps through the trees above: I freeze. It drops, lower, right over my hiding place. I only start breathing again when it continues beyond without pause.

Footsteps now. They get closer, then carry on, faint and farther away until they disappear from hearing.

Now, wait. I count out an hour; stiff, damp, cold. With every scurrying creature, every branch moving in the breeze, I start in fright. But the more minutes tick past, the more I start to believe. This time, I might succeed.

The sky is just brightening as I back out, inch by careful inch. Birds begin their morning songs, and my spirits sing along with them as I emerge. Have I finally won Nico's own version of hide-and-seek? Could I be the first?

Light blinds my eyes.

"There you are!" Nico grabs my arm, yanks me to my feet, and I cry out in pain at my ankle, but it doesn't hurt as much as this disappointment, hot and bitter. I failed, again.

He brushes leaves from my clothes. Slips a warm arm around my waist to help me walk back to camp, and his closeness, his presence, res-

onate through my body despite the fear and pain.

"You know you can never get away, don't you?" he says. He is exultant and disappointed in me, all at once. "I will always find you." Nico leans down and kisses my forehead. A rare gesture of affection that I know will in no way ease whatever punishment he devises.

I can never get away.

He will always find me . . .

2

A DISTANT *RRRRING* CALLS INTO DEEP NOTHINGNESS. IT pulls me to a moment of regret, half awake, half confusion, then a slow drift back to dreams.

The *rrrring* sounds again.

Wrongness!

Awake in an instant, I spring up, but something holds me and I almost scream, wrestle and throw it to the ground and crouch in a fighting stance. Ready for attack. Ready for anything . . .

But not this. Alien, threatening shapes blur and change, become ordinary things. A bed. An alarm clock, still ringing, on top of a dresser. My restraints, blankets; most on the floor now. Carpet under bare feet. Dim light through an open window. And a grumpy, sleepy cat, meowing protests and caught up with blankets on the floor.

Get a grip.

I hit the stop button on the alarm. Force my breathing to slow, *in, out, in out*; try to calm my pounding heart, but still my nerves scream.

Sebastian stares from the floor, fur bristling.

"Do you still know me, cat?" I whisper, reach a hand for him to sniff, then stroke his fur, as much to soothe myself as him. I pull the blankets back into order on the bed and he jumps up, eventually flops down, but keeps his eyes half open. Watching.

When I woke, I thought I was *there*. Half asleep I knew every detail. Makeshift shelters, tents. Damp and cold, wood smoke, the rustle of trees, predawn birds. Quiet voices. But the more awake I become, the more it is gone. Details fall away. A dream, or a real place?

My Levo says mid-happy at 5.8, yet my heart still beats fast. After what just happened my levels should have plummeted. I twist my Levo on my wrist, hard—nothing. It should at least cause pain. Slated criminals can't do violence to self or others, not while a Levo keeps guard of every feeling. Not while it causes blackouts or death if the wearer gets too upset or angry. With what I did yesterday, I should be dead: zapped by the chip they put in my brain when I was Slated.

Echoes of last night's nightmare fill my mind: *I can never get away. He will always find me* . . .

Nico! That is his name. He is not an insubstantial dream. He is real. Pale blue eyes gleam in my mind, eyes that can glint cold or hot in an instant. He'll know what all this means. A living, breathing part of my past that has somehow appeared in this life, as my biology teacher of all things. A strange transformation from . . . from . . . what? Slippery memory falls away. My fists clench in frustration. I'd had him there, clear, who and what he was; and then, nothing.

Nico will know. But should I ask? Whatever he was, or is now, one thing I do know: He is dangerous. Just thinking his name makes my stomach clench, both with fear, and with longing. To be close to him no matter the cost.

He will always find me.

A knock on the door. "Kyla, are you up? You're going to be late for school."

"Your chariot, ladies," Jazz says, and bows. He puts one foot up on the side of the car to yank the door open. I clamber into the backseat, Amy in the front. And though it has a feeling of ritual about it, every morning the same, it is so *alien*. A safe sameness that rankles.

I stare out the window on the way: farms. Stubbled fields. Cows and sheep stare, chewing and placid as we go past. Herded to school, not questioning the forces that channel us into our prescribed lives. What is the difference?

"Kyla? Earth to Kyla."

Amy has turned in her seat.

"Sorry. Did you say something?"

"I was just asking if you mind if I work after school? It's four days a week, Monday to Thursday. Mum isn't sure you should be alone so much. She said to talk to you about it."

"Truly, it's fine. I don't mind. When do you start?"

"Tomorrow," she says, with a guilty look.

"You already told them you could, didn't you," I say.

"Busted!" Jazz says. "But what about me? What about spending time with me?" And they pretend-argue the rest of the way.

The morning is a fog. Scanning my ID into each lesson, sitting down, pretending to listen. Trying to channel my face into attentive and eager to learn, so no one will have reason to focus any closer. Scanning out again. Lunch, alone; being ignored, as usual, by most of the other students who keep clear of Slateds. Though they mostly liked Ben—me, not so much. Especially now that he has vanished.

Ben, where are you? His smile, the warm certain feel of his hand in mine, the way his eyes light up from inside. It all twists like a knife in my gut, the pain so real I have to wrap my arms tight around myself to try to hold it in.

Some part of me is aware that I can't contain this much longer. It has to come out.

Not here. Not now.

Then, finally, it is time for biology. A queasy unease grows in my stomach on the way to the lab. What if I've gone mental and it isn't Nico at all? Does he even exist?

What if it is him? Then what?

I scan my ID at the door, walk across to the back bench and sit down, all before I dare look: not trusting my feet to still work if my eyes see what they can't stop imagining.

And there he is: Mr. Hatten, biology teacher. I stare, but that's all right, all the girls do. It isn't just that he's too young and good-looking for a teacher; there is something about him. And it's not just those eyes, that wavy, streaked blond hair, longer than you'd expect for a teacher, or that he is so tall and totally fit—it is more than that. Something about the way he holds himself: still, yet poised for attack. Like a cheetah waiting for the moment to pounce. Everything about him says *danger.*

Nico. It really *is* Nico; no question, no doubt. His eyes, unforgettable pale blue with darker rims, sweep across the room. They stop when they reach mine. As I stare back there is a warm touch inside, a recognition, an almost physical shock that makes it *real.* When he finally looks away it is like being dropped from an embrace.

Not my imagination. Right now, across the room, it *is* Nico. No matter that I knew it, from memories of then and now, compared and held up close together. Until I saw him myself, with these eyes that are new with understanding behind them, I didn't *know* it in my gut.

Then I remember that although the girls in his classes may stare, I don't; at least, not so much.

So through the lesson, I try not to, but it is a losing battle. His eyes flick to mine now and then. Do they hold curiosity? Questions? There is some dance of amused interest when they lightly touch mine.

Take care. Until I can work out what he is and what he wants, don't let him know anything has changed. I force my eyes down to the notebook in front of me, to the pen that skips across the page, leaving behind random blue swirls, half-formed sketches where notes should be. Hand on autopilot.

The pen; the hand . . . *left hand.* It is clasped, without thought, in my left hand.

But I'm right-handed. Aren't I?

I *must* be right-handed!

Breath catches in my throat; my gut fills with terror. I start to shake.

Everything goes black.

She holds out her hand. Her right hand. Tears trickle down her face. "Please help me . . ."

She is so young, a child. With such pleading and fear in her eyes, I would do anything to help her, but I can't reach her. The closer I get, the harder I try, the more her hand isn't where it appears. With some optical trick she is always turned to her right. It is always too far away to grasp.

"Please help me . . ."

"Give me your other hand!" I say, and she shakes her head, eyes wide. But I repeat the demand, until finally she raises her left hand from where she held it beside her, out of sight.

The fingers are twisted, bloody. Broken. A sudden vision flashes in my mind: a brick. Fingers smashed with a brick. I gasp.

I can't grasp her hand, not when it is like that.

Her hands drop. She shakes her head, fading. Shimmering until I can see through her like mist.

I lunge for her, but it is too late.

She is gone.

"I'm all right now. I just didn't get enough sleep last night, that's all. I'm fine," I insist. "Can I go to my last class?"

The school nurse doesn't smile. "I'll be the judge of that," she says.

She scans my Levo, frowns. My stomach clenches, afraid what my Levo will show. My levels should have dropped low after what happened; nightmares sometimes even made me black out when it was functioning as it is meant to. But who knows what it is doing now?

"Looks like you just fainted; your levels have been fine. Good, even. Did you have any lunch?"

Give her a reason.

"No. I wasn't hungry," I lie.

She shakes her head. "Kyla, you need to eat." She lectures on blood sugar, feeds me tea and cookies, and, before she disappears out the door, tells me to sit quietly in her office until the final bell.

Alone, I can't stop my thoughts spinning around. The girl with the broken hand in my nightmare, or vision, or whatever it was . . . I know who she is. I recognize her as a younger version of myself: my eyes, bone structure, everything. *Lucy Connor,* vanished years ago from her school in Keswick, age ten, as reported on MIA. Missing in Action, the highly illegal website I saw just weeks ago at Jazz's cousin's place. She was part of me before I was Slated. Yet even with my new memories, I cannot remember being her, or anything about her life. I can't even think of her as *I* or *me.* She is different, other, separate.

How does Lucy fit in this mess in my brain? I kick the desk, frustrated. Things are there, half understood. I feel I know them, but when I focus on details, they slip away. Indistinct and insubstantial.

And this was all brought on when I realized I was using my left hand. Did Nico see? If he saw I was writing with my left hand, he'll know something has changed. I'm supposed to be right-handed, and it is important, so important . . . but when I try to focus on *why* I am meant to be right-handed, why I was before, why I don't seem to be anymore, I can't work it out. The memory goes all distorted, like fingers smashed with a brick.